More Acclaim for RULE OF THE BONE

"To read *Rule of the Bone* is to want everyone you know to read every last word, to hear the story in Bone's words and see the world through his eyes. . . . One of the great rewards of the classic coming-of-age novel (and *Rule of the Bone* is surely one) is that the reader is allowed not only to observe but to partake in the protagonist's growing acumen, to watch the wide-eyed wise up and maybe to smarten up a little ourselves."
—*Washington Post*

"Ingenious. . . . It takes a very special and hard-to-achieve voice to make a first-person fictional character. And it takes something close to a miracle to achieve a first-person voice for a 14-year-old that will do vital and nuanced justice not only to the boy but to the age-old world he moves through. Bone's voice performs excellently." —*Los Angeles Times Book Review*

"Brutally, often fantastically picaresque . . . captures the mix of defiance and confusion, pride and remorse. . . . The moral underlying Banks' work up to now asserts itself with a new force. . . . He is at his characteristic best as he explores the combustible mix of fear, frustration and passionate feelings."
—*The New Republic*

"Veteran novelist Banks has finally done it: He has written the Great American Novel. Or, to be more precise, he has *re*written it. *Rule of the Bone* is Huckleberry Finn transposed to Upstate New York in the 1990s. Banks . . . excels at portraying lives on the edge. . . . In *Rule of the Bone* he gives us a searing wake-up call." —*People*

"What Russell Banks has given us in his fiction is the truth—sometimes creepily intimate—about what's going on in the underpasses of America's highways. . . . Bone's scary pilgrimage is a continuation of that journey, and an emotionally authentic one." —*Boston Globe*

"Banks has . . . pulled one adolescent from the drably dressed, drifting throng and found in his candor and freshness something like a diamond." —*Chicago Tribune*

"*Rule of the Bone* works because we are strongly moved by someone who can keep his integrity in a world that barely knows the word." —*Seattle Times*

Also by Russell Banks

THE SWEET HEREAFTER

AFFLICTION

SUCCESS STORIES

CONTINENTAL DRIFT

THE RELATION OF MY IMPRISONMENT

TRAILERPARK

THE BOOK OF JAMAICA

THE NEW WORLD

HAMILTON STARK

FAMILY LIFE

SEARCHING FOR SURVIVORS

RULE OF THE BONE

A NOVEL

RUSSELL BANKS

HARPER **PERENNIAL**

HARPER ● PERENNIAL

"All Is Forgiven" appeared in slightly different form in a *New York Times Magazine* special Christmas issue in 1992.

"Just Don't Touch Anything" appeared in slightly different form in *GQ* in May 1993.

"The Bone Rules" appeared in *Adirondack Life* in September 1994 and "Canadians" in *Antaeus*, Fall 1994.

Two more sections ran in the Spring 1995 issues of the *Ontario Review* and *Salmagundi*, respectively: "Presumed Dead" and "School Days."

"Red Rover" appeared in *Columbia* magazine in April 1995.

A hardcover edition of this book was published in 1995 by HarperCollins Publishers.

HarperCollins books may be purchased for educational, business, or sales promotional use. For information please write: Special Markets Department, HarperCollins Publishers, Inc., 10 East 53rd Street, New York, NY 10022.

First HarperPerennial edition published 1996.

Designed by C. Linda Dingler

ISBN 0-06-092724-0 (pbk.)   ISBN 978-0-06-092724-0(PBK)

11 ❖/RRD 50 49 48 47 46 45 44 43 42

To Ellen Levine
and always to Chase

CONTENTS

RULE OF THE BONE

ONE

JUST DON'T
TOUCH ANYTHING

You'll probably think I'm making a lot of this up just to make me sound better than I really am or smarter or even luckier but I'm not. Besides, a lot of the things that've happened to me in my life so far which I'll get to pretty soon'll make me sound evil or just plain dumb or the tragic victim of circumstances. Which I know doesn't exactly prove I'm telling the truth but if I wanted to make myself look better than I am or smarter or the master of my own fate so to speak I could. The fact is the truth is more interesting than anything I could make up and that's why I'm telling it in the first place.

Anyhow my life got interesting you might say the summer I turned fourteen and was heavy into weed but I didn't have any money to buy it with so I started looking around the house all the time for things I could sell but there wasn't much. My mother who was still like my best friend then and my stepfather Ken had this decent house that my mother'd got in the divorce from my real father about ten years ago and about that she just says she got a mortgage not a house and about him she doesn't say much at all although my grandmother does. My mom and Ken both had these cheesy jobs and didn't own anything you could rob at least not without them noticing right away it was gone. Ken worked as a maintenance man out at the airbase which is like being a janitor only he said he was a building services technician and my mom was a bookkeeper at the clinic which is also a nothing job looking at a computer screen all day and punching numbers into it.

It actually started with me roaming around the house after school looking for something that wasn't boring, porn books or videos maybe, or condoms. Anything. Plus who knows, they might have their own little stash of weed. My mom and especially Ken were seriously into alcohol then but maybe they aren't as uptight as they seem, I'm thinking. Anything is possible. The house was small, four rooms and a bathroom, a mobile home on cinderblocks like a regular house only without a basement or garage and no attic and I'd lived there with my mom and my real dad from the time I was three until he left which happened when I was five and after that with my mom and Ken who legally adopted me and became my stepfather up until now, so I knew the place like I knew the inside of my mouth.

I thought I'd poked through every drawer and looked into every closet and searched under every bed and piece of furniture in the place. I'd even pulled out all these old Reader's Digest novels that Ken had found out at the base and brought home to read someday but mainly just to look good in the livingroom and flipped them open one by one looking for one of those secret compartments that you can cut into the pages with a razor and hide things. Nothing. Nothing new, I mean. Except for some old photograph albums of my grandmother's that my mom had that I found in a box on the top shelf of the linen closet. My mom'd showed them to me a few years ago and I'd forgotten probably because they were mostly pictures of people I didn't know like my mom's cousins and aunts and uncles but when I saw them again this time I remembered once looking for pictures of my father from when he was still alive and well and living here in Au Sable and finding only one of him. It was of him and my mom and his car and I'd studied it like it was a secret message because it was the only picture of him I'd ever seen. You'd've thought Grandma at least would've kept a few other snaps but no.

There was though this stack of letters tied with a ribbon in the same box as the albums that my father'd written to my mom for a few months after he left us. I'd never read them before and they turned out pretty interesting. The way it sounded my father was defending himself against my mom's accusations that he'd left us for this female named Rosalie who my mom said had been his girlfriend for years but he was claiming that Rosalie'd only been a normal friend of his at work and so on. He had good handwriting, neat and all the letters slanted the same way. Rosalie didn't matter to him anymore, he said. She never had. He said he wanted to come back. I almost felt sorry for him. Except I didn't believe him.

Plus I didn't need the letters my mom'd written to him

in order to know her side of the story because even though I was only a little kid when this all happened I've got memories. If he was such a great guy and all how come he split on us and never sent any money or even tried to be in touch with his own son. My grandmother said just don't think about him anymore, he's probably living it up in some foreign country in the Caribbean or in jail for drugs. She goes, You don't *have* a father, Chappie. Forget him. She was tough, my grandmother, and I used to try and be like her when it came to thinking about my real father. I don't think she knew my mom'd saved my dad's letters. I bet my stepfather didn't know either.

Anyhow this one afternoon I came home from school early because I'd cut the last two periods which was just as well since I didn't have my homework anyhow and both teachers were the kind who boot you out of the class if you come in empty-handed, like it's a punishment that'll make you do better next time. I rummaged around in the fridge and made a bologna and cheese sandwich and drank one of my stepfather's beers and went into the livingroom and watched MTV for a while and played with the cat Willie who got spooked and took off when I accidentally flipped him on his head.

Then I started making my rounds. I really wanted some weed. It had been a couple of days since I'd been high and whenever I went that long I'd get jumpy and restless and kind of irritated at the world, feeling like everything and everyone was out to get me and I was no good and a failure at life which was basically true. A little smoke though and all that irritation and nervousness and my wicked low self-esteem immediately went away. They say weed makes you paranoid but for me it was the opposite.

I'd about given up on finding something in the house that I could rob—a personal possession that could be hocked like the TV or the VCR or the stereo would be instantly noticed when it was gone and all the rest of their stuff was boring household goods that you couldn't sell anyhow like electric blankets and a waffle iron and a clock radio. My mom didn't have any jewels that were worth anything except her wedding ring from my stepfather which she made a big deal out of but it looked like a Wal-Mart's ring to me and besides she always had it on. They didn't even have any decent CDs, all their music was seventies stuff, disco fever and easy listening and suchlike, on cassettes. The only kind of robbing I thought was possible was big time like stealing my stepfather's van while he was asleep for example and I wasn't ready for that.

I was taking one more look into their bedroom closet, down on my hands and knees and groping past my mother's shoes into the darkness when I came to what I'd thought last time was just some folded blankets. But when I felt into the blankets I realized there was something large and hard inside. I pulled out the whole thing and unwrapped what turned out to be these two black briefcases that I'd never seen before.

I sat cross-legged on the floor and put the first briefcase on my lap thinking it was probably locked until it snapped open which surprised me but then the real surprise came when I lifted the lid and saw a .22 automatic rifle broken down into three parts just lying there with a rod and cleaning kit and a box of shells. It wasn't hard to fit the parts together, it even had a scope like an assassin's rifle and pretty soon I was into a Lee Harvey Oswald trip standing by the bedroom window and brushing the curtain away with the tip of the barrel and aiming through the scope at stuff on the street going Pow! Pow! I blasted a couple of dogs and blew away the mailman and nailed the drivers of cars going by for a while.

Then I remembered the other briefcase and went back to the closet and sat down and opened it. Inside are all these Baggies, thirty or forty of them filled with coins, mostly old quarters and Indian head nickels and even some weird-looking pennies with dates from way back in the early 1900s. Excellent discovery. I figure the rifle must belong to Ken and he stashes it in this briefcase on account of my mom always saying she's scared of guns and the coins too, I'm thinking, because if they were my mom's I would've known it since she pretty much told me everything in those days. Besides she wasn't the hobby type. Ken though was definitely the kind of guy who would have a cool gun and never show it to me or even tell me about it, plus he collected things like exotic beer cans and souvenir coffee mugs from the various theme parks they'd gone to and put them out on shelves where anyone could see although he was always telling me not to touch them because I never left things the way they were which is basically true.

I took the rifle apart and put it back in the briefcase and then I took a couple of coins from each of about six Baggies so he wouldn't know any were missing if he happened to check. Afterwards I wrapped the briefcases back in the blanket and put the bundle behind my mother's shoes in the closet where it had come from.

I had maybe twenty coins, small change, nothing bigger than a quarter and I took them to the pawnshop on

Water Street near the old tannery where I knew some kids had hocked stuff they'd stolen from their parents, jewels and watches and so on. The old guy in there didn't say a word or even look at me when I spread the coins out on his counter and asked him how much he'd give me. He was this big fat guy with thick glasses and huge sweat circles under his arms and he scooped up the coins and took them in back where he had an office and a few minutes later he comes out and says eighty dollars which really blew my mind.

Sounds fine to me, man, I told him and he paid me in twenties and I went out already high just thinking about all the skunk I could get for eighty bucks.

I had this very good friend Russ whose mom'd kicked him out in the spring and he and a couple of older guys who were like headbangers and bikers were living in an apartment over the Video Den downtown. Russ was sixteen and had quit school and had this part-time job at the Video Den so that's where I went when I wanted to hang out and get high or just chill until I had to go home. Russ was okay but most people meaning my parents thought he was a loser because he was into heavy metal and all that and did a lot of drugs. At the time he wanted me to get a tattoo because he had one and thought they were cool which they were but I knew what my mom'd say if I came home with a tattoo. I was already driving her and Ken crazy with my lousy grades in school and having to go to summer school now and getting a mohawk haircut and nose rings and being a general pain in the royal ass around the house as Ken liked to say and not helping out enough and I could tell Ken especially was really getting sick of me. I didn't need any more trouble than I already had.

It's amazing how fast good weed goes when you've got the money to buy it with especially when you've got some friends to smoke it with like I had Russ and these older dudes who lived with him. They were what you'd call bikers not Hell's Angels and some of them didn't even have bikes but were the same violent type so they were hard to refuse when they'd come in and see me and Russ rolling joints on the kitchen table. In only a few days my stash was gone and I had to go back to the briefcase in the closet for some more coins. I'd always put the rifle together while I was there and stand at the window hitting imaginary targets coming along the sidewalk or just sit on the floor going Blam! into the darkness of the closet.

It was getting toward the end of summer school and I knew I was going to flunk at least two out of the three courses that I needed to pass just to get out of eighth grade which was going to make my mom crazy and deeply piss off my stepdad who already had his own secret reasons for disliking me but I don't want to talk about that right now, so I was smoking a lot of skunk, more even than usual and was cutting most of my classes and hanging out at Russ's place. Russ and the biker guys were my only friends then really. My stepfather'd developed this new habit of referring to me as *him* and never talking directly to me or even looking at me except when he thought I didn't notice or when he was drunk. He'd like say to my mother, Ask *him* where he's going tonight. Tell *him* to take out the goddam trash. Ask *him* how come he goes around with torn clothes and wearing earrings in his ears like a goddam girl and in his nose for chrissake, he'd say with me watching TV right there in front of him.

As far as he was concerned I was her son now not his

even though he'd adopted me when I was eight after they got married and he moved in with us. When I was a real little kid he was an okay stepfather with some significant exceptions you might say, but when I got to be a teenager he sort of pulled out of the family unit and did a lot more heavy drinking which now my mom was into blaming me for. I didn't care if he didn't like me anymore, fine by me but I didn't want her making it into all my fault. Some of it was his.

I went back to the coin collection in the closet a lot that summer always taking only a few coins at a time from six or seven different Baggies and I was starting to figure out which ones were worth the most like the dimes with the lady on it and the Indian head nickels and I'd just take those and mostly not bother with the others. Sometimes the guy at the pawnshop would give me fifty bucks, sometimes I'd get over a hundred. One day he says to me, Where'd you get these coins, kid? and I go into this sad story about my grandmother dying and leaving them to me and I could only sell a few of them at a time because it was all I had of hers and didn't want to let the whole collection go.

I don't know if he believed me but he never asked me about them again and just kept shelling out the bucks which I kept turning into weed. I was a good customer by now and had moved up from buying it off of the couple of older kids who were dealing at school and out at the mall to this Spanish guy named Hector in Plattsburgh who hung around Chi-Boom's which was a kind of club down on Water Street. I bought so much skunk Hector thought I was dealing and a couple of times when I had extra I actually did sell a few bags to friends of Russ's roommates but basically it was me and Russ doing most of it, and the bikers.

Then one night I came home around midnight from Russ's place. I still rode around then on one of those knobby-tired dirt bikes which my mother'd given me a couple of Christmases ago. It was like my trademark, that bike, the way some kids do with their skateboards and I had this habit of taking it into the house at night and parking it in the front hall. Only this one time when I come up the steps carrying my bike the door like opens in front of me and it's my stepfather standing there with my mom right behind him with her face all red from crying. I can see he's deeply pissed and maybe drunk and I naturally think he's been whaling on her which he's been known to do so I shove my bike right into his stomach and the handlebars hit him in the face and knock off his glasses and suddenly everybody is screaming, me included. My stepfather yanks the bike out of my hands and throws it back down the steps and this makes me go crazy and I start calling him all the worst names I can think of like faggot and fucking asshole while he's grabbing me by my arms and pulling me inside the house and telling me to shut the fuck up because of the neighbors and my mother is yelling at me like I'm the one who was whaling on her and tossing kids' bikes around not her own husband for chrissake.

Finally the door's closed and we're all panting and staring at each other and he says, Get into the livingroom, Chappie, and sit down. We have some news for you, mister, he says, and that's when I remember the coins.

On the coffeetable is the briefcase and it's closed and for a second I think it's the one with the rifle but no, when my stepfather flips it open I see right away it's the one with the coins and I realize for the first time that there aren't very many of them left. It was kind of a shock. None of the plastic bags had more than a few coins inside and some of the bags were completely empty although I didn't remember emptying any and leaving them in the briefcase but it definitely looked like that's what I had done. Dumb. My mom sat down on the couch and looked at the open briefcase like it was a coffin with a body in it and Ken said for me to sit in the chair which I did while he stood between me and the table and crossed his arms like some kind of cop. He had his glasses back on and was calmed down a little but was still steamed I knew from me hitting him with the bike.

I felt like a pathetic jerk sitting there looking at those few remaining coins. I remembered how I'd felt the first time I opened the briefcase and saw inside an endless supply of weed like it was the goose that laid the golden egg. My mom started crying then like she does when I really fuck up and I made a move to get up and comfort her by apologizing like I usually do but Ken told me just to sit there and shut the fuck up even though I hadn't said anything yet.

Chappie, this is the worst thing you've ever done! my mom said and she started sobbing harder. Willie the cat tried to get on her lap but she pushed him away hard and he got down and left the room.

Ken said he didn't give a shit anymore what I robbed from other people or how much dope I bought, that was my problem not his and he'd given up on me anyhow but when I stole from my own mother that's where he drew the line especially when I stole something irreplaceable like those coins. He said I was goddamned lucky I hadn't taken his rifle because he definitely would have called in the cops. Let them handle it. He was sick of feeding and housing and clothing a freeloader and a thief and a drug addict and as far as he was concerned if it was up to him he'd boot me out of the house this very minute except my mother wouldn't let him.

I said to him, I thought they were *your* coins, and he reached out and slapped me real hard on the side of my head.

They were your *mother's*! he said real sarcastic and she went sort of crazy then, screaming about how the coins had been *her* mother's and she'd given them to her years ago along with other precious and sentimental items and someday the coins were going to be mine and really valuable but now I'd gone and stolen them and sold them and spent all the money on drugs so she'd never be able to pass them on to me. Never.

They were only coins, I said which was stupid but I didn't know what else to say and I was feeling really dumb anyhow and lowdown so why not say something that sounded like I felt. They weren't worth much anyhow, I said and my stepfather whacked me on the head again right on the ear this time tearing out an earring which really hurt. But it was like the sight of my blood got to him because then he belted me a couple more times, harder each time until my mother finally hollered for him to stop.

He did and when he went out into the kitchen and got a beer I stood up and still shaking I said real loud, I'm leaving this place!

Neither of them tried to stop me or even said where do you think you're going so I walked out the door and slammed it as hard as I could and picked up my bike where he'd thrown it and went straight over to Russ's who let me sleep on a ratty old couch that was in the livingroom.

The next morning as soon as I knew my mom and Ken would be at work I went over to the house for my clothes and stuff. I took a few towels and a blanket from the linen closet and some shampoo from the bathroom and shoved everything into two pillowcases. I was just about to leave when I remembered the few remaining coins and said to myself why not try and find them and take what's left since they're supposed to be mine someday anyhow. I was feeling hard and cold like a criminal mentality was creeping into me, and it was funny to me that I'd gone and made up the story about my grandmother to the pawnshop guy and then it'd turned out to be almost true.

I put my stuff down by the front door and took a beer from the fridge and popped it and walked back to my mom's and Ken's bedroom. I knew that as the saying goes a friend in weed is a friend indeed and if I was going to crash at Russ's I'd better have some smoke to pass around until I got a job or something.

It didn't seem likely they'd put the coins back in the closet but it was worth a look and sure enough when I reached into the darkness there were the two briefcases wrapped in the blanket the same as the day I found them. Ken and my mom must've thought that after last night I'd be too scared to go back there again but it was like I'd gone too far by now to be scared of anything anymore. The first briefcase had what was left of the coins, maybe fifty or sixty of them in a half-dozen bags which I took. I opened the second case and put the rifle together as usual and loaded it this time just to see how you did it since it was probably my last chance.

I was standing by the window aiming through the scope at a little kid on a tricycle across the street when I heard the bedroom door behind me creak like someone was coming in from the hallway. When I spun around it was Willie the cat jumping onto my mother's bed. I must've been freaked because I aimed the rifle at him and pulled the trigger but nothing happened. Old Willie came down the bed and sniffed the end of the barrel and looked like he was ready to lick it. I pulled the trigger again but still nothing happened and then I realized that the safety was on and the trigger was locked.

I started to look for the safety but just as I found it Willie jumped down off the bed and disappeared into the closet which was lucky for him because as soon as he was out of sight I suddenly saw myself standing there with the gun in my hand and I could see what I'd been trying to do to him and I started to cry then, from my stomach up to my chest and into my head until I was standing there sobbing with my stepfather's stupid rifle in my hand and the last remaining bags of my grandmother's coins on the floor and the black briefcases open beside them. Nothing seemed to matter anymore because everything I touched turned bad so I just started firing. Blam, blam, blam! Mostly I shot at my mom's and stepfather's bed until the rifle was empty.

Then I came out of it like I'd been in a hypnotic trance. I stopped crying and put the rifle on the bed and got down on my hands and knees and tried to get Willie to come out of the closet but he was too scared. I was talking to him like he was my mom saying, I'm sorry I'm sorry I'm sorry, real fast and high-pitched like when I was a little kid and similar stuff happened.

But no way that cat was going to trust me now. Way back there in the dark end of the closet scared out of his mind, he looked like I felt so I figured the best thing I could do was leave him alone. I picked up the coins and walked down the hall.

I hauled my stuff over to Russ's place and stayed there until the last of the coins and the weed ran out and Russ said the older guys didn't want me hanging around anymore. Hector let me have a couple of bags on credit so I could start dealing on my own and then the older guys said I could have the couch in the livingroom at least for the rest of the summer if I kept them in weed and since I was a dealer now that's what I did.

Sometimes that first summer and during the fall too I thought about going back and trying to make peace with my mom and my stepfather even and offering to pay her back for the coins as soon as I got a job but I knew I could never pay her back because it wasn't the money. Those old coins of my grandmother's, they were like my inheritance. Besides my mom was scared of Ken and wanted to keep him happy and since for certain reasons that only I knew about he was relieved that I was finally out of sight and out of mind so to speak, there was no way now she'd let me come home again. So I didn't even try.

TWO

ALL IS FORGIVEN

Things went smoothly more or less like that for the rest of the summer and all fall. Unbeknownst to me however I was developing a criminal mentality. Dealing skunk to the bikers and so on I knew was illegal but that didn't make it a crime so it wasn't on account of committing any actual crimes that I became a criminal, it was because of my changing attitude toward my mom and Ken and other regular people.

I didn't go to jail for it or anything but I think of the time I got caught shoplifting at the lingerie store up at the Champlain Mall in Plattsburgh as the true beginning of my life of crime. I mean, that was when I first saw myself as a person who was a criminal. It was coming up on the first Christmas after my mother and Ken'd kicked me out of the house and I was still fourteen and crashing at Russ's place with the bikers down on Water Street in Au Sable Forks. They were still letting me sleep on this ratty couch they had because I kept them supplied with weed lots of times on credit even but mostly when I hung out there I stayed in Russ's room. The bikers were older than us and heavier into drugs. I saw one of those guys once rub a line of coke straight into his eye which kind of grossed me out. Plus they drank a lot.

Russ was sixteen and worked days part time at the Video Den so nights we used to ride up to the mall in his Camaro and I'd deal a little weed to the other kids and we'd hang out till the stores closed and hit on the girls. But mostly nothing was happening so we'd sit around on the benches and watch all these cheesy couples doing their Christmas shopping. At Christmas the malls're filled with people who feel rotten because they don't have enough money so they fight a lot and yank on their kids' arms. The carols and blinking lights and the guys in Santa suits are supposed to make you forget your troubles but in reality it's the opposite. At least for me it was which is one of the reasons I liked to get high before we went there.

This one night about ten days before Christmas I didn't have any weed and I was thinking about my mom and Ken, how it would be the first time they'd be alone and I wondered what they'd do on Christmas Eve. What they usually did was get smashed on this eggnog and bourbon mixture that my mom said was her mother's secret recipe and watch TV specials. Around eleven when the news came on we'd open the presents we'd got for each other and hug and say thanks and then they'd go into their room and pass out and I'd smoke a fatty in the bathroom and watch MTV with Willie till I fell asleep. It was okay but not exactly ideal. But we had a tree and lights in the windows and all and last year was cool because I got this excellent suede shearling jacket from my mom and Ken gave me a Timex watch. So I could start coming home on time, he said. I got her one of those long silk Indian scarves that she seemed to like a lot and for him I got a pair of lined driving gloves. Everybody was happy, in spite of the eggnog.

But a lot had happened since then. For one thing, the main thing that'd happened was me getting kicked out of the house. But it also had to do with my mohawk and getting my ears and nose pierced and screwing up in school and even though they never caught me at it my mom and Ken'd known all along I was heavy into weed which was why I'd stolen the coins in the first place. When I left home it was sort of by mutual agreement, I guess.

They would've let me come back if I'd wanted but only if I could be a different person than I was which was not only impossible but unfair because I didn't know how to keep myself from getting into trouble anymore. I must've crossed a line but didn't know it way back when I was a little kid like five or six after my real father took off and Ken moved in.

I knew it was hopeless but I started imagining this scene anyhow. I get Russ to drop me off at my mom's and Ken's house. All my stuff including my trademark dirt bike is in Russ's Camaro and we unload it and set it on the sidewalk. But also I've got this huge bag of presents for my mom and my stepfather, truly excellent items like a toaster oven and a microwave and maybe some jewels and a fancy nightgown for Mom and for Ken I've got a Polaroid camera and a portable sander and a Polo ski sweater. Then Russ takes off and I'm all alone on the sidewalk. The house is dark except for the string of lights around the front door and the deck railing in back and electric candles in the windows and I can see the Christmas tree lights blinking through the curtain in the livingroom where I know they're watching the Cosby special or something. It's Christmas Eve. It's snowing a little. They're really sad because I'm not with them but they don't know how to let me come home without acting like what I did to them doesn't matter—stealing the coin collection and smoking grass and getting a mohawk and all and living with Russ and the bikers and not going to school anymore which they probably know about by now and dealing weed for Hector the Hispanic guy at Chi-Boom's which they don't know about although I wonder what they think I've been living on all these months, charity? Also they don't know that so far I haven't gotten a tattoo even though Russ has this very cool tattoo on his forearm and is always after me to get one.

So in this scene I go up to the door and knock and when my mom comes out I say, Merry Christmas, Mom, just sort of flat and normal like that and hold out the bag in which all the presents are wrapped in this incredible shiny paper with bows and everything. She starts to cry like she does when she's excited and my stepfather comes to the door to see what's the matter. I say the same to him, Merry Christmas, Ken. And I show him the bag of presents too. My mom opens the door and takes the bag from me and passes it back to Ken and gives me a big maternal hug. Ken shakes my hand and says, Come on in, son. We go into the livingroom and I distribute the presents to them and all is forgiven.

They don't have any presents for me which embarrasses them naturally and they apologize but I don't care. All I care is that they really like what I got them and they do. Later we're drinking eggnog and watching TV and Ken looks out the window and sees my bike and all my clothes and things out on the sidewalk with the snow coming down and he says to me, Son, why don't you bring your stuff inside?

When I got busted for shoplifting it was in this fancy lingerie store called Victoria's Secret and I was already out of the store with a silky green nightgown stashed in my jacket pocket. The security guard, a black dude named Bart who I actually knew personally and had once sold some grass to put the arm on me and turned me around and took me into an office in the back where the manager of the store and the head security guy were and after they hassled me for a while I finally told them my mom's name and telephone number. Bart, the black guy who'd busted me had to go back on patrol and when he left the office I looked at him real hard but he didn't care, he knew I couldn't pin him for anything without pinning myself worse. And then of course a half hour later here they come, my mother and my stepfather, her looking frightened and upset and him just pissed off but neither of them talking to me, only to the store manager and the head security guy. While they talked they made me sit by myself in a storeroom next to the office where I stared at the No Smoking sign and kept wishing I could get high and a few minutes later my mother came out wringing her hands and her face all red from crying.

She says, They want to *arrest* you! And Ken agrees with them. He thinks it would be good for you, she says. But I'm trying to explain that we've *all* had a lot of trouble on the homefront this year and you're just reacting to that. She goes, I'm trying to get you off, do you understand? Do you?

I said, Yeah, I understand.

Then she said, If you will march in there and say you're sorry and say that you'll come home with us and stay away from the mall, I think they'll forget about the shoplifting. And Ken will go along. He's upset, naturally, and very angry and embarrassed, but he'll get over it if you'll make some amends and stay out of trouble. This could be your last chance, mister, she says to me. Come on, and she took me by the arm and led me back into the office where my stepfather was joking with the store manager who was a bald middle-aged guy in red suspenders and bowtie and the head security guy who had a gun strapped to his waist, a real cowboy type, probably an ex-cop. The three of them are buddies now and they look at me and my mom like we're insects.

Go ahead, my mom said to me and she pushed me forward a step. Just tell them what you told me.

I hadn't told her anything but I knew what she wanted me to say. I felt weird, like I was in a movie and could say anything I wanted and it wouldn't make any difference in the real world. They were all staring at me and waiting for me to say the desired thing but I looked down at my feet and said, My friend was going to lend me fifty bucks but he didn't get paid in time. I don't know why I said it but it felt good when I did, almost comical.

See, there you go! my stepfather says to his buddies. The kid doesn't know right from wrong! What the hell did you want with a woman's *negligee*? he said and laughed and held up the gown with his thumb and one finger like it was a porno costume or something and I was supposed to wear it.

No way I was going to answer him so I just stood there and after a minute or two with no one saying anything my mother grabbed me by the arm and led me back out to the storeroom. Listen, mister! she said, really upset. I'm going back in there one more time, and remember, I'm the one putting myself on the line for you! If I get them to let you go, you have to promise me that you'll come home with us and that things will be different. I mean it, *different*! Do I have your word on that? Do I?

Yeah, I said and she left and went into the office. I could hear them arguing through the wall, my mother's voice high-pitched and pleading and my stepfather's voice low and grumbling and once in a while some comments from the store manager or the security cop. It seemed like hours but it was probably only a few minutes before my mother comes out all sad smiles now and she gives me this big hug and kisses me on the cheeks. She held both my hands in hers and looked at me and said, It's all right. They're going to let you go. Ken finally came over to my side on this, but like he said, it's your last chance. Come on, let's get out of here, she said. Ken's going to meet us out front by the Sears entrance with the car. My goodness, she says smiling. You're getting so tall, honey. It wasn't true of course, I wasn't even as tall as her and she's short.

Then when we walk out into the mall I see Russ sitting on a bench over by the fountain chilling with a kid I didn't know and a couple of girls from Plattsburgh High who're smoking cigarettes and pretending that the guys aren't there. Listen, Mom, I said. All my stuff's over at Russ's place, okay? I'll go by there with him and bring it over. You and Ken go ahead without me.

She seemed a little confused. What? Why can't we just

stop off there with you and get it now? You don't need to go with Russ.

No, no, I said. The place is locked. I got to get it with Russ. I don't have a key. Besides I still owe him twenty bucks for the rent. And I can't get my stuff till I pay him. Can you give me twenty bucks, Mom?

I was broke and out of weed but I knew Russ was holding. I was already thinking about getting high with him and the girls he was talking to and riding around Plattsburgh in his Camaro.

No, she said. No! Of *course* I can't give you any money! I don't understand. Don't you know what just happened in there? Don't you know what I just went through?

Listen, Mom, just give me the money. I need the money.

What are you saying?

Give me the money.

What?

The money.

She looked at me in this strange fearful way, like she didn't recognize me but almost did and I got this sudden new feeling of power and didn't even feel guilty for it. Then she reached into her purse and pulled out a twenty and passed it over.

Thanks, I said, and I gave her a kiss on the cheek. I'll be back later, after I get my stuff from Russ's.

She put her hand to her mouth and took a few short steps away from me, then turned and disappeared into the crowd. And as I crossed over toward Russ and the other kids I remember saying to myself, Now I'm a criminal. Now I'm a real criminal.

THREE

CANADIANS

Christmas came and went like Thursday or Friday and nothing changed. I was still lurking around the mall but I wasn't exactly a homeless boy yet until this one night I went up there alone because the bikers at Russ's crib had been wired on meth for three days straight and finally they'd kicked me and Russ out for not having any weed. Russ said he was going to his mom's to chill for a few days but no way I could do the same, not with my mom and stepdad still hanging up on me because of what happened when I got caught shoplifting and all. Russ said I couldn't sleep in his car, he had it parked at his mom's and she was definitely against that so I didn't have anyplace to go which is why I decided to hitch up to the mall that night even though I didn't have any money and no weed to sell.

It was snowing and I caught a ride from this air force

guy heading back to the base and in the car I was like talking to myself saying, Asshole, asshole, asshole, all the way from where he'd picked me up in Au Sable. I really wanted to go home to my mom's now or anyplace actually that was warm and homey but I didn't know how to do it. The air force guy must've thought I was whacked on acid or something because he didn't once ask me what the matter was, just dropped me like a turd at the exit off the Northway and booked.

I cruised awhile and ended up hanging by the fountain at the center of the mall which is more or less a crossroad looking for somebody I could bum a smoke off of when I spotted this little girl who I figured was lost. Her face was red like from crying although she was not at that moment crying, she was peeping around the place searching for her mom probably so I go, Hey, kid, how's it going? You lost or something? She was maybe eight or nine, stringy blond hair, ratty red dress, and sneakers with no socks. I noticed the dress and no socks because it was cold and snowing out and it was unusual for a kid to be in a skimpy dress and almost barefoot. She stood by the fountain looking back and forth like this little alleycat caught in the middle of the road with cars whizzing past on both sides.

C'mere, kid, I said and got up and approached her a little too fast I guess because she jumped away from me. I'm not gonna hurt you, for chrissake, I said.

Then I felt the long arm of the law so to speak, a heavy hand on my shoulder and when I turn around I see the hand is black and it's connected to one of the security guys, Bart the same dude who I once sold some weed to and who busted me anyhow for shoplifting when I was only trying to do a little Christmas shopping to get back into my mom's good graces. He's ex-military from Rochester, sort of a dim bulb.

Chappie, he says to me, what the hell are you doing here again? I tol' you to keep your little punk ass out of here.

Hey, it's America, jerk-off. Remember? Land of the free, home of the fucking brave, man.

Don't give me no shit. You're loitering. Now g'wan, before I toss you out with the garbage.

Where you scoring for weed now, man? I ask him just to remind him of the true nature of our relationship which he seems to want to forget. You still smoking them blunts? I say.

Chappie, he says to me, don't fuckin' antagonize the cops. It's dumb.

You're only a rent-a-cop, man. I'm waiting to meet somebody, I say.

Wait outside. Do it now, he says and he spins me around with one hand which he can do because he's a sizable dude and I'm small for my age anyhow. He says, That's a nice shearling jacket you got, Chappie. Who'd you rob it off of?

I got it last year from my mom, asshole, I tell him which happens to be true and I ease off in the general direction of Sears.

Yeah, sure, he says and laughs and heads slowly in the opposite direction. Walking his beat. He knows I'm only changing seats, moving to another crossing in the mall and he's not especially worried because it's kids like me that make his otherwise boring job interesting.

A few minutes later I'm walking past Victoria's Secret, the same ladies' fancy nightgown and underwear store where Bart busted me for shoplifting last month so I look inside with a special interest in the place and I notice the little girl in the red dress from before. Only this time she's with somebody, this potbellied dude with a big soft nose and pockety skin and thin black strands of hair that he's combed sideways over his head like a bar code. He's got the kid by the hand like he's her uncle. Not her father. It's like they're supposed to be shopping for a present for somebody only I can't figure who. This guy was not the type who had a wife or a girlfriend even, he was all rumpled and the buttons of his navy peacoat were crossed up.

I don't know what but something about the guy held my attention, like I knew him from someplace else although I didn't. I watched them through the glass and the guy bought what looked like ladies' pantyhose stockings, a whole bunch, six or seven packages of them and while he blah-blahs the salesgirl in this over-friendly way the kid just stands there beside him like she's half asleep or maybe stoned. But she's too young to be high, I think. I figure maybe they're traveling someplace, like from Canada and she's tired. Must be Canadians, I think and then when I start to move off they come out and the guy gives me this long stare, like What the hell are you? He doesn't say anything but it's like he's never seen a kid with a mohawk or nose ring before which is probably true for Canadians.

I don't know why I thought he was a Canadian. My stepfather is supposedly from Ontario but the guy didn't look anything like my stepfather who except when he's drinking is this neat and trim sort of person, a control freak with a crewcut and creases in his jeans who my mom thinks is God and I'm supposed to try and be just like him. Right. Naturally he thinks I'm a total loser which is okay

because his idea of a real man is Arnold Schwarzenegger
or General Schwarzkopf or anybody with a name with
Schwarz in it because he's basically a Nazi with a drinking
problem plus a few others is how I see him. What bums me
is that my mom bought that crap and kept telling me I was
lucky to have Ken for my stepdad when I knew it was the
opposite and he knew it too.

You got a problem? I say to the Canadian because of
the way he looked at me and he smiles and says not at all
and takes the little girl by the hand and walks off, real
relaxed. I watch them for a minute wondering why they
seem so laid back and all, especially him if they're traveling so far from home because even if the border is only
about an hour from here Canada is a huge place and they
look definitely funky, like they've been on the road for a
week and you'd think they'd want to get where they're
going. Plus him buying the packages of pantyhose is
strange, unless they can't get those in Canada.

Anyhow I didn't exactly have anything better to do that
night so I followed them, keeping back a ways and out of
sight. I guess I was only curious about the guy but also I
was thinking maybe he has cigarettes. It was cold outside,
I remember and snowing. I thought maybe he's driving
one of those big RVs or a van that they're sleeping in and
he's parked it out in the lot and he'll let me crash there
till tomorrow or till the bikers run out of speed and Russ
and I can get back into our crib over the Video Den in Au
Sable. So I follow the guy and the little girl in and out of
the Wiz and then the Foot Locker where the guy actually
buys the kid some socks which she puts on right there in
the store while he waits and looks around and almost
catches me watching and after a while I realize that I'm all

hyped up, I'm like peaking out at a million RPMs and my heart is hammering in my chest and my hands are all sweaty. I didn't know what was happening at the time but suddenly it was like I'm looking down this tunnel at the Canadian guy and the little girl, especially at the little girl who I was really worried about now, like some terrible thing was about to happen to her and she couldn't see it coming but I could. I wanted to tell her something important about people but I didn't want her to have to know it yet, she was too young still.

It's weird but as long as I didn't look directly at her and watched the guy with her instead, her uncle or whatever, I didn't flip out, all I was into was maybe bumming a smoke from the guy. But the second I switched over to the kid it's like something terrible is about to happen, this huge heavy ugly gray thing shaped like a tyrannosaurus rex or the country of Canada on the map is hovering over the entire United States of America and is about to fall or break apart and avalanche down on me and cut off my breath, so I start to breathe in and out real fast like I remember once Willie the cat did when he had a hairball in his throat and got all humped over with his head down next to the livingroom carpet making these quick little gagging noises. My stepfather walked in from the kitchen and gave him a kick across the room because he was afraid Willie was going to make a mess on the carpet so Willie threw up in my closet instead and I never told anyone. I just cleaned it up myself.

Basically people don't know how kids think, I guess they forget. But when you're a kid it's like you're wearing these binoculars strapped to your eyes and you can't see anything except what's in the dead center of the lenses

because you're too scared of everything else or else you
don't understand it and people expect you to, so you feel
stupid all the time. Mostly a lot of stuff just doesn't get
registered. You're always fucking up and there's a lot that
you don't even see that people expect you to see, like the
time after my thirteenth birthday when my grandmother
asked me if I got the ten dollars and the birthday card she
sent me. I said to her I don't know and she started dissing
me to my mom and all. But it was true, I really didn't
know. And I wasn't even into drugs then.

The little girl in the red dress was wearing binoculars
over her eyes like I did when I was her age and she couldn't
see that she was in danger any more than I could have seen
it back then, only it was different for her now because she
had me to help her and I didn't have anyone.

They went into the food court and I followed a little
ways behind and when they stopped at the Mr. Pizza and
ordered slices I suddenly got too hungry to hang back
anymore so I came up behind the guy and I go like, Hey,
man, you got some spare change so I can buy me a slice,
man? I haven't eaten all day, I tell him which is basically
true except for some cold french fries in Russ's car this
morning that he gave me.

The little girl had her slice in one hand and a Coke in
the other and she was looking for a place to sit down. I
smiled at her like we're pals from before but she didn't
change her expression which was as serious as a spoon so
I'm thinking what the hell, she's scared, she doesn't know
friend from foe anymore, I can relate to that when suddenly it's like a hot white light has been thrown on my face
warming my cheeks and forehead and almost blinding me
with the glare. The Canadian guy is looking at me, he's

staring directly into my eyes almost which people never do with me, not even kids because of my mohawk I guess and my earrings and the nose ring and plus I try to discourage that type of looking. But this caught me by surprise probably because I was distracted by the little girl when the guy hit me with all the attention and before I can shove it back at him he's already talking a mile a minute which is definitely not like any Canadian I ever met.

Hey, you poor kid, you really do look like you're starving, he says to me. He goes, I'm gonna buy you some supper, young man, I'm gonna buy you something solid to eat, something to get some meat on those young bones, he says stepping back and taking a look at me and shaking his head.

I must've made a mistake, I think. All that stuff about the little girl being in danger and this guy being some kind of Canadian weirdo was only in my head, a product of my fevered imagination and I just thought it all up because of what I know about my stepfather who is from Ontario and what I remembered feeling when I was a little kid myself. The guy's just a normal American, I think, who happens to talk a lot. And he likes me. And he's real interesting too.

What would please you, my good man? he says to me. You're skinny as a rail underneath that jacket.

I told him anything and he ordered me a slice and a Coke, same as the girl which is not so much if I'm starving so I ask him for a smoke while we're waiting and it turns out he's carrying Camel Lights which sort of proved he's American. When my order came he carried it over to the table where the little girl was and introduced me to her. He said her name was Froggy, aka Froggy the Gremlin.

Hi, I say and tell them my name. Froggy doesn't seem to register anything.

Me Buster, the guy says pointing to himself with his thumb and I laugh.

Buster! No shit. How come Buster?

He goes, Hi-ya, kids, hi-ya, hi-ya, hi-ya! My name's Buster Brown and I live in a shoe. And that's Froggy the Gremlin, he said waving a hand at the girl who was mainly ignoring the guy like she was used to this stuff. Look for her in there too! he says.

He talked like that, in circles basically and different voices while I ate my slice and smoked my cigarette and mostly didn't say anything. I noticed the little girl Froggy, she didn't say anything either. She just kept her eyes on her food and chomped her way through to the end and then looked out at the people walking past in the mall.

I asked Buster if Froggy was his kid and he goes, More than my child, Chappie, and less. She's my *protégé*. I have had dozens of protégés over the years and they keep me rising like a phoenix from the ashes of my past. My protégés are my once and future acting career.

Cool, I say. What's a protégé?

Those who can, do, Chappie, and those who can't, teach. I could once but I can't now, and thus I teach. I was an actor once, my boy, not a very famous actor but a success nonetheless. I had my share of film and TV roles. Now, he said, now I train young actresses and actors, now I make protégés of young people like Froggy the Gremlin here and the process like a heart transplant prolongs my own life as an actor extending into the indefinite future my own early gifts and training.

You probably can't understand any of that, he says

offering me another cigarette. You're much too young.

I'm thinking no way this guy's an actor, not with those pockmarks and a nose like a mushroom although when he was young with a full head of hair and no potbelly he might not have been too bad-looking. His way of talking was cool though. I liked listening to him and it didn't really matter to me whether he was telling the truth or not. When he talked he looked right at me and made me feel like there was this spotlight on me and I was standing in the middle of a stage and anything I said would be listened to carefully and treated with total respect.

He said back in 1967 when he was a very young man he had been in this movie with Jack Nicholson and Peter Fonda called *The Trip*, I guess some kind of travel movie but I had never heard of it although I had heard of Jack Nicholson from *Batman* so I was pretty impressed. He asked me, what about me, wouldn't I like to become a TV star in New York City and Hollywood but I said no way.

I knew he was only this old gay guy hitting on me which I didn't care about because he was so interesting to listen to but also because I felt like I was baking in the sun with all the attention he was paying to me and of course he was feeding me cigarettes and even bought another slice of pizza for me, this time with pepperoni.

I wasn't afraid of Buster, not for myself anyhow even though he was a lot bigger than me because usually with these guys you just tell them what you'll do and what you won't do and they go along more or less. But I didn't know what was the deal with little Froggy. She was like dreaming at the table with her eyes open and I figured the guy must've been dosing her with something, 'ludes of pink ladies maybe but if I could get him to switch off of her and on to me then somebody like Black Bart the security cop would probably come by and latch onto her and get her back to wherever she came from.

It was like a plan from a movie or a TV show, I know but those shows are usually based on reality. Also I was really getting off on the guy Buster Brown and I was even starting to feel jealous of Froggy in this weird way so that if Black Bart didn't come along and find her and take her to the lost kid office or wherever I didn't care, as long as I could take her place with Buster.

So how come Froggy never talks? I asked Buster and he went off on this number about how frogs don't talk, they croak or they keep you up all night cheeping and peeping and then he was talking about all the different types of frogs there are until I practically forgot my question. That's how he handled questions. He constantly changed the subject and he talked about you yourself a lot and that kept you from thinking too hard about him or Froggy. It's funny, he was so ugly-looking he made you feel handsome which is normal but he was so smart he made you feel smart too instead of stupid like smart people usually make you feel, like my stepfather for instance and teachers I have had.

At one point while he was rapping away I noticed Froggy get up from the table and take her tray and paper trash over to the barrel. She dumped her stuff and set the tray onto the pile there and started walking, heading back down the mall toward the fountain where I'd first seen her. It wasn't like she was sneaking off or anything and Buster didn't seem to care one way or the other although I didn't think he actually saw her leave. He must've known that she was gone, once she was gone, but it was more like after I came onto his scene the little girl didn't exist any-more so it didn't matter to him if she was gone or not. Which was fine with me for various reasons so I wasn't going to be the one who pointed out to him that his pro-tégé had split and what did he think of that? I just moved in and took her place, so to speak.

I was wondering if Buster was high, coke I figured because of how he talked and could I get a little taste, when he asked me did I want to do a screen test?

Sure, I said. When?

Oh, anytime. Tonight if you want.

Sure, I said and got up from the table and dumped the trash in the barrel like Froggy'd done and Buster and me went back into the mall and headed toward the exit down past Sears and J. C. Penney's, opposite the way Froggy had gone. I was feeling lucky now because of how things were turning out after such a lousy start—me and Russ being kicked out of our crib by the bikers and Russ going back to his mom's which was not an option for me and the cold and the snow and no money and no drugs. Now as I walked past Sears with this cool dude Buster Brown it looked like all my problems were solved, at least temporarily.

If I'm going to your place, I said to him, you oughta give me some money. For the screen test and all, I say.

That depends.

On what? I say and I stop right there so he'll know I'm serious.

He's like, Well, various things, Chappie. It depends on how much the camera loves you, for instance. You may not be in the slightest photogenic, despite your beauty to the naked eye. That's why it's called a screen *test*, Chappie. You have to *pass* it.

I'm like, Gimme twenty bucks up front or find yourself another protégé. Plus I don't do no sex with you. No fucking or sucking. Just the screen test.

Just the screen test, he says smiling and he pulls a twenty from his wallet and hands it to me. You drive a hard bargain, Chappie, he says.

Yeah, well, I had a good teacher, you might say. I'm thinking at that moment of my stepfather, I'm like flashing on his face, the outline of his head in the dark really so not quite his face and his smell of booze and Brut and the sandpaper scratch of his chin on my shoulder and neck. I almost never think about that stuff anymore, except when my mom tells me how lucky I am that he's my stepfather which she doesn't do since they kicked me out of the house for stealing and me being into drugs and all.

So how come you bought those pantyhoses? I ask Buster as we pass out the door by Sears into the parking lot. It was snowing fairly hard by now and there weren't many cars in the lot. A couple of plows were scraping away at the far end.

Pantyhose! What makes you think that's what I've got? he asked and he held up the Victoria's Secret bag and wagged it.

I seen you buy them, man.

Ah, you were tracking me, were you? Playing detective, eh? And now you're thinking you've *caught* me, he said. Only maybe instead I've caught you. He laughed at that like it was a big joke.

Whaddaya got, a girlfriend or something? I was starting to think he was a Canadian again because of the pantyhose. You see a lot of Canadians down here buying stuff they can't get at home.

You'd look pretty terrific in pantyhose, he tells me.

Yeah, sure, I say. You can forget that. Forget all about it, man. I asked him where his car was and he said back alongside the J. C. Penney's building. Then I asked him where's his crib and he just said not far. Good, I said, because I ain't going to no Canada tonight.

He said, Hey, no problema, Chappie. No problema.

Yeah, sure, I say. We're walking side by side close to the building to stay out of the wind and snow and as we're passing the big J. C. Penney's windows I notice up ahead that there's a guy working inside on one of the window displays and he's got all these naked man-nequins that he's moving around. When we get closer I see that the mannequins are like in pieces with their arms and hands lying on the floor and some of them don't even have any heads and the ones that do are bald. They have breasts and all but no nipples or pubic hair. It's like they're adults but they're really little kids. Then the guy who's setting them up disappears through a door into the store to get some clothes for them or something and I stop by the glass and look in at all the body parts.

C'mon, Chappie, Buster said. We've done our window-shopping for tonight.

Yeah, wait a minute, I said. I'd never seen mannequins like that before, all naked with their arms and heads look-ing like they were sliced off. There were these bright over-head lights inside the window that made it look like a dis-secting room in a morgue or something. Definitely it was the grossest thing I'd ever seen, at least at that moment it was which is strange I guess because I'd seen lots of really gross things by then.

C'mon, let's get out of here, Buster says like suddenly he's afraid someone'll see us.

I say, I don't think I want to do that screen test, man.

Cut the shit, Chappie. We have a deal.

No, I say and I back off a few steps. I still couldn't take my eyes off the mannequins. It was like I was in a dream and I didn't want to wake up and this guy Buster Brown was standing by my bed shaking me by the shoulder.

He goes like, There's the matter of my twenty bucks, kid.

That's when I turned and started running. I ran back the way we'd come, past the Sears toward the entrance to the mall and I hear Buster's feet slamming along behind me and him hollering, You little bastard! Give me back my money!

Buster was definitely pissed and he ran pretty good for an old guy so when I go through the door he's only a few steps behind me. Inside there was no one in sight except way in the distance by the fountain but I spotted a fire exit sign a little ways down the mall and a door I could maybe lock behind me once I got through. I raced over to it and yanked it open and went in and slammed it shut just as Buster got there. There was no way to lock it from the inside though so I clamped onto the handle while Buster pulled on the other side until finally I couldn't hold it closed anymore and when I let go Buster went flying.

Before he could get up I pulled the door shut again and took off down this long narrow hallway. There were doors and other hallways running off the main hall like in a video game maze and with all these fluorescent lights it was very bright, but no people anywhere. At one point I stopped and peeked back around a corner and listened for Buster. I could hear footsteps in the distance, somebody running but I couldn't tell if it was water dripping or him or if he was going in the other direction away from me or about to pounce on me from behind. I didn't even know how to get back to the mall where the people were.

This time when I start to run it's like I'm a little kid lost in some kind of carnival funhouse and I'm panicking. I go down one hall and hang a left and come to a dead-end and make a U-turn back the same way I came. A second later I'm running along another hall and when I fly through a door with an exit sign on it I'm in a hall just like the one I left. I'm totally confused by now. It's like I've been taken off the planet earth and set down on this new planet where there's no people. I think I was almost crying by then.

Suddenly I smelled food cooking. There was a door ahead of me and when I pushed through it I almost knocked over a huge stainless steel counter with all kinds of steaming food in these big pans. I'm back in the mall but I've come out in the middle of the food court behind the counter of Wang's Pavilion the Chinese take-out place and these three Chinese guys and a tiny Chinese woman are staring at me very shocked. They all start jabbering in Chinese at once and waving their hands at me in this very pissed-off way.

I go, C'mon, man, chill out, willya fucking chill, for chrissake! But it's like they don't understand English. It was late and there were no customers in the place anyhow but these people were acting like I'm some kind of freako terrorist. I pull out Buster's twenty and go, Hey, man, I just want to buy some chopped suey, and they shut up for a second and stare suspiciously at the money like it's not

American. But then I glance over their heads into the food court and here comes Buster.

I freeze and the Chinese guys follow my eyes and slowly turn around and then they see him too and they must be figuring out that he's the bad guy I'm running from because they don't say anything, they just go back to work cleaning out their pans and stacking trays and so on. Then I noticed that Buster had Froggy the Gremlin with him. He was holding her by the hand like she was a rag doll. She looked really tired now, like she was in a nod.

They walked slowly past Wang's and out of the food court on down the mall toward the exit to the parking lot and I watched them the whole time until they disappeared from sight. I felt incredibly sad then. I felt guilty too because of losing my courage and deciding not to take her place when I saw those mannequins in the window.

What you want? the head Chinese guy said to me.

I pointed to a couple of green and brown things in the pans and he dished the stuff into a Styrofoam box and I paid and got my change. I was ready to book through the front when I spotted Black Bart cruising the food court looking spaced like he'd managed to score some weed. It was late, there was almost nobody left in the mall except the workers and Bart making his nightly roundup of the last couple of kids still hanging out and the bums sleeping on the benches and so on, driving them with his stoned smile into the cold snowy night.

Not me though. I slipped through the door behind Wang's Pavilion with my box of food and returned to the maze of hallways out back where I wandered around until finally I found this janitor's closet I could sleep in and Bart didn't find out about me crashing back there every night until about two weeks later. By then everything was cool with the bikers again and Russ's mom had kicked him out for drinking all her booze one night and busting the place up so we went back to our old crib over the Video Den in Au Sable. Russ had his same room as before and I had to sleep on the couch in the livingroom but I didn't mind, I knew then that as long as my stepfather was still living at my mom's I was never going back there.

FOUR

ADIRONDACK IRON

In the beginning and all winter I was only dealing small-load weed to the bikers which was cool because A, lots of kids in Au Sable were dealing then mostly in school where I never went near anyhow but everywhere around town too so we were like a swarm of flies and it was low-risk to be one of them what with so few swatters. And B, it didn't feel like a wrong thing to be doing even though it was illegal. Especially given the way I looked at booze in those days from what I saw of its effect on the bikers for one and my stepdad for another and even my mom, which is not something I want to go into right now. Plus it was the only way I could keep my crib in the apartment over the Video Den with my friend Russ and his biker roommates.

I was pretty heavy into skunk then myself but I could've dumped it off easy if I'd had a good reason to, which I didn't because like always high was better than low as those were my only two alternatives. It was cool though, so long as I had a warm squat and adequate food to eat and friends.

Russ was my friend. And the bikers were my friends too, even though they were older and kind of unpredictable. Russ had hooked up with them because of his job at the Video Den, which he'd had since before he quit school and got kicked out of his house by his mom for doing drugs. But the job was only part-time days and he couldn't afford the apartment over the store on his own so he offered to share it with this one guy he knew, Bruce Walther who was more or less a friendly biker in spite of how he looked.

But then Bruce'd started bringing his friends into the place because they were sort of a gang although he called them family. He like underlined it when he said it. These dudes're *fam-i-ly*, man. You don't fucking deny your *family*.

So they moved in, different ones, four or five of them at a time and sometimes their girlfriends who they called their old ladies or just split-tails or gash but the same ones never stayed long. The squat was this big funky apartment owned by Rudy LaGrande the guy who ran the Video Den with three bedrooms and a bunch of mostly broken old furniture. The stove partially worked though and the refrigerator but I remember the toilet was stopped up a lot that winter. Russ still paid half the rent but only got the pantry off the kitchen for his room where he had a mattress on the floor and his old stereo from home and his heavy metal tapes and *Playboy* collection all of which the bikers used whenever they wanted so Russ kept a lock on the door.

No question my mom and Ken truly did not want to see me anymore so I settled permanently onto this ratty old sofa in the livingroom which was okay except when the bikers were partying which they did a lot of and sometimes passed out on my couch and burned holes in it and barfed in their sleep. Once in a while like when they got whacked on crank they went crazy and Russ and I had to sleep in his car or someplace else but as long as I kept the bikers in skunk the apartment was free for me and usually peaceful so I didn't complain. I had to unload the weed pretty much at cost to keep the bikers from buying it off of other kids or trying to buy it themselves off of Hector the Spanish guy, who was only into selling sandwich bags wholesale to kids which I think is the safest way to deal in a small town. But I still managed once in a while to pull a few bucks out for myself plus the occasional nick. Besides all I needed money for then was smokes and food which I mostly ate at the mall because if I brought anything back to the squat the bikers ate it. It was smalltime dealing for sure and in spite of it I was usually broke but it wasn't very dangerous or wrong and my material needs were few.

Plus for a kid without a home it was an interesting way of life. The bikers for instance kept you pretty alert. Bruce was sort of the head biker because he'd been in the Gulf War and knew a lot about Arabs and desert life and weapons and he had these incredible tattoos all over his chest and back and up and down his arms of Arab guys with swords in their teeth and harem girls and suchlike. He lifted weights all day at Murphy's Gym where he said he was one of the trainers but he only hung out there and got to use the weights free because he was a good advertisement. He had arms and pecs as big as hams and because of them and his tattoos he almost never wore a shirt except for when he went out in winter when he just wore his leather jacket and kept it unzipped. He had an incredible body for a human being, like he was from the planet of the weightlifters, and he had these awesome nipple rings and shaved the hair off of his chest and stomach several times a week. Straights gave Bruce a lot of room and he took it like it was his in the first place, like he was a cop although he hated cops and called them pigs. Bruce used quite a few of those old hippie terms.

I think he was the smartest of the bikers who actually as a group were not very intelligent. Russ was intelligent. More than me anyhow and even more than Bruce although I was two years younger than Russ whereas Bruce was probably thirty. Smart or not, Russ was only sixteen then and thus he pretty much had to take shit not just from Bruce but from all the bikers which was often some pretty stupid shit, like when after they'd seen this old biker movie they made him stand in the middle of the Grand Union parking lot one night while they drove their Harleys around him in figure 8s to see who could come closest without hitting him. I sat in Russ's Camaro and watched and kept hoping they wouldn't remember I was there which they didn't because they were so whacked and into tormenting Russ who I think bugged them on account of his intelligence and the Video Den guy had put the lease in his name so Russ had to collect the rent. Also Russ tended to talk too much and too big especially when he was scared, and around the bikers he was scared a lot so they liked to punish him for that too.

Around big dogs if you're a kid you either learn to do the little dog or you book. Russ had trouble learning the little dog but he was stuck with the bikers due to his early friendship with Bruce and his job and the apartment, and

I was stuck with Russ due to my home situation and being too young to get a job yet, so in a sense like Bruce said we *were* a family whether we wanted to be or not which is true of real families anyhow.

Of course like always things could've been worse and that's why me and Russ didn't complain or go anywhere else. The town of Au Sable was like our home base. It was where our parents lived and where we had once been little kids and had lived with them. Plus it was where the friends were. There and up at the mall in Plattsburgh.

All the bikers rode strictly Harleys or else were planning to get one soon. Everything else was Jap shit or Kraut shit or Brit shit. What they liked was American shit—softtails, shovelheads. Bruce used to say, Harleys are iron horses, man. Fucking iron horses. He liked to repeat himself, probably because he was used to talking to people who didn't get it the first time. Due to his obsession with weightlifting he had given them the name Adirondack Iron which they had painted on their leathers and had gotten tattooed upside down under their left forearms so you could read it when they did a power salute, like they were an actual serious-minded motorcycle gang or one of those foreign skinhead bands. They looked more organized than they were. They talked like being a piece of Adirondack Iron was the whole point of their lives and maybe it was but some of them had wives and even kids someplace who they occasionally visited when they ran out of money.

Actually the Adirondack Iron and even to some degree Bruce were all assholes who couldn't get real jobs so they mostly stayed drunk or high all night and slept off the days or just chilled on the back porch listening to Russ's tapes or worked on their bikes in the yard. They were like dogs and Bruce was the lead dog, sort of a German shepherd or one of those big Alaskan huskies. He made decisions and gave orders and the other guys usually followed them or else carefully ignored him.

One of the guys, Roundhouse whose real name he once told me was Winston Whitehouse, was humongously fat and hadn't had a haircut since the third grade he said and had never once shaved or cut his beard and he'd ended up looking like one of those Sasquatches. Roundhouse's whole body from his eyes to his toenails, including his neck and shoulders down to his hands was covered like with a pelt and when he stood up you expected to see a tail. He was from New Hampshire or someplace like that where his uncle'd been a famous murderer and when he wasn't bragging about his uncle all Roundhouse talked about was fucking and sucking like he couldn't get enough of it. He had a bunch of stolen credit cards that he used strictly for phone sex with Orientals, Dial-a-Jap he called it, his favorite recreational activity, but whenever there were any real females around he plugged his headphones into Russ's box and got drunk and nodded out. He owned this truly cherry '67 Electra Glide though, much admired and he loved his bike and when he wasn't on the phone in the john jerking off he was down in the yard taking his hog apart and putting it back together again. Basically he was harmless and good-natured and after Bruce who due to his muscles I kind of admired I liked Roundhouse the best.

There was this other guy though named Joker whose real name I never knew, a short square-bodied guy with a head like a shovel and tiny flattened blue eyes and many facial scars. He had a bleached white buzz-cut and all his tattoos were words, Megadeth and Terminator and Suck, and even a few complete sentences, like Eat Shit and Satan Lives. All the bikers had guns I think but Joker had the most guns and he liked to clean and polish and fondle them the way the other guys did their bikes which was natural I suppose since he was one of the bikers who didn't have a hog of his own and was always thinking about buying one soon. He had a very cool little blue Smith & Wesson Ladysmith .38 which he called his pussy pistol and this huge single-shot .44 magnum Thompson with a sixteen-inch barrel that he said was his dick stick.

Generally though Joker showed very few signs of life and almost never talked to anyone least of all me but he was the one biker I was scared of all the time, even when he wasn't whacked. His neck went straight from his ears to his shoulders and he wore a heavy chain choke-collar around it in case you didn't get the point from the tattoos or the guns. Sometimes when Bruce was bored he'd grab Joker's chain and yank on it hard and say, Back, Joker! Back! Release! Joker'd growl and snap and drool and pull against the chain until his face got red and he couldn't hardly breathe and when Bruce let go he'd back off panting and whimpering like he'd been cruelly deprived of some primo meat-violence.

But I got through the winter okay because my stepfather probably thanks to my mom decided not to let the cops put me away for my Christmas shoplifting so long as I didn't try to move back in with them again, which was funny since the cops'd signed me over to my parents in the first place only on condition that I move back with them and take eighth grade over. The new rule was basically don't bother your parents and don't bother the cops or one of them will sic the other on you. All I had to do was stay out of the way of both and not flag either by going back to school who didn't want me anyhow. Which wasn't hard because they both tended to look in the other direction when they saw me, my parents on account of my bad attitude and drug use plus my overall funky appearance, which made them permanently pissed and ashamed of me at least my mom, and the cops because as a criminal I was more trouble than I was worth, just another homeless stoned dropout dealing small-load boom to the locals.

But even the cops know that a little weed can't hurt anybody. Most of them when they bust you are only trying to score for themselves anyhow and once they take your stash if you lick their boots and promise never to smoke reefer again so long as you live and thank them for saving you from a life of drug addiction and criminality they keep your drugs and let you go. Unless they're after you for something else you're not worth the paperwork. I've learned that's generally true of life, if you're not worth the paperwork adults won't hassle you. Except for the truly dumb and the nutcases of course, people who act on principle. They'll hassle you.

It was early spring and the nights were still cold but the days were getting warmer and the old gray snowbanks were starting to shrink and thousands of frozen dog turds and months of garbage and paper trash and lost clothes were coming up thawed and soggy all over town but especially in our yard behind the Video Den.

Not my favorite season. In winter the snow keeps reality like clean and covered in white but in spring you see everything too much for what it is. When the packed ice finally melts it leaves all these deep potholes behind and cracks in the streets and sidewalks and the snowbanks make these huge puddles of black oily water. The frozen ground thaws and turns into deep muck and soppy dead grass.

Nights are okay though because you can't see much and it's cold so everything freezes up but during the days the sky is always this pale yellowish color like old mattress stuffing. It makes a strange light and the town looks like it's been through this hundred-year war and everybody's forgotten what they were fighting about so it's hard for them to get too excited now that it's over.

On account of the long winter and still having to stay inside a lot I guess the bikers had lately been into slam-dancing. It was more slamming than dancing and they didn't even need music to do it, they just lurched around the apartment like a bunch of Frankensteins and bounced off each other's bodies and jumped against the floor with both feet which made a lot of likable noise because of their biker boots. Likable to them, I mean, and to me too although I myself didn't get into it but only watched from the kitchen door and tried to stay out of their way and kept poised to sneak out if necessary.

This one night they were more stoned than usual, really choked and there were a couple of decent females that Bruce and Joker had picked up at Purdy's over in Keene which is a respectable bar, not a biker place and to impress them the guys had started doing multiple tequila shots and beer and Roundhouse had put this old truly raucous Pearl Jam tape on Russ's box and started slam-dancing. I guess it was the only way he could figure out how to make the females notice him. He got pretty wild, all that hair and fat leaping and bouncing and pounding against the floor and then when the females seemed to like it and think it was funny the other guys joined in and pretty soon they were all slamming each other while the females watched.

The females definitely weren't skags but they weren't anything special either. *Not* babes. They had their own car and were in their thirties, my mom's age practically and thick in the middle and big-assed like her but they thought I was real cute. The one who said she liked my mohawk was named Christie and had on a Fuck You I'm From Texas tee shirt and no bra so you could see her nipples which was cool and the other whose name was Clarissa had on this tee shirt that said My Next Husband Will Be Normal but she right away put on Bruce's leather jacket so I didn't have a chance to see if she had a bra on. Bruce's nipples you could see though since as usual he wasn't wearing any shirt and also his little gold nipple rings which always made me nervous but if you didn't look at them especially if you're short like me you had to look at his shaved stomach and chest and tattoos too so you tried not to look at him at all, which I didn't. But then he always goes, What's your fucking problem, Chappie, you got a problem? You oughta look at me when I'm fucking talking to you, Chappie.

So I go, Hey, no fucking problem, man, and stare into his eyes which are blue and cold like Joker's but handsome and then he smiles down like he's triumphed over a major adversary even though if he wanted he could squash me like a flea.

The music was really loud, Pearl Jam is grunge but they play loud even when the volume is turned down and the men of Adirondack Iron had it cranked and I was starting to worry that the floor would cave in from the slam-dancing when suddenly I turn around and Russ is coming through the door behind me looking seriously pissed.

Shut the fuck up! he yells. The Old Lady's downstairs and she's ripshit!

The Old Lady was Wanda LaGrande wife of Rudy who owned the building and the Video Den and rented out the rest although except for our squat the rest was permanently vacant because of the decrepit condition of the building and I suppose the presence of Adirondack Iron. Plus the neighborhood was not the best.

Bruce stops slamming and comes over and puts his huge sweaty arm around Russ's skinny shoulders and says, What's the matter, little man? It's a party, man. It's a fucking party. Just chill, okay?

Russ pulls away from the arm and goes, The Old Lady's downstairs hitting on me for the rent and she's talking eviction again unless I come up with some money and you guys are making up her mind for her. I'm serious, man, I need some money from you guys, he said.

Bruce smiles like he does and reaches down and picks up Russ like he's a stuffed animal he won at the fair and kisses him on the nose. Still smiling he says, Fuck you, little man, and then he leaps back into the pack of slam-dancers sending them flying off his meaty shoulders against the walls and furniture. Clarissa, the one wearing Bruce's jacket was sitting in a corner with a can of Genny in her hand and she waves at me and pats the floor next to her for me to come over. She was definitely starting to look less like my mom and more like a babe.

But then Russ says to me, C'mon downstairs, man. Wanda gets off on you, maybe she'll lighten up and think of something else if you're there.

I think yeah why not, it's my squat too and I need to take some of the responsibilities once in a while, so together we go down the rickety outside staircase to the Video Den. Wanda liked to pretend that she managed the Video Den for her husband but mainly she was this dotty old lady married to a drunk who sent her out sometimes to collect the day's cash from the till and whatever rent money she could scrounge out of Russ and buy booze with it. I think they'd both been married a couple of times before and were together now more or less out of convenience. Luckily she had a weakness for talking about colon cancer on account of her father and several brothers and ex-husbands had died from it and usually Russ could get her talking about colon cancer a mile a minute until she forgot about collecting the rent and sometimes she even forgot to empty the till, which made it easier for Russ to skim a few bucks before making the night deposit and afterwards he could say she had taken it herself when she came in earlier.

People like Wanda and Rudy LaGrande on account of being drunk for half a century have very short and unreliable memories you might say and if you don't piss them off too much you can easily victimize them. Russ was into that. Although I myself was not and in fact I kind of liked her cancer stories. She always started in the beginning when her father or brother or whoever was healthy and unsuspecting and ended with all the disgusting details of his painful long-drawn-out death which was cool. The idea was you were supposed to be glad you didn't have colon cancer yourself and for me it worked. Afterwards I was always real glad I didn't have it and that made her happy.

This one night though Wanda happened to be unusually irritated with the world and was not distractable by anyone's apparent interest in colon cancer, even mine. It was cold out, close to zero and her husband Rudy's driving her into the night for money and more booze before the liquor stores closed had given her a crossed hair so to get even she'd been making all kinds of upper-level Video Den management moves and giving Russ a general hard time. Also the noise from upstairs must've reminded her that the rent was two whole months late. Which was why Russ'd come up to try and get the guys to chill.

But when we come through the door Wanda's standing behind the counter with the empty register drawer open in front of her and the first thing she does when she sees us is throw Russ's shearling jacket at him. It was mine actually, from my mom but I had sold it to Russ for twenty-five bucks to invest in half a bag of skunk on condition I could buy it back when I dealt the weed which I hadn't yet. Russ meanwhile'd been loaning me his old jean jacket.

She goes, Russell, you're a thief! Look here! Look! There is not a single cent in here! Not one penny!

Wanda's a small woman, round and energetic like a chickadee with frizzled black-dyed hair and heavy makeup that she puts on crooked and she always dresses like she's got a date with a traveling salesman, which is a sign I guess that she once had a good social life. She says to Russ, I happen to know for a fact that *Pretty Woman* was returned today and should have been paid for and also several more that were out when I went looking for them yesterday and the day before. Give me your key to the store, Russell, just turn it over now. As of this moment you're fired.

She was right, he had been stealing. Plus I knew Russ hadn't legally rented any videos that day or collected for any that were returned although he had loaned quite a few to his friends as he often did in exchange for a tray or even a roach sometimes or to impress girls. And *Pretty Woman* was one of those sensitive true-love movies that make girls hot so he'd kept it freely circulating among them ever since it first came out.

He says in his smoothest voice, Hey, hey, c'mon, Wanda, chill, it was ol' Rudy himself who checked out *Pretty Woman*. He does it all the time, you know that, and never even signs for them or pays either. He took it out probably for you. He himself returned it this morning, I think. He probably brought it home for you himself and forgot to tell you or left it in his car or else you guys got too busy or something. . .

Don't give me that fast talk! she yells. You're only trying to change the subject. Just get out of here, Russell, she says, calmer now. Go. And all your friends upstairs, the motorcycle gang. Get them out too. Chappie, I'm sorry, you too. Out.

Yeah, well, that's easier said than done, Russ says looking up at the ceiling which is rumbling and starting to shake off bits of paint and plaster. You could hear Pearl Jam pretty good and could almost make out the words even.

Don't you threaten me. I could always call the police, she says. They'll get you out.

You could. Yes, you could. You certainly could call the

police, Wanda. But the place is a firetrap, he pointed out. Then he told her if the cops came they'd probably condemn the building and she'd have to close down the whole operation. No more Video Den, Wanda. Nada.

This made her nervous. Just get out of there by the weekend, she said. All of you.

Russ was silent and downcast for a while. I doubt you could find anybody to replace us up there, he says. Who else would rent it?

She purses her orange lips. She's thinking. She says, Two months plus this month, two hundred and forty dollars you owe me.

Right, and he could pay it off a whole lot easier, he said, if she didn't fire him because then she could take part of the rent out of his pay, like thirty bucks a week and in a single four-week month she'd have half of what was owed her and he would definitely collect the rest from Bruce and the other guys. Definitely.

No, she says, very firm. You're still fired. You've been stealing from us, Russell. From now on she would run the store herself, she told him and he would just have to come up with the rent some other way.

He argued with her for a while longer but it didn't do any good, her mind was made up, we weren't quite evicted yet but Russ was definitely fired.

Finally me and Russ left the Video Den and sat out on the back steps in silence. I knew Russ was thinking hard which he's very good at. His chin was in his hands and there was like smoke coming from his ears.

I said, What're you gonna do, man? Get a job up at the mall?

Yeah, right, Chappie. The mall. The line forms at the

end, man. They got fucking college graduates up there flipping Big Macs and carrying out the garbage. Forget it, man.

Well maybe you could sell your Camaro. You could get eight, nine hundred bucks easy for it. More maybe.

You bet your ass more. A grand and a half easy. But no fucking way, man. That car's all I got between me and total nothingness.

What, then? I was more than idly curious because in a way I was dependent on Russ, him being two years older than me and all. Russ was the same for me as his Camaro was for him, the only thing this side of total nothingness.

Well, he says nodding in the direction of the bikers upstairs, there's a lotta empty bongs up there. Maybe I'll start keeping 'em filled. Plus Hector told me anytime I wanted crank to deal he had it available. Those guys may not have any money for rent but they always have it for booze and drugs.

Crank. Jeez, I don't know, I said. That's some heavy shit, man. I was thinking if Russ starts dealing drugs of any kind to the bikers he's going to put me out of business but also selling speed was different from the occasional bag of weed. I was just a kid then and not too good at telling right from wrong but Russ was smart and I trusted him so I said, Whyn't you deal just the meth, okay? You do the crank and leave the skunk to me, man. It's sort of my specialty, you know?

Yeah, sure. Sure, man. That's cool, he said but he was thinking hard, he was already making deep plans that probably did not include me. Except as his unwilling accomplice.

FIVE

PRESUMED DEAD

It was around this time that I started missing my mom again. Not really missing her because I knew she didn't want me back, more like wondering what she was doing at certain times of the day or night while I was doing strange stuff that would have made her think I'd died and gone to hell if she'd known about it. I wasn't *doing* strange stuff so much as witnessing it, but my mom would've tried to keep me from seeing it if she could. Anyone would've.

Like, I'd wake up in the morning on my sofa in the livingroom and one of the bikers, Joker or Raoul or Packer would be over in the corner on his hands and knees with his pants around his ankles humping some female from behind I'd never seen before while Roundhouse sprawled on a chair next to them jerking off and slugging back a quart of Genny. It was pretty gross.

I'd pull my blanket over my head and think of my mom

just getting up and coming out to the kitchen in her old flannel robe and fuzzy pink slippers to make coffee and feed Willie the cat. My stepdad would still be snoring in the back bedroom and my mom with these few minutes to herself would flick on the kitchen TV and watch the *Today* show and let Willie sit on her lap while she sat at the table and drank her coffee and smoked her first cigarette.

Willie I truly did miss and sometimes I thought about bringing a kitten back to the squat. They were all over town that time of year and people would give you a whole litter if you wanted. But I didn't trust the bikers not to kill it. So I'd just lie there on the couch all morning and let myself miss ol' Willie instead.

Meanwhile out in our kitchen Bruce would be standing in his jockstrap at the sink full of old caked dishes and pans shaving the stubble off his huge chest and washboard belly preparing for his daily pump at Murphy's Gym, and in the bathroom some weird thin gray-skinned pimply guy with a motormouth Bruce'd dragged back to the squat from Plattsburgh the night before was shooting up without the decency to close the bathroom door while he did it. Russ was in his crib with the door locked on the inside where he slept until late afternoon which he said he did because daytime was the only time the squat was quiet enough to sleep but I think he was starting to dip into the crank he was selling and liked to stay up all night yackety-yakking with his customers.

Russ was into the big subjects anyhow, God and the Universe and so on even when he wasn't high but the meth made it seem like all those things were linked together in this gigantic cosmic conspiracy, like algebra only real and since I wasn't very interested in math or any of the big subjects in the first place and it was all way over my head anyhow due to my youth Russ liked talking to the other guys instead especially when they were wired on crank. To me it was just talk but to them it was reality.

Most days I hitched up to the mall and hung there with some kids I knew until it closed and Black Bart the security cop or one of his little helpers ran us out and then I'd hitch back to Au Sable and crash at the squat and except when they wanted some of my weed the men of Adirondack Iron pretty much ignored me, like I was their mascot or something. They teased me about my mohawk a lot because to them it was retro but to me it was like my trademark. It was how people knew me.

Once Joker was going to cut it off. Get *bald*, man, he said, you look like a fucking hippie. Who's got some scissors, gimme some fucking scissors, he said and he grabbed me by the arm so I couldn't move.

Nobody had any scissors naturally. Use a knife, one of the guys said. Scalp the little motherfucker. He looks like a fucking Indian anyhow.

You cut my hawk, man, I'll slice off your balls while you're sleeping, I said to Joker.

Luckily Bruce was there and intervened. He grabbed onto Joker's choke collar and said, Release, Joker. Release! Chappie here's my little buddy and I like him the way he is. He's my little banty rooster, he said and ruffled my hawk.

Yeah, well fuck you too, I said and he laughed but Joker backed off permanently on the hair thing although he still tried to scare me whenever he had a knife in his hands which wasn't that often however since he preferred holding guns.

*   *   *

Then one night I hitched back from the mall late with this guy from town who worked at Sears and all the way home to Au Sable he played classical music from this station in Vermont which was cool and unusual and got me thinking a lot about my mom and Willie and my previous homelife but not my stepfather, so when I came up the stairs to the apartment I was feeling incredibly mellow. This was in April and most of the snow had melted and the black oily water had run off into the river and the mud had dried out and the air was warm and wet even at night and I could smell the buds of the trees and bushes, lilacs and such and the sound of the river a half mile away made me think of little kindergarten kids in a playground for some reason.

The door was locked which was not normal so I had to bang on it awhile until finally it opened a crack and Russ peeks out. It's only Chappie, he calls back.

Lemme the fuck in, I say.

He goes, Wait a minute, and locks the door again. So I wait and pretty soon he comes back and lets me inside my own apartment for Christ's sake. What the fuck's going on? I say. Right away I notice it's kind of dark. There's only candles burning in the livingroom and all the lights in the apartment are off.

Russ says, Just be cool, man.

We go into the livingroom and Bruce and Joker and Roundhouse are there and two other guys who've been staying at the squat lately, this guy Packer who's from Buffalo and has a classic '77 FLH with chrome drag pipes and everything and his buddy Raoul who drives a piece-of-shit Chevy pickup and is one of those bikers without a bike like Joker which always seems to put an edge on them, like they're pissed off at guys who do have bikes and also at guys like me and Russ who don't particularly want one. I'd barely graduated from skateboards and dirt bikes back then and Russ of course had his Camaro.

You holding? Bruce says to me. All around the living-room were these big unopened boxes that said Sony Trinitron and Magnavox and IBM on them and the guys were sitting around looking tired like they'd just finished lugging the boxes upstairs.

I had a bag of tropicana in one pocket for myself and another in my other pocket for sale so I said sure and passed it over. Forty bucks, man, I said. That's what it cost me, I said which wasn't quite true since I'd paid Hector twenty for it. What's with the boxes? I asked him.

Nobody answered. Then Bruce says to Packer, Give the kid thirty bucks, and to my surprise he did. I'm thinking I should've said fifty on account of it was tropicana not northcountry homegrown and maybe I'd have gotten forty and then I could've bought my shearling jacket back from Russ.

Bruce stoked up a bong and they all proceeded to get lifted for a while and didn't offer any to us which was boring so Russ and I went into his crib and split a blunt by ourselves. What's the deal with the boxes? I asked him.

Be cool, man. Like, you shouldn't've said anything out there. It's TVs, man. And computers and VCRs. All kinds of shit. Brand new.

This was excellent news because we didn't have a TV or a VCR in the squat although I didn't care one way or the other about a computer. But a VCR would be good because I hadn't watched a video since Russ lost his job at the Video Den. And I was missing my MTV, especially late-night shows like *Headbangers Ball* and other heavy metal programming.

But the electronics were not for our personal use, I quickly discovered. Bruce and the guys were stashing the stuff until they could deliver them to a guy from Albany he'd met who had a warehouse and sold them wholesale to these Arabs and Jews who had stores down in New York City. Bruce and the guys were paid by the pound, Russ explained. So much for TVs, so much for computers and so on and the boxes couldn't be opened because they ended up being sold in New York as brand new with guarantees and everything.

Where'd they get them? I asked.

Service Merchandise, man. Up to the mall.

No shit. *How'd* they get them though? They just break in and steal them?

Naw, man. Took 'em right off the loading dock while the store's still open. They just drove up earlier tonight in Raoul's pickup alongside real customers picking up the shit they'd actually paid for and filled the truck, man, and drove off. The security guy, the black dude, Bart, he arranged it. Bruce worked it out, it's his deal.

Cool, I said and took a big hit off the blunt.

Russ said, Yeah, I'm trying to get the guys to cut me some of the action. There's a shitload of money in this and with Black Bart on the inside there's no way we'll get caught, man. There might even be something in it for you too.

Cool, I said but I was thinking it was wrong to be stealing stuff on this scale. It was different from me stealing some old coin collection from my mom or the Christmas shoplifting that I got busted for when I was only trying to get back in her good graces. Besides I'd gotten swiftly punished for both those crimes and as long as I stayed away from home I didn't feel guilty about them anymore. This was different and the punishment to fit the crime was going to be heavy so I didn't want any part of it. Plus I'd already done enough in my life that was wrong and didn't need any more.

So it was only Bruce and his gang, Joker, Roundhouse, Raoul and Packer, and Russ if they'd let him, not me who were into stealing the TVs and stuff and for a while every few nights they brought more of it back to the apartment until the place was like a warehouse and all the rooms were filled with these huge cartons so that we had to climb over them just to get in and out. I guess the guy from Albany wasn't ready for delivery or something. The door stayed locked and nobody else was allowed in the place anymore except me and Russ, probably because Bruce and the guys were afraid if they kicked us out we might go home to our parents and tell them or the cops and besides we were more or less responsible for keeping them in drugs. One or two of the bikers were always in the apartment on guard, usually stoned or asleep though and they sent me and Russ out for food and smokes and on minor errands besides drugs which for once they paid us for.

There was a fair amount of money flowing then, expense money from the Albany guy I figured or maybe some sales to private individuals on the side so for the first time I had enough cash on hand to indulge in some amusements at the mall like video games and the occasional movie. Russ bought a set of new sheepskin seatcovers for his Camaro at Pep Boys and screwed a girl who was a senior at Plattsburgh High on them the first night and told me about it later. It sounded like fun but I still wasn't ready for that.

Russ talked a lot about the TVs and all. The whole deal really had him stoked and he wanted to be a partner in crime with the bikers and bring me in as a partner too but the men of Adirondack Iron were not interested in cutting Russ or me a piece of their pie so to speak and they got very pissed off whenever Russ tried to talk them into it especially Bruce.

Then one night when they were lugging another load of boxes into the apartment Russ ran down to help them and grabbed onto a box and Bruce said, Get the fuck outa here, kid! Don't you ever touch this shit! You understand me? *Ever*!

I was standing at the top of the stairs holding the door open for Raoul and Joker to carry this huge 27 inch Zenith inside and I'm thinking Russ should not push this, Bruce is the one guy not to cross. But Russ keeps it up. He goes, Hey, c'mon, Bruce, I'm cool, and besides, I've already been incriminated. You might as well make me a partner and put me to work like the other guys. Adirondack Iron, man! he says with a grin and gives Bruce a power salute with his tattoo showing.

I start down the stairs to see if maybe I can distract Russ or something before he gets in too deep but Bruce has already gently set the box he was carrying on the tailgate of Raoul's pickup as if to free his hands to beat the living shit out of Russ and he says, Just what the fuck do you mean *incriminated*?

Well, you know what I mean, like I'm in the presence

of stolen goods, man. So I'm an accomplice to a crime. I mean, I could always say I didn't know what was in the boxes or where you got them, but who knows, they might not believe that.

Are you threatening me, you little asshole? Are you?

Moi? Mais no, man! All I want is the same as the other guys're getting, since I'm running the same risk as them. You can use the help anyhow. Like, whaddaya say to only a half a share? Since I'm a minor and all and can't be charged with a felony.

Bruce sees me on the stairs a few steps behind Russ and he says, What about you, Chappie? You in on this shit too? Are you threatening me like this asshole?

I didn't want to abandon Russ so I tried to answer in a way that might help him without necessarily hurting me. He's just high, man, I say which was true anyhow, Russ had been gobbling inhalers all afternoon and was speeding pretty good. C'mon, Russ, let's go cool out, I say and grab his arm but he yanks it away.

Nobody's threatening nobody, he says. I'm negotiating, that's all.

Bruce goes, I don't fucking negotiate with assholes. I fuck 'em. I fuck 'em with my fist. He leans in real close to Russ then, Do you know what that is, kid? Fist-fucking?

I don't know if he did, I sure didn't but it sounded real undesirable so I said, He knows, man, don't worry, he knows. He's only high, I said and grabbed Russ by both shoulders hard now and practically dragged him away from Bruce although Russ didn't resist this time and was secretly glad probably that I was there to save him without him having to back down on his own.

Although he didn't admit it of course. He acted like I

had saved Bruce's ass instead of his. I got him into the driver's seat of his car and pretty soon we were driving down 9N along the Ausable River toward Jay and Keene, country villages where everyone had long since gone to bed. Russ's Camaro was the only car on the road, a good thing because he was wired and pissed and the combination made him a good talker but a lousy driver. But he didn't object or even seem to notice whenever I reached across and adjusted the steering wheel and got us back onto the road which was pretty narrow and windy and had the river on our left.

Russ wanted to get even but he also wanted to make a profit at it and he had this new idea how we could get both, although I definitely did not like his use of *we*. What we gotta do, he said, is take one or two VCRs at a time and sell them ourselves. Just the VCRs, man. They'll never miss them, those assholes don't even have an inventory. The VCRs don't take up much room, we can stash them in my trunk until we unload them. We specialize in VCRs, see, and sell them one by one at half price. New they go for what, three hundred, four hundred bucks apiece. We'll sell 'em for one fifty, or less, even. No matter how much, it'll still be one hundred percent profit. We can split two ways, seventy-five twenty-five, since I've got the car and I'll be doing most of the negotiating with the buyers.

Who're you gonna sell 'em to? I asked swerving the car back onto the road with my left hand and just missing a parked van and a whole row of maple trees.

Well, lemme think. For about ten seconds he thought. Rudy LaGrande for starters, he said. Ol' Rudy used to tell me how he wanted to rent out VCRs from the store only he couldn't afford to buy new ones and used weren't any good because you hadda keep paying to have 'em fixed. Yeah, Ol' Rudy'll probably want five or six at least.

Bruce'll notice five or six gone.

Not if we take them outa the squat one at a time and from different stacks. We just walk out with 'em early in the morning when whoever's there is sleeping and the next day we take another and so on. Simple.

I don't know, man. It's risky with those guys. They all got guns, man.

Chapstick, he said, we're already risking being busted so we might as well profit from it. Fuck those guys, man.

Yeah, but it's stealing.

Stealing from thieves is not the same as stealing from straights. Remember, thieves are not victims, man. Besides, he explained, this is kind of a step up. Morally speaking.

What d'you mean, a step up? I said and grabbed the wheel again and pulled the car back to the right and avoided hitting a railroad crossing sign by maybe a foot.

From dealing to stealing, man. I mean, which is better? Think about it. They're both fucking illegal so which is better? Didn't your parents teach you anything?

Not about the difference between dealing drugs to asshole bikers and stealing already stolen VCRs from them, I said. But that don't mean there isn't one.

One what?

A difference, man. I was thinking like Russ'd said there *was* a lot about right and wrong that my parents hadn't taught me and now due to my situation I was having to work out most of it myself. Everybody, Russ and the bikers, Black Bart and Rudy LaGrande and probably Wanda too and that creep Buster Brown at the mall who tried to get me to act in his porn movie and my stepfather and maybe even my mom, everybody but me seemed to think the difference between right and wrong was obvious. For them I guess what was right was what you could get away with and what was wrong was what you couldn't, but it made me feel stupid that I didn't know it too. It was like the difference between dealing small-load weed and dealing crank—there was one, I knew but I didn't know what it was. The whole thing was scary. It made you feel like once you stepped across the line you could never get back and were doomed from then on to a life of crime. Since everybody stepped across the line and did a wrong thing at least once in his life then everybody was doomed. Everybody was a criminal. Even my mom. You had to be a cat like Willie or a little kid like I once was not to be a criminal and for a human being like I was now that was impossible.

I decided that for the time being I didn't want to be any worse a criminal than I already was so I told Russ I wouldn't help him steal the VCRs from the bikers. He thought I was being stupid and a wuss but basically he was relieved I think because now he could keep all the profits for himself although I had to convince him first that my lips were sealed so to speak. And they were. No way I'd fuck over my best friend, my only friend actually if you didn't count Bruce and the bikers and some kids I knew a little up at the mall.

We drove along for a while and then he said he was worried about me because of how I wasn't taking advantage of opportunities to advance in the world.

Yeah, I said, like stealing stolen VCRs from psychos with guns.

It's freight forwarding, man. That's all. I'm into freight forwarding, and it don't matter to me what I ship or where it comes from or where it's going. That's someone else's problem.

It matters to me, I said.

Yeah, well, that's the difference between us, Chapstick. Which is what worries me about you. You can't spend your life dealing weed to Adirondack Iron, man. You've got to start thinking about the future. Biker gangs, they come and go, man.

I said yeah but I didn't mention that the main reason I hadn't gotten one of those Adirondack Iron tattoos of a winged helmet on my arm was exactly that, biker gangs do come and go. They really *aren't* your family.

Afterwards we didn't talk much and finally Russ turned around in Keene and drove back to the squat where to my surprise Bruce and the guys seemed glad to see us, I guess because in our absence they'd gotten scared and had figured out that we'd respond more favorably to kind treatment than to harsh. They were dumb but not totally dumb. I could tell they were nervous about having all that stolen stuff on their hands and two kids around who knew where it came from.

The very next morning bright and early Russ started up his freight forwarding company. I was on my couch asleep but when he walked past I woke up and with one eye half open watched him scoop a Panasonic VCR off a stack of boxes by my head and put it under his arm and stroll out the apartment door with it like he was taking out the garbage. I didn't move until he was gone and then I slowly lifted my head and peeked around the corner into the next bedroom where Bruce was crashed facedown and bareass except for his jockstrap on a mattress on the floor snoring like a chain saw. I looked back at the stack of VCRs beside me but even though I'd seen Russ take one away only a few seconds ago the pile seemed the same size as before which relieved me a lot although I was too nervous to go back to sleep afterwards.

But none of the guys noticed anything missing. The next morning Russ did it again, and the morning after, and even when he took two VCRs one each from different piles and then one day a portable computer it was the same. The livingroom and the rest of the apartment still seemed to be filled with big unopened boxes of electronics. I myself could see the difference of course because I'd watched him take them. But every day around ten or eleven the bikers'd eventually wake up and start prowling around the place looking for food or a morning beer and cigarettes like they usually did and no one noticed anything missing.

Except Russ, he was missing, which was unusual and noticeable even to bikers so finally one morning Bruce says to me, Where's your buddy? He got a job or something? The fucker usually stays in his room sleeping all day.

Beats the shit out of me, I said but I could see Bruce was suspicious although he didn't say anything, just stood there in his jockstrap by the kitchen door with a half-empty jar of this powdered muscle food he mixes up in a quart of orange juice and drinks every morning. He had his own special glass and everything that nobody else was allowed to use but he never washed it so who would. He poked the door to Russ's crib open a ways with his foot and looked around inside and then went back to mixing his breakfast.

He didn't lock his door like he usually does, he says.

Must be coming back soon, I said but I'm thinking

Russ probably didn't lock it so they'd think he was inside sleeping instead of up in Plattsburgh or someplace peddling stolen electronics.

If you see him today find out can he get me a dozen hits of acid by tonight. 'Cause tonight we're finally gonna deliver all this shit, Bruce says. And I'm gonna party hearty, man.

No problema, I say. That was an expression I'd picked up from that guy Buster Brown at the mall and I noticed that I used it only when I was wicked scared.

Yeah, he says laughing and chugging down his orange grunge and wiping it off his chin with the back of his hand. No problema. You are one funny little dude, Chappie, he says taking a few steps toward the livingroom. One funny little piece of shit. But then his expression changes like an unfamiliar and not particularly welcome thought has penetrated his brain and he goes, You been moving any of this stuff around, Chappie?

Me? No way, man. You told me not to touch any of it. I obey you, man.

Yeah, he said and then he walked slowly into the livingroom where I was lying on the couch with my blanket wrapped around me up to my chin and he studied the scene carefully. Something's wrong here, man. Something's very wrong.

I decide to say nothing. I'm thinking just be ready to run even though I've only got my underpants and a tee shirt on. I'm thinking up my escape route via Russ's crib which I can lock from inside, then out the window onto the back porch roof and down to the ground and out to the street. . . and then where?

It looked pretty hopeless. I was almost wishing Russ

would walk through the door and see what was happening and confess everything and save me but I knew he'd never do it.

Bruce says, You and your little buddy, I believe that you have stepped in some very deep shit, Chappie.

Whaddaya mean?

All kinds of stuff is missing from here. VCRs it looks like. And some of those portable computers. Which makes sense. Everything else is too big for you two little assholes to swipe without someone noticing. You've been lifting stuff from me, Chappie. Amazing!

I of course denied everything which was half the truth since I myself had not stolen anything off of Bruce and half a lie since I said Russ hadn't either. Not that I knew of. I added that. I guess to cut down on the lying part a little. But the second I said it I felt lonely because I was separating myself from Russ and then I felt guilty, real guilty because I knew how Bruce would hear it. The more power you've got the more you're able to do the right thing which is whatever you can get away with and at that point in my life I had no power whatsoever, I couldn't get away with anything so I had to do the wrong thing and tell the truth. I was the ultimate little dog and it was all I could do to keep from pissing down my own leg.

Not that you know of, he said. Yeah, right. Thanks very much. I was gonna do the both of you just to be sure I got the guilty party but now I'll only have to whack the one. I always liked you better than him anyhow. Whacking Russ'll be easy, the little bastard.

Joker was standing next to Bruce now and I guess he'd heard the whole conversation. If you whack one, he said, you got to whack the other, man.

Yeah, you're probably right, Bruce said sighing. Unless you help us out, he said to me.

Sure. Whaddaya want me to do?

Where's Russ at right now?

Joker stood leaning against the doorjamb fondling his little blue .38, his pussy-pistol. I could hear the other guys getting up in the back bedrooms. Roundhouse stumbled into the room rubbing his eyes with one huge fist and scratching crumbs and other items out of his pelt with the other. Wussup? Chappie goin' out for food?

The little assholes've been stealing our TVs and shit, man, Joker said.

Wow. Jeez, that's pretty fucking stupid.

Bruce asked me again where Russ was and I said I didn't know which was the truth and I think he believed me. Then I told him I was asleep when he went out which was a lie but he knew not to believe it. So me and him were at least still communicating. Bruce said for Roundhouse to get some duct tape from his toolbox which Roundhouse did and then he taped my hands together behind my back and my feet at the ankles and lifted me up and slung me over his shoulder like I was a lamb ready for slaughter and carried me into Russ's crib off the kitchen and put me down gently on Russ's mattress.

I don't know yet what I'm gonna do with you, he said. We'll just have to wait and see what Russ says for himself when he gets back. But for now this'll keep you out of trouble.

Joker stood behind him watching. When Bruce stepped away he brought the barrel of his gun down close to my head and smiled and said, Bang. Then he laughed and went back into the livingroom with the others.

From the door Bruce said to me, If you keep your mouth shut I won't tape it. Not one fucking peep, you understand?

I nodded yes and he went out and closed the door but I could hear them talking in the livingroom trying to figure out what to do next. Joker was clear on what he wanted to do which was blow me away and then Russ but the other guys were undecided and a little scared, I think. Even Bruce who was maybe into a lot of things but not murder. He was secretly gay or S and M or something weird like that because he liked to hassle gay guys when he saw them in public and make fairies in parks or the Greyhound station bathroom give him blowjobs and then he would beat the shit out of them and brag about it, and despite his body building and health foods he was a drug addict, plus he was a serious thief. But unless you're a true psycho like Joker everyone draws the line somewhere and I think Bruce drew the line at cold-blooded murder of teenaged boys. I did not take a whole lot of comfort from this however.

For a while I lay there looking up at Russ's Anthrax and Metallica posters. Russ'd decorated his crib to make it home-like, lots of nice domestic touches like the yellow and brown plaid curtains he'd found in somebody's trash and hung over the one window and the iron floor lamp and busted easychair. Pretty soon though I was getting cold because of only having my underwear on and no blanket so I hollered for Bruce to c'mere a minute which must have sounded like I was going to tell him where Russ was.

He came right in but looked disappointed when he found out all I wanted was for him to turn on Russ's electric heater and give me my blanket. Also it pointed out to

Joker and the other guys that I could holler for help if I wanted to risk it so they told Bruce to tape the little fucker's mouth shut, meaning me which Bruce did, being careful not to block my nose so I could breathe okay. Then he got my blanket from the livingroom and tossed it over me. He unplugged Russ's box by the window and plugged in the space heater and flipped it on high.

He picked up the stereo and a handful of tapes but when he got to the door he stopped for a second and looked down at me like he was saying goodbye forever. I blinked twice for goodbye, once for hello, but he didn't get it. He just shook his head like he felt sorry for me and disgusted at the same time. Then he closed the door and locked it on the outside with Russ's padlock which wasn't too smart since Russ had the key. But I never really thought Bruce was smart anyhow. Just interesting, and maybe not as dumb as the other guys.

Pretty soon I can hear Megadeth thumping through the walls and I can smell dope smoke and pizza and can hear the refrigerator being opened and closed and the top-popping of beer cans. Adirondack Iron is having its breakfast and I know it'll last till tonight when the guy from Albany finally comes for his stuff or Russ makes the mistake of his life and returns home, whichever comes first.

Somewhere around the middle of the afternoon I guess it got really hot in Russ's crib so I squirmed my way out from under the blanket and realized that I could actually move around a little. I managed to stand up and then I hopped over to the window and with my head pushed the curtains back so I could see out. Directly below the window Raoul's beat-up old Chevy pickup was parked in the narrow driveway that ran between the Video Den and the old abandoned state liquor store. I thought maybe if someone looked up they'd see me all taped up and blinking like crazy to come up, come up and save me.

For a long time I stood up there in front of the window like a store dummy advertising boys' underwear but I was waiting to see somebody, anybody, a passerby, a cop, Rudy LaGrande, Russ parking his Camaro behind Raoul's pickup or a Video Den customer, anybody but one of the bikers and just as I felt myself starting to fall asleep I saw Wanda come out of the Video Den and lock the door, closing early I guess. She didn't once look up and was making her way down the driveway toward the street so I banged my head against the windowpane which caused her to stop and look around for a second like maybe the noise was coming from inside the store. I did it again but that just told her it wasn't coming from the store so she went on and disappeared around the corner.

Pretty soon it was dark and I knew no one could see me by the window now even if they happened to look up at it. Hopping backwards over to the floorlamp I managed to turn and tip it toward me with my hands and flipped it on, then dragged it back by the window so it shone on me. The party in the livingroom was still going so no one had heard me.

Finally about an hour later I saw Russ's Camaro pull into the driveway and park behind Raoul's pickup. He shut off his headlights and I couldn't see him anymore but as soon as I heard the car door shut I started banging my head against the window glass. I did it in a steady but varied way so it would sound intentional but after three or four minutes I figured either he heard me or he didn't and it was too late if he didn't, he was already coming up the stairs and walking into the livingroom where the bikers were lying around stoned listening to his tapes and waiting to kill him first and me afterwards.

Suddenly there was a tap on the window next to my head and I jumped. It was Russ standing on the roof of the back porch. He grinned at me and lifted the window open and climbed into the room like he did it every night. The wind blowing through the open window was cool and fresh and I'm thinking freedom, man, freedom.

Russ smiles and looks me over and says, Yo, wussup? I just shook my head and rolled my eyes in the direction of the livingroom. You look like a fucking mummy, he said and proceeded to pull the tape off my hands and ankles. I undid the tape around my mouth myself because it yanked on my hair and earrings and hurt a little.

Don't talk, I whispered to him as soon as the tape was off my mouth. We got to get the fuck outa here, man. They found out about you stealing their stuff. They're gonna kill us.

Russ scoped the room a second and listened to the noise from the livingroom. Where's my padlock? he asked. They use it to lock you in?

Yeah, but hurry up, let's get outa here. And keep it down, man, they're next fucking door!

Chill. They'd hafta break the door down to get to us. Wait a minute, he said, you oughta put some clothes on. It's cold out.

Forget clothes, man, I'm just trying to save the body.

But he went over to a corner where there was a pile of clothes and pulled out some old jeans and a flannel shirt for me which I quickly put on and rolled up because they were too big. He also had some socks and a beat-up pair of sneakers. Then he did something strange. He took off my shearling jacket and gave it to me.

It never fit me right anyhow, he said. Too small. Where's my jean jacket? he asked looking around the room.

In the livingroom, man. Don't even think about it.

He shrugged and smiled and went into the pile of clothes and pulled out an old Islanders hoodie which he put on.

Okay, c'mon, let's book, he said but when I turned to the window I suddenly smelled smoke and saw that the curtains were blackening along the bottom where they lay against the space heater. It was my fault, I'd pushed the curtains against the heater myself.

They were probably made out of some highly combustible man-made fabric and they'd heated up to the burning point and with the breeze and fresh air blowing from the open window they looked like they were ready to burst into flames. And then sure enough just as I moved to pull them away from the heater a flash of blue zipped up one side and crossed over the top and shot down the other and the curtains practically exploded like they had been covered with gasoline or something.

Oh shit, let's go! Russ said. He dove out the window like a circus lion jumping through a ring of fire and I followed him straight into the darkness.

By the time we got to the edge of the roof and turned to shinny down the pole to the ground the flames had completely filled the window and it looked like the whole room was burning. It was a combination of beautiful and scary probably like war. The room went up like one of those smart bombs'd hit it and when me and Russ reached the ground we turned and stood there and looked up amazed at the sight.

We should've gotten into Russ's car and beat it the hell out of there but I guess we wanted to watch the fire. We staggered backwards away from the house across the yard to the garage where the Harleys were and a few minutes later we saw Roundhouse and Joker and Raoul and Packer come running down the stairs from the apartment so we slipped away from in front of the garage into the bushes on the side.

Russ said, C'mon, follow me, and we climbed through a broken old fence and came out behind the abandoned liquor store. He walked up to a rear door and opened it and we went inside this large storage room where we could safely look out the side window and watch the fire. All around us were these empty whiskey and wine cartons and then in the center of the pile I noticed a stack of ten or twelve unopened boxes. VCRs and laptop computers. I touched Russ's shoulder and when he turned I just pointed to the boxes.

He goes, Oh, yeah, I know. I had a little trouble unloading them locally. I thought maybe I'd make my own deal with the Albany guy. You know what I'm saying?

Yeah, I said and turned back to the fire. Already there were two fire engines blocking the driveway. Lights were flashing and sirens and cop cars were pulling up and firemen were running hoses down the alley and driveway and rushing up the stairs with their axes.

The bikers still stood in the shadows at the front of the garage looking up at the apartment. Bruce wasn't with them I noticed. They were only a few feet from us and I could see they were scared shitless, even Joker who was telling them they had to book. Forget the electronics.

So where the fuck's Bruce! Roundhouse said in a loud voice, very upset.

Packer said, I think he went back for the kid.

Fuck the kid! Joker said. Fuck Bruce. Fuck the stuff. We gotta get outa here, man. There's cops everywhere.

Moving fast Roundhouse and Packer rolled their bikes out of the garage and got the engines started. Joker climbed on behind Roundhouse and Raoul got on behind Packer and the two huge Harleys and four bikers went roaring down the driveway past the pickup and Russ's Camaro bumping over hoses and dodging firemen and at the street they turned right and disappeared.

You hear that? I said to Russ.

What?

Bruce is still up there, man. He thinks I'm locked inside your crib. He's trying to save me!

Yeah. And I've got the key, Russ said in a strangely calm voice.

I gotta tell him I'm okay!

But when I turned to leave Russ grabbed my arm and said, You can't get up there, man. It's too late now.

I looked back at the fire and he was right. The whole apartment was in flames and the attic above and the empty storefronts and even the Video Den were burning now. A couple of firemen who had gone up the stairs to the apartment came stumbling back out the door and got safely down to the ground just as the whole staircase and porch fell in a huge shower of sparks and flame.

The noise of the fire was incredible, like a jet plane tak-

ing off with sirens and firehorns and firemen giving
orders over loudspeakers. They had hoses snaked all over
the place and were shooting hard heavy streams of water
into the fire but it was like the fire was alive and the water
was its food that only made it grow larger and hungry for
more. I spotted Wanda and Rudy LaGrand out on the
street with a crowd of people but then the cops pushed
everyone back out of sight and a third fire truck pulled
into place. On the far side of the street I thought I saw a
bunch of people I knew, including my mom and my stepdad but I think it was an optical illusion due to fear and
excitement.

Pretty soon the firemen must've realized there was no
way they could save the house so they started spraying
water on the buildings on either side of it including the
one me and Russ were in to try and keep them from
going up too. I could hear the water pounding on the
roof and a bunch of firemen ran past the window toward
the back. The storage room was filling with smoke and we
were coughing from it and our eyes stung and sparks were
starting to float down from the darkness near the ceiling
like fireflies.

We better book, man, I said.

He goes, What about my stuff? I can't leave my stuff!

It's not your stuff. Never was.

Bruce and the other guys, they're the ones who *stole* it!

Yeah, and you stole it from them. Now Bruce's dead
and the other guys're gone.

Like it's the first time he's thought it Russ says, The
cops'll think I stole it too.

Fucking duh, man. Let it burn. It's our best chance.

What about my car? I need my car.

Forget it. We're criminals, man. You'll have another chance. Maybe we'll get lucky and people'll see your car and think we died in the fire too, I said and ran for the door thinking that was the way it should be, me and Russ and Bruce burned up in the fire together, our bodies turned into three piles of char surrounded by burned-up tons of stolen electronics.

I didn't know how Russ's mom would take it but mine would be sad at first and then she'd get over it and my stepdad would be secretly happy especially since he could carry on like he'd lost something important to him.

Nobody else would think much about it though. Except Black Bart maybe since he'd lost a lot of freight forwarding business with the bikers plus a homeless kid who used to sell him his daily blunt. But nobody else'd care.

Russ was a step behind me and when I pushed open the door I freaked a pair of firemen who had their axes all ready to chop their way in.

Jesus! What the hell are you doing in there! the lead guy hollered. Get the hell outa there! he said and I said, We're gone, man! and we were.

SIX

SKULL & BONES

We booked like mad through a bunch of backyards and cut down to the river where there's this narrow brick walkway from the olden days when the mill was running that snakes under the Main Street Bridge. You can stand down there next to the water which in spring comes right up to your feet and smoke a J if you want or just hang out and talk without being seen or heard which is why kids have been going there for generations I think.

Due to the fire and everybody in town wanting to watch it, us getting out of Au Sable without being seen was easier than it probably should've been but of course nobody was actually looking for me and Russ yet. They didn't know yet that we were missing and presumed dead.

It was my idea not to let anyone see us. Russ said, Maybe they'll be so busy putting the fire out and keeping it from spreading and all that they won't notice my stuff and we can go back later for it. Plus he was worried about his car. Russ is a very material guy.

I said, No way, man. Firemen are really smart and they hate unanswered questions. They're not like cops, I told him, who would've just grabbed up all of Russ's stolen VCRs and computers for themselves like it was Christmas and then busted us for some other crime than stealing. Like arson, even though it was only accidental. And once they found Bruce's body up there in the apartment which unless he was burned to a crisp they could identify easy because of all his Gulf War tattoos they'd try and nail us for murder although a lot of people'd want to give us a good citizenship medal for getting rid of the bikers regardless of how we'd done it.

Either way I didn't want to be connected to what had happened to Bruce. I didn't even want to think about it. He was my friend and he'd tried to save me. It was just bad luck that I'd already been saved by Russ.

What we got to do now, man, I told him, is disappear off the face of the earth. If anybody sees us they'll have more questions than we've got answers for.

Boy, is my mom going to be pissed, he said.

Forget that, man. Your mom is like my mom, I said. They'll both think we died in the fire with Bruce and will be real sad or else as usual they won't know where we are and won't really give a shit. Russ's mom wasn't married with a regular job like mine, she was sort of a hooker who worked in a bar near the air force base and lied about her age and told the guys she brought home that Russ was her nephew which is why he left home when he was fifteen in the first place. She was a babe but I actually preferred my mom to his although he was better off than I was having no stepdad like mine to deal with.

We stayed there under the bridge in the dark for about an hour listening to the cars and trucks rumbling overhead and the steady roar of the river which was only a few inches below the walkway and the occasional siren as fire trucks from the towns around came in to help. A fire is one of the few things that gets people together nowadays. The bridge was a big stone arch and when we looked out from under it we could see a piece of the sky which was all lit up like there was a night baseball game over where we used to live with the bikers and it did make me want to go and join the crowd so I tried not to look.

What I really wanted was to get high but neither of us had any weed so Russ and I talked for a while about Bruce and what a cool dude he was and what bastards the other bikers were to leave him like that. He had soul, man, Russ said. White soul. You know what I'm saying?

I said, Yeah, but actually I didn't want to talk about him anymore because of how my feelings were all mixed up. Then one time I peeked out and noticed that the sky was getting dark again so I figured we should book while people were still somewhat distracted by the fire and thinking maybe we had burned up in it. Russ had about ten bucks and an almost full pack of cigarettes and I had nothing but the clothes on my back but Russ said he knew these excellent guys in Plattsburgh who lived in a bus where we could crash as long as we wanted and no one would know because there were always different kids who stayed there between squats, nobody permanent except the dudes who owned the bus.

We couldn't get out of Au Sable though and hitch over to Plattsburgh without being spotted and we didn't have Russ's Camaro anymore so we decided to sneak up by Stewart's which is like this late-night convenience store where people drive in for last-minute items like cigarettes or beer and sometimes leave their car running outside. By keeping to the alleys and backyards we got to Stewart's without anyone noticing us and then hid behind a dumpster next to the store and waited. It was pretty cold but I had my shearling jacket and Russ had his Islanders hoodie so we were okay.

Quite a few cars and pickups came in and a lot of them were people we actually knew but they were locals and knew not to leave the motor running. After a while the out-of-town fire engines and some of the volunteer firemen with their blue bubble lights on the dashboards started passing by and two or three of them stopped for gas or went in for supplies and the such but even though they were from away they shut off the motor and took their keys with them.

Then this one pickup, a red practically new Ford Ranger pulled in. It was a volunteer fireguy probably heading home to Keene or some other small town where nothing was open this late. After a few minutes he came out with a bag of groceries and got into his truck and started to back out but then he suddenly stopped and jumped down from the cab and with the motor still running walked slowly back inside the store like he'd forgotten something he was supposed to bring home for the wife and was pissed.

Russ ran around to the front of the store, took a quick look through the window and came back to the dumpster and said it was cool, the guy had his head in the ice cream freezer. We scooted across the lot and Russ jumped in on the driver's side and I climbed in beside him and we were outa there.

At first I thought Russ was going the wrong way but it was only a deceptive maneuver to make the guy or anyone who saw his truck leaving the lot think we were headed west in the direction of Lake Placid instead of east to Plattsburgh. As soon as we'd gone a few blocks he cut left and zipped back on River Street which turns into River Road and then crosses the river on this old wooden bridge outside of town a ways where it connects a few miles further on to the main road to Plattsburgh.

A few minutes later we were doing eighty headed east on Route 9N smoking the fireguy's cigarettes from the carton of Camel Lights I'd found in his grocery bag and laughing like crazy. There was other good stuff in there too—a twelve-pack of Bud kings, Fritos, some chips, and some Kotexes probably for the guy's wife which naturally caused Russ to make a couple of his cruder jokes but I didn't mind because for the moment at least we were like free, free to just be ourselves, driving fast with the windows down and the heater blasting, smoking cigarettes and eating junk food and drinking beer and crankin' with Nirvana's Serve the Servants on WIZN screaming from the speakers. It was definitely cool. We even switched on the blue bubble light so if anyone saw us they'd think we were heading for a fire.

Russ said, Yesss! and pumped his fist and I said, Yesss! and did the same although it felt a little stupid because of everything that'd happened. But life is short I guess and you have to celebrate it when you can so that's basically what we did.

*   *   *

We stayed off the Northway and shut off the bubble light because there was likely to be staties cruising and took the back roads into Plattsburgh and parked the pickup in a used-car lot out on Mechanic Street where there were fifty or sixty used trucks for sale. It was around midnight by then and not much traffic and only a few local cops who were probably drinking coffee over at Dunkin' Donuts so there was very little danger of us getting caught.

After Russ took the number plates off the truck with this screwdriver he found in the glove compartment the fireguy's Ranger looked like all the other pickups on the lot. Russ figured it wouldn't be discovered there until somebody tried to buy it or else they did an inventory and when they did no way it could be tied to us. Russ was good at criminal activities and even when he was doing something for the first time it seemed like he'd already done it twice last week.

The number plates he put in the bag with the beer and stuff because he figured maybe we could sell them if we met somebody who was into stealing cars and then we booked on foot for the dudes who lived in the bus, which wasn't very far, Russ said.

It was out past these old warehouses and junkyards where there weren't any regular homes or stores and you had to go through a break in a chain-link fence and cross a huge field where people had dumped old tires and refrigerators and such. It was kind of spooky out there in the dark lugging the grocery bag over the rough crumbly ground with the wind blowing and everything smelling wet and rusty like it was a hazardous waste site or something. Russ said he'd only been out here once when he took home this girl he'd picked up at the mall and it turned out she was crashing at the bus with these crack-heads from Glens Falls who were going to Montreal for a Grateful Dead concert but never made it.

Was she a crackhead too? I asked him. I didn't think I'd ever met one. I knew lots of kids who'd done crack a few times but they were just normal like me.

She was into rock, yeah. She said she was sixteen but I think she was real young. Fourteen or something. Maybe thirteen.

Wow. Thirteen. That's young. For crack, I mean. You didn't screw her or anything, did ya?

Jesus, no, Chappie. Whaddaya think I am, a goddam pervert? All she wanted was money for rock anyhow and I was broke. There were these other guys there though that she gave blowjobs to for only two bucks apiece and then she got her kibbles and bits and got high. I couldn't relate, you know what I'm saying?

Yeah, sure, I said and we kept walking for a while with-out talking. These guys who own the bus, I said, are they crackheads?

I don't know. I guess so, maybe. But they're cool, he said. They're college guys or something.

I didn't see the bus until we were practically in front of it. It was this old dented beat-to-shit regulation schoolbus like from before Vietnam with broken headlights and the windows which were mostly busted were covered over inside with cardboard and no tires or wheels even. It was lying on the ground at a slight angle and looked like it had been dragged there and dropped in the middle of the field with the rest of the junk. It was still yellow but

faded and people had painted peace signs and hippie
flowers and a few deadhead slogans on the sides and it
stank pretty bad when we got close to it like people had
been shitting and pissing a lot in the immediate vicinity.

There was the one door at the front and Russ knocked
on it and said, Yo, man, anybody home?

Somebody lifted a corner of the cardboard on the window next to the door, checked us out and dropped it
again. There was some rummaging-around noise from
inside and then this guy's voice says, We don't want any
we don't got any it's fucking late go away.

Russ goes, Hey, c'mon, man, it's me, Russ. Me and my
buddy, we got some beer.

The wind was blowing pretty hard and it was definitely
cold out there and weird so I was getting anxious to get
invited inside even though maybe it wasn't such a good
idea. The vibes off this wrecked schoolbus were way nega-
tive. We waited a few minutes and I was going to suggest
to Russ that we should forget it although I didn't know
any other place we could go. Maybe we could break into a
furniture warehouse or something, I thought. I once
heard about some kids who did that and lived there for a
whole winter, when suddenly the door opened and this
tall skinny dude with a scrawny rat's-ass beard and pimples and hair down over his shoulders stepped outside
and the first thing about him I noticed is that he smelled
really ripe like he hadn't taken a bath in a year.

Yo, man, Russ says, wussup. Remember me? I came
here once, man. I brought the chick who was with the two
dudes from Glens Falls.

The guy only looks at Russ with a stoned smile and
then at me the same. Who's he? the guy says pointing a

long bony finger so Russ told him my name and the guy said his. Richard, man. Richard. He leaned down then and poked his face into my grocery bag and all of a sudden it's like he's in a completely different head and he says, Well well well what have we here a little beer a little bit o' chips a little o' this and a little o' that. And number plates! *Stolen* number plates I bet! Yummm! We even got us some *sanitary* napkins, he says pulling out the Kotexes. We don't need *those*, do we? and he tosses them into the darkness and goes back into the bag and pulls out a beer and says, It's like Halloween only the trickers come a-treatin' and the treaters come a-trickin'. He goes on talking like that, real fast and spindly, sort of to himself but not really, like he basically can't think of anything to say so he lets his mouth do it all for him.

He didn't seem to remember Russ from before or not to remember him either—it was like he was empty inside and stuff you said to him bounced around in his head like BBs or pinballs for a few seconds and then rolled to the bottom. After a few minutes of Russ trying to have a regular conversation with the guy he suddenly turned around and walked back inside the bus leaving the door open so we followed him in.

It was dark but they had a couple of candles burning so you could see things okay and I could tell right away that there was this one other guy there who looked just like Richard, tall and real thin, same long hair and ratty brown beard and pimples, same filthy tee shirt and raggedy jeans. He was sitting in the busdriver's seat with his bare feet up on the steering wheel, staring straight ahead like he was driving someplace and steering with his feet.

Russ goes, What's happening, man.

You got to pay your fare, the guy says and Russ handed him one of our beers and the guy popped it and instantly started chugging like he was starving.

This's James, Russ says to me. Him and Richard are brothers.

No shit, I said.

Even though most of the passenger seats had been yanked and the place was surprisingly big inside like a house trailer, it wasn't exactly homey. There were three or four old mattresses on the floor and some really moldy-looking sleeping bags and a couple of livingroom chairs with stuffing coming out that looked like they came from the dump and a table made from boards and cin-derblocks with piles of dirty pans and dishes all over it and old clothes and newspapers and magazines and some kind of old brown rug on the floor that smelled and looked like they got it off a sunken ship and posters on the ceiling and against the cardboard walls from like a two-year-old Red Hot Chili Peppers concert and retro bands like Aerosmith which I guess college guys are into.

Actually I was kind of grossed out by the place but I fig-ured it was better than no place and Richard and James seemed nonviolent types which after the bikers was almost relaxing so I came inside and sat down on one of the old bus seats like I was a passenger and opened a beer and ate some Fritos. Russ did the same although he also talked to Richard and James for a while but that's Russ, he'll talk to anyone and most people will talk to him.

He was going on about the bikers and the fire and all although not about the stolen VCRs and TVs I noticed, when I got sleepy and lay back on the seat. It was made of imitation leather and felt cool against my face and smelled the same as the schoolbus seats when I was a little kid, like cheese sandwiches and sour milk. I remember just before I fell asleep that night which was the first night of my new life that it would be wicked cool to have a real bus, one that worked and all and fix it up inside like a home and drive it around the country your whole life, stopping wherever you felt like and making a little money off a job for a while and if you got restless just taking off again. You could have friends and family with you some of the time and be alone some of the time but basically, and this would be the best thing, you'd be in complete charge of your life like those old pioneers in their covered wagons.

This bus, man, this bus is the same one me and James used to ride to school in when we were little kids, Richard said.

Cool, Russ said. It was morning but pretty late, like noon I think when I finally woke up and James was gone but Russ and Richard were smoking the fireguy's cigarettes and talking like normal people for a change so I ate some more Fritos and just listened. I couldn't talk anyhow because the Fritos made me too thirsty and the beer was finished I noticed and there wasn't anything else to drink, no running water or electricity for a fridge or anything although in the daytime the place didn't look as creepy as before. Rays of sunlight were streaking through cracks in the cardboard and the door was hanging open so there was some fresh air coming in. It still smelled a little like a hazardous waste site though, like they'd buried a million old car batteries out there.

Richard was going on about how him and his brother and sister used to ride the bus to school every day but this one time him and his brother stayed home sick and that was the day the bus went off a cliff and crashed in a quarry. A *shitload* of kids were killed, man, but my sister, man, she was okay, he said. Well not okay, she got busted up pretty good, broke her back and everything and now she's in a wheelchair and all that. But check it out, this fucking bus, man, me and my brother James, we wasn't *on* the bus that fateful day, so this bus was like good karma for us and bad karma for my sister Nichole and bad karma for practically every kid except me and James in the whole town of Sam Dent. That's where we're from, man. You know it, you're from Au Sable, right?

Russ said yeah, he knew where Sam Dent was which is over near Keene where Russ had an aunt, his mom's sister who was supposedly his mom. But I never heard of no schoolbus accident there, he said. I woulda heard, I think.

Long time ago, man. Eight, ten years. You're too young to remember. It was big though, TV and everything, lawsuits, the whole thing. But lemme tell about the fucking *bus*, man. After the accident and all, nobody wanted to touch it, you know? It was like *cursed*. Except for me and James, on account of how we'd stayed home that day. So when we graduated and came up here to State thanks to our unusual skills at the game of basketball the bus was still around but nobody wanted it so we got it off the school district for free and the guy who ran the garage in Sam Dent hauled it up here for us and dumped it right where it sits today because from when before me and James dropped out of State I knew the guy whose father owns this field and he didn't give a shit. We just needed a place to party and all, us and the team and our friends from school, and the place got fucking *famous*, man! But then we started living here because our old man, who was like pissed because Nichole was in the accident and we weren't, he wasn't about to let us come back home, and anyhow he knew we were doing drugs and all which is why we got shit-canned from the team and fucked up at school in the first place. But fuck the old man, I'm going back next fall, he said. No shit. Me and James, man, we'll get our shit together easy. I'm only twenty and he's nineteen, we can get in shape easy and make the team and get the old scholarships back and *boom*! Fix this bus up *right*, you know? Get us one of those diesel generators and a portable toilet and run some water out here in a hose from one of the warehouses. It'll be cool, man. 'Cause this thing has good karma, man. You can *feel* it, he said and he shut his eyes and let his hands float out to his sides and flutter like fish fins. This ol' bus is going to *rock*, man! Parrr-*teee*!

What an incredible asshole, I'm thinking and got up to leave and try to find something to drink.

Where you going! Richard says real loud and harsh.

Thirsty, is all I can manage on account of my throat was so dry from the beer last night and the Fritos this morning. Plus he'd scared me.

Listen, you little shit! he says suddenly all feverish with excitement. I don't know you, man, so you stay put until I *say* you can go. People can't just come and go out here like they please, man! You can come in and you can go out, but only when *I* say so. Me or my brother James. Nobody else. Me and James rule, man.

Just then brother James himself came in and he slung his backpack down on the driver's seat and started pulling out groceries and stuff that I guess he stole, mostly canned goods like chili and hash including a half gallon of Diet Coke which I took the liberty of opening and swigging from because I was so nervous but nobody said anything so I passed it around to the other guys.

James tossed a newspaper at Richard and Russ who were laid back on one of the mattresses and said, These dudes are famous, bro. That's your fire, ain't it? he said to Russ. You're right up on the front page of the *Press-Republican*, man.

Richard spread the paper out on the mattress in front of him and Russ, and I scooted over to the mattress and read over their shoulders. There it was, AU SABLE FORKS FIRE DESTROYS 3-FAMILY HOME, and in smaller print, *1 Dead, 2 Local Boys Missing*. There was a picture of our old squat and the Video Den with smoke and flames and fire engines and ladders, the whole scene from the front, a crowd's-eye view. The one dead was Bruce of course, but burned beyond recognition, it said. And the two boys missing was me and Russ whose names were not released pending notification of next of kin. By now they must've been notified though, Russ's mom and mine and my stepfather and my grandmother. I kind of wished they could've notified my real father too since he was as much next of kin as anybody else. You'd've thought the cops'd try and find him. But he was like me I guess, missing and presumed dead. Still, I'd wanna know if my own son was burned up in a fire.

Cool, Russ said. Excellent.

What's so excellent about it? I said.

There's nothing about my stuff. You know what I'm saying?

Yeah, I said. Russ is pretty single-minded. He was thinking no one'd noticed his stolen electronics and they were still just lying there in the back room of the old state liquor store waiting for him to pick up someday for freight forwarding.

So you guys are missing? Richard said.

Yeah. And presumed dead, I said.

Wow. That's truly far out. It's like you don't exist, man.

The idea of us not existing really got Richard excited and he started asking Russ and even me all these questions about what we were going to do now. It's like you're *invisible*, man! You don't have fingerprints or footprints or anything! Check it out, you don't have a *past*, man! It's like being dead without having to die first. That is so cool! I truly envy you guys, he said.

Then he switched off and got suddenly serious and tense and he said to James, You bring the rock, man? The dude show up? You get it okay?

James said, Yeah, yeah, yeah, and the two of them went to the back of the bus where I guess they had their bong or whatever and left me and Russ alone with the newspaper since they didn't invite us to join them. I don't know if I would've although Russ I think would've but I don't think crackheads are into sharing anyhow. Just knowing Richard and James were getting high made me wish I had me a J but there was some bread with the groceries and some bologna so we made a couple of sandwiches and ate them and drank the rest of the Diet Coke. We kept reading and rereading the article about the fire like it contained some secret coded message from Bruce or from our moms like, Come home all is forgiven.

Finally Russ said, I got to get rid of my tattoo.

Yeah, I said. But it's permanent, isn't it? Actually I'd almost forgotten that he even had a tattoo.

He rolled up his sleeve and held out the underside of his forearm and examined it for a minute like it was somebody else's. Fuck those guys, he said. You know? After what they did to Bruce and us, I hate them, man. I never shoulda got this thing.

It was a green Nazi helmet with these black and red eagle wings attached and the words *Adirondack* on top and *Iron* below and not too big, about like a half-dollar. Whyn't you go to a tattoo guy and just get him to turn it into something different? I said.

Like what?

I dunno. Something bigger, with a lot of black in it. Like a humongous black panther all ready to leap and rip and tear living flesh with his fangs bared and claws and yellow eyes and everything. Or maybe one of those black and orange butterflies, whaddaya call 'em, monarchs. Or a black guy. I saw a tattoo once of that guy Malcolm X that they made a movie out of and it was cool because the guy who had it was a white dude and it really stood out.

Russ liked the panther idea the best. It'll be my new identity, he said. My trademark. I'm going underground, man. I might even change my name.

What to?

I dunno. Buck maybe. Whaddaya think?

Your last name is Rodgers, asshole. You wanna be Buck Rodgers? A fucking astronaut?

I'll change my last name too.

How about Zombie, that's cool. You can be Buck Zombie, the living dead boy.

Maybe I will, he said but I knew he wouldn't because in spite of everything Russ isn't radical enough to be a true criminal. Basically he is an astronaut.

You oughta get a new identity too in case the bikers ever come looking for you again, he said. They'll be pissed you got away.

It's you they're really pissed at, Buck. For stealing their stuff. I'm the one they think is dead, man. Me and Bruce.

People will tell them they seen a mall rat named Chappie. Homeless kid with a mohawk. You got high visibility, man. Myself though, I'm gonna be fucking underground. New name, new tattoo, papa's got a brand-new bag. You know what I'm sayin'?

Yeah, well, I guess I will let my hair grow out. I was thinking of doing it anyhow, I said. I ran my hand over the shaved part of my head and it was already surprisingly nubbled.

You oughta change your name too. Don't get me wrong, man, but I always thought Chappie was sort of a cheesy name.

It's better than fucking Chapman, I said. But Zombie sounds pretty good.

He laughed and said, Yeah, Zombie! Fucking Zombie. Buck 'n' Zombie. No last names either. Road warriors, man. American gladiators! Like in Mortal Kombat! he said and he gave me these karate chops and kicks and I did it back—high kick, low kick, high punch, low punch, block, flip, jump, and duck, and pretty soon we're cackling uncontrollably and falling down on the mattress almost like we're stoned although the truth is we were really scared and were laughing and falling down to keep from thinking about what had scared us.

*   *   *

Russ figured we needed about a hundred bucks to get his tattoo changed although I wouldn't have minded saving some of it for the future for basics like weed and food, but the number plates were mainly his since he took them off the fireguy's truck and he was the one who'd done all the driving which meant that the truck was mainly his too, so I guess it was okay for him to say what we did with the money. I actually never would've thought of trying to sell the plates and the truck to Richard and James in the first place who I didn't think had any money anyhow except for buying crack with but Russ has this instinct for selling things. He knows when people want stuff and he knows they can come up with the money for it even before they do themselves.

It helped I guess that Richard and James were pretty lifted when they made the deal but I had to admit Russ made it sound very attractive especially after he gave them his idea of stashing the truck in a used-truck lot when they weren't using it. Just keep moving it around to different dealers, he said, and put it in with the trucks for sale and take the plates home with you and they'll never figure it out. If somebody wants to test-drive it they won't be able to find the keys, they'll just think it's a fuck-up, and the next night you put the truck somewhere else. The rest of the time it's yours. Like right now it's ours.

That is so fucking *smart*! Richard said. Isn't it, James? Isn't it smart?

Yeah, James said. But what's it gonna cost us?

Five hundred bucks, Russ said. And I'll throw in the plates free. You'll definitely need the plates. It's a four-by-four Ranger, man, almost new.

They said no way and Russ dickered with them for a while until finally he agreed to come down to a hundred bucks, five twenties which Richard peeled off a roll and Russ accepted with a sad face like they'd really screwed him. He told them exactly where to find the truck and they naturally threatened to kill us both if it wasn't there. They seemed to have a lot of money for crackheads or even for college guys for that matter but Russ said they had these old college loans that they were still spending even though they'd gotten kicked out of State last fall.

Then Russ put on my shearling jacket and made me wear his hoodie and put the hood up so my mohawk wouldn't show and we took off for this well-known tattoo place downtown. First though we cut down to the town park and this little public beach where kids hang out by the picnic tables and cop weed which we did in a minute from this big redheaded dude I knew slightly from the mall and me and Russ split a blunt and just chilled for a while. We hadn't chilled in a long time.

The sun was out and when the redheaded kid left there was nobody but us there and it was warm and peaceful. We sat on a picnic table and didn't even talk. Just thought our thoughts. Lake Champlain is huge and you can see all the way across to the Green Mountains in Vermont twenty-five miles in the distance and the water was glittering like it was covered with brand-new silver coins and the sky overhead was bright blue with these towers of puffy white clouds on the Vermont side. Seagulls screeched and swooped past the beach like tiny paper kites and the breeze blew off the lake and you could hear it behind us swishing through the trees which were hazy red and light green because of all the new buds. It was a true spring day and although I wasn't all that anxious to think about what was coming next for the first time I felt like the worst winter of my life was over at last.

Finally we realized we were hungry so we got a couple of slices and Cokes at the pizza joint on the corner of Bay and Woodridge Streets and headed for the tattoo place which was only a few blocks away. A couple of times I noticed the *Press-Republican* for sale in street boxes and stopped to check out the picture and read the front page again.

Wanna buy one for a souvenir? Russ said since he had the money. Maybe we should take a bunch, you know? For our grandkids.

Zombies don't have grandkids, I reminded him. And neither do Bucks, I said although I was thinking they can if they want and knowing Russ he probably would.

Suit yourself, man, he said and he put a quarter and a dime into the machine and cleaned it out, nine or ten copies and stuck them all under his arm like he was a paperboy in those old movies. Extra, extra, read all about it. Homeless boy disappears in fire. Local biker burned to death. Parents in shock. I can't believe he's gone! Mother cries. He was basically a good kid, stepfather says. Whole town mourns.

The tattoo place was called Art-O-Rama due to the tattoo guy's name being Art. It was in this funky old storefront on an alley off of a side street which didn't look like much but it was famous in the area for doing air force guys from the base as well as kids who were more or less of the punk type so long as they had IDs that said they were eighteen or over which me and Russ did, of course.

Neither of us'd met the guy before but we'd seen his work on miscellaneous kids we knew at the mall and liked it. Besides, Russ's original Adirondack Iron tattoo he'd gotten from a softtail specialist down in Glens Falls who was a guy who only did Harleyheads and was a biker himself and knew all the other bikers in the northcountry so no way we could've gone to him.

Art was this old guy way up in his forties or fifties and his whole body at least what you could see of it was covered with these incredible tattoos, mostly fire-breathing dragons and colorful Oriental symbols with nothing cheesy like stars 'n' stripes or Betty Boops or valentines with arrows the way some old guys do. When he moved even a little all the tattoos moved with him like his skin was alive and had a mind of its own and his body inside was following orders from the skin the way a snake's does.

Russ told him what he wanted which is called a cover-up and Art showed him a bunch of panther pictures and after a lot of back and forth Russ finally settled on the one that I thought was the best too because of the eyes which were emerald green and the fangs. Art said it would cost fifty bucks for the one or seventy-five bucks for the cover-up plus another the same size and Russ couldn't resist negotiating with the guy, except he was negotiating for me not himself I suddenly realized when Art says to me, Okay, kid, what the hell it's a slow day, pick what you want from here, and he hands me this beat-up old book of drawings.

Thirty bucks for the panther and thirty for the second, so long as you pick it from these here, he said and he lit a cigarette and went right to work on Russ's forearm while I leafed through the tattoo book.

The buzz of the needle was like a hummingbird's wings and didn't sound dangerous at all and whenever I glanced up at Russ he wasn't wincing in pain or anything. Does it hurt? I asked him.

Naw, he said. It feels like you got a ice cube on your arm except at first when it feels hot and sort of stings.

I was attracted to some of the drawings more than others, like palm trees with a sunset and a howling wolf on a mountain but I figured they were more for ecology freaks, vegetarians and suchlike than kids like me. The severed heads with snakes coming out of the eye sockets and the knives dripping blood and jokers with huge red tongues were okay too but obviously for metalheads and I might be into heavy metal a little now but you never know about the future. A tattoo is forever even if you get a cover-up like Russ so you want to pick a design you can grow with.

Then I saw what I wanted. It was like a pirate's flag only without the flag, just the skull and the crossed bones behind it which reminded me of Peter Pan from this book I had when I was a little kid that my grandmother used to read to me anytime I wanted. I loved that book. I remember studying the pictures up close like you do when you're real small and asking Grandma about the flag because it kind of scared me but she said it was just something Captain Hook and the pirates did to make people think they were evil when all they were really interested in was finding buried treasure. It's a good story. Peter Pan goes to this big city looking for his lost shadow and he meets these rich kids whose parents don't like them so he teaches them to fly and takes them back to his island hideout where they have all kinds of adventures against Captain Hook and the pirates. There's an Indian princess and an invisible fairy named Tinker Bell and they help Peter Pan and the rich kids defeat the pirates and it's like a very cool place for them, this island which is called Never-Never-Land because there's no adults and you get to stay a kid forever. But eventually the children start to miss their parents and want to go home and grow up like regular people so they have to leave Peter Pan behind on his island alone. The ending is actually sad. Although he does have his shadow.

Anyhow I figured a tattoo is like a flag for a single individual so I decided on the skull and bones flag like Captain Hook's only without the skull in it. Just the crossed bones. The skull kind of grossed me out and I was pretty sure after a few years of looking at it I'd get bored by it, so I was thinking X marks the spot and Malcolm X like in the movie and Treasure Buried Here and RR Crossing and suchlike. Plus when they saw it people'd still think I was evil even without the skull part which was cool. And whenever I looked at it myself I'd remember Peter Pan and my grandmother reading to me when I was a little kid. Russ thought it was an excellent decision too but he only picked up on the evil part. I didn't see any point in telling him about the rest.

I had Art put it on the inside of my left forearm like Russ's so I could show it to other people by making a power salute or a high five and could show it to myself just by turning my arm and looking down at it. The tattooing part actually stung a lot more than Russ said and stayed hot the whole time while Art made it and was sore afterwards but it really looked wicked excellent when he was done except my skin all around it was red and inflamed-looking. But it was a real work of art. The crossed bones had big joints at the ends like thighbones or something and were very detailed. The guy could draw.

Fucking A, man! Russ said and we both high-fived with our left hands. You got the *bones*! he said to me. I could tell Russ was wishing he hadn't gotten a panther now but it was too late.

That's what your name oughta be, he says. Bone. On account of your tattoo. Forget Zombie, man, it sounds like you're into voodoo or some weird occult shit like that. Bone is *hard*, man. Hard. It's fucking universal, man.

Yeah. Forget Zombie. Bone is cool, I said and I meant it and was already viewing myself as the Bone. You still gonna use Buck for a handle? I asked him. I was thinking Buck 'n' Bone didn't sound so good. Country and western. How about Panther? I suggested so he'd maybe feel better about his tattoo but I didn't really think Panther was such a cool name for a talkative dude like Russ, I just said it.

Naw. I'll stick with Buck for now, he said. Like the Buck knife company. Or like one of those big twelve-point deer, man. You know, in that insurance ad.

Yeah. Or like in Bambi.

Fuck you, asshole, he says. I could see he was pissed and I'd hurt his feelings about his name and his tattoo.

C'mon, man, I'm only kidding you. The Bone's a great kidder, y'know.

He said sure and paid the guy for the tattoos and we walked out. Except for Russ being bummed I was feeling truly excellent, like I was a way new person with a new name and a new body even and my old identity as Chappie wasn't dead, it was only a secret. A tattoo does that, it makes you think about your body like it's this special suit that you can put on or take off whenever you want, and a new name if it's cool enough does the same thing. To have both at once is power. It's the kind of power as all those superheroes who have secret identities get from being able to change back and forth from one person into another. No matter who you think he is, man, the dude is always somebody else.

SEVEN

THE BONE RULES

After we paid Art for the tattoos Russ only had thirty-some bucks left which limited our options so to speak and we had nothing to sell except maybe my shearling jacket. That and the nine or ten copies of the *Press-Republican* Russ tried to unload for spare change as we walked along but it was afternoon already and the citizens weren't interested. Plus we didn't have any safe place we could crash except the schoolbus and Russ wisely thought better of that when I reminded him that the Bong Brothers were definitely going to fuck up and get themselves busted driving around in our stolen pickup.

Crackheads, man, they do dumb things, I reminded him.

Yeah but these're college guys, he said.

Fucking duh, man. It doesn't matter they're college guys. Nobody but a pipe sucker'd give you a hundred bucks for the license plates and keys to a pickup stolen from a Stewart's only twenty miles away, I told him. And the minute those assholes get busted they'll try to blame us and will reveal our secret identities to the cops who if we go back to the bus will instantly try to entrap us.

Russ said yeah but like Richard and James didn't know our secret identities, they only knew our old ones which I had to point out were the same thing, it was Chappie and Russ that were our secret identities now, not Bone and Buck. I don't know why but I really hated referring to him as Buck. He did look a little like a buck, a young one, a four-pointer maybe, gawky and long-faced with big brown eyes and straight brown hair and ears that stuck out, but whenever I had to call him by his new name I could only say it in a somewhat sarcastic tone or else I stumbled over it and almost said Duck or Fuck or Suck. You'd've thought a guy who talked as good as Russ would've picked a name easier to say and more inspiring to think about.

Anyhow he agreed it was too dangerous now to go back to the schoolbus and he had to admit that even if nobody believed the Bong Brothers when they spilled their guts trying to squirm out of a stolen vehicle charge by blaming it on two poor missing and presumed dead kids that they read about in the newspapers, the cops would definitely be watching the schoolbus for a while anyhow.

But we had to go someplace. We couldn't hang out up at the mall or on the city streets where Joker or one of the bikers might see us never mind the cops although I figured the bikers by now had split for Buffalo or Albany. And with or without our new identities we still couldn't hitch out of town to someplace like Florida or California, someplace far away where we could start our young lives over again. At least not until they decided to remove us from the missing and just left the presumed dead part and people stopped watching for us at the side of the southbound lane of the Northway with our thumbs out. That could take months.

I wondered if they'd put our pictures on milk cartons with the other missing kids. I kind of hoped so although the most recent picture my mom had of me was my sixth grade school picture when I was eleven and had long hair and looked really dumb and even younger than I was then. I used to think all those missing kids were living together in some squat like in Arizona and they were all close friends now getting a big laugh every morning over breakfast when one of them went to the fridge and brought out the milk carton for cereal.

Russ did some thinking and said he knew of this summerhouse over in Keene that was down the road from his aunt's whose kid his mom used to say he was when she brought guys home from the bar. He liked his aunt, she was his mom's cool older sister and was married to this guy and had some kids of her own although not Russ of course. Sometimes before he officially left his mom's Russ used to crash at his aunt's house and him and his cousins used to break into the summerhouses in the neighborhood when the people who owned them were away. There was this one house he said was way in the woods a half mile in from the same road his aunt lived on and it didn't have any alarm system or anything and was real easy to break into and the people only came up from Connecticut or someplace in the summers. It's like a fucking hotel, man. They even keep food stashed there for emergencies and a TV and everything.

Since we had enough money left for the bus to Keene which dropped you off only a couple of miles from the house that's what we decided to do. Russ finally gave up trying to peddle his newspapers for spare change and dumped them in the trash except for the front page that he tore off of one copy, For the scrapbook, man, he said. Then we went over to the Trailways station to check out the schedule.

There was a bus to Glens Fall and points south that stopped in Keene leaving in about an hour so while Russ bought our tickets I hung out in the bathroom. He figured we might be spotted by a cop if the two of us were seen together in public like that. So I waited and while I waited I started remembering how Bruce used to like coming here to get blowjobs from fags and would then beat the shit out of them afterwards which seemed weird to me although nobody else saw anything wrong with it. He'd brag about it later and the guys would get all psyched to do it themselves but I don't think any of them ever did. Not because it was against their principles, they practically didn't have any principles but more because they were afraid of getting blowjobs from a guy. They only liked getting blowjobs from females. What they did to fags was just roll them for their money and watches. I never really saw the big difference, a blowjob is a blowjob I figured but I was only a kid.

Pretty soon the bus was ready to roll and Russ came and gave me my ticket and told me to get on separate from him and sit way in the back and watch for when he got off in Keene and we'd join up again there. He went first and after a few minutes I followed and stood in line with about ten people between us. The whole time I was half-expecting to feel a cop's hand yank me back just as I boarded but I got onto the bus without a glitch and walked past Russ who was in the third seat from the front like I didn't know him and sat alone in the back.

I wasn't alone for long though. As soon as the bus pulled out of the station this musclebound red-faced guy around eighteen with a big adam's apple who I recognized as air force because of his buzzcut in spite of the fact that he didn't have a uniform on left his seat and came and sat beside me. Right away he pulled out a pint of peach brandy and took a swig from it and offered me one which I silently declined because except for beer booze makes me sleepy and I was afraid of missing my stop.

The guy was a motormouth going home to Edison, New Jersey to see his girlfriend who better not be fucking anybody or he was gonna kick her ass blah blah blah. He'd joined the air force because of Desert Storm and the Gulf War which was big right when he got out of high school but he was pissed because the only thing the American military was doing now was feeding starving niggers in Africa blah blah when what he really wanted to do was fucking kick some fucking Arab ass, did I know what he meant blah?

I didn't answer which wasn't smart because he got curious and asked me where I was headed.

Israel, I said which was the first place that popped in my mind.

No shit, he said. Well you got plenty of Arabs to fuck with there, man. All that PLO and shit. You Jewish?

Yes I am. But not your regular Jewish, I told him. I said I was an ancient type of wandering Jew called the Levitites, a name I made up which I said translated into Bark Eaters who're the descendants of the Lost Tribe that'd settled in Canada and upstate New York back before the Vikings. Although over the years some of us'd married into the Indians and had given up the old Jewish ways a few of us'd stayed faithful right up to modern times and now we were slowly migrating back to our homeland which was Israel where certain skills we'd learned from hundreds of years of living alongside the Indians in Canada were highly desirable.

No shit, he said. In Israel? Like what kinda skills?

Oh, like tracking enemies over rock and going for days in the desert without water and enduring torture.

But you don't know that shit, he said. You're just a kid.

It's part of our early childhood training. We spend a certain number of years on the reservation learning Indian skills in case there's ever another Nazi uprising and then during summer vacation and afterwards our fathers pass on to their sons all the rest of the ancient Jewish lore. The mothers teach their daughters different things.

Like what?

They don't tell us. Jews and Indians keep the boys and girls pretty much separate, you know. The guy was really into it now and I was too so I sat there and spun him my tale all the way to Keene and almost didn't notice Russ get up from his seat when the bus pulled in next to a restaurant there and stopped. I gotta get off, I said to the guy.

I thought you were going to Israel.

Yeah but my aged father lives near here and I gotta say goodbye to him and stop by my mother's grave. He's one of the Jews who married an Indian, I said and pulled my hood back and showed him my mohawk which even though it wasn't spiked anymore from no hairspray and the hood and I had all these nubbles of hair growing back it still made me look like a half Indian at least to this guy from New Jersey.

Hey, good luck, man, he said and shook my hand with a power grip. What's your name?

Bone.

Cool, he said and waved as I hurried down the bus and joined Russ who was standing in the restaurant parking lot waiting impatiently for me.

It took us about an hour to reach the turnoff to the summerhouse, all uphill on this old winding dirt road where the houses next to the road were mostly small and beat-to-shit with plastic over the windows and rusting old cars in back. Every now and then we passed a driveway disappearing into the woods with stone pillars by the road and fancy carved signs with names like Brookstone and Mountainview. Rich people don't like you to see their summerhouses from the road but I guess they don't want you to forget they're still around either.

The sign where we turned off said Windridge and they had a chain stretched across the driveway to keep cars out which we just stepped over and a big No Trespassing sign and all these No Hunting signs with bullet holes in them from the locals saying fuck you. The driveway was this long narrow lane that led through tall old pine trees with the wind blowing through. It was dark in there and kind of spooky and the ground was soft under our Doc Martens from the pine needles as we walked along not saying anything due to our nervousness, not so much from the Keep Out signs back at the road but the general atmosphere which was like in a kid's scary fairy tale where there's an evil witch waiting in a cabin in the woods at the end of the lane.

But when we came out of the woods instead of a witch's cabin there was this huge dark brown log house with all kinds of porches and decks set up on the side of a hill with acres of lawns and a swimming pool with a cover over it and a tennis court and garages and little houses for guests and the such. They even had their own satellite dish. It was definitely the biggest fanciest house I'd ever seen in person. It was like a plantation.

These people only live here like on their vacations? I said to Russ.

Yeah. My aunt works for them as a housecleaner when they're here, he said. The guy's a big professor or something and the wife's an artist. They're pretty famous, I think.

The windows had wooden shutters over them and the place looked like it might be hard to break into but Russ said he'd scoped out a way one time when he came over to help his aunt haul trash to the dump in his uncle's pickup. You wouldn't believe the excellent shit they throw away, man. Good stuff. My aunt just keeps most of it. Half her house is furnished with the stuff these people toss out with the garbage.

We walked up the hill past the house and around to the back where there was this little screened porch that stuck out from the second floor. Russ climbed up one of the supports and while he was hanging there with one hand he used his pocketknife to cut through the screen with the other and climbed up onto the porch. I followed him and by the time I got up he'd already jimmied open a sliding glass door and gone inside so I pushed the curtains away and strolled in too like we lived there and this was how we always came in.

The house was dark on account of all the windows being shuttered and the curtains so it was hard to see anything but I could smell fresh paint and figured this must be where the wife did her artwork. I started to pull open the curtains on the glass doors but Russ said, Don't do it, man. My uncle's like the caretaker. They pay him to come over here once a week and check it out mainly for signs of a break-in.

For a while we stumbled around in the darkness looking for candles and then moved into this hallway off of the art studio when all of a sudden right next to where I'm standing a phone rings and scares the shit out of me. Then we hear a man's voice. Hi, you've reached Windridge! If you wish to speak with Bib or Maddy Ridgeway, they can be reached at 203-555-5101 and they would be delighted to take your call. This machine, I'm sorry to say, won't take messages. Bye-bye!

Jesus! What the fuck is *that* all about? I said.

It's an answering machine, asshole. But what it means is the electricity must be on, Russ said and started patting the wall by the door until he found a switch and turned on an overhead lamp. Let there be light, man! he said.

After that it was like we were living there. We wandered all over the house looking into closets and drawers and cabinets, checking out everything like our parents'd gone away for the weekend. The one room we closed the door to and didn't go into anymore except when we needed to go outside was the art studio because Russ was afraid his uncle if he came by could see the lights through the curtains. But there were plenty of bedrooms to rummage through that had shuttered windows and a den with all these bookcases and a bunch of stuffed animal heads and birds and a way huge kitchen and a pantry with hundreds of cans of tomato sauce and soups and beans, all kinds of food in cans including some weird stuff I'd never even heard of like smoked oysters and anchovies and water chestnuts. They also had these humongous jars full of funny-colored spaghettis and fancy kinds of rice and oatmeal and instant coffee and instant iced tea and Tang, everything we needed plus a big freezer and two complete refrigerators but unplugged with nothing in them.

The furnace was off naturally and the house was colder inside than out and smelled damp and moldy from being closed up all winter but it was comfortable anyhow and Russ said we could build a fire in the fireplace in the living-room after it got dark when nobody'd see the smoke and he thought there was probably some space heaters around. Not a good idea I thought after our last go-round with a space heater and I kind of hoped he wouldn't come across any which he didn't.

When I tried a faucet in the kitchen nothing came out and I said to Russ, Hey, the water's off. So how're we gonna piss and shit, man? We can't even wash up.

Russ said he thought maybe we could figure out how to turn on the water ourselves so we hunted around awhile until we found the door to the cellar and when we went down there we saw all this incredible camping equipment on shelves by the stairs including sleeping bags which we took two of to sleep in because the beds didn't have any blankets or sheets on them. It took a while but eventually we found the pipe where the water came into the house from the well and Russ just turned the handle on the pipe

and flipped the pump switch to On and in a few seconds
we could hear the pipes gurgling and banging all over the
house. Let there be water! Russ said. Then he turned on
the electric water heater and said, Let there be *hot* water!

Our sleeping bags we laid out on the two beds in the
main bedroom on the second floor which had its own
bathroom with lights all around the mirror like a movie
star's and then after we each squeezed some pimples and
studied our tattoos because of the good light and took a
piss in the toilet we went back down to the kitchen and
cooked up some of this weird green spaghetti they had.

It was pretty good spaghetti but a little on the clumpy
side. We made it with tomato sauce and tuna fish from a
can mixed in and sat at the long diningroom table and
ate it off these great gold-edged plates with instant iced
tea in fancy wine goblets but no ice of course. Russ sat at
one end of the table and me at the other and we talked
like Bib and Maddy Ridgeway's teenaged sons home on
vacation from their fancy prep school while Bib and
Maddy're down in Connecticut making more money to
buy us more good stuff.

Pahss the salt down, would you, deah brother?

Why I'd be *dee-lighted* to, and would you care for
another helping of this most exquisite green *spaghetti*? It's
the color of old money, isn't that the most *charming* idea?
I'll have the butler Jerome bring us some.

Why *thank* you, deah brother, how *thoughtful* of you.

That first night in the summerhouse was the best I'd
felt in a long time even though I knew it was only temporary and we were like burglars more or less. Of course
now that I was a fugitive from justice and definitely committed to a life of crime I didn't worry much about being

a small-time burglar. Once you cut your ties to the past like we'd done you've gone the whole route. There's no more near or far, it's all the same thing—gone.

After supper we watched TV for a while but since we couldn't figure out how to work the satellite dish the picture was lousy and all we got was Channel 5 from Plattsburgh. We kind of watched Sally Jessy Raphael and then the local news came on with some stuff about the fire which was basically the same as the newspaper had only with not as many details except that now we were presumed to have perished in the fire and weren't missing anymore. That got us really psyched and we pumped our fists and said All *right*! and kept hoping there'd be interviews with our moms and all but the news guy just went on to some boring stuff about taxes being due today.

When *Jeopardy* came on after the news we shut the TV off and went looking through the Ridgeways' tapes and CDs for some tunes but all they had was classical and Russ said no way with that shit although I wouldn't've minded a little classical. I remembered liking it that one time when the guy gave me a lift back to Au Sable from the mall. There was a portable radio in the kitchen though and we found a pretty good rock station from Lake Placid that came in loud and clear and played old guys like Elton John and Bruce Springsteen and me and Russ amused ourselves by dissing them for a while.

Later when we knew it was dark we went looking for some firewood and when we couldn't find any in the house we noticed that a lot of the furniture especially in the livingroom was made out of old sticks and logs, mostly birch branches and rough with the bark still on and everything, all these wobbly chairs and tables like a kid'd made them for his clubhouse. It didn't seem like anything rich people would give a shit about and they came apart real easy so we made a fire with one of the chairs and then just lay back in front of the fireplace on some pillows from the couch and got real mellow.

At a certain point we realized that it'd be perfect if we had some weed and Russ got it into his head that the Ridgeways were dopers because they were like famous artists and his aunt had even said she'd seen some once when she was cleaning house.

Where'd she see it? I asked him.

I dunno, she never said. But let's start sniffing, man, Russ said and he jumped up and began to feel around in all the table drawers and in the desk and even behind the books on the shelves. C'mon, Bone, give me a hand, will ya? he said. I didn't think there was anybody who'd leave their smoke behind when they locked up their house for the whole winter but I helped him look anyhow just to shut him up.

I checked out the kitchen for a while and then went upstairs to the big bedroom where we had our sleeping bags and went through the closets and dressers but didn't find anything. Then I pulled open the drawer of this table that was next to one of the beds and suddenly I was staring at a sandwich bag of about twenty of these neat little already rolled joints.

Excellent discovery.

Then I saw a bunch of condoms and I thought maybe there's even some coke in here because you get greedy when you're this lucky so I reached way into the back of the drawer and felt what I instantly knew was a gun and a small box of bullets.

The joints and the condoms I took downstairs with me and showed to Russ but not the gun and the bullets which I didn't even tell him about although I don't know why not except maybe because he's so excitable and all I didn't trust him with it. Anyhow we split up the joints fifty-fifty and I gave him all the condoms because I didn't know when I'd get to use them if ever and he said he wanted them because it was always better to be safe than sorry and he was looking forward to screwing some of the local babes. Then we sat down on the rug in front of the fire and each smoked a joint and the evening was way perfect.

Later I asked him how long before the Ridgeways come up from Connecticut.

Long time, man, he said. Not till June probably, they won't come till after blackfly season. Relax, man. For the next couple of months, man, this place is ours.

What about your uncle, doesn't he ever like come inside and check things out?

Naw. He just does what he has to. He drives up and looks around and most times he doesn't even get out of his truck. Then about a week before they come up I guess the Ridgeways call him and he drives over and turns on the water and the furnace and all that.

How'll we know when to split?

We'll just hafta keep listening for his truck to drive up and I guess we'll go out the same way we came in.

What about after that?

What?

After he comes and we leave. Where do we go then?

I dunno. Jesus, Bone. Cross that bridge when we come to it, man.

I was thinking somehow Russ wasn't into this new way

of life as deep as I was. Every time I brought up the subject of Florida or California or life after now he'd try and
talk about something else or he'd say we'll cross that
bridge when we come to it like it wasn't already staring at
us in the face. It was like I had gone and changed completely who I was, my name, my whole attitude, my hair
even, and he hadn't changed anything. I was the Bone
now for sure but Russ was still Russ.

After the first few days time passed slower and slower
until finally it didn't seem to be passing at all. It got
incredibly boring. We couldn't even look out the windows
at the view of the mountains because the windows were all
blocked up and it was dark inside so we kept all the lights
on day and night and slept whenever we felt like it which
was most of the time. We watched TV a lot, the one lousy
channel from Plattsburgh which came in all snowy and we
tried playing some dumb board games that we found
which are no substitute for video games that's for sure but
the Ridgeways weren't the type for video games I guess.
They did have these Jane Fonda exercise tapes that we
watched on the VCR though and we got off on those for a
while on account of Jane's tights and all until neither of
us could stand the squealing anymore. We ate mostly
spaghetti and then sometimes for variety rice or oatmeal
and drank powdered iced tea and instant coffee and Tang
which is a diet you can get sick of really fast.

In the den where the animal heads and stuffed birds
were they had hundreds of books but even they were boring, at least the few I tried because of the titles that made
me think they might have a little sex in them like
Evolution and Desire, a dog turd of a book that I couldn't

get through the first page of. And this one book I remember, *Beyond the Pleasure Principle* which I thought was a sex manual only it didn't have any pictures and one called *Finnegans Wake* that I hoped would be a murder story with some good plotting but it turned out to be in like some strange language that was made up of mostly English words but was actually foreign. They had a whole bunch like that. I don't know why people write books that normal people can't read because I sure couldn't and I was always pretty good at reading.

Russ's uncle did drive up a few times and turn around and leave without getting out of his truck but in case he decided to get out and like check the doors we didn't unlock or use them at all and instead went in and out of the house through the same upstairs porch we'd come in by, making sure each time to put the screen we'd cut back in place so you couldn't hardly tell anyone had broken in unless you got right up close to it. Generally we stayed inside the house though and when we did go outside we only lurked around the yard since there really wasn't anyplace else to go, A, because we didn't have a car or any money and were way out in the boonies where there wasn't anyplace for kids to hang except a Stewart's and this one restaurant down on the main road. And B, because of Russ's aunt and uncle and his cousins and numerous other local citizens who if they saw us would recognize Russ instantly and know we weren't dead.

Anyhow after the first few times even going outside got boring. We'd walk around the yard awhile and check out the no-net tennis court for the fiftieth time and the empty pool and all that but they didn't have any good stuff out there that we could use like a basketball and hoop or dirt bikes. We found some split firewood in a woodshed but it was too hard to haul it inside via the porch so we kept on busting up the furniture when we wanted a fire in the fireplace at night. We only used the stuff that was made of sticks and twigs though, not the good things.

The inside of the house was getting real funky and our source of firewood was disappearing fast and there were all these dumb cluster flies buzzing around now especially in the kitchen where the dishes were stacked like to the ceiling and the garbage can was overflowing. Neither of us were into washing dishes so we kept on using new plates until after a while we couldn't find any more and would just turn them over and eat off of the other side and the pans we figured it was okay to keep on using without washing because when you cook things it kills the germs. Plus there was a lot of stuff lying around that we hadn't put away because we'd forgotten where it came from originally or just didn't feel like it, things we'd used or only fooled around with like jigsaw puzzles we'd given up on as soon as we saw how cheesy the picture was going to be and bath towels and emptied tomato sauce cans and Mr. Ridgeway's clothes that we'd started wearing even though they were baggy and definitely uncool, green plaid pants and alligator shirts and old-guy boxer underwear which I actually liked wearing but outside the green pants not inside. The house was a real mess.

Maybe it was the strain of being confined like that and bored out of our minds and the house getting all grunged out, I don't know but after a few weeks of it Russ and I started having these little fights, just dumbass arguments over nothing like who was going to cook the spaghetti or whether or not to watch *Jeopardy* which in desperation I had gotten into but Russ said he hated the smartasses who knew all the questions to the answers before he did, which he faked knowing anyhow.

It was no real biggie but we started avoiding each other so to speak. We even took our sleeping bags and put them in separate bedrooms and used different bathrooms and all so we'd some days go the whole day without seeing each other although we no longer even knew if it was day or night except from what was on TV or unless one of us happened to go outside the house.

Of course we'd used up all the weed long ago and didn't have any cigarettes either and that probably contributed to the tension too. When we weren't sleeping we were too wired and too bored for normal conversation. A couple of J's and a carton of Camel Lights and a couple malt 40s would've helped civilize things between us for sure but it still would've lasted for only a day or two. When you've been high for most of your life it's hard to be nice when you're not.

I'd already started thinking about what it would be like if me and Russ were traveling alone instead of stuck here together when this one night, or maybe it was morning—I didn't know because I hadn't watched any TV in a long time and hadn't been outside in at least a couple of days—Russ comes slumping into the guestroom I was using for my crib then and he goes, Chappie, I gotta have a talk with you.

Bone.

Yeah, Bone. Sor-ry. Listen, I think I'm leaving, man, he said. Real casual like he was gonna take a shower or some-thing.

Whaddaya mean? Leaving?

Well, going back, I mean.

Back? Like where? To your mom's?

Not exactly, he said. What he had in his mind was going to his aunt's house and in fact he'd already called her on the phone. Just to feel her out on the subject, he said. But he hadn't told her where he was calling from he assured me because I was like freaked, plus he hadn't told her he was with me. She'd asked of course, like what about the other boy who was in the fire and he'd said that he didn't know what'd happened to him. He told her he'd come back to the apartment in Au Sable alone that night and he'd seen the place was on fire and he'd split because he was scared on account of knowing about all the stuff that the bikers'd stolen and stashed there. He'd been afraid of getting busted for accessorizing a crime he didn't commit.

So what'd she say? Come home to Auntie, Russell, all is forgiven?

C'mon, man, chill. She just said I could stay at her house for a while until I got everything straightened out like with the cops and my mom and so on. So I guess that's what I'm gonna do, man.

That's cool.

Yeah. I'll tell them all this time I've been staying by myself up at the Bong Brothers in Plattsburgh. You know, in the schoolbus.

Yeah. Whatever.

Don't be pissed, man.

What about the truck we stole? You mention that to Auntie?

No one can prove we did that, man.

Okay, I said. Whatever. That's cool.

He seemed real happy and put out his forearm and the stupid panther tattoo like he wanted me to kiss it. I was lying in my bed with my sleeping bag all around me and my arms inside but Russ looked so foolish and pathetic standing there with his forearm out that I squirmed my own arm free and reached up and like kissed it with my crossed bones tattoo.

All *right*! he said.

Yeah. So when're you leaving?

I dunno. Now I guess.

Okay. See ya 'round, I said and rolled over and faced the wall.

Hey listen, if you need me, man, you should like call my Aunt Doris. Even if I'm someplace else she'll know where I am. He'd already written down her phone number on a piece of paper which he handed to me like it was his business card or something. I don't think my mom and me are going to get it together again, he said. I'll probably stay here in Keene and maybe go back to school and get a job in construction or something.

I said thanks but couldn't think of what else to say to him so I didn't even try. He rattled on for a while longer about his Aunt Doris and Uncle George and his plans for his new life with them until he finally ran out of words too and then he was silent for a few minutes and I could hear him shifting his weight like he finally felt guilty and he said, Well, see ya 'round, man, and he left the room.

Then a few minutes later when I knew he was gone from the house I started to cry. That only lasted a couple of seconds though because the more I thought about it the more pissed I got at Russ for running out on me like that. First he commits a bunch of crimes like skimming the take at the Video Den and dealing meth to the bikers and stealing their electronics and so on like hey no big deal, Russ's only a young criminal working his way up the ladder of crime, and then pretty soon I start to see the wisdom of a life of crime myself and we steal a pickup together and run from the cops and deal the pickup to the pipesuckers and get tattooed and break into the Ridgeways' nice fancy summerhouse and fuck it all up. Because we're criminals now and criminals don't give a shit about owning property, they just take what they want and drop it when they're through and the kind of high that regular people get from having jobs and owning things like houses and pickups and stocks and bonds us criminals get from other activities like taking drugs and listening to music and exercising our basic freedoms and being with our friends. Russ goes the whole route with me, my partner in crime and then all of a sudden he decides that he can't pay the price anymore which is basically that regular people, the Ridgeways and the Aunt Dorises and Uncle Georges of the world don't respect you anymore. Tough. Big fucking deal. They never did respect us in the first place unless we were willing to want the same things they wanted. They never respected us for ourselves, for being humans the same as them only kids who people are constantly fucking over because we don't have enough money to stop them. Well, fuck them. Fuck him. Fuck everyone.

I threw my sleeping bag off and marched straight to the bedroom where the gun was and took it and the box of bullets and then I went down into the cellar and got a backpack and put the gun and bullets and a bunch of the camping equipment inside, a cook kit and canteen and hatchet and even a first aid kit and tied a fresh sleeping bag onto the pack frame. Then I walked through the whole house selecting various items I thought I'd need for survival like a flashlight and a couple of towels and the rest of the canned smoked oysters which I'd developed a definite fondness for and some of the other food that was left. I took one of Mr. Ridgeway's sweaters and the last of his clean socks and underwear and some other clothes and put on a cool flannel workshirt I found in the closet, the only thing of his I actually might've bought myself if I'd had any money and a loose pair of old jeans with paint stains that kind of fit me when I rolled up the bottoms practically to the knees and of course my old shearling jacket which Russ'd been decent enough to leave behind. In one of the pockets I found the folded-up clipping about the fire which I guess he no longer wanted to be reminded of but I sure did, I never wanted to forget it.

Then I checked myself out in the movie star mirror in the big bathroom and the clothes looked pretty decent on me in a grunged sort of way. I remember thinking suddenly that I didn't look like I used to anymore. I was still a kid and all and small for my age but I looked more like a true intentional outlaw now and not so much a homeless kid pretending not to give a shit that no one wanted him. I took out my nose ring for the first time in a year and my earrings too and laid them on the counter. For a second it felt funny like I was going to sneeze but then it felt more normal than ever. Same with my hair. I found a pair of scissors in the medicine cabinet and snipped off the mohawk so that I had short hair all over like a guy just released from jail.

It was strange to stand there in front of the mirror and

see myself like I was my own best friend, a kid I wanted to hang with forever. This was a boy I could travel to the sea-coasts with, a boy I'd like to meet up with in foreign cities like Calcutta and London and Brazil, a boy I could trust who also had a good sense of humor and liked smoked oysters from a can and good weed and the occasional 40 ounces of malt. If I was going to be alone for the rest of my life this was the person I wanted to be alone with.

One other thing I did before leaving the Ridgeways' was look around for stuff I might be able to sell for cash. There wasn't much except for things that were too big to carry like the TV and VCR and the fancy plates with golden edges and some antique furniture and pictures that I thought might be worth a lot but couldn't be sure of. I took one of the smaller stuffed birds that I personally liked though, a woodcock I think it's called and put it in a plastic garbage bag and a bunch of the classical CDs but they were things I might keep for my own private enjoy-ment and not sell unless someone offered me a substan-tial amount of cash. Otherwise there wasn't much left in the house for me to exercise my criminal mentality on that I hadn't already used or eaten or burned in the fire-place or just trashed and left in the middle of the floor.

I stood there in the middle of the huge livingroom with the high ceiling and this enormous picture window at the end because of the terrific view of the Adirondack Mountains on the other side which you couldn't see because of the wooden shutters outside, and I kept think-ing there was something important that I'd forgotten to do or some final thing I needed to rob. I must've still been incredibly pissed at Russ for running out on me or something because what I did then was sort of stupid and pointlessly violent but it felt good. I reached down into my backpack and drew out the gun and the bullets. It was a small black Smith & Wesson niner, heavy and solid in my hand and when I checked I saw it was already loaded like Mr. Ridgeway'd kept it right next to his bed so he could reach into his dope and condom drawer and without even getting out of bed he could blow away whoever'd sneaked in to rape his wife and rob his valuables.

I didn't have to aim but I did anyhow, holding the gun with two hands like on TV and said, Freeze, asshole! and fired at the plate-glass window in front of me. It was incredibly loud like from the world of nature instead of a little metal handheld instrument. I fired again. The third shot was the one that did it, killed the window so to speak and the whole thing shattered at once and fell like a curtain crashing to the floor in a million pieces. It was beautiful to see and I stood there for a minute playing it back in my imagination a couple of times.

Then I crunched across the broken glass and shoved hard against the wooden shutters and busted the hooks holding them and when they swung back it let the light of day pour into the house and fill it like a tidal wave. A couple of bluejays squawked and I saw a hawk making these slow loops overhead and heard the wind float through the pine trees like a river sliding over smooth rocks. I stood there with the warm spring air and the early afternoon light hitting me full in the face and looked across the wide acres of sloping yellowed lawn below the house and the wide forested valley beyond and then up the further side to the dark blue and purple mountains, all cragged and hooked and bulky making this huge bowl of space spread out before me and it was like I was up on the balcony of a castle and could see the whole world from there.

I put the gun on the windowsill and cupped my hands around my mouth and like I was a lone wolf howling at the moon I hollered as loud as I could, The Bone!

The *Bone*!

The Bone *rules*!

The Bo-*own-n-n* rooo-oo-*oool-l-ls*!

EIGHT

THE SOUL ASSASSINS

Probably it would've been more polite if I'd've cleaned up the Ridgeways' summer place a little before I split especially with the busted picture window and all but I figured if I left the house funky and more or less trashed like it was they'd have to pay Russ's Aunt Doris and Uncle George extra to do the job for me. They might even put Russ to work, he was so hot to get a job and all. Pumping a little extra outside cash into the local economy was mainly how I looked at it so with no further a due or thought I slung on my backpack and grabbed the garbage bag with my CDs and stuffed bird and truly glad to be out of there at last I stepped through the window frame onto the deck and strolled down the stairs to the driveway and out to the road.

When I reached the bottom of the hill by the Stewart's in Keene I had to ask myself for the first time in a while

which way to go, west or east. The road through town ran
two ways. West wound across the Adirondacks to nowhere,
to Fort Drum and parts of Canada I guess, hundreds of
miles of little country roads and small towns and the occasional ski resort. But east went to the Northway which is
the highway that runs between Montreal and Albany and
from where I was standing Albany looked like the gateway
to the rest of America and to the wider world itself.

I set my pack and bag down on the road there and
started hitching east. I didn't have any map or anything
or any money and I didn't have a detailed plan except to
get out of the northcountry where I had so far lived my
whole life and to just go limp so to speak and let fate take
care of the rest like I was the pod boy from Mars freshly
arrived on earth.

Quite a few cars and pickups flashed past without a
look or a pause or else they pulled into the Stewart's for
groceries or gas and I was starting to get discouraged and
wondering if maybe I should try to hoof it the whole goddam fifteen miles out to the Northway where all the traffic wasn't local like here in Keene, when this old dark
green Chevy van that had CHURCH OF THE DISADVANTAGED
SAINTS painted on the side comes speeding around the
bend. It slows like the driver is looking me over and
finally stops a ways up the road and I think what the hell,
Christians are people too, although it looks like there's
only the one inside and I run up to where it's stopped
and pull open the door and throw my pack and bag
inside and climb in.

I hadn't even got my bearings yet and the old van is
already rocking along at about eighty and all this neat

mountain scenery is flying by in a blur and the tape deck is blasting Bodo B Street's No Mo Hoes 4 Bo, this gangsta-rap song that was pretty popular then at least with black kids I think it was. I'm thinking for a Christian this guy really wails, maybe he's not even a white guy so I turn and take a good look at him for the first time and it only takes a second for me to recognize him. He's white all right. All I can say is, Fuck.

He grins over at me and goes, Hiya, kid! Hi-ya, hi-ya, hi-ya! Remember *me*?

Yeah, man. I remember you.

It's the pockmarked porn dude from the mall, Buster Brown. He's got both hands clamped onto the wheel and his foot mashed flat to the floor and the van's flying across Keene like a stealth bomber on a search-and-destroy mission. We're like swooping under the radar and moving too fast for groundfire. I look out the window and it's way too far to the ground so I'm definitely going to get busted up on the trees and rocks if I open the door and jump and we're like slipping up on the sound barrier, flying too fast and too low for me to push the eject button without breaking every goddam bone in my body from the force of the ejection so I say the hell with it, man, just go limp and let fate take care of things.

So how're they hangin', Buster? I say to him.

Oh! He laughed. High and dry, my boy. High and dry.

Yeah? Where's Froggy? Your protégé. She still with you?

Ah, yes, La Froggella. The dear old dear-old. Right behind you, lad, he said and hooked his thumb toward the rear of the van. I turned and searched around the junk in back, boxes and suitcases and concert posters and a mattress and so on and finally found her curled up in a corner sleeping it looked like with a Walkman on and her thumb in her mouth like a baby. She was barefoot and had the same old red dress on as before and she didn't look any too healthy either. Worse than before.

She taking a nap? I asked him.

Yes. Napping. He smiled and then he asked me where I was headed.

I figured I'd just say the opposite of wherever I thought *he* was headed so I said north, to Plattsburgh even though that was the opposite direction of where I wanted to go.

Not too smart as it turned out. Buster is going to Plattsburgh too, he says, right into town to a bar called Chi-Boom's, had I ever heard of it?

Yeah, I say but he doesn't even hear me, he's on one of his speed raps or maybe it's coke except I don't think he's got the money for coke. He rips along at about the same speed as he's driving, yakking about this and that like he's trying to sell me something only I can't figure out what it is unless it's himself. He's going to meet up at Chi-Boom's with this band he manages and pay them off and after one more concert dismiss them. He's gotten back into show business, he says. Only now he's on the business side instead of the performing side and while the money is much better the responsibilities are also greater, especially since musicians today are not professional in the old-fashioned sense of the word and cannot be relied upon, they have to be treated like children. Especially the niggers, he says which surprised me to hear him dissing black people since he'd been playing the Bodo B Street tape like he couldn't get enough of it and I'd noticed that there was all kinds of badass gangsta-rap tapes scattered all over the front seat of the van and on the floor in back.

But Buster Brown is a man of contrasts I guess, a guy who at first glance seems to be taking care of a child that he later turns out to be doping for his porn movies, a guy who wants to help kids who're homeless and all that but also he wants to suck and fuck them too, a Christian in a Christian van who turns out to be a has-been actor with an English accent looking for kids to be protégés and turns out to be a white guy who likes gangsta rap and manages a band and calls them niggers who turns out to be a doper on speed or coke or maybe crack and turns out to be taking care of a poor lost little homeless girl, and so on in a vicious circle like that. Buster Brown was possibly the weirdest dude I'd ever met and I was pretty sure he was capable of almost anything even cold-blooded murder of a teenaged kid so I treated him with the extreme caution and humor that he deserved.

Also I was once again thinking about saving Froggy but this time the idea of substituting myself for her did not occur to me I'm proud to say, as a sign of how much I'd changed in the last few months, since Chappie had become the Bone.

So what's with the church van? I asked him. You into Jesus and all that now? You finally seen the light, man?

He laughed. The light! Ah yes, I've seen the light all right, my witty little friend. You'd be amazed how useful an actor's skills can be in this vast and wonderfully religious country of ours. A man who gives every appearance of being a man of religion, that is, a man such as myself, can always find shelter and sustenance in America. To become known as a man of religion all you need, my boy, besides a certain verbal dexterity and the usual appearances of sincerity, is a *sign*. Look for a sign! he said and he laughed like crazy. It's your only required prop. The rest, lad, is pure acting. But don't look for the sort of sign those we-three-kings-of-Orient-are happened to see one night arise in the eastern heavens. Or the sort of sign seen by the two Marys when they went to the tomb and found it empty. No, rather you must seek the more mundane sort of sign, the sort you saw painted on the side of my van, the sign of the Church of the Disadvantaged Saints, a sign which having been writ moves swiftly on.

Yeah, I said. How come *dis*advantaged saints? You mean like crippled?

Hardly crippled but, yes, disadvantaged indeed, for they are the saints who are not yet known to the world at large. They are known, let us say, only to one another. And of course to the Lord above. Him too. My sign is thus a sign of recognition, a fraternal flag, a secret handshake and a greeting, and wherever I go others like me come forward and offer me shelter and, as I said, sustenance, or as in the case at hand I am able to come forward myself and offer shelter and sustenance to others even less fortunate than I. Which is basically how I've been able to get myself started booking musical acts here in the north-country, he said suddenly switching voices and turning into the band manager and booking agent who'd put together this huge rap concert, at least he said it was huge with four or five downstate rap bands none of which I'd ever heard of but that didn't mean much since I'm not really into rap anyhow, even the Beastie Boys who're white and pretty good.

The concert'd been booked by the student council or something at the Plattsburgh branch of SUNY which is the state university of New York. Buster handed me this

printed brochure that said Get Assassinated at the Soul
Assassination Concert and promised to have all these
bands appearing at the SUNY field house like House of
Pain and the Stupid Club and so on. I was impressed. In
spite of everything I knew about him Buster was definitely
cool.

He then said he remembered I owed him some money
which was true, twenty bucks and I didn't deny it or anything but I did say he could forget about any fucking or
sucking and no screen test either. I'm like a free agent
now, I said. You understand what I'm saying, man?

Not to worry, mio caro. Not to worry. He was on his
way to meet one of the bands called Hooliganz who were
from Troy and they'd just cut a record and everything
and he was supposed to take them to the motel where
they were staying for the concert. It was a little too complicated to follow especially the way Buster explained it
due to his being high although I probably wouldn't have
understood even if he wasn't. Anyhow he owed this
money to the Hooliganz from some other concert they'd
played down in Schenectady and unless he paid it to them
they wouldn't do the Soul Assassination concert so now
because he'd already spent the money on expenses he'd
been forced to take up a special collection from the
Brethren of the Disadvantaged Saints and he was hoping
I'd be able to contribute my twenty bucks to the pot since
I owed it to him anyhow.

Fuck that shit, I said. I can't do that. Besides, I'm stone
broke, man. And all I got's a few CDs. Classical, man, in
case you want to buy 'em. How about I sell you twenty
bucks' worth and we'll be even. Two, maybe three CDs.
Like new, man. From rich people, professors.

He said forget it, but I could work it off if I wanted by helping him deal with the Hooliganz in Plattsburgh.

What do I hafta do, man? I don't feel like doing anything dangerous, I said. I'm still just a kid, remember. I wouldn't mind being a roadie for the concert though.

Yeah, yeah, yeah, he said. I could be a roadie, that was fine and tonight all I had to do was follow orders and like hold on to the money he owed the Hooliganz and give it over to them when he said and not until he said because first he needed them to sign some kind of contract that he had from the student council so that he could get his cut later when they paid the bands. I was supposed to hold on to the money in case the Hooliganz wanted to grab it off of him and do the concert the next night without signing the contract Buster needed for getting his cut.

I guess being a manager of a band is sort of like being a leech and it's hard to get yours without letting the band get theirs first but you don't want them to think they'll get theirs unless you get yours first or else they'll just rub you off against the nearest rock. It's complicated. Anyhow I said sure.

Do you have a good hiding place there in your pack? he asked me. These fucking niggers may decide to search me and they may search the van but they won't bother you. You're just a child, he said and he made this sickening dry-lipped smile.

I was going to have Froggy hold the money, he told me. But she's a little slow on the uptake let us say. And then when I saw you standing there by the side of the road. . . Well, my boy, my boy, talk about heaven-sent! Halleloo-yah. And praise the Lord.

Yeah. The Lord works in mysterious ways, I said which

is something my grandmother used to say for explaining weird things.

We were all the way out to the Northway now and Buster turned the van left onto the ramp heading north, not the direction I'd originally planned on going but there really wasn't much I could do about it now. Besides my criminal mind was already kicking in and telling me that if Buster was stupid or high enough to trust me with holding the Hooliganz's money there was the distinct possibility of me getting some of it off of him before I split. And then there was the matter of Froggy which frankly I was now into viewing as a total green-light rescue operation, a definite Go.

Around five which was when Buster'd arranged to meet these guys the Hooliganz we pulled into the parking lot of Chi-Boom's but Buster looked over the cars and said they weren't there yet. There was a McDonald's two stores down on Bridge Street so Buster went off to get everyone some Big Macs and fries and left me and Froggy in the van. I asked her, You wanna book, man? You wanna get away from Buster?

She looked at me from her corner in the back like she was a suspicious beaten old dog instead of a regular little kid and didn't say anything, just glanced up at me and then looked at her bare feet and picked at the bottom hem of her dress. I could see she didn't know anymore what she wanted which was of course how Buster preferred it and why he kept her stoned so I decided then and there that if I was going to help her I'd have to take Buster's place so to speak and tell her myself what she really wanted and then go ahead and get it for her. That wasn't my style, I usually let people do what they want to do or even do nothing if that's what they want but this time I was fully prepared to take over her decision-making powers and rule her myself at least temporarily.

We'll get the fuck outa here together, I told her. You just be cool and leave everything to me, man. I know a place we can hide till I find out where your real home is. Maybe you got parents.

Then Buster was back with the Big Macs and all, yack-ety-yakking about this and that like we were great lifelong buddies, me and him and Froggy, and these rapsters the Hooliganz from Albany or Troy or wherever were out to rip all three of us off and not just him and not him being out to rip them off either. Buster took this thumb-sized roll of bills, mostly fifties it looked like and tucked it into my hand and said to stash it deep inside my pack where no one would think to look.

There wasn't anyplace like that in my pack, I told him because there actually wasn't and plus I didn't want him or anyone else to see my gun which is how I now regarded the niner I'd taken from the Ridgeways', *my* gun. But hey, I got this stuffed bird, I said and pulled the ol' woodcock out of the garbage bag. And it's all hollow inside. I can stick the money inside the bird, I said to Buster and did it, just shoved the roll of bills up what would have been its asshole if it hadn't been turned into this neat little pouch-like interior that I had already examined long ago to no avail for drugs. See, I said to him and then I put the CDs and the ol' woodcock into the backpack but on top of everything else right out there in plain sight.

Genius, pure genius! he said and he leaned back in his seat and took a nap for a while as it slowly got dark and cars started pulling into the lot and after a while the place was rocking pretty good and there were pickups and motorcycles and all kinds of cars coming and going. Buster was wide awake now and watching every car that pulled in but still no black rapsters from Troy, just white people, locals it looked like, big guys with mustaches and shaggy hair and thick necks and some females in tight jeans and cowboy boots and the occasional biker when speak of the devil there they were, the men of Adirondack Iron, at least a few of them, Joker and Roundhouse and Raoul and Packer, all four riding their own Harleys this time.

Naturally I didn't say anything to Buster about them, I just slid down low in my seat so they couldn't see me even by accident as they walked right past the van and went inside Chi-Boom's. It wasn't bad enough I had to deal with Buster Brown the psycho porn king, now I had to worry about the men of Adirondack Iron too. Those guys I definitely did not want to see me even from a distance.

And then pretty soon after that Buster's rapsters finally arrived, four black dudes in a rusted-out '79 Galaxie, big guys wearing doo-rags on their heads and Chicago Bulls sweats and hoodies and Filo sneaks looking straight out of the projects only there aren't any projects within a hundred miles of here so they really looked like they were men from another planet like Pod Boy except Pod Boy was traveling incognito tonight and the Hooliganz definitely weren't.

Buster jumped out and ran around and greeted them with all these high fives and get-down street talk which is almost embarrassing for a fellow white person to have to witness with his own eyes and ears and the first thing they do is ask him for the money.

They talked for a few minutes out there and I could pick up most of it. The rapsters wanted Buster to hand over the expense money up front or they wouldn't sign and he was saying he couldn't get it from the promoters until after they signed the contract blah blah but he does have a couple of motel rooms for them, he says and he'll spring for food until they all get paid after the concert and so on.

The rapsters know Buster is lying and why, but they don't know exactly *where* he's lying which is his forte so to speak. The biggest Hooligan was wearing sunglasses and looked bad enough to rip Buster's brains right down through the roof of his mouth. He draped one of his arms the size of a tire around Buster's slopy shoulders and very pissed he says, Man, we be needin a drink and you be buyin cause they ain't no other *fuckin* way for us to get a muthafuckin drink, you know what I'm sayin. Let's us go inside an talk this whole muthafuckin mess over, he says and as requested Buster like a good boy scoots along into Chi-Boom's with them leaving me and Froggy alone in the van with various things but most important with the money.

C'mon, man, let's get the fuck outa here! I said and grabbed her by the hand and yanked. But she pulled her hand out of mine and didn't seem to want to leave. What's the matter, Froggy, don't you want to get rid of this guy? He's a creep, for chrissake.

He's gonna be mad, she says in this tiny voice, practically the first time I've heard it and I think maybe she's only about six or seven, even younger than I thought. I'm s'posed to stay here an' wait for him to come back, she says.

C'mon, man. This is our only chance, the rapsters've got him scared, I said and reached for her hand again but she pulled away and shrank back against the side of the van. I climbed around the seat and got in back with her and she scrunched herself up like she was afraid of me. Aw c'mon, Froggy, I ain't gonna hurt you. All I wanna do is help you out a little, help you get away from this creep and maybe find a regular family to live with. Maybe even find your own mom and dad. You got a regular mom and dad someplace? I asked her. Actually I was starting to wonder if anyone had a regular mother and father anymore except on television.

She said yes.

Whereabouts are they?

I don't know. At home, I guess.

Where's home then?

I don't know. Far. Milwaukee, she said.

Jeez, that's far. How the hell'd you get mixed up with Buster Brown? He your uncle or something?

No, she said. He was somebody her mom knew and her mom had given her to him.

Gave you to him?

I guess. Yeah. She couldn't take care of me anymore, and my daddy was gone someplace. In jail.

Jeez. Didn't she even maybe *sell* you to him? I mean, it ain't like Buster is fucking Doctor Spock or some kind of child care expert. If you give your kid over to a guy like him you want to get *paid* for it, you know?

She said yeah he must've paid her mom something which to me made more sense especially if her mom was cracked out and maybe had AIDS or something and really needed the cash and couldn't take care of her kid anymore. I'd heard a few stories of mothers doing that and while it didn't exactly cheer me up about family life it at least made sense. But it also meant I was going to have a hard time getting Froggy situated with a regular family and all, assuming I could even convince her to run out on Buster in the first place. Loyalty is weird, it kicks in when you don't expect it and the people who deserve loyalty the least seem to get it the most especially when it's coming from little kids.

Look, we gotta get the fuck outa here before Buster makes peace with the rapsters and comes back and wants his money. This is our one chance. I know this great place where we can chill for a while, it's an actual schoolbus only it's been turned into like a housetrailer where you can live in it. I told her then that if she didn't like it better there with me than here being Buster's prisoner she could come back to him or she could even go home to Milwaukee if she wanted, I'd buy her a bus ticket with some of Buster's money. You know it's illegal to buy and sell little kids, I told her. So it's okay for you to cut out on him and go wherever the hell you want. This's America and America's a free country, Froggy. Even for kids.

I think I pretty nearly had her convinced when all of a sudden I heard this crash and a few feet in front of the van the window of the bar comes down like when I shot up the Ridgeways' picture window and a bottle comes flying out and then a couple of people come flying out too, one white and one black and the white guy is Joker and the black guy is a rapster, not the huge guy but one of the smaller ones, and then there's Buster in the middle of it trying to pull Joker off of the rapster when Packer comes out and coldconks Buster on the head with a beer bottle and then there's Roundhouse and Raoul hollering racist stuff like kill the fucking nigger which of course brings on the rest of the Hooliganz who whale into the bikers like this is the most fun they've had all month, beating the shit out of a bunch of white asshole bikers from the northcountry. Buster is down on the ground all bloody and getting tromped on by both sides and the lead Hooligan is smacking Joker around like he's a carpet and the other Hooliganz're fending for themselves pretty good against a rapidly growing gang of white guys from inside the bar who normally wouldn't take the side of bikers except when the white race gets into it.

Now suddenly it's like we've got a full-scale race riot going on in the parking lot of Chi-Boom's and I figure the cops'll be next to join the fray and are probably already on their way over from Dunkin' Donuts or wherever. C'mon, girl, let's us be invisible, I said to Froggy and I opened the side door of the van and grabbed her by her wrist and with my other hand hefted my backpack which actually weighed more than Froggy and dragged her out of the van and around behind it. Then we were running side by side, she was really into it with me now, the two of us scuttling along between the cars until we were out there on Bridge Street and ducking down Margaret Street toward an alley I knew and there came the cops only they didn't see us.

Half an hour later we're at the secret hole Russ'd shown me in the chain link fence by the field out behind the warehouses. I held the fence back while Froggy slipped under and then I followed and took her hand and led her across that creepy windblown dark field toward the old wrecked schoolbus in the high grass in the middle. When we got there it looked the same, no signs of life but it didn't stink so bad all around as before. I knocked on the door a couple times and waited and did it again but no answer.

I guess the ol' Bong Brothers got busted or else they split, I said and pulled the door open and looked inside. Nothing. No one. Looks like we're home, I said and went inside and set my pack down. Froggy followed and stood there by the driver's seat examining the place which wasn't all that bad although it probably helped that it was dark and all we could see were the outlines of the few bus seats that had been left and the mattresses and the old boards on cinderblocks.

What d'ya think? I said.

It's dark.

I remembered the flashlight in my pack then and when I had it turned on we checked the place out carefully and saw that the Bong Brothers seemed to've cleaned all their stuff out and left just the furniture so to speak and from the smell nobody'd been here for a month or more. It smelled clean and dry like it had been aired out and I noticed that some of the cardboard that'd covered the windows'd been taken down and a few of the windows were open. I walked down the length of the bus toward the rear shining my flashlight into the corners and behind the seats and so on until I got to the end where I shined it across the back seat and I saw a body lying there.

I didn't say anything because of not wanting to scare Froggy who was behind me a ways and I let the light go slowly up the guy's legs—it was a guy, I could see that much, wearing Wal-Mart sneaks and jeans—on to his hands which were on his belly and I saw then that he was a black guy with a plaid flannel shirt on but no wounds or sign of blood so far and then I came to his face and there he was, lying on his back and smiling up at me like he'd just overheard me telling Froggy this funny joke, gray eyes crinkly and open in the middle of a broad coffee-colored face with a humongous flat nose and deep lines almost like trenches around his wide mouth and over his eyebrows and a huge mass of dreadlocks wrapped all around his head like a pillow of blacksnakes.

He puckered his lips and said, Would y' mine shinin down de torch, mon. I-Man cyan see nuttin wid de light shinin in him eyes so.

Cool, I said and dropped the beam of my light.

Mon got to shine de light from *out* him eyes fe seein good, he said and he laughed from way down deep in his chest.

Racially this was getting to be quite an unusual night for me. I hadn't seen this many black people on the same night in my whole life practically and these weren't your usual black people either like Bart the security guard at the mall and the occasional Air Force dude you saw around town. These guys were seriously black, like Africans almost.

What're you doing here, man? I said keeping my light pointed down like he'd asked.

Same as you, mon.

What's that?

Tryin to get home, mon. Me jus' tryin to get home.

Yeah, well, I guess us too, I said. Then I introduced myself and Froggy and he said his name was I-Man and shook my hand like a regular white person so as to make me feel normal which it did. Afterwards me and Froggy settled on one of the mattresses and I covered her with my jacket and she fell straight to sleep. I was lying there thinking about all that'd happened when suddenly I smelled the sweet familiar aroma of burning marijuana and I-Man calls down from his seat in the back, You wan' smoke some spliff, mon?

I said sure and went back there and we smoked and talked a while and before the night was gone I knew that I had met the man who would become my best friend.

NINE

SCHOOL DAYS

It's hard to think back to those days of living in the bus with I-Man and Froggy and not get all gummed up with feelings of like thankfulness although I don't know who to thank and didn't know then either since I-Man himself never took any credit and everything that seemed unusual to me was only normal to him.

Maybe it *was* normal and maybe what was unusual or weird was basically my life up to then. Because up to then for me living was the same as running through hell with a gasoline suit on.

You got to give thanks and praise, mon, he used to tell me whenever I'd say how cool things were now with me and Froggy and him living together in the schoolbus out there in the field behind the warehouses north of Plattsburgh.

I'd say, Yeah, right, who'm I supposed to give thanks and praise to? and I-Man always smiled that soft smile of his and said Jah which I guessed was his idea of God or maybe Jesus but different on account of I-Man being an old black guy and a Jamaican and all that. I wasn't sure who Jah was really, the whole thing being still pretty new to me and when he told about how Jah was actually this African king of kings named Haile Selassie who drove the whites out of Africa and freed up his people I figured this was something white people probably couldn't get or else I-Man was working from a different Bible than ours, one I hadn't heard of yet.

Actually there were some Rastafarians who were like white Americans that I'd seen at the mall and elsewhere hitching et cetera, kids mainly who were into reefer but wanted a religion to go with it so they grew their hair out and twisted it into locks and put wax and other crap into it so they could make like dreadlocks out of it and these white Rastas when they talked about Jah and said give praise and thanks, mon, stuff they'd picked up mostly from Bob Marley songs they never mentioned the Haile Selassie guy. I knew they were in reality talking about God though and Jesus and suchlike only picturing Him as a way older black guy like Malcolm X with a gray beard so they could picture themselves as black too, like that was the whole point, to not have to be an American white kid worshiping the god of your parents which is why the Haile Selassie stuff got overlooked by them but it was important.

The thing is, reality, at least that part of reality which includes gods and saviors and so forth was different for I-Man than it was for us American white kids. Probably different even than for American black kids too but I can't say much about that of course since I'm not one myself. I mean, who knows how black kids from America picture God? I guess if you judge from their parents' artworks and church songs and suchlike it figures that they picture Him pretty much the same as white kids do only He's a little less uptight maybe.

Anyhow whenever I-Man told me to give thanks and praise to Jah because I'd just said how cool everything was it was like he was telling me to thank the monkey god or praise the hundred-armed god with the elephant face or something weird like that. But when I thought about it since for the first time in my life I was actually happy it made more sense for me to be thanking and praising foreign gods like that than the bearded white American Methodist God and His skinny son Jesus that my mom and stepfather and my grandmother'd told me to thank and praise in church when I was a little kid. I would've been lying then since I didn't exactly have a lot to be thankful for unless you count my real father taking off on me and my stepfather's sicko visits to my room when he was drunk and my mom's weepy dumb belief that everything was cool and my grandmother's constant complaining. Giving thanks and praise to God and Jesus back then, that would've been the really weird thing and they probably knew it too. Then or now they themselves never went to church regular anyhow, not even one Sunday a month but only often enough so people knew they weren't Catholic or Jew which I think was the main point.

It's funny about religion, whether it's the religion of white Rasta kids or even my own mom it's usually got some other point than thanks and praise. For the people doing the thanking and praising, I mean. I'd actually never thought much about this stuff until I met up with I-Man that summer and then for a while before I realized it I really got into it and started making up some ground-breaking new opinions for myself. In religion I-Man was different than anyone else I'd ever met, he was actually sincerely religious I guess you could say but religious in the way that God or Jesus or whoever must've had in mind back in the olden days like in Israel when they first started thinking religion might be a pretty good idea for earth people since earth people were so selfish and igno-rant and all and went around acting like they were going to live forever and deserved it too.

For I-Man religion was mainly a way to give thanks and praise just for being alive because nobody exactly *deserved* life. It wasn't like you could go out and earn it somehow. Plus for him religion was a way to straighten out his diet and in general get his act together due to the fact that true Rastafarians weren't allowed to eat any pork or lob-sters or any of what he called deaders which meant meat basically and no salt on anything on account of Africans being allergic to salt he told me. And they didn't allow alcoholic beverages either, he said due to the connection between rum and slavery days, a connection I didn't quite get till later. Anyhow everything had to be natural, he said which was one reason why he'd run away from the farm camp, because of the unnatural food they had to eat there and because of all the insecticides they put on the apple trees was the second reason why he'd split.

He'd come up from Jamaica in April with a crew of migrant farmworkers and the hiring guy hadn't told him in advance that he wouldn't be able to practice his reli-gion here in spite of America being a free country

because of how the food in America was all full of deaders
and salt and chemicals. So I-Man'd just walked. The deal
was they were supposed to work on the apple trees in the
spring and then in June the same crew was supposed to
go to Florida on a bus and cut sugarcane all summer for a
different company and come back north in the fall and
pick apples. Once you signed on you couldn't quit until
six months were up without losing all the money that
you'd earned so far and your work permit so if you left
the camp you were like an international outlaw, an illegal
alien plus you were broke.

I said I was an outlaw too and Bone wasn't my real
name and I-Man said every honest man was an outlaw and
every free man if he didn't want to carry a slavery name
had to choose a new one. He wouldn't tell me his slavery
name, he said he couldn't actually say it anymore and I
didn't tell him mine either, the same as my stepfather's.
Although I did say I used to have two names, Chappie and
something else but now I only had one, Bone. He
thought that was cool.

He was definitely the most interesting guy I had met in
my life so far. I dug his dreadlocks, these long thick black
whips about forty or fifty of them that hung down almost
to his waist which actually wasn't as long as it seems
because he was pretty short for an adult, my height but
very muscular especially for an old guy who I think was
around fifty. The dreadlocks were only two and a half feet
long or so but probably if you straightened them out they
would've reached all the way to the ground because his
hair was springy and like coiled the way black people's
hair is naturally and he'd never cut it since he'd come to
his lights, he said which was when he first came to know I-

self. That's how he talked. Rastas weren't supposed to cut their hair, he told me or shave either which wasn't a problem for him since he almost didn't have any more hair growing on his face than I did which was basically none. I thought he might be part Chinese on account of some of his looks but when I asked him once he said no, one hundred percent pure African blood.

Of great interest to me naturally was the fact that like it was a commandment from the old African king of kings himself all good Rastafarians were required to smoke ganja pretty much on a daily basis. They smoked it in order to ascend to the heights and penetrate to the depths was how I-Man put it when what I think he meant was just getting high. Getting high was like a religious experience for him which was cool but from the way he talked about it religion was also a way to be free of control by white people, English people mainly who he said had taken his ascendants out of Africa and made slaves of them in Jamaica and many other places. Then later on when the English found out how colonization was a cheaper and less vexatious way than slavery for getting rich without having to leave London except on vacation, they went and freed all their slaves and colonized them instead. And after that when the English queen finally died and they had to let Jamaica go free the Americans and Canadians invented tourism which was the same as colonization, he said only without the citizens of the colony needing to make or grow anything.

I liked his words, ascendants and vexatious and so on which made the subject of history interesting to me for the first time, and considering it was a religion Rastafarianism made a lot of sense too, at least the way I-Man explained it.

I didn't think a white boy could get into it without fakery like the kids wearing dreads I'd seen around but he said sure if you smoked enough ganja you could because once you got to the depths of understanding and came to know I-self you'd see that everything and everyone was the same I-and-I. One love, he said. One heart. One I.

I told him I wasn't really into going that far yet but maybe when I was older and had put travel to foreign lands and sex and eating meat and some other important experiences behind me I'd be willing to check out the depths of understanding where everything and everyone was the same. For now though I was still into differences.

That first night when me and Froggy showed up at the schoolbus the reason it smelled so good was because I-Man had turned the bus into like a greenhouse. I couldn't know it until the next morning of course because it was dark when we got there and I was high for the first time in a while and a little confused by everything that had happened but the first thing I saw when I woke up was the sunlight streaming in through the windows and then I saw all these incredible plants in cans and jars and wooden tubs and old barrels. They were set all over the bus wherever the sun could hit them, on boards and bus seats and plastic boxes and hanging from the ceiling by wires, even on the driver's seat up front and the dashboard and it was like I was waking up in this beautiful tropical garden instead of what used to be a crack den and before that a regular schoolbus.

I sat up on the mattress and studied the place. The plants were mostly young and not too leafy yet but they looked real heathy and green, all kinds of vegetables growing, some of which I could recognize myself like corn and tomatoes and others that I-Man had to tell me later like potatoes and peas and string beans and cabbages and yams and chili peppers and this Jamaican stuff called calalu but it looked like spinach and even carrots and some cucumbers and squashes. Naturally he was into growing weed. I didn't have any trouble recognizing that even though the plants were only a few inches high. You smoke enough skunk you develop a sense for spotting it, like you turn into one of those drug dogs they use. When you water it or after it rains the smell enters the air and you can pick it up from a long ways off like lilacs or roses and that first morning when I woke up I inhaled and knew it was the smell of freshly watered cannabis. I-Man had all these small pieces of hose and tubing connected to each other and running into the pots and jars and on to the next ones with water dribbling at the connectors and out of these tiny holes he'd poked in the hosing and you could hear the drip-drip-drips and the light breeze coming through the windows and the new leaves brushing each other and with the smell of fresh green mari*juana* in the air it was a nice way to wake up. A supernice way. It was like the Garden of Eden.

I noticed that the hose came into the bus through the window by the steering wheel and when I stood up and looked out I saw that it led back across the grassy field and there was I-Man in floppy green shorts and yellow tee shirt way in the distance by one of the old cinderblock warehouses where I figured there was a water spigot he'd tapped into. Then I looked around for Froggy but didn't see her anywhere. I yelled, Hey, Froggy, where are you, man? No answer so I'm thinking she must've gotten scared when she woke up and found herself in this weird garden with a little old black dude who talked funny and as soon as he left to turn on the water she must've sneaked out and gone back to find Buster although I sure hoped not. I didn't want him or anyone else finding out where I was presently located and also I kind of felt Froggy was my personal responsibility now and with I-Man's help I might get her situated with some real parents instead of a guy who maybe he did manage rap groups and run a religious organization but as far as I was concerned he was still the psycho porn king of Plattsburgh who kept kids on junk.

Then I looked out the window again and saw I-Man coming across the field toward the bus and beside him is Froggy holding his hand like she was his kid. As they get closer I can see that he's talking to her a mile a minute and pointing out the different kinds of weeds and grasses and flowers, teaching her things it looks like, probably the first time anybody'd taught her anything good in her life.

They made a real nice picture, the two of them and it made me think of that book *Uncle Tom's Cabin* which I got from the library and read in seventh grade for a book report but my teacher was wicked pissed at me for saying it was pretty good considering a white woman wrote it and gave me a D. My teacher was a white woman herself and thought I was being disrespectful but I wasn't. I just knew it would've been different if it'd been written by a black man, say or even a black woman and it would've been better too because the old guy Uncle Tom would've kicked some serious ass and then he'd've probably been lynched or something but it almost would've been worth it. In those old slavery days white people were *really* fucked up was what I meant in my book report and the white lady who wrote it was trying not to be, that's all. Of course white people are still fucked up, no surprises there but sometimes I forget like with the book report.

Anyhow Froggy made friends right away with I-Man and trusted him and started telling him things I think she was afraid of telling me probably because I was more like Buster than I-Man was, being white and all and somebody Buster'd once been friendly with. Plus she knew I'd copped Buster's wad which maybe he deserved having it copped but it didn't make me look exactly trustworthy. Although you can be an outlaw or a criminal and still be trustworthy, just like you can be a cop or a minister and not be. But Froggy was young and more or less still in other people's hands and she didn't know that yet. I knew for instance that even I-Man did a certain amount of lying like where he got his reefer which he said came up from Jamaica with him but I could tell instantly from the flavor that it came from ol' Hector who doesn't give it away unless you deal for him so I-Man was probably dealing. And he did some stealing too, like the water and probably some of the materials for his greenhouse even though he said he only found them in people's trash and dumpsters and odds and ends like soap and candles and shampoo and even the seeds that he said he got from vegetables that'd been thrown out at Sun Foods, this huge grocery store over at the mall which was where until his garden came in he was getting all his food now for eating.

That was all he ate, fruits and veggies cooked the Ital way, he said which is this special Rastafarian method of cooking that I guess old Haile Selassie used in Africa and basically meant no salt plus you had to use shredded coconuts for oil and flavoring and lots of hot peppers. It was a little strange but I got used to it pretty fast, especially the few specialty items like the Zion juice which was made from carrots and these great fried bean cakes called akkra that you cover with this sauce made out of chili peppers and onions and tomatoes and limes and the Ital stew made from pumpkins and yams and bananas and coconut was real good and dreadnut pudding made from peanuts and sugar. I-Man had made himself like this whole kitchen outside the bus under an old piece of corrugated tin he'd set up on sticks so he could cook even in the rain. He'd built a stove with rocks and some iron bars for a grill and he had a couple of old pans and so on to cook with and some dishes to eat off of that did look like he'd found them in somebody's trash but they worked fine and for a sink he had an old plastic dishpan and running water from his hose and since his food was only veggies and fruits and we went out to Sun Foods on a daily basis he didn't need a refrigerator or anything.

I don't know why, probably because it made me feel independent like I was hunting and gathering but I really got into the shopping part, hanging out in the bushes behind the supermarket and waiting for them to toss out the stuff that was just going bad or was bruised or broken a little so they couldn't sell it and then diving in as soon as the store guys had left and filling my backpack with some incredible stuff, coconuts that only had a crack in them and squashes that'd been dropped and split and all kinds of lettuces and greens and loose onions and potatoes from ripped bags and so on, enough to feed all the homeless kids in Plattsburgh if they'd gotten organized about it. Mostly homeless people aren't vegetarians though or they're not Rastafarians with their own outdoor kitchen like us, they're more into fast food or restaurant leftovers like from Chuck E. Cheese and Red Lobster which we wouldn't go near anyhow on account of the deaders so we more or less had the stuff at Sun Foods to ourselves. Except for the guy we called Cat Man who was always there prowling around in the trash mewing like a cat and a couple of really old guys who came on Tuesdays and Fridays, gay guys I think with one of them bald and crippled with these metal crutches and he'd lean on his crutches and hold a cloth bag for the stuff the other guy'd dig out of the trash. They were mostly into pastries and old bread though and Cat Man was looking for things like hot dogs and bologna and the such that'd gone bad but was still okay to eat at least maybe if you thought you were a cat it was.

We'd make our daily grub run out there to Sun Foods, me and Froggy and I-Man and that was our main activity away from the bus except for when I-Man disappeared once every few days for a couple hours when I knew he was doing a little dealing to keep himself and now me in reefer which was cool. I knew where he bought it but not where he sold it and didn't ask him about either, I guess because it would only give me bad memories of when I was living in Au Sable over the Video Den with Russ and Bruce and the men of Adirondack Iron which seemed like years ago and in a way different country.

Now every day early in the morning after the plants'd all been watered the three of us'd cut across the fields behind the warehouses and come out on the edge of the mall parking lot behind the Officemax which was right next to the Sun Foods so we could basically come and go without being seen or having to cross a single street. This was good because I think we would've stood out, a little girl and a black Rastafarian with dreadlocks and a white kid although without my mohawk I wasn't as obvious as before. Still, it was the combination. And there was always Buster to worry about.

We were happy then, I know I was anyhow and little Froggy seemed happy too for the first time. Without junk she started acting normal after a few days which made me think Buster'd had her on 'ludes mainly, probably in her food and hadn't been shooting her up with anything which was good because a kid can get off of 'ludes without getting sick, and I even caught her laughing on several occasions like when I-Man made these little Rasta dance steps and hip-hop motions when he was busy cooking supper and had two or three pots going at once or when I screwed up with the hose and sprayed water all over myself. That sort of thing'd cause her to crack up and put her hand over her mouth in case anyone saw like she was covering up bad teeth although her teeth were fine except for a couple in front that she'd lost because she was only seven and still had baby teeth. She was wearing one of I-Man's old tee shirts for a top now that said Come Back To Jamaica and one of Mr. Ridgeway's plaid boxer shorts safety-pinned to fit her and I-Man had made some sandals for her out of an old tire and leather strips and for me too instead of my old Doc Martens which I-Man'd explained were military. I was into wearing just a tee shirt and cutoffs myself, same as I-Man.

Now that it was warm and I-Man was transplanting the bigger plants from the bus like the cornstalks and tomatoes and expanding the garden generally we spent a lot of time working together outside and me and Froggy were getting tanned and real healthy looking. I even had a pretty good muscle in my arm for the first time and when I showed Froggy she was impressed. I didn't show I-Man of course on account of his being so much more muscular than me although he was an adult so it was more or less natural for me to look puny beside him but I still would've been embarrassed.

Anyhow he brought home a couple of old shovels one day and a rake that he said he'd found in a park downtown which was probably true but I don't think they'd been tossed out in the trash exactly by the park department guys or accidentally misplaced and the next day he got us out there in the field digging and turning over the sod and shaking all the dirt out of it and so on, making a regular garden only it wasn't like any garden I'd ever seen before. It was a single row a foot or so wide that went in these goofy loops and circles following some mysterious map in I-Man's head that wound around the bus and beside the kitchen and then spun off through the tall grasses of the field. I wondered how it would look if you saw it from above, if it'd resemble those animals and gods that the space people made down in South America and when I asked I-Man about that he said he didn't know, only Jah knew and Jah was guiding I-and-I.

He was very clear on where to dig though and laid it out exactly with string and stakes and all while me and Froggy came along behind with our shovels turning over the soil which was surprisingly free of rocks and dark and crumbly and rich-looking. It was like I-Man was following this vein of good soil, the only good soil in the whole area actually and if he'd gone and cut a regular garden plot in the field twenty or thirty feet square like a normal person nothing would've grown there because most of that field like most of the whole county was rocks and gravel and in lots of places was chemical waste. Definitely the field we were working and living on then was pretty much on top of old chemicals from when they stored poison and radioactive stuff out there for the air force years ago in case the Russians attacked but somehow I-Man was able to sniff out the one narrow strip of dirt that wasn't like contaminated and dangerous or rocky even because I never saw such dark thick dirt in that part of the country and everything he planted came up and grew wicked fast and looked as healthy as food from the olden pioneer days.

It stayed light pretty late then because we were coming up on the end of June and nights after supper the three of us would sit out on the steps of the bus with the door open and me and I-Man would knock back this blunt-sized spliff and we'd talk about stuff, him doing most of the talking actually and me and Froggy just trying to understand because he was like our teacher in life and we were the students, her in the first grade or kindergarten and me maybe in the third and there'd be these long silences in between I-Man's words of wisdom and we'd all three just sit and listen to the crickets together and the breeze rustling the long grasses and the cornstalks and all the other plants in the garden and we'd watch the sun go down and the sky turn all red like jam and these thin strips of silver clouds would float across and one by one stars would pop out of the dark blue sky overhead like genuine diamonds and then the old moon would drift up over the tops of the trees in the distance and the field in the moonlight would look so incredibly peaceful and beautiful that it was hard to believe that at one time not so very long ago I'd seen this place as spooky and kind of nasty and couldn't hardly wait to get away. Now it was like for the first time in this old wrecked schoolbus on this funky field I'd found a real home and a real family.

But it wasn't a real family of course and me and I-Man couldn't be like Froggy's parents or even her older brothers because she was such a very young child and I was only a kid myself and an outlaw and I-Man was a Jamaican illegal alien trying to get by and eventually get home without getting busted by the American government. Plus Froggy was somebody's real daughter and no matter how fucked up that person was we had an obligation to try and return Froggy to her if she wanted to be with her mom, or if not then we had to find her somebody else for a mom. It was obvious that being a female and such a little kid Froggy needed a mom more than she needed me and I-Man, we understood that and accepted it and tried talking to her about it.

I-Man'd say to her, Somewhere out dere, Froggy, in de cold wild hinterlands of America, dere mus' a mama be cryin fe you t' come home now, chile, him cryin it time to come home. Him sorry now, Froggy, dat him sold him baby off into Babylon.

I said maybe we could call Froggy's mom on the phone and kind of feel her out on the subject and then decide what to do and I-Man thought that was okay if Froggy wanted it but she just said, No, talk about something else.

It took weeks but her mom was named Nancy Riley, we finally got that much out of her and Froggy thought she lived in Milwaukee, Wisconsin or she used to anyhow before Buster came and got her but that was a long time ago and she probably wasn't living there anymore anyhow. Froggy didn't cry or anything when we talked to her about returning to her mom, she'd say a few words and then just look out in space and bite her lower lip and let her eyes go dead. I knew she hadn't been away all that long, only six months or a year and it only seemed long to her because she was still a little kid so I kept saying let's go call information and find out if your mom's listed, that won't hurt, until finally she seemed to give in and said, O-*kay*.

It was a warm night early in July, the Fourth of July actually because I remember the fireworks later down by the lake and it was around seven-thirty that we finally got permission from Froggy to try and call up her mom. Basically I think up to then she'd been too afraid that her mom would tell her don't come home if she called which was a natural fear I guess or that her mom wouldn't even talk to her at all but she'd been getting some serious attention from me and I-Man for quite a while by then and a lot of description of what moms really feel for their kids regardless of how they act sometimes so she was starting to trust people a little more. It was like a major breakthrough I guess.

But it'd taken a lot of coaxing mainly by me because I don't think I-Man was all that into talking people into doing what was good for them even little kids like Froggy who're supposedly too young to know what's good for them, but finally this one night when she'd said O-*kay* she would talk to her mom if I got her on the phone the three of us headed on our usual path across the field which had lots of flowers on it now, daisies and goldenrod and suchlike and slipped under the old chain-link fence and walked to the Officemax and around to the front of Sun Foods where there was a pay phone and not many people on account of it being Fourth of July and pretty late. I led and Froggy followed and I-Man was last.

I-Man did have a point although he didn't make it in words, just by example instead which was typical plus it kept you on your toes and thinking on your own. But getting kids to do stuff for their own good when they don't want to can be dangerous and only works out for the best once in a while. Actually I don't know if it ever works out unless you're standing in the middle of the street and don't see the ten-ton truck coming and this good guy pushes you out of the way and says it's for your own good. But even in situations like that if you'd've known the facts you'd've gotten out of the way on your own and with a lot less stress too and wouldn't've been pissed for being shoved.

Generally it was true that in my own life so far I myself had not done anything just because my mom or stepfather or teachers I have had or any of the adults who had me in their power told me it was for my own good. No fucking way. And whenever somebody told me that, there was like this alarm that went off under the hood and all I could hear was *whoop-whoop-whoop,* somebody's trying to steal something valuable, I'd think so I'd usually do the opposite. Most of the time that didn't turn out so hot either but I'd've never done it in the first place if somebody hadn't've been out to get me for my own good to do the first opposite thing.

Yet here I was practically begging Froggy a kid littler than me to call her mom on the phone like E.T. calling home when it was obvious she didn't want to. Her mom'd sold her to Buster for money probably to buy rock with but still I guess I just couldn't believe her mom wouldn't be real happy and incredibly relieved to hear from her lost child no matter what and vice versa too.

I went inside the supermarket and cashed one of Buster's fifties which got me a good close once-over from the customer service guy after the lady at the cash register refused to break it for me. I think they both thought the bill was a phony which happens a lot here on account of it being so close to the border and all the smuggling et cetera that goes on but I told the guy my father's outside driving a special handicapped van because he's a Vietnam vet in a wheelchair and it's a huge deal for him to come in and do it himself so I was doing it to make a call to his lawyer for him due to his having to go to Washington to testify about Agent Orange. Which finally got to the guy so he broke the bill in a hurry. I don't know why but I always like to drop that in just to say it, ever since I read about it in the newspaper and thought Agent Orange was like this cool spy who'd worked for the CIA in Vietnam and when he saw how the war was so fucked up he went over to the side of the vets and agreed to testify for them in Washington like in that movie with Tom Cruise. It might've been MTV news I saw it on because I don't really read the newspapers except by accident like if I sit on a park bench and there it is on the ground staring back at me.

Anyhow I came out with a bunch of quarters and a handful of small bills and called information in Milwaukee, Wisconsin for Nancy Riley. There was a number listed for N. Riley so I dialed that and a woman answered on the first ring like she'd been sitting beside the phone waiting for her daughter to call.

She goes, Hello? and I say, Is this Nancy Riley? and she says yeah and I go, Do you have a little daughter? and she's all of a sudden wicked suspicious and starts in like who is this and whaddaya want and so on and whaddaya talking about.

My daughter's with her grandmother, she says. I can tell she's a pipesucker, you can hear it instantly from the buzz behind her voice like she's got a lousy speaker.

Froggy's looking down at her rubber tire sandals all this time and I-Man's checking out the few customers coming from the store with their grocery carts full of food and he's offering to push their carts to their car for them, spare-changing in other words but people of course say no real fast, no way they're going to entrust their precious groceries to this grinning little black dude in floppy shorts and Come Back To Jamaica tee shirt and a red and green and gold mushroom-shaped Rasta cap on his head with all his dreadlocks curled up inside like mystical thoughts of Jah. Although suddenly this one humpbacked old couple says, Yes, thank you very much young man, and off he goes pushing their cart across the lot one happy Rasta, so you never can tell although in my experience with white people when it comes to dealing with kids and blacks it's the really old and feeble ones who're more trusting than the healthy middle-aged and younger people, probably due to the elderlies not having very long to live.

Look, Mrs. Riley, I said to her, I've got a little girl here, she's my friend and she says you're her mom. Or at least her mom is the same name as you.

There's silence for a few seconds and I can hear her smoking a cig and wished I had one and promised myself to buy some with Buster's bucks as soon as I got off.

Cigarettes'll make you do that, spend other people's money. Finally she sighs and says, What's her name? and suddenly I realize that all I know is Froggy so I panic and put my hand over the phone and say, Froggy, what the fuck's your real name, man?

She takes a minute like she can't remember herself, then she looks off toward the parking lot and just says Froggy.

C'mon, man, that's *Buster's* name for you. What's your *real* name? What name did your *mom* give you?

Rose, she said.

Wow, I said. Rose. That's in*cred*ible! I wish I'd've known that.

Her name's Rose, I told her mom.

Where're you calling from? the lady asks. Is she okay? My daughter's been visiting with her grandmother, I want you to know. That's where she stays.

Yeah, fucking duh, man.

Are you with the police or anything? You sound like a kid to me, I think you're just a goddam kid. Some goddam kid screwing around, fucking with my head. I don't need this.

I *am* a kid, lady. My name's Bone and I'm in Plattsburgh, New York. And your daughter Rose ain't with her grandmother. She's standing right here beside me and she's okay if you want to know. She's with friends now. You oughta talk to her, man. And if you want and she wants I'll send her home to you on a bus tomorrow no questions asked.

She laughed at that. You will, huh? I think you're just some kid who wants to fuck with my head. Is this Jerry? I think I probably know you somewhere and you've got a weird sense of humor is all. This is Jerry, right? Jerry from over by Madison.

I was starting to hate this bitch. Does the name Buster Brown mean anything to you, man?

That did it. She said, Okay, lemme talk to her, and I handed the phone to Froggy. Rose.

She took the phone and said, Hi, Mom. She didn't cry or anything. She almost didn't show any feelings at all, just went on saying like yeah and no and so on while I guess her mom told her various stuff. I really wanted to know what but from the way Rose was acting I couldn't tell anything. It might've been, I'm sorry, please come home, I love you, my child. Or just as easy, Don't ever call me again, you sonofabitch, you're *nobody's* child. Either way Rose looked and sounded the same.

I-Man circled back and checked in before some more spare-changing and I told him what had happened so far and he just nodded like it didn't make no nevermind to him which was an expression he liked to use and took off looking for more old people with grocery carts because it looked like he was doing okay. It always surprised me how if people gave I-Man a chance to talk they liked him even though they couldn't understand him. He was one charming African dude.

Finally Rose passed me the phone and just said, She wants to talk to you.

I held my hand over the mouthpiece and said to her, Everything okay now, Rose? You want to go back there? and she shrugged her shoulders like whatever which was definitely not a good sign. I was starting to feel sorry I'd ever broken Buster's fifty and gotten her into this. You don't hafta go back if you don't want to, I said. But you've got to go with *somebody*. A regular person, I mean. For school and all.

She said, Yeah, I know. It's okay.

I said to her mom, Wussup.

Listen, I don't know you from Adam but I guess you're okay. Is Rosie living with you or your family or something? What's the deal?

The deal is I'm only a homeless boy you might say and she's sort of crashing with me and a friend here and we're like outlaws. She's too young for that. She's only a little girl, for chrissake. So I need to find her a real home. And you looked the logical place to start.

Nothing. Just the buzz of her bad speaker.

It's simple, Mrs. Riley. You're her mom. And thanks to this guy Buster Brown I happen to have enough money to buy her a ticket to Milwaukee, Wisconsin. If you want me to. She's willing. What about you?

Still nothing. What an incredible bitch, I'm thinking.

What the hell, Rose's only a little girl and you're her mom. Doesn't that mean anything to you?

Yeah, she finally said. Then another long silence.

So what about it, Mrs. Riley? Rose told me about her dad being in jail and all. What's the deal with you?

Yeah, she said. That all sounds great. But c'mon, how'm I gonna pay for her when she gets here though? I'm outa work. I'm sick. You understand what I'm saying? It's a problem. I'm broke. And I'm sick. Various things.

There was a heavy dragged-out sigh like she was waiting for me to say something sympathetic but I didn't want to so finally she goes, All right, whyn't you do that, then. Buy her a ticket home to her mother. It's a good thing to do, right? I need her and she needs me, a kid needs her mother. I mean, I can tell you like her and she likes you, you're friends, I guess, which is real sweet and all. But I'm her mother. Also, listen, if you want you can put some money in an envelope with her, like when you put her on the bus. In a little pocketbook or something safe. You know? For Rosie. You can probably do that for her. So I can take care of her when she gets here. Like buy her some decent new clothes and so on. Maybe find a better place to live. So she can have her own room. You know what I'm saying? God, I love her. I truly do.

Yeah, okay, I said and then I asked her if she wanted to say anything else to Rose but she said no, that's fine. Just put her on the Trailways tomorrow morning, she told me and write down the phone number and give it to Rosie so she could call when she got into the Milwaukee station and she'd come down and get her. It wasn't far, she said. And don't forget the extra money. So I can buy her some clothes and maybe find a new apartment for her. And it's summer and we could really use an air conditioner, she said.

Yeah, I bet. I hung up then. I was feeling a little sick about the whole thing but it was too late and besides I didn't have any better ideas and neither did I-Man, although I knew that wouldn't bother him because except for things like his veggie patch and other day-to-day activities I-Man wasn't really into ideas and plans and suchlike. Mostly he just took things as they came and made all his adjustments on the spot. He was like the opposite of my friend Russ and most people in America who flip out if they don't have a plan for the rest of their lives and I have to admit there was a little of that in me too.

* * *

It was pretty dark by then and we started hearing some rumbles and crackles in the distance and I-Man jacked a look in the direction of downtown Plattsburgh and the lakeside park and with his eyebrows pulled down and his lips pursed he said to me, Sound like de army-dem comin fe kotched I-and-I.

I said no it was just the fireworks but he was definitely scared, I could tell and it surprised me because it was the first time I'd ever seen I-Man even a little bit scared.

It's only the Fourth of July, man, I explained. Birth of the nation and all that. We do it every year, just blast the shit out of the sky with tons and tons of fireworks to remind us of all the wars won by America and all the people who got killed doing it. It's like a fucking war dance, man. We're celebrating our hard-won freedom to like kill people.

Come wi' I, he said and grabbed Rose by the hand and waved for me to follow and led us back around behind the Sun Foods store to where the dumpsters and loading docks all were, our personal one-stop food-shopping spot. There was this steel ladder back in a corner attached to the cinderblock wall and I-Man helped Rose up onto it saying, Gwan, chile, up to de top now. Gwan, don' be 'fraid, chile. Jah protect de pick'nies-dem.

She started climbing slowly hand over hand and I-Man signaled for me to follow which I did and then he came along behind me peering kind of wild-eyed from side to side and behind him as if any minute he expected the marines to come roaring into the lot back there and start firing at us with M-16s or something. I guess the illegal alien business was a more serious offense than I'd thought on account of it being a crime against society instead of an individual person or store like with stealing and the other kinds of illegal stuff that were in my range of criminal acts. With the blasts from the fireworks getting louder and louder I could almost see his point, it did sound more like an invasion or some kind of heavy military action was going on than a celebration and maybe the roof of the supermarket was the safest place in town.

We climbed over the top and crunched across the flat gravel roof with I-Man crouched over and in the lead taking us to the front where we settled down behind a low concrete wall there with a perfect view of the parking lot below and the rest of the mall beyond all washed in this pale orange light. There was no traffic on the roads and only a few cars down there in the lots and no pedestrians that I could see which made it a strange lonely scene like from a science fiction movie when everyone drives out of town to see where the flying saucers've landed and somehow we get left behind all alone.

After a minute or two I-Man started to feel safe I guess and he relaxed a little and we began watching the fireworks going on down by the lake which we could see pretty good from up there. Actually we had probably the best seats in town. They were shooting up the big red, white and blue dazzlers now with the long *whoosh* as they go up and the big sprays of color across the dark sky and the huge booms like thunder after, over and over again the same way but with different sprays of color, gold and green and bright blue and pink and yellow even, until it was obvious even to I-Man now that this wasn't a military action out to round up all the illegal aliens in town who probably numbered no more than ten if that.

Later on of course I learned that I-Man was basically

right though not on that particular night but it *was* a good idea to always find yourself a safe hiding place whenever you hear what you think might be gunfire because it generally *is* gunfire and if there's more than one or two shots there's usually more than one or two guns and if there's more than one or two guns then it's probably the police or the army shooting people. And the people, as I-Man would say, is *we*. I learned it in Jamaica later on but that July night in Plattsburgh I-Man knew it already and I didn't yet or I probably would've panicked just like him.

After he'd calmed down some though I told him about most of my conversation with Froggy's mom and revealed to him Froggy's real name which he liked as much as I did.

De name irie, mon. Fe trut', mon, you never was no frog in de firs' place, he said to her. I-and-I know dat. Bone know dat too. You a rose, mon. Like de famous Rose of Rose Hall in Jamaica, de 'oman who kilt all she deadly enemies an' she lovers wi' obeah him got from Africa. Gone from bein a Froggy to bein a Rose, mon, an' dat de way fe come to know I-self more properly and move more to de true depths of I.

He smiled down into her somber face and said, *Ex*-cellent! which was an expression he'd picked up from me and was using now whenever he could fit it in which was cool because I'd been picking up a lot of little phrases and words from him and needed to feel useful to him once in a while in exchange. Although I knew that his way of talking was much more interesting than mine of course and he was only being polite. Still, I always got a little hit when he said things like *Ex*-cellent! and *Yes-s-sss*!

I told him how I'd agreed to send Rose back to her

mom in the morning and he looked a little skeptical at
that with one eyebrow cocked and his lips pressed
together and didn't say anything one way or the other. It's
for the best, I said.

Mus' be, he said.

You think so too, don't you, Rose? I asked but it wasn't
really a question and she knew it. She just nodded up and
down like she was obeying me instead of saying what she
really thought.

Check it out, I-Man said then using another one of my
trademark expressions and meaning for us to view the
fireworks. They were really filling the sky now and it
looked like Star Wars or something, more like the birth of
the planet than the nation with these huge blasts like
supernovas going off and spreading out in circular waves
of red and orange and purple and then *boom-ba-boom*s in
long spine-rattling chains. Great draping clouds of smoke
hung down like gray rags and you could see the bright
roofs of the whole town spread out below and the trees of
the lakeside park all lit from above like from flares and
out on the lake you could see the fireworks reflected off
of the water where way beyond in the darkness was the
city of Burlington, Vermont. And if you squinted you
could see the Vermonters' fireworks going up into their
darkness too. Further down along the shore on the far
side of the lake you could see the fireworks from the
smaller towns and harbors and boatyards and on the near
shore to the south along the New York side of the lake
there were fireworks going off at Willsboro and the people of Westport were shooting rockets into their version
of the same darkness as we had over us. And even inland
back up by the Adirondack Mountains we could see the

pale yellow glow and the red and blue and silver pulsa-
tions of the fireworks from Lake Placid and over in Keene
where I figured Russ must be watching with his Aunt
Doris and Uncle George and his cousins, and back along
the valley in Au Sable where they were shooting off their
fireworks at the ballfield I knew my mom was in the
stands with some of her friends from work maybe or my
grandmother and all saying *Ah-h-h!* and *Oh-h-h!* when the
rockets went up and splashed the bright beautiful colors
across the darkness. And my stepfather was probably
there too, although I knew he'd be hanging around with
his beer buddies in their plastic and aluminum folding
chairs talking about teenaged pussy and putting down
kids generally while he kept an eye peeled for a cheek-
shot under some girl's cutoffs or a glimpse of kiddie tit
and thought his ugly thoughts without anyone but me
knowing them and me far far away, and all he could hope
was for me to be dead or gone forever.

Early the next morning I woke up before Rose and I-
Man and took a little string bag that'd come with onions
in it originally and filled it with stuff for Rose to take with
her, a clean tee shirt and Mr. Ridgeway's wool sweater in
case the bus was cold and some miscellaneous food,
mostly fruits but a jar of Ital stew and a couple of pieces of
dreadnut pudding too. I didn't know how long it was
going to take to get to Milwaukee by bus, two or three
days maybe, a long time anyhow and she'd be hungry so I
figured she'd enjoy having the kind of food with her that
she was used to and that way wouldn't have to go into any
bus stop restaurants if she didn't want to because those
places can be creepy for a little girl late at night.

I also put some extra cash into the bag. I wrapped in a sock the small bills I had from yesterday after buying a pack of cigarettes plus another fifty which I was thinking might possibly end up buying her a few new dresses but probably wouldn't. Still, it was worth the gamble.

Pretty soon I-Man was up and had a fire going and breakfast was ready, hard-boiled eggs and bananas and Zion juice and then Rose was up and wearing her traveling clothes which were her old red dress nice and clean and her sandals and a Montreal Expos baseball cap that I-Man'd given her a few weeks ago and I'd shown her how to curl the brim and wear it in back so it looked cool. We all ate very quickly without saying much until it looked like it was around eight and I said, Well, let's go, Rosie, and I handed her the bag.

Rose, she said. Don't call me Rosie.

No sweat, I said and explained to her about the money in the sock, how it was hers and no one else's and she should use it any way she wanted or needed to and not to give it over to anybody not even to her mom although I was thinking especially not her mom.

She said thanks and all and then I-Man came over and gave her a long hug and a kiss on each cheek like she was his daughter going off to visit relatives for the summer and in a real low voice he said to her, One love, Sister Rose. One heart. One I. Heartical, mi daughter.

She nodded like she understood and then took my hand and we walked off leaving I-Man standing behind us at the fire watching. We got about halfway across the field and I turned around and looked back and saw him still standing there with his hands down at his sides and all of a sudden a thought entered my mind that was like a radical thought and completely unexpected. At the same instant I-Man raised both his hands to the heavens as if giving praise and thanks to Jah, like he knew my thought.

Wait here, I said to Rose. I'll be right back.

I ran back to the schoolbus and rushed inside and grabbed my backpack and shoved all my loose clothes and other items inside it like the flashlight and CDs and my stuffed bird with Buster's money that had been hanging around on my mattress and came back outside with it.

I-Man had this wide smile on his face when he saw me and his hands on his hips. So, Bone, you goin to trampoose off to Milwaukee Wisconsin wid Sister Rose. Dat be real irie, little brudder.

No, I said. Not that, man. She'll be okay without me. No, I think I'm gonna go home too. Like Rose. I need to see *my* mother too, I said. You know what I'm saying?

Irie, Bone. Dat be real irie, he said but he could use that word irie a hundred different ways just like he could use the word I and this was almost sarcastic mixed with a little sadness and surprise.

I didn't know how to answer him so I just said, Thanks. Thanks for everything, I mean. You really taught me a lot, man. That's actually why I think I can like go back home now. On account of what you've taught me. I think I can face my mother and my stepfather even and figure out what they want me to do and like do it. I just *got* to go there, man, I said to him like it was an explanation and maybe it was. Me and Sister Rose are sort of alike, I told him.

Brother Bone and Sister Rose, he said.

One heart, one love, right?

Yes, mon. De trut'. One I.

You want the rest of Buster's money? I said and reached into my pack for my woodcock and the roll of bills.

No way, mon. Keep it. Dat fe you own self, mon. I-and-I can make plenty money pushing carts at de market, he said grinning and he showed me a handful of quarters which I guess was all he really needed out here, especially with me and Rose gone.

Well, thanks, I said. I reached out my hand and we shook hands in a power grip and then I was running back over the field toward Rose and this time I didn't look back because I was afraid I'd start crying if I did.

TEN

HOME AGAIN, HOME AGAIN, JIGGETY-JIG

I didn't think of it until we actually got there but me and Rose must've looked a little weird that morning at the Trailways station, Rose in her Little Orphan Annie dress and Expos cap and me in one of I-Man's trademark Come Back To Jamaica tee shirts and the baggy cutoffs I'd made from old Mr. Ridgeway's lime green pants with the red anchors on them and the both of us walking on I-Man's fantastic homemade tire sandals. Plus in those days I was into wearing like a doo-rag on my head made out of one of those red farmer's handkerchiefs that I found one morning in the Sun Foods parking lot and took it home and washed it up and dried it and I-Man showed me how to tie it around my head the same as a lot of cool black dudes do for keeping their hair from burning red in the sun, he said.

No problem for me, I told him since my hair was already on the reddish side anyhow.

But I-and-I got to have a lid fe protect him brain from de sun, he said, an' to heat it up fe when de air come cold an' wet. White man or black man, de brain be de key to de whole structure of I-self, an' if it not too hot an' not too cold, it be cool an' jus' right, an' de res' of I-structure be cool an' jus' right as well, no matter how de sun him go an' him come.

At first I thought the doo-rag made me look like a cancer kid covering up his baldness on account of my head being big for my body which was kind of on the scrawny side but then I got into it like I was a Crip or a Blood from L.A. only the white kid from Plattsburgh, New York version and after that I almost never took it off day and night. Plus it went pretty good with my crossed bones tattoo I think which I liked to show off by doing many small tasks with my left hand that I used to do with my right. I-Man said using the off hand was good for me anyhow, that it'd improve my mental balance. So when I bought Rose's ticket to Milwaukee I naturally held out the money with my left hand and the ticket guy saw my tattoo and said, Nice tattoo, kid, real sarcastic, and then, Jesus, you kids today. I was gonna say something like fuck you, man, but didn't since it meant the guy didn't give us any shit after that because basically he didn't want to look at us like he would've if he'd felt sorry for us instead of pissed at my tattoo.

It was maybe an hour while I waited there beside Rose on a bench for the bus to Albany where she'd switch for the Chicago bus and after that she'd have to change again for Milwaukee. She was real quiet and nervous and I hoped she wasn't mad at me or anything but I didn't know how to ask if she was without sounding stupid or making her worry about what she was doing even more than she already was so I just sat there and didn't say anything either, until finally the bus pulled in from Montreal and a few minutes later they announced all aboard for Albany.

There were only a few other people getting on with her, a couple of air force guys and a little old lady saying goodbye to her son and daughter-in-law it looked like. The old lady was normally white for someone her age but her son who kept his arm around her to show her he still cared while he watched the clock for her to leave was the whitest guy I'd ever seen, short pure white hair and beard and eyebrows and eyelashes, pale blue eyes, pink skin, like he had a pigmentation deficiency disease or something and his tall skinny wife looked like that movie actress with the short hair, whatzername Jamie Lee Curtis but the little old lady seemed nice enough so I was hoping she was going to Chicago or maybe even all the way to Milwaukee too and could kind of help take care of Rose.

Get a seat next to Grandma, I whispered to Rose and then I walked up to Mister White and said loud so he and Jamie could hear, Be careful now, sis, and remember what Pop said about don't talk to strange men or anything.

She traveling alone? Whitey asked. He was wearing raspberry pink pants and a white polo shirt which didn't help to cut the glare. Also he had a diamond stud in one ear which was cool but definitely not normal. The wife was wearing this long jean skirt and a striped tee shirt and a duck-bill cap that said Mountaineer on it and looked fairly normal so I was more drawn to her than him but he was obviously the boss.

Yeah, she's alone, I said. Going home to Milwaukee, to be with our mom. I live with our dad.

No kidding, he said. Where's your dad?

Drives a schoolbus. Can't be here this early, so I'm seeing her off.

Too bad. Then he said to the little old lady beside him, Mother, maybe you can keep an eye on the little girl. At least as far as Albany. Be good company for you too, he said smiling down at her and it was like he'd taken her off a leash the way she went forward toward Sister Rose already talking and in deep grandma mode after weeks probably of feeling old and in the way around Mister White and the wife.

That's the moment I chose to back off and then slip away and head quickly out to the street before I started to cry or worry too much about what was going to befall Sister Rose when she got to Milwaukee and had to reunite with her mom.

Maybe ten minutes later I'm standing out there on Bridge Street with my thumb in the air and this flashy new silver-colored Saab Turbo 9000 stops and it's Whitey and Jamie Lee Curtis. Jamie's driving and Whitey goes, Hop in, kid, and I jump into the back seat and we're off. A minute later we're out of town headed west into the mountains aiming toward my old town of Au Sable on the way to where they lived in Keene, it turned out. We were out on 9N yakking about this and that, me and Whitey mostly because his wife was really into the driving. I think the Saab was hers and brand new or something because of how it smelled and out of the blue I asked them if they knew the Ridgeways up on East Hill Road in Keene and they both said oh yeah, sure.

Nice people, he said and she laughed like maybe they weren't.

Yeah. I used to work for them, I said but I don't know why, the words just popped out like marbles. It was like I wanted to confess or something.

You did, eh? he said. Doing what?

Oh, mostly yardwork, raking grass and cleaning out their swimming pool and so forth.

So you've been there, Whitey said sounding suspicious. I wondered did he hear about the break-in and all that.

Yeah, but mainly I was only helping out a friend of mine who worked for them regular, I said back-pedaling like mad.

Is that so? Whitey said. And who might that be?

You probably wouldn't know him. He lives in Au Sable, except for when he lives in Keene with his aunt and uncle. Russ Rodgers is his name. Friend of mine.

Oh, we know Russ! the wife chirped and Whitey shot her a look like keep out of this and I'm thinking oh shit I've blown it, the guy is on to me somehow and he knows more than I thought or else he knows stuff I don't. Russ's probably been busted and confessed all and told everyone about me to keep from going to jail himself. He probably even said I was involved in stealing all the electronics and the fire. Suddenly I was incredibly pissed at Russ not for confessing but for copping a plea like that and at my expense too. He should've taken his punishment like a man and not ratted on a friend.

You know Russ? I said. No kidding. How is ol' Russ? We kinda had a falling out actually. I haven't seen him in over a year and in reality to tell the truth I only helped him out there at the Ridgeways' one or two days. Way back last summer, I think. In the spring maybe, before the Ridgeways came up from wherever they live.

Connecticut, Whitey says.

Yeah, Connecticut. How're they doing, the Ridgeways? Nice people, I understand.

Oh, fine, fine, he says.

We were coming into Au Sable then and I said to drop me off wherever, right there by the Grand Union'd be fine, so the wife pulled the Saab over and I got out and pulled my backpack out and shut the door when the guy, Whitey, he leans out the window and says, What's your name, son?

Bone, I said.

Bone, eh? What's your last name? Who's your dad?

My last name's different from my dad's. On account of being adopted, I said and I gave him a wave and said see you around and started walking off in the opposite direction real fast. No more questions, man. I heard the Saab start up and after a few seconds I turned back to make sure they were definitely on their way and the car was maybe a hundred feet down the road. I saw then that it had Connecticut plates. It was them, the Ridgeways, I suddenly realized and then in a flash I remembered seeing pictures of them in the house with tennis rackets and horses and with their kids and even with the little old lady they'd just been putting on the bus.

And then it came over me like a huge wave of cold water from the Arctic Sea and I felt really sorry for the

first time that I had done so much damage to their house
and burned all their antique furniture and shot up the
picture window and used all their food and stuff and left
it a mess. I wondered if they had a clue who they had
given a ride to and I decided they did. They weren't stupid. I wondered if Mr. Ridgeway'd noticed that my cutoffs
were originally his green pants with the red anchors or if
he'd recognized the backpack I'd stolen from them and
knew that practically everything inside it was his, the
woodcock and the gun and the clothes and the sleeping
bag and the cook kit and the flashlight and the classical
music CDs. The only thing I owned that I hadn't stolen
off of them was the roll of money, and that I'd stolen off
of Buster. What a stupid wasteful thieving little bastard
I've turned out to be, I thought as I walked out to the
edge of town and crossed the bridge and came up to the
light blue mobile home where my mom and stepfather
lived and I used to live with them.

My old dirt bike was out back by the deck getting all
rusty and it looked almost like I still lived there. Nothing
was changed really, at least on the outside so I just walked
up onto the deck to the back door like I'd been sent
home early for screwing up at school again and tried the
door as if expecting it to be unlocked and it was which
surprised me some since usually when my mom and Ken
were at work they locked the doors and left the key under
the mat.

Inside the place was really all messed up with beer bottles and overflowing ashtrays and furniture out of place
and the TV busted and on its side and dirty dishes and
glasses everywhere like the bikers had been living here

not my mom and her husband Ken. The place smelled of wicked ripe BO and stale beer and old food and cigarettes like they'd been partying for a week. It was weird. In the past they were capable of really getting lifted at times and staying there for whole weekends and longer and forgetting all about me but usually they sobered up by Monday and cleaned up the place and went to work and so on like regular citizens. This was so unusual that I stood at the door and for a few seconds wondered if maybe they'd moved out but everything was theirs, the furniture and kitchen stuff and even Ken's beer can and mug collections although they were spread around and not lined up like little soldiers the way he always told Mom to keep them when she dusted and cleaned the shelves and me if I even touched one.

I put my backpack down by the door and then I thought of ol' Willie and started looking around calling, Here, Willie, here, Willie, c'mon out, Willie, and when I walked through the breakfast nook into the livingroom there's my stepfather Ken standing at the hallway that leads from the two bedrooms in back. He was in his bright blue bikini underpants and a tee shirt and looked pretty fucked-up like he hadn't shaved or showered in a week and he even had a boner.

I was just looking for Willie, I said.

No shit. Willie's dead. What the fuck are *you* doing here? What the fuck are you doing *alive,* for chrissake?

Willie's dead? How?

Killed by a car. Right out front. Who knows? Who the fuck cares.

I care! Who hit him? You?

Yeah, sure, *you* care, he said coming into the room and

standing there in the middle of the mess while he scratched his stomach and looked all over and finally found a crumpled pack of cigarettes on the coffee table. Maybe I hit him, maybe I didn't, he said. Point is, he was standing still when he should've been running. He rummaged through the cigarette pack and pulled one out and lit it and inhaled slowly and for a few seconds just looked at me like he didn't quite recognize me and then he said, So what's the story, morning glory?

Whaddaya mean?

You been having plenty of fun? That's some outfit you got on.

You ain't exactly Ralph Lauren yourself, I said and he kind of laughed at that.

We never bought the story about you being dead in the Video Den fire, y'know. Especially after they only found the one body and a few weeks later your little buddy turned up at his auntie's in Keene. So where've you been all this while? Peddling your ass in New York City? That's what all you little druggies do, isn't it? Head for Times Square and sell your ass to rich old cocksuckers with AIDS and then come home to Mama to die.

Sounds more like something *you'd* like to do, I said. Where's my mom?

At work. Where I oughta be, he said and he sighed and sat down on the sofa and put his bare feet up on the coffee table and I saw that he didn't have a hard-on anymore. Well, Chappie, I am glad to see you, he said. No shit, I am. I'm sorry for being such a hardass there. It's just, there's been a lot of people upset since you disappeared. Especially your mom. Your grandma too. And me too, believe it or not. Even me.

Yeah, well, I've been fine, I said. Living with friends is all. So what's happening, Ken, you guys been partying? I said and kind of waved my hand at the debris and he smiled and told me he'd been laid off at the base a few weeks ago because the Democrats were going to close it and the first ones to get let go were always the building services people but my mom was pissed at him for that and some other things beyond his control and not worth mentioning and they'd had some fights, he said, and then she'd moved in with my grandmother for a while. He guessed he wasn't much for housekeeping and I said yeah, from the look of things. He seemed like a real sad sack flopped there on the couch surrounded by his filth and even though he was still the same guy he'd been before, still in pretty good shape for his age which was around forty I think, he seemed older and softer and sadder like he'd finally received some bad news that he'd spent his whole life trying to avoid.

I asked if him and my mom were splitting up and he said no, they just needed to give each other a little space on account of she had gone into AA, he said and now he was going to have to do the same if he wanted her back and he did. He was going in today as a matter of fact.

My *mom*? I said. In Alcoholics A*non*ymous? Like she's an alco*holic*?

Yeah, AA or something like that, one of those groups that meet over at the hospital. AA or Al Anon or Ali Baba or PLO or some damn thing, it don't matter, they all say the same shit. They're right though, Chappie. They are. They get you straightened out and keep you there. But your mom, she's turned into a real hardass on this drinking thing.

It turned out she herself wasn't exactly an alcoholic he explained, or at least she said she wasn't but she was like in this group of people who all claimed their husbands and wives were alcoholics and drug addicts et cetera and they got together once a week and talked to each other about it and according to Ken if you wanted to get your wife back you had to go into AA and give up booze or drugs or whatever they said you were addicted to.

Sounds weird, I said and he said yeah, it was but he really wanted her back so he was going to do it.

You want some help cleaning up? I said. She might be willing to come back home if the place is clean and all and I'm here now. I was thinking I kind of needed her to be living here with or without Ken because my grandmother's place was this small one-room apartment in the Mayflower Arms in town with no kitchen and only this tiny alcove for a bed which meant my mom was sleeping on the couch so no way I could live there with her.

Ken thought that was a terrific idea and smiled for the first time but first would I check the fridge and see was there a beer. I did but didn't enjoy it especially because the fridge was so filthy and I knew I'd be the one to have to clean it. In spite of Ken being such a neatnik and all I'd never seen him lift a finger to clean anything himself. It was always me or my mom.

I brought him his beer and handed it to him and when I did he grabbed my wrist real hard. What the fuck's *this*? he said meaning my tattoo.

Nothin', I said and tried to get away but he wouldn't let me. You little *pussy*! he said. You fucking *twat*, getting yourself tattooed like some kind of fucking fag. You got one on your ass yet? Lemme see, fag, lemme see your ass, he said and he made a grab for my shorts and when he did I slipped out of his grip. I ran back into the kitchen and he hollered, Get the hell back here, I'm gonna fuck you right once and for all!

I could've gotten out the door easy then and he wouldn't've caught me, he was drunk and half naked and I'm a good runner but instead I reached into my backpack and pulled out the gun and turned and very calmly walked back into the livingroom just as he was coming around the coffee table and I saw he had his boner again.

He saw the gun though and stopped. He goes, Oh c'mon, Chappie, just give me that. You don't know how to use that.

Try me, you sonofabitch. C'mon, let me burn you with it, man. I mean it. *Please*! I said. I really wanted him to take one step toward me or to call me a fag again or a twat or a pussy. I really wanted him to say he was gonna fuck me right. I wanted to hear the words one more time, that's all, and for him to take one more step toward me. Just one. Because I wanted to kill him. I have never wanted anything in my life as much as I wanted to kill my stepfather at that moment. But I knew I couldn't do it unless he said one more bad thing to me or took one more step toward me. It was like a deal I had made with God, like I had been given legal permission by God to shoot the fucker in the face but only if he went one step further than he'd already gone in my life, only if he went one step beyond all the nights he'd sneaked into my room and made me touch his dick and suck on it for him and then called me a little cocksucker, one step beyond all the lies he told to my mom and made me tell too so she wouldn't know, all the times he said he'd cut off my dick if I told and no one'd believe me anyhow because everyone knew that whatever happened was my own fault because I was the one who sucked the cock, one step beyond all the times he hit me and then was sorry and came into my room to apologize and lay down on my bed and ended up jerking off in the dark next to me. Please, please, Ken, call me a twat, call me a fag, come at me now, reach out and try to take this gun away, try to grab my wrist, *please!*

He didn't. The sonofabitch. He fell back onto the couch and put his head in his hands and started to cry. It was the first time I'd ever seen him cry and he cried like a little kid, sobbing and drooling with snot running down and everything, his shoulders and back jumping like he was throwing up. It was pretty pathetic but I didn't feel one bit sorry for him. I was only sorry that I hadn't been able to shoot him in the face, a lost opportunity that I knew would never come my way again.

I turned around then and went into the kitchen and picked up my backpack and put the gun inside it and stepped out the door and shut it behind me. Standing out there on the deck I felt incredibly calm and almost old, like I was an elderly and had already lived my whole life and was only waiting around now to die. It was a cool gray day and looked and felt like it was going to rain. The leaves on the trees'd turned upside down and silver. The wind was blowing and a bank of dark clouds was building up over toward Jay which is where a lot of summer storms come from in Au Sable. Slowly I walked down the steps past my old rusting dirt bike and out to the street where I stopped for a minute and thought about Willie and wondered if he'd still be alive if I hadn't run away. Probably none of us'd be alive if I hadn't run away, I decided and then I turned left toward town and after a few minutes of walking real slow like in a fog I speeded up some. I was thinking I'd better walk fast if I was going to get to the clinic where my mom worked before the rain started.

ELEVEN

RED ROVER

By the time I got to the clinic I'd gone all trembly and loose in the limbs. Even my jaw hung down and my mouth was open like I'd been shocked by the sight of something awful, a way bad accident or a bloody crime and I suppose I was. My hands were wet and my knees felt watery and I was afraid I was going to flip out if anybody looked at me the wrong way like with suspicion or even a hint of disrespect. And I was dangerous, wicked *dangerous* because after the deal back at the house with Ken I was aware now that I was carrying chrome, I was a dude with a loaded niner in his backpack who could start blasting if he wanted to and who could blast an actual person and not just some rich guy's view of the mountains. For the first time I understood how these pissed-off ex-employees or some divorced guy who didn't get child custody can walk into a post office or a Pizza Hut full of people and pull out his heater and start firing and not give a shit who gets hit. I didn't *want* to do anything like that of course but I felt like if one little thing went wrong in the next hour or two I wouldn't be able to stop myself, that's how far gone I was on account of my stepfather and the collapsed situation at our house and family and the fact that ol' Willie was dead and no one seemed to give a shit and I was trying to come home again but no one seemed to quite get that either, not even me.

The clinic is a low brick building at the edge of town near the ballfield where there was a Little League game going and some parents sitting in the bleachers watching like it was the World Series so nobody noticed me when I walked by. I almost felt invisible or like I was watching a movie with me in it even when somebody passed me on the sidewalk or drove past on the street. Everything was weirdly normal except for the storm coming up and the trees swirling around in the wind.

The waiting room at the clinic was empty of customers and silent like a morgue, spooky. I walked up to the receptionist, this blond mound of renown around town named Cherie who I knew by her reputation from guys but also slightly from before when she used to come around the house with my mom after work sometimes for a beer, and I said, Is my mom here?

She slowly looked up from the *People* magazine she was reading and said, Huh?

My mom. Is she here? I wanna talk with her, man.

Who's your mom? she asked evidently not recognizing me on account of my hair grown back and no more mohawk or nose rings and earrings which in the past'd kept people from actually looking at me and seeing my face for what it was which was the whole point of course. But now I was into accepting I-self as I-Man would say and as a result I didn't give a flying fuck what people thought when they looked at me.

I said my mom's name and suddenly everything registered in Cherie's mind, meaning who I was and that I wasn't missing and presumed dead anymore which raised up a whole lot of new questions in her small mind that I did not particularly want to answer so I said, She's still in bookkeeping, ain't she?

Oh yeah, sure. But listen, Chappie honey, where have you *been*?

Call her in bookkeeping, willya, and tell her that I'm out here in the lobby and I want to talk to her about something important, I said and I turned around and walked across the room to a far corner behind this big plant where I set my pack on the floor and took a seat and crossed my legs and folded my arms. I studied the No Smoking sign and waited.

A minute or two later here came my mom looking all frazzled and scared like thanks to Cherie she expected to see me covered with blood or something. I love my mom, I really do, despite everything. And I especially loved her then when she came running out from the bookkeeping office and rushed past Cherie at the receptionist's desk and by the time she got to me she had her arms opened wide like a real mom so when I stood up I kind of walked right into her and disappeared inside. That's what it felt like anyhow. Then she was like crying and saying things like, Oh Chappie, Chappie, where have you been? Let me see you, let me *look* at you! I've been so worried and all, honey, I thought you were *dead*!

She told me she'd been sure I'd been burned up in
that fire but Ken had kept saying no and then when my
friend Russell showed up again she'd started to hope
maybe Ken was right. And now here you *are*! she said
brightly and stood back and held me by my arms and
smiled and I smiled and then she hugged me again and
so on back and forth like that until we'd pretty much covered the reunion scene and were ready to move on to
more serious stuff.

She wanted to know where I'd been all these months
and who I'd been staying with naturally and I lied a little
bit so she wouldn't think I'd been hiding out in Keene
and then Plattsburgh just down the road practically and
could've come home easy anytime I wanted. Instead I said
I'd been across the lake over in Vermont almost to New
Hampshire living on a commune with these old hippies
who ran an organic school. I didn't know what that was
but I could tell the words organic and school eased my
mom's mind somewhat although she's a long ways from
being a hippie. She's just not scared of them is all and
believes anything organic is good, just too expensive and
of course school is the magic word. So it was like I was
hanging out with rich people.

She hugged me some more and commented on how
healthy and tanned I looked and I told her how I'd been
doing a lot of gardening for the hippies and lately with
the garden in and all I'd had a little free time and I'd
started to miss her a lot so I'd come over from Vermont
for a visit maybe, in case she wanted me to visit or stay a
while or whatever.

I was being careful because I wasn't sure if she'd want
me back again after everything I'd put her through this

year and once she knew I was okay she might get mad like before and slam the door on me again, although to tell the truth it was never really her who slammed the door last summer when I left home, it was Ken and in a sense it was me myself. My mom just kind of went along with the boys which sad to say is how she's always dealt with her problems. Until now that is, with this new AA program she was into and which seemed to've gotten her to move out on Ken and all even if it was only to move in with Grandma. Still, this was a promising set of developments, I thought.

I told her I'd already gone by the house and had seen Ken and knew about Willie getting whacked. Yes, she said, she was sorry about that, it was sad and all, he was a good cat. But it was an accident, you know, just one of those things that happen in life. She said Willie changed after I left and didn't come home much anymore so she wasn't all that surprised when she found him pancaked on the road a few houses down one morning when she went out to work.

I didn't want to hear about it. Yeah, well, lots of things've changed, I guess. Ken's pretty messed up, it looks like. And the place is too, I said. You oughta see it. You'd be disgusted. By the way, Ken explained to me what happened, I told her. About you guys separating, I mean, and you staying at Grandma's.

He did, did he? Did he say separating?

I don't know. I guess I just thought it. But he's really one messed-up dude, you know? I mean, the guy's kind of sick, don't you think? He's like a pervert. You know what I'm saying?

I was trying to figure out how to tell her for the first

time about Ken, about what he'd done to me when I was a little kid. I wanted her to know about the ugliness that still connected me and him and how I hated it and was dying to get it out of my life but couldn't as long as I had to deal with him as the price for being with her and keeping everything a secret. It meant that I couldn't actually *be* with her, I couldn't be with my own mom in a clean way until her husband, my stepfather was out of her life once and for all and there weren't any more secrets, none and it didn't matter about the drinking and the AA and all his promises to get straight because it was the secret of the past that he carried with him, *my* secret past, it was the ruined part of my life that he brought into the room with him like Dracula's cape over his shoulders and a werewolf's mask over his eyes so that whenever I saw him I was scared and felt ugly and dirty and weak. With Ken anywhere in the neighborhood I felt the exact opposite of how I felt when I saw my mom alone with just me and her for instance like now or when I was with I-Man or Rose or even ol' Russ. With them I was the Bone whether they knew it or not but with my stepfather I was still little Chappie lying in the dark alone. Except when I had the gun.

It's the drinking that makes him sick, Chappie, she said. It's the alcohol. He's allergic to alcohol, that's why he acts the way he does. You have to understand that.

Bullshit, I said.

Oh come on, Chappie, please, let's not get into this. Let's just leave Ken out of this, okay? It's *our* reunion, okay? Don't spoil things, honey. And I wish you wouldn't swear.

Yeah, well, are you gonna get a divorce from him? Are you? 'Cause you oughta. I mean it. There's things about Ken that even you don't know. Stuff I heard. Stuff I *know.*

I don't need to hear whatever you *heard*.

Yeah well you oughta kick him out of your house right away anyhow so we can move back in and clean it up. He's completely fucked it up, sorry about swearing. But it's your house, ain't it? Didn't my real father give it to you? Ken, he's just the stepfather, you know. He doesn't have any right to live in that house unless you say so. Besides you should see what a mess he's made of the house, it's really gross and disgusting.

Chappie, *please*. I want you to keep out of my business. Ken and I are trying to work things out, and we will, if you'll just stay out of it.

Me? I said and my voice went all twinky and high like a bicycle bell. *Me?* You think *I'm* the problem? Ha! That's a laugh.

She looked over my head like she was enjoying the breeze.

It's *Ken* who's the problem, not me, I said but it was useless I knew.

That's just not true, Chappie! she yelled. She was mad now and here it all came again, the same story as before. She said, As a matter of fact, young man, over the last year or so you *have* been very much a problem, wouldn't you say, and otherwise I think maybe Ken and I would've gotten along better. I certainly wouldn't have been so upset all year and he might not've turned to alcohol to deal with his problems and frustrations so much. Really, who knows how many things would've been different if you hadn't gotten into drugs and stealing and all? If you'd've stayed in school for instance and had some decent friends and all, who knows how things would've been different? Only now you're fine and you're back, and that's wonderful, Chappie. I know we'll be able to work things out now, sweetie, all three of us.

No. Fucking. Way.

What do you mean? Don't you *want* to work things out?

Not if it's the three of us, I told her. I mean, I want to be with you, I said. With you I can work things out. But not him. Not if he's there.

Where?

Wherever you are.

Well, excuse me, mister, but you can't make that decision. It's mine to make, if Ken and I are going to stay together. Mine and Ken's, not yours. We're still trying to work things out and I'm at Grandma's only temporary. Until Ken decides to deal with his drinking problem, that's all. And you certainly can't live at Grandma's with me, there's barely room for me there. So if you want to live at home with me, and you're welcome to, I want you to know that, then you'll just have to let me and Ken work things out first. Which we will, and when we do you'll have to put up with Ken, I'm afraid. And you'll have to like it, too. And be nice to him for a change. Many things will have to change, Chappie, for the three of us to go back to living together like we used to, back before you started getting into trouble. And you, mister, are the one who has to do the most changing, she said. You and Ken too, Ken will have to make a few changes too, she said like she'd made a big compromise. Then she stood back from me and crossed her arms over her chest which always meant that she'd made up her mind, she'd staked out her territory and there'd be no more arguing with her now. Only defiance, only open in-your-face fuck-you-mom defiance.

Nothing's changed! I said. And it never will! Nothing! I

guess I was shouting because she stepped back like she was scared of me. You're just trying to set up the same old thing as before! I think I was crying by then. Look, Mom, please please please! Just try, please? Just try and see it my way. I was practically begging her but I knew she wouldn't even *try* to see it my way and probably couldn't anyhow, not without knowing my secret and there was no way I could tell it to her now. It was too late. So I kept on hollering and I made all these stupid demands instead, not because I thought or even hoped she'd meet the demands but because I was pissed at everything that was going down and frustrated because it was too late to change anything and also because I didn't know how else to express myself.

You know what, Mom? You wanna know what? I'll tell you what. *You* should choose! Yeah, you should choose between me and Ken! I said. That's right, choose which one of us you want. 'Cause you can't have both. That's the one thing I can guarantee. So c'mon, Mom, choose one or the other. Ken or me. Let's get serious.

Stop this! she said. Stop it right now!

Who d'ya want standing there beside you, Mom? Is it gonna be your stupid sicko drunk of a pervert of a husband, or the homeless boy who's your own flesh-and-blood son? Red Rover, Red Rover, who're you calling over, Mom? Is it me or is it Ken?

I was remembering how when I was a little kid in the schoolyard we used to play Red Rover and the teachers thought it was cute and all but it was scary, two lines of kids holding hands facing each other across a distance and the one in the middle says, Red Rover, Red Rover, let Chappie come over, and I'd get all excited like I'd been chosen for something special. I'd let go of the hand of the kid on either side of me and I'd step out there in like no-man's-land between the two lines all alone and exposed and everyone looking at me and I'd wind up and start running straight at the line opposite as fast as I could. I'd slam against the linked hands of the kids who I only remember as being bigger than me because although I didn't realize it then you only call come over to the littlest kids, the ones who are too small and weak to bust through the line. Otherwise if you break through you get to go safely back to your own line and now it's your team's turn to call for the littlest kid to come over and try to bust through and when he fails he gets captured. Back and forth you go until finally there's only one kid left on the other side facing a huge long line of everyone else opposite him, and the last kid realizes that he can't call anyone over anymore because he's all by himself. It was usually the biggest strongest kid in the schoolyard like a fifth or sixth grader who ended up standing there all alone and it was interesting because he was the loser. Anyhow I was never him. Instead I was always called over early in the game and got captured and even though I said like Oh no and all, I was secretly glad to be captured. I never wanted to be the big tough kid who ended up on the other side all by myself and unable to say Red Rover, Red Rover, let even the littlest kid in the schoolyard, let Chappie come over.

You—you're—you're just a *terrible* son! she sputtered and she started to cry but more from being mad than sad.

Yeah, well, that should make it easy for you to choose, I said. So who's it gonna be, Mom? The terrific husband or the terrible son?

She wrung her hands and I knew I was totally screwing up our relationship forever probably but I couldn't stop myself. Her face was dark red and had more lines in it than I'd ever seen before like she was aging right before my eyes and I truly wished that I didn't have to force her to make this choice. But I felt like I myself didn't have any choice and it was her husband, the man she had chosen to marry after my real father left, who had taken it away from me and had made it so that neither me nor my mom had any freedom to choose, and the one who had taken it away from us, Ken, he wasn't even here.

She said in a low voice, almost a whisper, Then go, Chappie. Go away.

I'll always remember that moment. I've played it back in my mind a hundred times at least since then. But not much of what came afterwards. I think I said okay. I was calm and picked up my backpack and I remember thinking about the niner inside and I remember noticing with relief that I hadn't the slightest interest now in becoming a mass murderer.

I'm gonna go by and see Grandma first, I said. Just to tell her like goodbye. I didn't do it before, I said. Then I guess I'll go back to Vermont, to the organic school.

Whatever, she said. She looked definitely downcast, like her only son had died only of course he hadn't, he was standing right there in front of her saying goodbye. But I think she kind of wanted me dead, that she actually had all along preferred me missing and presumed dead to being where and what I was now. In a sense by cutting out I was only giving her what she really wanted but didn't dare ask for.

What a good boy am I, thought I. See ya 'round, Mom, I said and left her sitting there in the chair behind the big green plant in the lobby of the clinic looking dreamy and sad and when I got to the door and turned she looked relieved too.

TWELVE

OVER THE RIVER AND THROUGH THE WOODS

It was raining pretty hard when I left the clinic so by the time I got to Grandma's at the Mayflower Arms Apartments down by the bridge I was soaked even though I jogged most of the way and must've looked like a kitten somebody tried to drown in a bag because when Grandma came to the door she didn't recognize me at first and I had to tell her my name. It's me, your grandson. The only one incidentally but never mind, she's old and surprisingly self-centered for a person who doesn't have long to live. Plus she'd probably decided right after the fire that I'd been burned up in it so I was like a ghost to her and nobody wants to recognize a ghost, even the ghost of their only grandson.

She clapped her hand over her big bosom and said, Chappie? It's really *you*? My God, I thought you'd been burned beyond recognition in that fire over the Video Den. You know they found the one body, she added and I said yeah I knew.

She gave me the usual hugs and all, carefully holding her cigarette out to the side so's not to burn me and keeping her head turned so I wouldn't knock off these big clip-on earrings that she always wears day and night. She was real glad to see me though and liked holding my hands in her old soft ones once she'd put her cigarette in an ashtray and she enjoyed standing back and looking at me and smiling in a teary way and saying like how *happy* she was to know that it wasn't me who was burned beyond recognition. I think that particular phrase pleased her because she used it a lot more than necessary especially if she was trying to make me feel lucky for not being dead which is what she told me, that I should feel lucky for not being burned beyond recognition in that terrible fire. Did I know about the fire, had I *seen* it? she asked like it'd been the highlight of her year.

I like my grandmother and always have since I was a little kid but I never really know what she's thinking. Part of it's she doesn't either. Also she plucks her eyebrows off and then draws in new ones with a pencil or a special crayon the way she'd want them to look in a fashion magazine which is up high on her forehead practically like she's stuck in a state of cute permanent surprise so most of the time you actually can't read her expression very well. It's sort of a mask. Plus she has this habit of reversing how people are supposed to ask you about yourself so that it comes out she's really telling you about herself only you aren't supposed to know it and most people probably don't. Even I didn't until I got used to it. Like once on my thirteenth birthday my mom had a special family dinner and Grandma when she sat down at the table took my hand in hers and looked into my eyes and said, Did you ever think you'd be old enough to have a grandmother who'll be seventy-five in September?

I said, No kidding, Grandma. Happy birthday in advance then, in case I don't make it to September, but then my mom started dissing me because she knew what I was doing even if Grandma didn't. I was only kidding though and Grandma likes being kidded. She knows attention when she sees it.

This day she said to me, I bet you never thought you'd see your old grandmother again, did you, Chappie?

Yeah, it's pretty amazing, I said. But I've been over in Vermont, I told her and added the bit about the organic school and the hippie family who were these wicked decent older people with kids and this huge farm they all lived on with some other kids like me who were like foster children and they grew all their own food and ran their own school in the barn and made all their own clothes and shoes even, I said showing her my sandals.

Those are nice, the sandals. I once had a pair that they remind me of, she said. Made by Indians from Mexico or one of those places. I got them at an Indian souvenir place in Lake George. They didn't last though. But yours look fine, she said. I see you got rid of that weird haircut and all the earrings and that ring in your nose and so on, she said.

Yeah, I said. On account of the rules of the school and all. That's the one drawback, I told her in case she thought I'd done it to please people like her. At the door when I took off my doo-rag on account of it was soaked she'd seen my hair and she just had to like nod with approval which'd made me instantly want to shave my head and grow back the old mohawk as fast as I could. That's why afterwards I kind of exposed my arm a few times so she could see my crossed bones if she wanted to comment on something, but I guess she was distracted and didn't see it or probably she just thought I'd had it all along and couldn't get rid of it like the haircut and the rings so she'd rather not think about it and didn't. She was like that, she could think about anything she wanted whenever she wanted or she could decide not to think about it at all and then didn't. Grandma always had her fingernails to paint, her eyebrows to pluck, her TV shows to watch, plus church and her AA meetings. She's been in AA for half a century or at least since my mom was a kid and her husband, my mom's dad who would've been my grandfather got killed in a car crash when he was drinking, an event Grandma refers to as her wake-up call and still talks about like it happened a year ago and was a blessing in disguise.

At her weekly meetings in the basement of the Methodist Church Grandma is the one who makes the coffee and cleans up afterwards and gets to complain how they take her for granted. I knew she was the one who'd gotten my mom hooked into the AA, she'd been trying for years and it was probably an okay thing and the reason why my mom was living with her nowadays, and I figured once my mom was sure she'd be able to keep going to AA meetings on her own she'd move out of Grandma's and back in with Ken.

It couldn't've been much fun living at Grandma's anyhow. It was a crummy old building full of old people on social security and derelicts and drunks and her whole apartment was smaller than a standard-sized bedroom jammed with all kinds of furniture she couldn't let go of. Plus I knew when it came to food, TV, housecleaning and so forth it was bound to be Grandma who ran the show, not Mom even if Mom was contributing money for rent and food and all Grandma had to live on was her social security check. Grandma was totally self-centered and strong but my mom who was equally self-centered was weak. I kind of preferred my grandmother's version though because you could see it coming from last Tuesday and it didn't make you feel sorry for her all the time. Even when I was so pissed at my mom I could hardly look at her like now I was still feeling sorry for her and guilty. Which is why I probably acted the way I did that day at Grandma's.

I flopped down on her couch and didn't move when she started wringing her hands and complaining about how I was getting it all wet. She was like a bird whose nest'd been taken over by a bird of a different breed, fluttering and squawking around while I sat there and ignored her. I picked up the remote and started surfing the TV in a dazed way and put my feet on her coffee table which wasn't cool I know but I was incredibly pissed off way down deep inside and scared too but I couldn't say to myself or to anyone else what it was exactly that I was upset about. Except of course that it obviously was about my stepfather and my mother, and me not being able to live a regular life with them.

All that'd been true for a long time but somehow it hadn't upset me before as much as it did now. All at once it felt like everything was way too complicated for me to control and nobody else was in control either so I didn't have anyone to turn to for help. Except Grandma and with her the second I walked through the door and she didn't recognize me I realized she wasn't going to be any help either. It was like I really was invisible or something and no one could see me. No, actually it was more like I was this human mirror walking down the road and all people could see when they looked in my direction was some reflection of themselves looking back because the main effect was nobody saw me myself, the kid, Chappie, Bone even, no one saw me except as a way to satisfy their desires or meet their needs, the nature of which sometimes they didn't even know about until I showed up on the scene, like my stepdad's needs for instance.

I guess I shouldn't've been so pissed off at my grandmother for being unable to deal straight with me though. She was old and poor and uptight and probably scared of things I hadn't even imagined yet, monsters and demons that only visit old people whose lives are completely behind them now and from that angle look wasted and stupid and unhappy and there's no chance left of them ever changing things for the better. It's like the party's over and it was a bummer of a party and there ain't gonna be any more. No wonder so many old people act like animals that were mistreated in their youth. I should've been helping Grandma to mellow out in these last years of her dumb life and maybe help her see how it hadn't been all that bad after all but instead I was only making it worse by reminding her of what a poor imitation of a regular family we were, her and my mom and me. It was like she was the seed and my mom was the plant and I was the rotten fruit and what I should've done if I couldn't be the good grandson to her was just leave her alone, stay hidden and let the old lady go around telling people that she's the grandmother of the poor boy who was burned beyond recognition in the Video Den fire last spring. Then they'd feel sorry for her and make a fuss and she'd be happy as a clam.

She had cable so I watched MTV for a while but she kept trying to butt in and get me talking to her by asking me if I'd seen my mom yet or Ken and I'd just nod or say yeah and go on watching TV, flicking up and down the channels when the ads came on and back to MTV for the music videos which didn't seem any different from the last time I watched about a year ago before I got kicked out of my mom's. Mostly music videos're visual headtrips with a sound track and a good one is a quick low-grade contact high requiring no effort on the part of the user to get high which is cool and if you're already bummed it's actually enough.

Beck this singer with only one name like me and I-Man was standing in this orange and purple haze with the silhouettes of the leafless trees of death against a pink sky and singing about how nobody understood him either when Grandma finally lost it and she goes, *Chappie*, please at least have the decency to turn that down! And pay attention to me when I talk to you, young man! You're not in your own home, you know, you're in mine!

I flicked off the TV and stood up and said, Yeah, I'm not in my own home. You sure got that one right. I went over to the fridge and opened it and poked through like I was looking for something in particular but I wasn't even curious, I just didn't know what else to do at that moment. I think I was only trying not to cause any more damage than necessary but it probably didn't look that way to Grandma.

You got anything good in here? I said but I wasn't hungry, I was just filling the air between us with words.

Do you like egg salad? You used to *love* my egg salad, she said.

Yeah. I was wondering, I said and closed the refrigerator door pretty hard I guess because she jumped. I was wondering if you could loan me fifty bucks.

Me? Her eyes started darting from side to side like she expected me to rob her and was looking for an escape route. I...I don't have any money, Chappie. I can't...you'll have to ask your mother, she said. Or Ken. Ask your stepfather. What do you want it for?

I don't *want* it, Grandma. I *need* it. There's a difference.

Oh.

Forget it, Grandma. Forget the fifty bucks. I was only kidding.

She was silent for a minute, we both were, then she said, Are you in some kind of trouble, Chappie? You can tell me, honey. You can trust me, you really can. She was like trying to think her way onto a TV show, one of her afternoon soaps because that's where her lines were coming from now. I'm your grandmother, honey, and if you can't trust me who *can* you trust?

I grinned into her face up close and that snapped her back and I said, *Yumsters*! Yumsters, Grandma! Me want yumsters! Can Grandma give Chappie some yumsters? 'Cause if she can he'll be one happy Chappie, all his problems over at last.

Stop that! You...you're just like your father! She goes, You do the same things to me that he did!

What d'you mean, man! I'm *nothin'* like him! That's why my mom and him tossed me out, isn't it? Get a clue, Grandma.

I don't mean Ken. I *know* you're nothing like him. Although if you really want to know, it might help if you *were* a little more like him. Except for the drinking maybe. She puffed herself up a little and after a few seconds remembered what she'd been saying. No, I mean your *real* father. Paul. He used to talk to me exactly the way you're doing now. He used to make me feel afraid that he was going to get all crazy on me, although he never actually did. But still that man could make me very very nervous. He wasn't normal.

My real father used to make you nervous? How'd he do that? Why?

Oh, you know, just by talking in a funny way, real fast and about things that didn't make sense like you were doing just now, and he didn't seem to care one way or the other. I used to think he was on drugs or something, the way he talked, and your mother told me after the divorce that she thought he took cocaine and was possibly an addict because of how he went through so much money. He made very good money.

No way! Coke? My father? Wow, I said. Cool. I was suddenly for the first time since I was a little kid very eager to hear about my real father. Usually I just shut down whenever his name came into the conversation and it was like they were talking about somebody I never met and who didn't have any impact on my life anyhow so why should I care et cetera. But I was like five years old when my father left and I had memories of him and I knew things, although my memories were fuzzy and I couldn't really see him in my mind except for the picture I once found in one of my grandmother's albums. It's this snapshot of him and my mom standing in front of his '81 Blazer in the driveway of my mom's same house which they had just bought then and she got in the divorce later. He's a lot taller than my mom, taller than Ken too and skinny and he looks kind of good-humored like he knows there's a joke going on but no one else has caught it yet, and I can see from this long leather coat he's wearing that he's on the flashy side, he's cooler than my mom, he's a guy who likes new 4x4s and wouldn't be caught dead in one of Ken's turquoise nylon jogging suits. Anyhow I never wanted to know much about him, on account of his leaving me to Ken, I guess although he didn't actually leave me to Ken, I'm pretty sure he never even met Ken, that was after. The point is I just sort of numbed out on the subject of my real father for years and didn't even want to hear his name. Paul. Paul Dorset.

Now though suddenly I was asking Grandma all these questions, like what kind of work did he do back then and where did he go after the divorce and so on. I think she was relieved to have a normal conversation with me no matter what the subject because she started rattling away and pretty soon didn't need any questions from me to grease her wheels.

She said that my father'd worked as a medical technician which was cool. An x-ray expert she called him and he made big bucks but she didn't think he was much of an expert on anything except lying to people since she knew for a fact that he never went to medical technician school or even to x-ray school and he had lied about his so-called military record where he was supposedly an EMS ambulance driver. My mom who worked in personnel at the clinic then knew the truth because she was supposed to check that sort of thing out when they hired anybody and she'd told Grandma all about his lies after the divorce when she was no longer protecting him. Although she had to swear Grandma to secrecy because of Mom being the one to cover for him. He was smart, he'd known to ask my mom out on a date the same day he applied for the job and she fell for him and when it came back that he'd never gone to the schools and that he'd been dishonorably discharged from the air force and all she didn't tell anyone because by then she was head over heels in love with him.

My father was a fast talker, a smoothie was Grandma's word which struck me as funny, the idea of my old man being a smoothie and wasting it on Grandma and Mom who were both unusually gullible let's say especially when it came to men which they pretty much worshiped. But I liked picturing my father's talents being wasted on them and on the whole town of Au Sable actually, a place that smoothies may come from but if they're any good at smoothing they never stay. Was he from Au Sable? I asked her. Did he grow up here and have like a family? I'd be related to them if he did. I'd have cousins.

No, he was from away, she said. He was from someplace downstate although you couldn't believe him about that either and in fact he had a funny accent like he was originally from Massachusetts or Maine where they talk like President Kennedy, all nasal and without any *r*'s which was attractive and made him sound smarter and better educated than he really was.

I thought that was cool and remembering the picture

of him decided that he actually looked like JFK too. The same haircut anyhow. Sort of a young Jack Kennedy, that was my real dad.

So tell me the truth, Grandma, why'd they get divorced? I asked her. I'd been told stuff over the years but mostly it'd come down to him having this girlfriend Rosalie on the side which from letters I found once and read he didn't really care about, not the way he cared about my mom anyhow. At least that's what he said in the letters. But usually people don't go to all the trouble of a divorce especially when they have a little five-year-old kid who loves and needs both his parents equally unless there's something more wrong than the fact that somebody hooked up with somebody else a few times or even a bunch of times. So I wondered what the real story was.

Well, it didn't disappoint *me* they got divorced, she said. The man was no good, he was a drug addict probably which I didn't know at the time and he drank too much although that's no sin. But I told your mother that she should be strong and she was.

What?

Strong.

About what?

About getting divorced from him. After she found out he was seeing other women. It was all over town, she said.

You *wanted* her to divorce him?

She said, Oh sure, of course. She was much better off without him.

According to Grandma my father'd claimed to be sorry and all and cried and begged and told my mom he didn't want the divorce but Grandma made sure my mom got a good lawyer and the judge gave her the house plus a hun-

dred dollars a week child support which she never saw a
penny of, and he gave my father liberal visitation rights
which he never used since he would've had to pay a little
child support if he wanted to see me.

So she didn't let him have any visitations with me? I was
wondering if things would've been different if I'd've had
my real father to go to when I was seven and Ken first
started in. I think I would've gone to him and told and my
real father would've taken me away with him and for a
second I flashed on that, it was like a picture of me and
him riding in his Blazer 4x4, he's like JFK and I'm his little son. With my real father to help me I wouldn't have
been scared to tell like I was with my mom who I couldn't
go to or didn't think I could because Ken was her husband and she loved him supposedly and never let me
complain about him even a little without telling me how
lucky I was to have him for a stepfather.

No, Grandma said, I didn't want that man in the same
house with you two. Of course not. Not unless he was willing to pay up the child support he owed your mother.
Grandma said she'd offered to move in with me and my
mom but by then Mom was seeing Ken and he moved in
instead. I could tell that had given Grandma a crossed
hair but she couldn't say it of course or people might
think the reason she'd pushed so hard for the divorce was
so she could have a nicer place to live for herself.
Grandma's a person with permanent ulterior motives.

I asked her if she knew where my father took off for
after the divorce because so far as I knew he hadn't stayed
in Au Sable or even Plattsburgh. No one in town'd ever
once mentioned him to me. It was like he was this mysterious stranger named Paul Dorset who looked and talked

like JFK and he rode into Au Sable one day and married
the prettiest gal in town and then he knocked her up and
married her and one day after a little nastiness the
stranger rode out of town again and except for the gal
and her immediate family no one remembered him as
having even been there. They were like, Who *was* that
masked man? And he was like, Hi yo, Silver, awa-a-ay!

Grandma said after the divorce he went to the
Caribbean, one of those foreign countries down there like
Jamaica or Cuba or at least that's what she'd heard from
someone at the bank, a friend of hers who was a teller who
a year or so after the divorce was told in a letter to close
out my dad's account and send the balance to a bank in
Jamaica or someplace like that which she happened to
remember because right after she did that a whole bunch
of checks came in that bounced like rubber balls but there
wasn't anything the bank could do since my dad was out of
the country now. They had a warrant for his arrest,
Grandma said, for bouncing checks and for nonpayment
of child support which she had encouraged my mother to
file for since it was criminal for a man not to help pay for
his own son's food, clothes and housing, didn't I agree?

I guess so, I said. But maybe if he'd been able to get to
know me a little he'd've been more willing to kick in and
help pay for things. The way it is now he'd be busted if he
tried to even see me, I said.

You better believe it, mister! Grandma said. She could
get fierce when she wanted to, a regular wolf in grandmother's clothing. And you should be more appreciative
of everything your mother's done for you, she said. And
Ken, him too. He's been more of a father to you than
your real father ever was.

Oh yeah, wow, fucking A, man! Dear old Daddy Ken, I almost forgot about what a great guy *he's* been all my life. Thanks for reminding me, man, I said and I was up and stomping around now wanting to knock something over, wanting to trash the place or start tossing all the furniture out the window and see it break down on the sidewalk so I figured I'd better get the hell out of there before I did something that I'd really regret afterwards because I didn't want to hurt my grandmother or harsh on her too much or wreck any of her stuff. She didn't know any better than to be the way she was.

Look, I gotta get outa here, Grandma, I said to her and grabbed up my backpack and tied my doo-rag back on which had dried out on the radiator while we were talking.

She was wringing her hands and all, saying how she hoped she hadn't upset me with all this talk about my father and I said no way and if it was up to me I'd go to Jamaica or wherever tomorrow and find him if I could because I had a few things he might be interested in hearing. Stuff about my stepfather, I said to her.

That lit up her screen. Really? she said. About Ken? Like what?

I smiled at her and said, Wouldn't you like to know. Hang in there, Granny, I said. If things work out you may end up living in Mom's house with her after all.

She smiled in that innocent way of hers and she goes, Well, I did point out how they had an extra bedroom now. With you gone, I mean.

Yeah, well, don't worry, I'll stay gone. The place needs a little bit of a clean-up though, I said. I gave her a kiss on the cheek and went down the ratty old smelly hallway to the stairs and down the stairs to the street. I couldn't much blame her for wanting to get out of that place and my mom was an incredible wuss to be staying there with her. The whole scene gave me the creeps.

Out on the street it was almost dark and the rain was still coming down. I didn't put out my thumb or look for a ride or anything though, I just walked straight out of town and along the side of Route 9N toward Plattsburgh. With my luck if I hitched I'd get picked up by Russ or the Bong Brothers, or maybe the Ridgeways in their Saab or why not ol' Buster Brown in his church van? Better to walk all night long in the rain if that's the only way to get back to the bus and I-Man. Besides I had plenty of new stuff to think about now, especially about me and my real father.

THIRTEEN

MISTER YESTERDAY

I'd say the night that I walked out of Au Sable forever in the rain was one of the weirdest nights of my life except that nothing happened. Plus later I went through some even weirder nights and of course I'd already experienced quite a few by then that not many normal people go through, due to drugs and the bikers and some of the stuff maybe that me and Russ'd done together like at the Ridgeways' summerhouse in Keene. But even though nothing was happening it was only on the outside because inside I was like tripping only I wasn't high or anything.

After a while I didn't think about my real father and me anymore because there wasn't enough real information to feed my thoughts so to speak. It was like my brain ran out of things to say to me. I was walking along 9N on the shoulder of the road in the darkness with the rain pouring down on me stepping steadily straight ahead like

I was marching to the edge of the planet so I could drop right off it into cold black empty space. My mind was empty and my body was this machine that walked. Every once in a while a car or a truck would go by and catch me in the lights and slow down to check me out and a couple of times drivers stopped and rolled down the window and said did I want a ride but I kept on moving so they probably figured I was just a stoned freaked-out kid or a mass murderer or something and went on their way.

I actually kind of was a mass murderer. Boy slays family and self. I'd started having these incredibly realistic visions of firing my niner at my stepfather, shooting him in the right temple from about six inches away while I stood with my foot on his neck and him lying on the floor begging me not to. It was pretty vivid, with blood and brains splashing over my foot and all.

And then my mom comes into the room, it's my old bedroom at home and she sees what's happened to Ken and me with the gun and blood spattered all over my pantsleg and sandal from where I had placed it on his neck and my hands from holding the gun so close to his head when I fired, and she takes off down the hall and I go after her and catch her as she gets to the door only it's locked and she can't get it open in time so she goes, No, Chappie, *don't*!

I do though. I give her one straight in the heart. It was like in a video game only real.

I looked out the livingroom window and there was Grandma coming up the walk so I opened the door for her and she came inside and saw my mom lying there with blood all over her chest and her eyes rolled back and her mouth open with blood bubbling out and Grandma says, *What's* going *on?* and that's when I blast her too. In the heart, same as my mom.

Afterwards I walked around the house for a while calling Willie and finally I remembered that he was dead too and it was Ken who ran over him and then I realized that if ol' Willie was still alive maybe none of this would've happened. It's amazing but all I needed was that little black and white cat who really liked me and I probably wouldn't have slain my family. He only weighed nine or ten pounds, about like a bag of sugar and he couldn't talk or anything but it was like there was the concentration of a person inside his furry head who truly liked and was always sincerely glad to see me when I came home and slept on my lap whenever I stayed up late alone watching MTV and purred with contentment like I made him feel safe in a dangerous world.

I remembered the time I got Ken's .22 rifle with the scope out of the case that was stashed in his and my mom's bedroom closet and aimed it at Willie and pulled the trigger but the safety was on and it didn't fire so I used the gun to shoot up Ken's and my mom's bed instead. I felt incredibly guilty then for almost killing Willie. Sometimes I guess you do a bad thing in order not to do a worse thing that you can't stop yourself from doing. Boy slays cat and self they would've said if that day Ken's .22 hadn't had the safety on. Ken and Mom and Grandma would've been okay and even would've gone to the funeral and after that normal life would've resumed for them.

Lucky for Willie I guess, even though he bought it later. But unlucky for them because now I'd ended up doing the worst thing instead of only the bad thing. It was like being inside a snuff video on the VCR and watching it at the same time with a remote in my hand and I could play the same three scenes over and over, noticing new details each time, pressing Rewind after I whacked Grandma—she gets up and goes backwards out the door and down the steps to the street and Mom stands up and yanks on the locked door and then comes toward me down the hall with her back facing me like we're playing blindman's buff when suddenly she turns and sees Ken on the floor his head all bloody and I stand up and put the gun into my backpack and by this time Ken is slipping back out the bedroom door—and then pressing Play and now I notice when he comes sneaking into my bedroom that Ken's wearing only his bikini underpants and he's got a boner and that glazed boozy look in his eyes that makes me feel like bread dough, and my mom's first reaction actually is to be pissed off at me for making such a mess and firing off a gun inside the house instead of for what in reality I've gone and done with it, killed her husband, and my grandma's first thought I can tell from her face when she sees that my mom's lying dead on the floor is that maybe she'll get something out of it for herself, the house even.

Hours passed, it was probably like three in the morning and there weren't any more cars on the road but it kept raining and my body kept walking while the rest of me was trapped inside the family massacre video examining and thinking about every gross detail. Over by Keeseville where the road crosses the Ausable River I got halfway out on the bridge when I noticed the wind was blowing and suddenly it was like the VCR had jammed with everybody but me dead in the house and it wouldn't rewind or go forward. It's stuck on the scene at the end where I go around the house looking for ol' Willie. Here, Willie, c'mon out, Willie.

For the first time since leaving my grandma's apartment I stopped walking. I looked over the railing and down about three hundred feet into the chasm and the rocks and the rushing water below which I could hear in spite of the rain beating down and the wind. It was too dark to see the river or the rocks down there and I thought now was the time and place if he was going to do it right for the boy to slay self. No muss, no fuss. Behind him nothing but waste and scenes of carnage. Ahead more of the same.

I took off my backpack and set it down on the walkway and climbed up onto the flat top of a concrete post that the iron railing was attached to and with my hands out at my sides stood there for a while listening to the water way below churning over the rocks and felt the cold wind push against my soaked tee shirt and cutoffs and looked up into the black sky and let the rain fall straight onto my face. I was shivering from the cold and the wet and except for that I couldn't tell anymore what was real from what was only in my head.

The concrete post was slippery under my feet though. And when I noticed that I realized I didn't want to fall off the bridge into the chasm and bust myself up on the rocks by accident. I figured I'd better get down and think about this some more. I don't know why but it seemed that the worst thing I could do now was accidentally kill myself. I wanted to do it strictly on purpose. Not some dumb slipup.

Just then I saw the lights of a car approaching from the direction of Willsboro still a long ways off and I started to turn and get down so I could get off of the bridge before the car got close enough to see me because at this hour it was probably a state cop. But when I turned, my right foot slid off the edge of the post and my left followed and for a second I was floating in the air and then I flung out both hands and grabbed at the darkness and found the iron bars of the bridge railing. I clamped on and hung there with my whole body dangling below the bridge while the steady gush of the rain above and the overflowing river far below filled my brain like that classical music from the Burlington station I heard once on a car radio when I was hitching home to Au Sable from the mall. The music was real mellow and relaxing and all, with violins and clarinets and hundreds of other instruments playing this smooth powerful song that rose like in spirals and fell and swirled around and rose again like it could do that forever or at least for a very long time.

I was starting to think the music was strong enough to lift me up and carry me off like on a beautiful soft cloud if I let go of the iron railings which I clung to like they were the bars of a jail cell and my hands were pretty cold by then and I probably couldn't hold on for more than a few seconds longer anyhow, when the car I'd seen before got to the bridge and splashed across and cast its lights over everything and made me see clearly where I was, dangling a hundred yards above a killer river in a wicked rainstorm. After the car passed on it was like it'd left its lights behind because I could still see exactly what I'd seen in that split second and it freaked me so I pulled myself up and got one foot onto the bridge and then the other and managed to clamber back over the rail to safety.

I was breathing real hard. My teeth were chattering

and I was soaked through and my heart and liver felt like they were frozen solid. I went over to my backpack which was all I owned in the world, my rain-soaked worldly effects it would have been if they'd found it there in the morning and my body all smashed up on the rocks below. Opening it I reached in and pulled out the pistol I'd used or thought I'd used and still kneeling flipped it over my shoulder. I watched it sail into the air turning like a tiny dead animal and then disappear into the darkness and down into the chasm. Then I stood up and put the backpack on again and started walking toward Plattsburgh. That was the closest I ever came to committing mass murder and suicide and until now I've never told anyone.

By the time I got to the field behind the warehouses and spotted the schoolbus out there in the middle it was dawn and the rain had finally stopped. The sky was a shiny gray color like it had wet paint on it with these wispy white cloud-tails floating underneath here and there. I crossed through the chain-link fence and the tall wet grasses and ragweed and goldenrod in the field slapped against my bare legs and pasted their seeds to my skin as I made my way toward what I guess I now thought of as home. Although the truth is I wasn't thinking much of anything then, I was dizzy and shivering and probably had a hundred and ten fever and a couple of times during my nightlong hike I'd been really sorry I'd given the sweater I'd taken from Mr. Ridgeway to Sister Rose at the bus station. It was only yesterday morning but back then I'd figured she was going to places unknown and I was going home to where I had parents who'd buy me clothes of my own so I could afford to be generous.

I don't really remember arriving at the schoolbus, only crossing the field and the weeds and the seeds and hundreds of daisies and black-eyed susans and the bus getting bigger and bigger until it was the only thing I could see, this big banged-up yellow schoolbus with huge green leafy plants instead of kids looking out of the mostly broken windows, and then I was knocking at the door like I was a kid who wanted to be picked up for school and that's all I remember. It was like once I'd gotten there I could finally let go the way I'd wanted to let go when I was hanging off the bridge because the next thing I remember is waking up inside the bus on a mattress with a blanket around me and a dry tee shirt on that's too big like a nightshirt.

I felt like a newborn baby. Sunlight was splashing through the windows and I was warm and dry and there was music playing, reggae music, this light bouncy sweet tune with the words, Hey, Mister Yesterday, what are you doing from today? It was so different from the music that I'd heard on the bridge which I now realized was evil and weird and probably sent from Satan like you're supposed to hear when you play heavy metal backwards that I became at that moment like a complete convert to reggae. It filled my head with light and for the first time I could remember I was happy to be alive.

I ached all over though, like my body was a box of rocks and I could barely turn my head to see where the music was coming from, somewhere above and behind me when suddenly there was I-Man dancing barefoot and wearing his floppy shorts and flipping his head and switching his dreads to the beat with this big spliff in his mouth which smelled like freshly turned earth and sunbeams. He kept on shuffling in this excellent reggae dance around my

bed smiling down and nodding his head like he was glad
to see me awake but didn't want to say anything to inter-
rupt the music, just bopping by to check on Mister
Yesterday and then moving on down toward the rear of
the bus and returning a few seconds later with a steaming
bowl in his hand, still dancing and puffing on his spliff
until finally the song ended and he said how I was coming
forward now and mus' drink dis herb fe return to de
structure of life an' de fullness dereof.

Which I did. It took a while and sometimes I got the
chills again and then I'd sweat for hours especially at
night and I was so weak I could barely sit up and had to
piss in a jar and so on. But I-Man knew all these old
African and Rastafarian cures from herbs and other
plants he could find in the field and out among the shady
woods behind Sun Foods and downtown in the park by
the lake that he'd go out for at night and bring back and
mash up and boil into like a tea that he actually spoonfed
to me for quite a few days, and every morning I woke up
feeling a little bit better until pretty soon we were having
regular conversations like before. I-Man still had a lot of
Rasta wisdom to impart and I still had a lot to learn about
life in general and about the spirit of truth and goodness,
as I'd discovered from trying to go back home again so I
just tried to relax and listen and watch.

The reggae tunes were from some tapes and a box, a
cool Sony probably stolen that had been given to I-Man
by a local kid he called Jah Mood but I knew he was only
Randy Moody who was heavy into reggae and dope and
had grown these matted white-kid imitation dreadlocks
that he thought were cool and they sort of were if you
didn't know about the real thing. Randy though was too

dumb to know the difference between black people and white people or too racist to admit there was a difference and he was stuck forever being a white kid from Plattsburgh.

When I mentioned that one morning to I-Man he smiled and patted my hand and said Jah Mood will come to I-self in Jah's own time and way and not to worry, Bone, him na gwan displace m' heart. That's when I decided I'd better do more listening and less talking.

Nobody knew we were crashed at the schoolbus, not even Jah Mood. After the Bong Brothers'd been busted the place had bad vibes locally and kids'd stayed away and the cops forgot about it I guess. I-Man's ganja crop'd started coming in by then so he was even more careful of the cops than before when he was only an illegal alien and he didn't leave the place during the daytime now except when he absolutely had to which was almost never, not even to Sun Foods now that his vegetables were ripe and he didn't tell any civilians he knew, mostly mall rats and other homeless kids where he lived or who he lived with or where he had his plantation. His ganja plants were from seeds he'd sneaked in with him from Jamaica, he said and he'd started them in old egg cartons in the bus. Then he'd slipped them in among the weeds around the field and he'd cropped them off when they were young so they grew in low and broad and you wouldn't even know they were there unless he pointed them out to you. They were genius plants and I-Man was like this mad scientist when it came to growing and processing herb so we ended up blowing pure lamb's breath, all we wanted and probably the best dope in the whole northcountry that summer. Maybe in America.

It's funny, when you have all the quality dope you want and no stress about getting more you find out pretty fast what you need and you never smoke more than that. With I-Man once the crop came in I never went into deep buster-freak mode like I used to. I'd just hit a J in the morning after breakfast and chill around sunset with another so I could talk with I-Man I-to-I so to speak. In the old days me and Russ'd cop some weed from Hector or someplace and scoop up some malt 40s and go bust our brains with bongs and brews until we ran out or passed out whichever came first and we'd never learn anything from the experience about ourselves or the world. Now my head was like permanently located halfway between being bummed from no dope and unconscious from too much, only it was like my true self that I'd locked onto there, the self that hadn't been fucked up by my childhood and all and the self that wasn't completely whacked in reaction. I-Man said I was coming up to my lights, de Bone him coming to know I-self an' placin him on de way to natty. He said I was taking my first baby steps along the path of truth and righteousness which would soon lead me out of Babylon and I said, Excellent, man, that is truly excellent, and he laughed.

Then this one night late in July after my health had been completely restored and in fact I was stronger than I'd ever been on account of I-Man's roots and herbs and the Ital vegetarian diet and all and from working on the plantation in the summer sun, I woke up a few hours after I'd fallen asleep and heard this strange slow tune from I-Man's box being played real low back in the rear of the bus. That was where I-Man slept and kept his personal stuff. My crib was in the front near the driver's seat and we used the middle space for socializing and making things or just hanging out on rainy days. Anyhow I woke up to the sad slow sound of this old song Many Rivers to Cross which is about life in Jamaica and Jimmy Cliff sings it although it's not a reggae song, it's more like a regular black American religious song about slavery and patience and getting over to heaven and suchlike.

I got up and went back to his crib just because of this strange strong feeling I had that I-Man was sending me a message with the song, and he was because as soon as I sat down on the bus seat next to his mattress his voice came out of the darkness all gloomy and slow and weary. Bone, Bone, Bone, he said. I-and-I got too many rivers to cross.

He needed to get home to Jamaica, he explained. He needed to return to the forests and the mountain streams and the deep blue Caribbean Sea to live among his brethren again. It was the first time I'd heard him talk about Jamaica as a real place and not Babylon, with real people living there, people he loved and missed and I could fully understand that and felt sorry for him. Which was a whole new feeling for me and scared me a little but I quickly overcame my fear and started asking him questions like where in Jamaica he was from and what was it like there and did he have a wife or kids or anything.

He was from this village called Accompong way up in the hills, he said which was this independent nation of Ashanti warriors who'd like escaped from slavery and had beaten the British in a war in the olden days, in the 1900s I think. He told me he had a small plantation up there in Accompong and listed everything that grew on it, bread-fruit and afoo yams and coconut and calalu and akee and

banana, his groundation he called it, and he had a
woman up there and some kids too, four or five, he said
which sounded funny due to its vagueness but by now I
was used to I-Man being vague about things Americans
are real exact about and then turning around and being
incredibly exact about stuff that Americans are vague
about like history and religion which to him were as personal as his teeth and hair.

He spoke real slow and his voice was sadder than I'd
ever heard him and I thought I was going to cry without
even knowing for what but I kind of knew what was coming. I got up and went down to my end of the schoolbus
where my pack was and got my old stuffed bird, the woodcock and took Buster's roll of bills out of it. I didn't know
how much was there, I'd never bothered to count it probably because I felt guilty for stealing it even off of someone as evil as Buster. It was dirty money made from kiddie
porn probably or worse although Buster'd claimed he'd
gotten it from producing rap concerts which I'd never
believed so I'd kind of decided not to spend it except in
ways that were completely clean like buying Sister Rose's
bus ticket. I lit a candle there by my mattress and counted
it out, seven hundred and forty bucks which was a lot
more than I'd figured.

Then I went back to where I-Man was still playing his
Jimmy Cliff tape. It's the sound track of this famous
Jamaican movie *The Harder They Come* actually which I
never saw but I heard it was incredible. I put my candle
down on the floor and handed him the money, all seven
hundred and forty bucks of it. He raised his eyebrows and
pursed his lips which was how he always said thanks for any
favor, small or big and folded the bills without counting

them and put them in the pocket of his shorts. He said, Heartical, Bone. Then he smiled and said he'd be going to sleep now, he'd have to rest I-self for the long trampoose home was how he put it and I said sure, me too.

I'll be going with you, I said. Only as far as Burlington on the Vermont side of the lake though, where the airport for international flights is. I'll wave you off, man. I've never done that before.

Excellent, he said copying me which was his cool way of thanking me again for the money although giving it up hadn't exactly been a big sacrifice on my part. I was actually glad to get rid of it. But I was already missing I-Man more than I'd ever missed my own mom even or my real father and when I went back to my mattress and blew out the candle I cried to myself like a little kid as quiet as I could although I knew I-Man could hear me. But he was the type of person who was wise and kind enough to just let me cry and not embarrass me by trying to make me feel okay about everything which is one of the reasons I loved him and so I did until just before dawn as the sky was starting to turn gray over Vermont in the east where in a few hours we would be going on the ferry, I finally fell asleep.

FOURTEEN

CROSSING THE BAR

The next day was bright and warm, a good day for traveling at least for I-Man it was and I ran around behind him trying to catch up with his pleasure while he bopped through the bus packing his stuff into a blue plastic flight bag and walked me one last time through his garden and gave me final instructions on how to harvest and dry his ganja crop and take care of the vegetables although I pretty much by then knew how to run the plantation on my own.

At one point he got sad for a few minutes I think mainly on account of not being able to see all his crops come to their fullness as he put it and he took a few leaves off of each ganja plant like for souvenirs and nestled them inside his red and gold and green tam among his coiled dreadlocks.

He wanted to leave his boom box and the reggae tapes

that he'd got from Jah Mood with me as a sort of present but I could tell he really wanted to take them home with him so I said forget it, man, I won't have any trouble replacing them and you probably will so he raised his eyebrows and pursed his lips like he does and dumped the tapes into his flight bag. Then after a breakfast of refried Ital beans and hot sauce and leftover roasted dreadnuts and chicory tea we sat on the steps of the old schoolbus and smoked a spliff together and finally took off for the ferry dock downtown.

I'd packed a few things into my backpack myself, clothes and my stuffed bird and so on, personal items in case I ran into an opportunity to explore the state of Vermont a little although I wasn't actually thinking too much about my future just then, it was too scary and lonely to contemplate any possible futures without the company and teachings of I-Man to guide me so I was just going to float awhile on an hour-to-hour basis and see what developed.

When I mentioned that to I-Man he said I was on my way to being a brand-new beggar and gave me this warm smile. No plans, no regrets, he said. Praise an' thanks mus' be sufficient unto ev'ry day.

I said yeah but it'd be hard to do that the rest of my life. Making plans and having regrets, man, they're like second nature to me.

Y' first nature, dat be what you got to come to, mon, he explained and I made a mental note to remember his words which I was doing to just about everything he said that morning since I never expected to see him or hear from him again. I didn't think I-Man'd be much of a letter writer.

He was carrying his box which was pretty big—it was like this humongous quadraphonic the size of a regular suitcase—on one shoulder and his flight bag slung over the other and in his free hand he lugged his Jah-stick which was this incredible long snake with the head of a dreadlocked lion at the top that he'd been carving all summer while we sat around the bus at night exchanging views. The Jah-stick was about a foot taller than he was and made him look like this old African prophet or something which I guess is what he had in mind because he didn't really need it for anything else.

When we got down to the ferry dock and there were other people waiting around who were like staring at us I saw I-Man for the first time in months the way he must look to straight people who aren't used to seeing even regular black people let alone African prophets and I realized that he sure was one weird-looking little dude and I probably was myself although not as weird-looking as him because I was only a white kid. But I was wearing my doo-rag and we both had like these baggy surfer cut-offs on and our old faded orange Come Back To Jamaica tee shirts and our homemade sandals and a bunch of hand-woven bracelets that I-Man'd showed me how to make out of the hemp we'd found growing wild in the ditch at the end of the field one day.

We were cool though and I liked how people'd flick us with their eyes and then when they thought we weren't paying any attention they'd elbow each other and stare and I was wishing I had a couple more tattoos like maybe a Rasta lion or Jah Lives or a green ganja leaf to flash with. I was thinking I'd get some after I-Man was gone, like for helping me to remember these days when they were long gone. The crossed bones on the inside of my forearm even though it was the source of my name seemed kind of cold and harsh to me and too connected to my past life back when I was with Russ and before I'd met I-Man to make it known to people that I was now in the process of becoming a brand-new beggar. The bones was like Mister Yesterday's tattoo but that was okay I guess, it wasn't like I'd lost my memory or anything.

In about twenty minutes the ferry came and I-Man bought the tickets peeling the bills off of Buster's roll like he was an experienced big-time spender. I was surprised by how huge the boat was, a triple-decker luxury ocean liner, the Love Boat practically bringing a load of tourists and their cars over from Vermont twenty-five miles away and taking another load back. They were mostly families on vacation in stationwagons piled high with folding chairs and ice chests and grills, fatback suburbanites with sunburns and their fatback kids who looked sick of having to enjoy their parents' idea of a good time. There were some sporty young couples too though who drove aboard in Audis and Beemers and Volvos and suchlike and groups of college kid types in their parents' cars and some overweight middleaged bikers in shiny new leathers out on a cruise, the Mild Ones Bruce used to call them who rode Jap shit with sidecars, plus a few pickups and RVs and a small number of people who walked on board like us. Most of them though were exercise freaks with money and tans, slim people in J. Crew shorts and tee shirts printed with fortune-cookie political advice carefully wheeling their ten-speed bikes aboard like greyhounds, plus a bunch of whole-earth hikers with beards and ponytails and high-tech backpacks and huge suede tractor-tire shoes looking righteous and environmentally safe all over like they'd been recycled in a previous life.

More than before like at the mall and so on I really felt out of it here. I felt different from everyone else like I was watching a science show on the Discovery channel, Life Styles of the Mindless Wusses or something and anyhow after all these weeks of being crashed at the schoolbus and all I wasn't used to mixing with so many people, especially straight people and it made me nervous and a little paranoid so I said to I-Man who actually looked like he was enjoying himself watching the wusses and being watched back, Let's go up on top and check the scenic splendor, man.

He smiled and said excellent and up the stairs we went ahead of the others and got good seats on the top deck way in the front of the ship where I-Man as soon as we sat down pulled his stash out of his flight bag and rolled a fat spliff and lit up like we were back home at the plantation and all alone.

I was scared we'd get busted naturally but didn't say anything. I-Man being a Jamaican and all maybe didn't know the ways of Americans yet I thought, but he was older than me and a lot wiser about people in general and I hadn't seen any cops on board so I said to myself what the hell, let come whatever comes, Jah rules, et cetera and when he handed the burning spliff across to me I took a big hit and went with it and was high in a second and by the time the boat was moving out onto the glistening waters under a cloudless blue sky I was moving too.

We got up and walked as far forward as we could to a little fence where we could look down and see the whole boat below us and we gazed out as far as Canada in the

north and as far south as Ticonderoga practically and the
Green Mountains in front and the Adirondacks in back
and all around us were the glittering waters of Lake
Champlain. I could feel the engine chugging under my
feet like somebody was playing a huge drum down there
in the hold. The wusses seemed to've disappeared or actually they'd like turned into the crew of the Love Boat and
were harmless now and me and I-Man were the first mate
and the captain of our own ship crossing the ocean with
seagulls darting around overhead and little green tree-
covered islands dotting the water as we pulled away from
the continent into the open sea.

I looked back over my shoulder at New York State and
the city of Plattsburgh watching my past get smaller and
smaller in the distance while next to me stood I-Man the
prophet with his staff in his hand staring into the future.
We're crossing out of Egypt into the Promised Land, I
thought like I was becoming some kind of baby Rastafarian
myself. That was the effect of hanging with I-Man obviously
and I didn't know if it was good or bad especially since I
had such a dim view of white Rasta kids like Jah Mood but I
had to admit it was hard not to go slipping and sliding into
his way of thinking and talking on account of it being so
much more interesting than the way most people are
raised to think and talk especially us white Christian
Americans.

I remember thinking you live from moment to
moment and the moments all flow into one another for-
wards and backwards and you almost never catch one like
this that's separate from the rest. It felt like a precious diamond and I was holding it up to the sunlight between my
thumb and forefinger and all these cold blue and white

and gold colored sparks of light were jumping off of it.

I turned to I-Man and said to him then, What d'you think, man? Maybe I should go to Jamaica too. You know?

He nodded but he didn't say yes, no or maybe. He just kept looking at the distant shore like Columbus or something with the birds all wheeling and diving overhead and the front of the boat plowing through the water.

What d'you think? I asked him.

Up to you, Bone, he finally said.

Yeah, I guess it is. I should do what Jah wants me to do. That's what I think. Jah rules, I declared.

Fe trut'. You got to.

Yeah but how do I know what that is? How do I know what Jah wants?

Jah don't trouble wid de small t'ings, Bone.

I decided then to leave it up to Jah anyhow which is not quite the same as deciding whether to go to Jamaica, I know but it was as close as I could get. I said, If Jah makes it so there's enough of ol' Buster's money to buy us two tickets, then we'll go ahead and buy two tickets and I'll go to Jamaica with you. If not, I mean if there's not enough money then I'll just check out Vermont for a few days and hitch on back to the plantation.

That was cool with I-Man, I guess. He nodded anyhow but he didn't say anything. I think he would've liked it better if I hadn't bothered Jah with the small shit. But that was my Christian upbringing. It's not easy, changing religions and no matter what I-Man said just to be polite I knew I was still a long ways from being a brand-new beggar. Plus when you get down to important moments in life like this your upbringing always seems to kick into over-drive no matter what religion or philosophy you happen to prefer as an adult or as an older kid like me. In a crunch us Christians like to think God even sets the price of airline tickets.

Anyhow we got off the ferry at Burlington about an hour later and got some directions from a cop who looked at first like he wanted to bust us but I-Man had this royal bearing and all like he was the President practically or a movie star so the cop just told us how to get to the airport and even said, Have a nice day, fellas. Which is how they talk in Vermont. I think Vermont's a lot like California only cold and without many people.

When we got to the airport which is about three or four miles up on the heights above the town I-Man said Delta was the kind of plane he'd ridden on before so we walked up to the Delta ticket lady and right away found out that in less than an hour we could get a plane from Burlington straight to Montego Bay with only one stop in Philadelphia or someplace and another in Miami. You won't have to change planes, she said. Plus thanks to Jah's attention to detail Buster's seven hundred and forty bucks was enough to cover the cost of two tickets with even a few bucks left over.

I-Man looked at me and he goes, Well, Bone? You comin'?

I waved him to step aside so the Delta lady couldn't hear us and whispered, Do you think it's wrong for me to be using Buster's dirty money for this? I'm like worried, man. Sending Sister Rose home to her mom was one thing and sending you home is sort of like the same. But using it to send me *away* from home, that's another, isn't it?

He shrugged like he didn't really give a shit.

Help me out on this one, man. I'm only a kid and

spending dirty money is new to me. Is this what Jah wants?

He said, Jah knows *you*, Bone, but you don't know Jah. Not until you first know I-self. Him cyan be no daddy fe I-and-I. I-and-I mus' fin' him own daddy. Then he kindly pointed out that I'd already made my decision back on the boat.

I said, Okay, go ahead, man, buy two, and he handed the whole roll of bills to the woman behind the counter.

She scooped up the money and counted out the bills and gave I-Man the change and started punching a bunch of keys on her computer. Let me see your passports please, she said and me and I-Man looked at each other and both of us raised our eyebrows the same way. Like, Passports? He was an illegal alien and I was a homeless youngster missing and presumed dead, practically a milk carton kid and it suddenly looked like the truth was about to come out.

He leaned his Jah-stick against the counter and went rummaging through his bag and pulled out this red Jamaican passport which'd probably been stamped when he came to America to show he'd only been allowed in for picking apples in New York and cutting cane in Florida and couldn't go home until the company said so. They'd want their money back for the ticket they'd bought for him to leave Jamaica in the first place and the computer'd probably have a bill for it next to his passport number. That'd be the end of my ticket money. Besides, all I had instead of a passport was this phony ID I'd once bought off a kid at the mall that said I was eighteen but except for Art the tattoo guy no one believed me whenever I tried to use it which I only did a couple of times.

But I figured what the hell, Jah's will be done and pulled the ID out of my backpack and slapped it down on the counter next to I-Man's passport.

The Delta lady picked them up but at the same time she happened to see I-Man's Jah-stick which I guess distracted her because she just glanced at my ID card and his passport at the same time keeping one eye on the stick until she says to I-Man, I'm sorry, sir, but you won't be able to take that on board the aircraft with you.

Mus' be, he said.

I'm sorry?

It's like a religious item, I said. He's a priest.

A what?

I was pretty paranoid by then and also still a little high from the spliff on the boat which didn't help and so I like go off on this long rap about how I-Man can't be separated from his Jah-stick on account of he's like the Pope of Rastafarianism, a world renowned religious leader *par excellence* and besides it'll protect the plane and the rest of the passengers and all which confused her and by then there was a bunch of other people in line behind us who even though they were from Vermont they were getting restless.

I go, The stick's *alive*, man. Nobody can touch it but him without getting bitten.

She smiles like yeah sure and grabs the stick and yells, *Ow-w!* and lets it go instantly and sticks her hand in her mouth like a little kid.

I-Man took his Jah-stick then and his passport and his bag and boom box and I grabbed up my pack and ID and our tickets and boarding passes and we split from there without another word. We found our gate and went through the x-ray machine and sat down to wait for the boarding announcements.

Finally after a few minutes of just sitting there I turned to him and said, How'd you do that, man?

Do what?

You know. Get the stick to bite her. How'd you do that?

He just shrugged his shoulders like he didn't know and didn't care either.

I sat back in my chair and crossed my legs and smiled inside and I thought, This is gonna be some wicked strange adventure. I'm thinking, Bone, man, wherever you were before you're on the other side now.

FIFTEEN

SUNSPLASHED

Even though it was summertime our fellow passengers after the Miami airport anyhow were mostly tourists I guess taking advantage of bargain rates which is how the one guy who was sitting next to me explained it when I asked him why he was going to Jamaica now instead of waiting for winter.

It's off season, kid. Cheapereno, he said. Plus it's a package. Which means you don't have to leave the hotel for *anything*. You know what I'm saying? Whatever you want, they got it right there at the hotel. You get me, kid? he says like wink-wink nudge-nudge.

Yeah but don't you want to travel around some? You know, like maybe get out and see the country, do some trampoosing, man.

Naw. We're comin' to *party*!

Meaning him and about thirty or forty of the others on

the plane who all had these couch-potato bodies and big hair and wore acid-washed designer jeans and tanktops, both the guys and the females who were about half of the group. Some of them were already wearing these straw hats they'd gotten in the airport. Miller-timers I call them. People who don't like to leave home without their ice chest.

Jamaica's a long ways for a party, I said.

He goes, *Yeah*! like that's the point. They looked like they were into getting seriously laid a lot and by black people if possible and smoking some heavy reefer and snorting coke only they were too uptight to do it in America so I didn't push it. I guess you do what you can where you can.

They were older singles in their twenties and thirties from Indiana and I think they all lived in the same condo development and had cheesy jobs like in malls and I guess they didn't travel much because when the plane landed even though it was dark down there and you couldn't see anything out the window yet except the lights of Jamaica which are the same as the lights of anywhere they all clapped and cheered and hollered *Yes-s-sss*! and All *right*!

The guy beside me pumped his fist and grinned and said, Let the games be*gin*!

Go for the gold, man, I said and pulled my backpack and I-Man's flight bag and boom box down from the over-head bin and brought I-Man his Jah-stick from where the lady had asked him to stow it up front and he'd said no problem. Up to now I'd never even been as far as Albany and here I was like in a foreign country which the first time can be a real shock to the system. Except I was with I-Man who even though he was a foreigner to most people to me he was my homeboy practically and my spiritual guide and on his native ground now so I could be cool and just follow along behind him like I was only going to Albany instead of Jamaica and I went there all the time.

When we'd stopped off and the plane was waiting I guess for gas in Miami me and I-Man'd walked around the airport a little and took a piss and so on and watched the Indiana party animals so it wasn't like we were actually anywhere then except normal America where it's mostly white people running things. But when we got off the plane in Jamaica it was real different. All the people in charge were black for starters and that can throw you off if you're an American. I was pretty used to that from hanging with I-Man of course but it was weird to see my fellow white Americans getting suddenly all nervous and loud and dumb like they couldn't read the signs and the black people couldn't speak English.

They were scared I guess and when they were getting their suitcases off of the conveyor belt they started yelling and grabbing their stuff and dropping it and generally fucking up so the Jamaican airport guys had to pay a lot of attention to them to get them to go where they were supposed to for having their bags checked for drugs and such and for getting their papers stamped. Plus it was really hot even though it was night and everybody was sweating like mad which they weren't used to and which I think pissed them off like they'd expected the whole country to be air-conditioned. Me and I-Man already had our bags and didn't have any papers to get stamped on account of I-Man'd said not to bother filling them out when they gave them to us on the plane. No need fe deal wi' Babylon, Bone, he'd said when I asked the guy next to me for his pen when he was through. Forget-tee, he said which was one of his favorite words. Forget-tee.

Now though I wasn't so sure with all these soldiers and customs guys checking everybody out but I just followed I-Man and his magic Jah-stick as he stepped away from the Americans struggling to find their bags and crossed the room to this one guy who stood by the gate and looked like he was the head customs guy, this big potbellied black dude with sunglasses and a mustache and a toothpick in his mouth and a clipboard in his hand.

He would've been the main guy to avoid if I'd've been alone but I-Man just comes right up on him and they start talking in Jamaican which I'd never heard I-Man do before, he'd always talked English before which I'd thought was his native language. But they have this other native language that they only use with their fellow Jamaicans. It has quite a lot of English words in it but it's mostly African I think. I got so eventually I could understand it pretty good but the first few times I heard it they could've been jabbering in French or Russian for all I knew.

Anyhow from what I could figure the customs guy and I-Man were like true homeys or something because after they exchanged views for a few minutes he just waved us through this separate little gate and we're suddenly out in the main part of the airport which is open to the street and there's all these Jamaicans with vans and taxis waiting, fifty or a hundred of them, some with hotel signs and even buses waiting and a whole bunch of women carrying huge trays of souvenirs and Jamaican shirts and straw hats and so on and some skinny kids standing around ready to panhandle or whatever and these tall cool dudes in sunglasses even though it's night with short natty locks and their belts undone and their flies half open, evil-looking guys who're probably coke dealers or just trying to look generally available for white chicks from Indiana and everybody's watching the gates and waiting to pounce as soon as they see a regular American come out. There were some cops too in striped short-sleeved shirts and blue pants who were mainly watching the Jamaican civilians, probably to keep them from scaring the party animals when they came out and realized that they hadn't been safely herded inside their hotel yet.

Me and I-Man though, we were like invisible I guess because nobody even noticed us. We walked past everyone down the crowded road to the main road where I-Man turned left and then we walked at a good clip away from the airport into the darkness and suddenly we were surrounded by this strange silence although I thought I could hear waves of the ocean breaking off to our left a ways. I could tell from the lights behind us that the town which I guessed was Montego Bay was in the opposite direction so I said to I-Man, Where we headed now? and he goes, Not far, Bone. We gwan jine de lion in his kingdom.

That's cool, I said. For a long time though we kept walking along the side of the road. Now and then I could see the light of a house in the distance and here came a bus or a car that blew by and I could hear a dog bark sometimes. Otherwise darkness and except for the sound of our sandals and the click of I-Man's Jah-stick against the pavement, silence. I had about a thousand more questions to ask but I knew I wouldn't've understood the answers, it was still too soon so I just marched along behind I-Man and didn't say anything. I was like a clueless newbie. It was incredibly hot and the air was soft and really wet, it smelled like woodsmoke and curried ocean water or something which was a whole new smell to me, strange and not a good one either and I'm thinking like maybe I'm on a different planet than the one I originally came from, maybe I'm actually the pod boy from earth not Mars and for the first time since the plane took off in Vermont which was the first time in my life I'd done *that* I got really scared, I'm thinking like maybe I won't be able to breathe right, maybe there's too much oxygen here or maybe there's some weird Jamaican marsh gas in the air and it's fine for I-Man, he's got gills or whatever but me, on account of growing up in New York State and all I'm not physically equipped to do this. Travel is good for you, I kept saying to myself, it broadens you and extends your horizons et cetera but way down deep I was wishing I was back in Plattsburgh in the schoolbus again, just another homeless northcountry mall rat dodging the cops and copping a J now and then and spare-changing my way from day to day until my mom finally saw the light and split from Ken so I could go home and grow up living with her as her son again.

Just then I-Man turned off the road and went down into like a ditch and over a low rock fence. There was a little moonlight now and I could see this goat standing on the fence gazing at us with these glazed pale eyes and I watched back because I'd only seen goats in pictures before and didn't know if they bite. Come, Bone, I-Man said so I followed him and the goat didn't do anything.

It turned out we were on this path that cut through some palm tree woods and pretty soon we were down on the beach walking along on the sand. There were waves coming in, these strange low peaceful kinds of waves, not surfer waves like you'd've thought from it being a real ocean and suddenly the clouds broke open and a big silver moon came out and I could see a little of where I was then, on a long strand of beach with a tangled hedge of low bushes on one side and silhouetted palm trees in back like on a postcard and mountains humped up behind and the water was dark and velvety soft in the moonlight and the clouds got all bright and were edged like in melted silver. It was wicked beautiful.

Now that same warm soft wet air seemed totally natural to me and the smell was like a flowery perfume instead of like somebody'd just pissed on a woodfire and I wasn't wishing I could go back to Plattsburgh anymore. I was reminding myself that with I-Man and Sister Rose gone and Russ making it in the straight world I'd be all alone up there and pretty soon it'd start getting cold again and the snow would come cruising in from Canada and all the plants and vegetables in I-Man's groundation would freeze and die and I'd probably start getting into panhandling for crack I'd be so bummed from that kind of life and it'd be downhill from there for sure. And my mom I knew wasn't going to see the light. No way. No, I was definitely going to have to become a brand-new beggar. Just like I-Man said.

After a while we ended up cutting off from the beach and went back into the bushes on a zigzaggy path I'd've never seen on my own if I hadn't been following I-Man. Finally we came to this bamboo fence with a gate that had a red and green and gold lion's head painted on it and when we went through the gate there was this little sandy yard and then I-Man picked up a candle from a shelf beside a door and lit it and went through the door into a bamboo cave which was actually a house, this incredible house with high steep ceilings that were thatched like in Africa and walls built entirely out of bamboo tied together with vines and there were all these little circular rooms and hallways going off of each other in a hundred different directions like an ant farm I once made for school.

The rooms had bunches of huge pillows placed around the walls for sitting on like in a harem and hammocks for sleeping in and low tables and curtains made out of beads hanging at the doors and pictures of Rasta heroes on the walls like Marcus Garvey who I-Man said was the first Jamaican to figure out how to get back to Africa and Martin Luther King who I recognized on my own and an African king in a suit named Mandela I-Man told me when I said who's that and of course the head Rasta, Haile Selassie himself, Negus of Bathsheba, Emperor of Ethiopia, Jah Rastafar-i. I was learning a lot.

Except for the pictures and the pillows and hammocks and the bead curtains everything else in the house was handmade including the picture frames out of bamboo. It was like Bamboo World, a Rasta theme park and definitely the coolest squat I'd ever seen. It really blew me away so I go, This is cool, man, which sounded so stupid I couldn't believe I'd said it. Plattsburgh, New York, that's where I belonged.

Lion in his kingdom fear no one, Bone. Nyah Bingh in his kingdom, twelve tribe in his kingdom, Bobo in his kingdom, he's like chanting from a pillow where he'd sat down and was now filling the biggest best bong I'd ever seen from a huge bowl of ganja. No matter where we go, we de lion in his kingdom. Sattar, Bone, an' smoke from de chalice.

He was off on a Rasta-rap, a kind of homecoming high I guess and I could dig that even though it sort of weirded me but by now everything else was so different from my previous life that there probably wasn't much left that could make me freak and besides I was interested in doing a load myself so I said, This is like your squat, right? Your Jamaican crib? And nobody else knows about it?

He was pulling these huge draws in by now, his head surrounded by spiraling clouds of smoke, the chalice bubbling and burping away and I was already lifted just from the secondhand smoke. He goes, I-and-I gots to be smart to prevent dem from tumble down on I-and-I. People of de world who see I-works an' know of I wants to tumble down on I, backbiters-dem wants to tumble down on I, criticism-dem wants to tumble down on I, badminded-dem wants to tumble down on I. . . .

That's excellent, man. Lemme have a hit, I said and he handed me the chalice and off I go, more toasted in a few seconds than I actually want to be and suddenly I'm scared of losing my brains which almost never happens to me when I smoke so I tried to fake it by not inhaling so much and handed the chalice back to I-Man who was lying back on the pillow across from me a few seconds ago only he was gone now but it was too late, I was flying, the harem room was flying, the bamboo ant farm was flying, the whole world was flying through the known and unknown universe into like deep space where no boy has dared to boldly go before. I thought I saw I-Man but he turned into this tall Rasta guy I'd never seen before with dreads tied up like a huge soft bow on his head and there were a couple of other Rastas who walked past all drifty and mellow and I could hear reggae tunes coming from someplace sometimes real loud with words and chants and then just the heavy beat real quiet and no words and pretty soon it was silent.

I was slumped over sitting on one of the pillows watching the candle flame when suddenly this spider came drifting down from the ceiling and hovered over the flame for a minute and then like it'd gotten too hot the spider started trying to climb back up on its web. It struggled and fought but it was too late, the web turned into a gold wire and the spider lost it and dropped onto the flame where it got instantly crisped and its tiny ashy body floated up on the heat a ways and then it disappeared into thin air.

I was almost crying then. I'd done it, I'd moved the candle under the spider on purpose, it was all my fault. I tried to stand up but couldn't so I crawled around the room on my hands and knees like a baby looking for I-Man and then down this dark hallway thinking maybe if I could find a peaceful corner I could curl up in with my back to the wall nothing could sneak up and surprise me, goats or lions or avenging spiders but the hall kept curving around until finally I came to a door and pushed it open and I was outside in the sandy yard and the sky was clear and there were millions of stars swimming overhead like fish in schools or birds flying in flocks and the moon was splashing everything on earth with this dry white powder like flour.

I could stand up now so I did and managed to get to the gate in the bamboo fence and out and then I let my

feet kind of lead me along the path in the general direction of the ocean which I could locate okay from the
sound of the waves until I came out on the beach and
plopped down there on the white sand and just watched
the waves coming in over and over friendly and slow and
no surprises until my heart stopped pounding and I wasn't
breathing so hard and fast anymore. I didn't think I could
find my way back to the ant farm again, I actually didn't
want to go back there yet so I decided to just chill on the
beach for the night and wait till daylight to figure out what
to do next. I was totally bummed. This was a new kind of
loneliness for me. It made me want to stay away from people forever.

That didn't last, naturally. The next morning I'm sitting on the beach watching this atomic sunrise going on
way out at the horizon beyond the gray ocean with sheets
of red and yellow and pink clouds going nuts out there
and the water all streaky like with blood which is definitely not what you see at dawn in upstate New York after
blasting your brains on skunk the night before, and suddenly there was I-Man squatting down beside me. I was
real glad to see his familiar brown face, like it was a rela-
tive's face and I didn't feel lonely anymore.

He put his hand on my shoulder and said he had some
food fe strengthen de structure and fe repair de damage
from our long journey out of Babylon so I followed him
back up to the ant farm where there were these other
Rastas squatting around on their heels in the yard smoking spliffs and makin' chat as I-Man says who he introduced me to, Fattis and Buju and Prince Shabba that he
said were his posse.

Prince Shabba I recognized from the night before on account of his humongous bowtie hairdo and the other two were kind of familiar too. They were younger than I-Man, in their thirties or forties maybe, it's hard to tell because they were skinny dudes and their huge long dreads were kind of distracting and white people even me have trouble telling the age of black adults except by their clothes until they're really up there like I-Man. They talked to each other in their native language so I didn't catch much of what they were saying and basically they ignored me, even I-Man which was cool because I figured I'd be smart to just hang and watch and learn what I could before branching out on my own again because these dudes who were basically different from me inside as much as out were also very well adapted to their environment which gave me a good idea of the danger I was in every time I took what I thought was an innocent step.

Like their environment was now mine and the ant farm was definitely not some package-tour hotel for Miller-timers from Indiana. So I just did what I-Man told me, ate when he said and what he said, drank what he gave me and only took real light nips of kali off of the chillum pipe when he passed it over to me and kept the spliffs moving down the line like I had plenty at home for later. No more buster-freak for Bone.

I-Man's posse was a little like the men of Adirondack Iron except more mellow and at first I thought nonviolent until sometimes they'd be rapping and sucking on a chillum and they'd get all psyched from telling stories which I couldn't understand and suddenly Fattis or Prince Shabba'd whip out an actual razor-sharp machete and start chopping the air with these vicious swipes and everybody'd laugh and holler like crazy. By then I knew enough of the language that I could tell they were talking about chopping people's heads off and suchlike. Level de devil wid de bevel! Prince Shabba'd yell and he'd whack his machete into a coconut and split it in half.

And just like the bikers the Rastas didn't seem to have any regular jobs or families at least not at the ant farm and they spent most of their time hanging and getting high and fixing up the ant farm the way the bikers used to work on their hogs and instead of listening to headbang the Rastas were into constantly playing reggae on I-Man's box which they called his master-blaster until the batteries ran out and then the same way the bikers used to send me and Russ out for pizza they'd send Fattis or Buju who was the youngest I guess into town for more batteries although I didn't know yet what they did for money unless I-Man was spending what was left of Buster's stash. Which was cool by me. I didn't want it for myself, that's for sure. I wanted it gone completely and batteries for I-Man's blaster seemed a harmless way to make it disappear.

We ate mainly stuff they cut off of the trees with their machetes and dug out of the ground and cooked over a fire in the yard, breadfruits which look like grapefruits only taste like bread and akee which are kind of like scrambled eggs when you cook them and your standard hairy green coconuts which they grind up the meat of and mix with everything and these long bananas you cut up and fry called plantains and soursops which're sweet and creamy inside like custard and regular oranges and these long white yams and calalu and so on, a whole garden of excellent tropical food that grew around the ant farm among the trees and bushes in the same kind of screwy wandering garden as I-Man'd planted in the field around the schoolbus only here it seemed more natural.

Sometimes we'd all go down to the beach and swim and they'd wash their dreadlocks and rub these green leaves all over them afterwards that left them shiny and black as licorice and then the posse'd play this game with a paddle and ball called cricket that was like baseball only slower and more like dancing and originally came from Africa I think although they threw the ball and hit it and caught it and ran back and forth more like a bunch of antelopes than crickets unless they have those kind there that leap about and run and stop. I-Man was good at what they called bowling and they always let him go first and he'd bowl for a long time only it was overhand and upside down from the kind of bowling I knew.

Quite a few different people came by the ant farm, fellow Rastas and some regular Jamaicans and even a few Chinese guys and a couple of buff females one time who'd hang and smoke for an hour or two and then split and pretty soon I came to understand that I-Man and his posse were doing some serious ganja dealing on the side which explained a few things. They had like tubs of it stashed in the back rooms of the ant farm and they moved it in these paper bags like it was rice a pound at a time it looked like. The ant farm was a factory outlet for ganja and for a heavy pot smoker hanging there with I-Man and the posse was like dying and going to heaven except I was pretty cautious now due to so many things surprising me every day and only took my toke when it would've been weird or embarrassing not to.

I was getting my picture of I-Man slightly revised you might say. I'd even seen some guns by now, Prince Shabba had one, a .45 I think and so did I-Man which he kept in his old flight bag that he took with him everywhere and of course the flashing machetes which these guys treated real casual like they were Swiss Army knives or something. Plus quite a lot of money was being passed around including to and from cops. One night the same potbellied dude who'd let me and I-Man walk through customs at the airport without checking came by the ant farm and left with a free pound of primo boom loaded with buds like he'd phoned in his order ahead. And there were the same cool dudes with their flies open as I'd noticed at the airport who came around every few days for a load and I pictured their customers the Miller-timers rolling joints in their hotel rooms getting too choked to think and paranoid and all and I almost felt sorry for them.

I-Man and Prince Shabba and Fattis came and went from the ant farm a lot, making home deliveries I guess or bill collecting and whenever I-Man left the premises he took his blue bag and his Jah-stick and looked like a priest going on a pilgrimage. He was cool and I was proud to be under his protection which is basically how people treated me. Mostly though I did chores like sweeping the yard every day and lugging water with Buju from this spigot pipe up by the road where a lot of other Jamaicans came for their water with plastic buckets and pans, women and little half-naked kids and some wicked good-looking teenaged girls who I didn't dare talk to or anything so me and Buju'd chat while our buckets filled about how he was going to Miami soon to work cutting cane or New York and pick apples like I-Man'd done and buy stuff. Not, I figured. He was like into video cameras and VCRs and big-screen TVs and so on that he wouldn't've been able to even use at the ant farm on account of there being no electricity but he thought everything ran on batteries.

He wasn't much older than me and on the dim side but friendly and he had a good singing voice and knew all the reggae songs from I-Man's box but I still couldn't understand the words so I didn't talk much, I mainly listened. I think except for I-Man they thought I was on the dim side myself, especially for a white American kid but it doesn't hurt for people to think you're not as bright as you are when you don't know all the rules yet.

Then this one afternoon Prince Shabba was gone off to Kingston or someplace and Fattis was asleep and Buju was making mugs out of bamboo for drinking and I-Man wanted to head out fe deal wi' de brethren so he said for me to come along too. Come see de sights of Jamaica, Bone.

Cool, I said and off we went through the bushes to the road where we caught a bus crammed full of regular Jamaicans and rode about five or six miles into Mobay which is their word for Montego Bay, this fairly big town the size of Plattsburgh only a lot more crowded. I didn't know for sure how long I'd been at the ant farm, two or three weeks maybe but a long time so when I started seeing white people like you do here and there on the streets of Mobay or in cars they really stood out and looked like extra-terrestrials with their chalky skin and long narrow noses and scrappy hair and I kept checking them out like I wasn't one myself on account of how weird they looked, even the quick jerky way they walked and how they waved their hands but not their arms when they talked and how they didn't get right up in each other's face and all when they met like I was used to by now but stood back a ways and talked from a distance.

The streets were hot and crowded and muddy from a morning shower and where we got off the bus there were ten or twenty more buses unloading crowds of people with big burlap-wrapped bags of stuff, vegetables and fruits and even animals like chickens and pigs and goats and I saw that we were at this huge outdoor marketplace jammed with tables all loaded up with different kinds of goods, everything from rubber flip-flops and canned Spam to sugarcane and huge yams the size of your arm. It was the Jamaican equivalent of a mall I guess, with a special emphasis on food. And just like in a regular mall people were into socializing and hanging out and eating these little meat pies you can hold in your hand like tacos and sucking on stalks of sugarcane and cruising each other for different things from sex to gossip I guess or drugs.

I-Man I soon realized was making his regular once-a-week deliveries to people who probably lived too far from the ant farm or were too busy to come there in person. He was carrying a dozen or so one-pound bricks of grade A sinsemilla inside his old flight bag and he'd come up on some guy selling green parrots in homemade cages and they'd rap for a few minutes about this and that and then he'd just pull out the ganja which was wrapped in brown paper and pass it over in plain sight of the cops who were all around the place. The parrot guy'd say thanks and stash the dope under his table and count out the hundred and fifty bucks or whatever was the going wholesale price, something I could never quite figure since I never saw any scales or anything and they mostly used Jamaican money which I wasn't used to yet. I figured I-Man and his posse were middlemen though, not producers and there was wholesale which they did mostly at the ant farm and there was retail which they did out here on the streets and the more you bought the less it cost per pound unless they didn't know you or you were a rich white guy which I guess is the same free enterprise system as everywhere.

Speaking of money by now I wanted some of my own because of getting pissed from having to always bum cigarettes and beers and suchlike off of I-Man and the posse although nobody ever got uptight about it or anything due to the ant farm being like a commune and whenever I apologized for bumming another Craven A or a Red Stripe when the guys'd kick back over a few brewskies and cricket on the beach I-Man'd say, From each accordin' to him ability, Bone, an' to each accordin' to him need. Which was irie with me except that without a little cash on hand my needs kept exceeding my abilities. My only previous work experience though was in dealing small-load dope and spare-changing neither of which was a useful skill here especially spare-changing. That is until at the marketplace in Mobay I started seeing all these white people mixed in with the Jamaicans.

So I split off from I-Man for a while and tried hitting on some sunburned tourist types weating straw hats and carrying video cams and checking out the natives, male and female couples who sometimes are easier to spare-change because one of the two will try to harsh on the other for being too suspicious and he or usually she will give the poor kid a couple of quarters. I tried to look worried and scared and said I was on a class trip and my teacher and everybody else in the group'd left for Kingston in the van early without me and I just needed seventeen dollars to meet up with them or I'd miss the plane back to Connecticut and get left behind in Jamaica, which would've worked probably except that both the couples I hit on turned out to be German or Italian or something. They just shrugged and smiled and wagged their heads no comprendo until finally I gave up and held out my hand and said, Spare change, man? which I guess is universal because they said no loud and clear and acted disgusted that a white American boy'd act that way in front of all these poor starving Jamaicans.

I was wishing I'd run into some of the Indiana party animals who I figured would be relieved to buy some ganja from a white kid who spoke regular English instead of having to deal with a scary black Jamaican like I-Man, exploit my fellow Americans' race thing in other words, and who knows, if it worked turn it into a regular job with I-Man and the posse, specializing in paranoid package tourists at the hotels. Having their own white kid on the staff so to speak'd give I-Man and the posse a definite advantage over the competition when it came to the tourist trade, I thought and then I wondered if I-Man'd already figured that out long ago, back in Plattsburgh even and had just eased me along without me knowing it, recruiting me and this was all a sort of apprenticeship in the ganja trade and if I came up believing it was my idea instead of his I'd never feel like he'd victimized me or anything or that he'd taken advantage of an innocent kid.

It wasn't like Buster and Sister Rose. I mean, either way, whether it was my idea first or I-Man's plan all along it didn't matter once I was doing it because at any point along the way from the ferry ride across Lake Champlain to this morning in Mobay I could've said I'm outa here and I-Man would've said, Up to you, Bone. It's important for me to remember that even though I-Man usually knew what I was going to do before I did a thing he never tried to make me do it.

So anyhow just when I'm in the middle of deciding to reenter my old life of crime you might say I spot another white couple on the other side of the marketplace. They're easy to pick out of course due to practically everyone else is black or at least brown and the couple is getting out of this big mud-spattered Range Rover and walking over to I-Man who greets them like he knows them from before. I could tell instantly they weren't tourists. They were both older, like in their forties and tanned like they'd been living in Jamaica a long time and incredibly cool-looking, definitely cooler than any white people I'd seen here so far.

The guy was real tall and skinny and clean-shaven but with a long ponytail and wearing a tan safari jacket and one of those great-white-hunter helmets like you see on lion tamers and reflector sunglasses. The woman had a Rasta tam on her head with brown matted dreadlocks sticking out and was wearing all these Rasta bracelets and necklaces and even though she was on the heavyset side and older she was surprisingly sexy even to me because of her red and green striped belly dancer pants with only a yellow bikini bra on top, plus she had great tits.

I'm watching from across the market and I-Man passes the tall dude a brick of sens and the guy hands him some money and everybody does a power handshake even I-Man and the woman and touches fists a couple of times and then when the couple turns to go back to the Range Rover the man pulls off his shades and helmet and wipes off his face with his sleeve and suddenly my mouth goes dry and my eyes practically bug out of my head.

I know him. I know his face, way down deep inside me, like in my chest I know him. And for the first time I understood why I'd decided to follow I-Man to Jamaica. I knew he'd be here. It's my *father*! My real father! My mouth flopped open and I couldn't say anything but in my mind I'm like calling him in this little boy's voice, Daddy! Daddy! Over here, it's me, your son Chappie!

I didn't once think it might be a case of mistaken identity, I knew absolutely it was him. I'd recognized his face the second I saw it from how I remembered it when I was a little kid and from the picture my grandmother had and he still looked a little like a tall thin JFK even with the ponytail. I remembered him from when I was with him all the time and he was still married to my mom and life was perfect. It was definitely my real *father*!

I started running then, dodging around people and jumping over goats and chickens in cages and shoving my way up and down the long jammed aisles until I finally got to the other side of the huge tin-roofed market building where I blew by I-Man just as my father and the white Rasta woman slammed the doors of the Range Rover only about a hundred feet beyond and drove out of the lot between a bunch of buses onto a narrow street. My father was driving and they weren't moving very fast due to the mud and deep ruts so I ran after them, right down the middle of the street with people jumping out of my way and dogs barking as I blasted past running faster than I've ever run before, stretching my legs out in front of me as far as they'd reach and pumping my arms and hollering, Wait up! Wait up! It's me, it's your son Chappie!

I chased them down one street and then up another and was only a few yards behind them and even got close enough almost to jump onto the back bumper where I could've hung on to the spare tire and ridden there, when they turned onto a bigger street and the Rover speeded up some but I kept on running after and hollering even though my chest was burning and my legs felt like iron. I slipped once and fell down and scraped myself and got mud all over me but I scrambled back up and saw them still ahead of me but further away now and I ran after them anyhow but limping and both knees and the palm of one hand bleeding from when I fell. They got to the center of the town where there's this big traffic circle but when I came to it the Rover was already on the far side with a big fountain in between us and it turned off there onto like a highway that led out of town and I heard my father shift into fourth gear and hit the gas and the Rover disappeared around the bend probably doing fifty already.

For a long time I stood there with my heart pounding and my chest on fire and the only thought in my head was that at last I'd seen my father. My real father! Finally after all these years I'd come to Jamaica not knowing that I was looking for him even and then one day completely by accident I'd found him. And even though I'd lost him again I knew it was only temporary this time. I was bleeding and muddy and all but I felt like I'd finally woken up from one of those nightmares that trick you into thinking you're awake and this is really happening. It was like this incredible *relief*.

SIXTEEN

STARPORT

After a minute or two of just standing there by the fountain like an idiot child sweaty and panting and bleeding from the knees and hands I came back to my senses and turned around and walked slowly back through town. As I walked people who must've seen me when I was running came up and patted me on the back and made sorrowful faces like they knew somehow that it was my father I'd been chasing and that I'd lost him again. I didn't think I had though since this was the closest I'd ever been to finding him and now we were at least on the same island together but it was nice they sympathized. In the States the whole thing would've been a big joke.

Finally I made it back to the marketplace where next to a table with all these Rasta carvings of African lions and noble black men with dreadlocks and such I saw I-Man standing in the shade smoking a spliff and chatting up

the woodcarver who looked a lot like one of his own statues. There was this cop there, a young red-striper who
seemed more interested in me than I-Man's spliff and
when I came up the cop says right away, You know 'im?

Who? I-Man? Yeah, I guess so, I said thinking maybe it's
a trick and he's going to bust the both of us or something
although so far I hadn't seen any signs that selling ganja
was illegal in Jamaica except maybe in stores and even in
stores you could buy it if you talked to the right guy.

No, mon. I mean the white man. Doc. You know 'im?

Yes I do, I proudly said.

So why're you chasin' him, mon?

He's my father. Only I haven't seen him in a long time,
and I've been living in the States and he didn't know I was
coming back to Jamaica. That's why he kept going, I said.
He probably just didn't see me.

Doc be cool, I-Man said. Him come an' go alla time, fe
trampoosing all across de lands, him settin' de pace.
Time, material an' space, mon, gas, clutch an' brakes.
Technology controls, Bone, techno set de pace.

I said for them to c'mon, cut the shit and tell me what's
up with Doc because I only knew what my mom and my
grandmother'd told me which wasn't all that much and
the cop laughed and said the same as I-Man, Doc be cool.
Didn't know he had a son in the States though.

Baby Doc, I-Man said and he laughed too. Papa Doc
an' him baby.

They were like slipping around the subject but I kept
asking and pretty soon it came out that my father was an
actual doctor working for the government in Kingston
about a hundred miles away and he lived over there in a
big government apartment and the woman he'd been

with in the Range Rover was his girlfriend named Evening Star, this rich American who lived near here in a greathouse whatever that was and who he visited sometimes and came down to Mobay driving her car and so on.

Papa Doc a man you can deal wi', I-Man said. Don't know him 'oman though. Him call Evenin' Star?

The cop said oh yeah he knew her all right, most everybody in Mobay knew Evenin' Star and knew her house too, big fancy place with lots of different people hanging out including Doc. Dem mostly jus' limin', the cop said and he told us where the greathouse was located which wasn't far, this town called Montpelier maybe eight or ten miles into the hills. I-Man shrugged and said we could go up there by bus if I wanted and I said, Excellent. Let's go now.

No problem, I-Man said and off we went with the cop kind of smirking after like he smelled something we didn't but I just figured it was because he knew I-Man was going up there to check out the ganja-selling possibilities, not just to help me find my father which was okay by me. Everybody's got his own agenda and that's cool. The good thing about I-Man was he never laid his agenda down on top of mine. Unlike certain people. He always just said, Up t' you, Bone.

We rode this old top-heavy wheezing green bus that was all decorated with Rasta designs like lions wearing crowns and even had a name on the front, Zion Gate up a long curvy hill with cliffs that dropped away from the edge of the narrow road into gorges and you could see rusting cars and trucks and even a crashed bus way at the bottom with the jungle growing back over them and little cabins close by the side of the road where kids stood at the door and watched as we passed and women were washing clothes next to a stream and so on. Until finally we came to a village which I guessed was Montpelier with a couple of one-room convenience stores the same as we have Stewart's and 7-Elevens at home only smaller and when we got off the bus and went inside one of them for Craven A's it had hardly anything to sell, like canned milk and yellow cheese and rum and beer was about it.

I-Man asked the woman behind the counter for directions to the home of the Evening Star which she rattled off in Jamaican too fast for me to understand. Then we came back out and walked along the road a ways and cut off it up this long winding lane to the left where there were little cinderblock houses with tin roofs set back in the bushes with goats lunching on the brush and pigs wandering loose or sleeping in the yard and little blond dogs yapping at us as we passed, a white kid wearing a doo-rag and a Rasta with a Jah-stick from away heading slowly uphill. As we walked we got occasional peeks and views of the bright blue ocean way below. Hummingbirds and regular birds too flew alongside us and there were loads of butterflies making loops and there weren't any more houses after a while, just the lane and the trees and vines and the birds and butterflies and those big black buzzards they call John Crows circling high overhead. It was real quiet and we were sweating pretty good from the climb by now and I was wondering if maybe I-Man'd heard the lady with the directions wrong.

But pretty soon we came over the top of this one mountain where we could see down through the hills and valleys below gaining a sudden wideview panoramic look all the way to the ocean and could even see Mobay down there looking like a regular seaport town with boats and white buildings and orange rooftops and all, and for a minute I was remembering the terrific view of the Adirondacks from the Ridgeways' summerhouse. Then when we walked a little ways further we came around a corner and saw this fancy old sign that said STARPORT which I knew was the house's name, not the people who owned it and I almost lost my locale and was back on East Hill Road in Keene with Russ instead of I-Man that day after I first got my tat and took the name Bone.

A small black goat with blue eyes stood in the bushes though and stared at me and I-Man and that brought me straight back to Jamaica, and then there were these big stone pillars that we went through and suddenly we're in this fantastic terraced yard with green grass and all kinds of flowers growing and these strange statues all over the place of life-size American-type animals like rabbits and foxes and beavers and suchlike painted white except for their eyes and nostrils and mouths which were bright red. They were a little on the strange side. It was definitely an unusual kind of yard, like you expected them to be making a movie there or a fancy restaurant.

The driveway curled up a long ways to this huge white-stone two-story ancient house from France or England set on the side of the mountain looking down on Mobay and the sea ten miles away like it ruled the countryside and a duke or a minor king lived in it. We came up on it from below peering up at its majesty like on our hands and knees showing reverence only we were just walking along the driveway trying to look cool, leastways I was. The house was real old, I think from slavery days but fixed up with lots of columns along the front and huge high win-

dows and like patios all around and more animal statues
with the red eyes and mouths placed here and there on
the patio walls. There was a swimming pool over at the
right side of the house and you could see some white people and black people standing around up there with
glasses in their hands and a couple of white females with
bikinis in the group who didn't have anything over their
tits the same as the guys. Then on the left over at the
other side of the house and toward the front I saw a few
parked cars, including the Range Rover.

All of a sudden I got incredibly nervous. Like what if
he told me to fuck off? I knew he was my real father for
sure so I wasn't worried it was a case of mistaken identity
but what if he denied he even had a son my age named
Chappie who he'd left behind in upstate New York almost
ten years ago? What if he didn't like me personally? What
if he thought I was too short or something?

Then there was this roaring noise and I thought it was
a bomb going off but it was a humongous blast of music
coming from the pool area like from a live reggae concert. It was Baldhead Bridge by Culture which I recognized from the ant farm tapes and it was booming out of
these two huge black speakers up on the wall by the pool
that were the size of refrigerators, the kind you see at outdoor concerts in the States and they were aimed away
from the pool and rocked the universe out there, slamming reggae down through the gardens and the jungle-
covered hills all the way along the steep valley to Mobay
practically and the folks up at the pool now were dancing
around with the females' tits jiggling and the guys bobbing and snapping along, everyone with spliffs and drinks
in their hands. The music was so loud and the bass was so

heavy it controlled your heartbeat and I was thinking the leaves'd start coming off the trees any minute and the white animals might crack and crumble from it.

As we went up the long set of wide steps to the front door I-Man leans into me and he goes, Jah-sniffers, Bone, and looked suddenly real serious instead of how he usually looked which was only curious and patient. Then we were standing on this long wide porch in front of a huge open door and could see inside the house to I guess the livingroom which was dark and all paneled and filled with fancy couches and long tables and a big set of stairs disappearing above and a bunch of bamboo birdcages with green parrots and other birds in them and all these weird paintings on the walls of wild animals and tropical scenery like they'd been painted by a little kid on acid and for a second I wanted to get out of there and back to the ant farm where things were more normal.

But just then here comes Evening Star, the white Rasta lady of the house in this flowing red and gold and green gown and her dreadlocks swinging and her bracelets clanging and I notice she's holding a pretty-good-sized J like it's a cigarette. Her skin was this professional sunbather's color almost like a wallet but she was pretty goodlooking for her age like she worked out a lot and dieted and all because even though she was on the heavy side I could see she had a lot of muscle. Coming along beside her was a big old black Lab and trotting behind the Lab was one of those tiny blond Jamaican yard dogs who're usually scrawny but this one's fat like a taco and both the dogs look and act like they're used to strangers and almost glad to see us which is not like any dogs I've ever known.

Evening Star smiles at I-Man and goes, Greetings, Rasta! Respect, mon. Everyt'ing irie, mon?

He just nods and turns to me like I'm supposed to say something but nothing comes. I don't know why but suddenly it was like my tongue wouldn't work. I even opened my mouth but no words, no sounds came out at all.

Finally I-Man said, De bwoy him be Baby Doc, an' him lookin' fe him fodder, Papa Doc.

The reggae was blasting away outside by the pool and we could barely hear even normal words never mind I-Man's Rasta-rap so she asked him to tell her again which he did until she seemed to get it and smiled at me real warm and almost motherly and drawled, Oh, y'all want to look at the *paintings*! The Haitian pictures. Are you an *artist?* she says to me like I'm in kindergarten which kind of pissed me off and I said no and very relieved to be talking again I said, I'm looking for somebody.

I *see*, she said real serious but I could see she didn't see so I went ahead and told her I was looking for the man she'd been with at the marketplace in Mobay. I'm looking for Paul Dorset, I said.

Paul? You mean *Doc!*

Yeah, whatever.

You're an American, aren't you? Nobody from *here* calls him *Paul*, she said. Except *me*. She had this weird slow way of talking that put a lot of emphasis on certain words and when she spoke she kind of leaned forward and wrapped her lips around the word like she was kissing it which was distracting so you tended not to notice that she wasn't saying anything very important or interesting. She sounded like she was from down South maybe, like Alabama or Georgia. Also due to her not wearing any bra when she leaned forward like that you could see her tits which I think she liked but that too made you forget what she was saying.

O-*kay*, she said. Y'all and the Rasta just sattar, everyt'ing be irie, mon, an' mi bring Doc, she said and she whirled and split and took off up the wide curving stairs with the dogs following her like shadows leaving me and I-Man to look at each other like, What kind of crazy shit is *this*?

We wandered around in the livingroom looking at the birds and then the pictures which were from Haiti I guess and actually when you studied them they were basically peaceful and kind and made you feel relaxed even though they were definitely strange. The room was like a ballroom with high ceilings and windows from the floor to the ceiling almost that were open to the wide porch out front and a breeze blew through and it was shady and cool inside and with the reggae playing and now and then the sound of people laughing by the pool and the splashes when they dove in and suchlike I was thinking this is a pretty cool life my father's got. Better than anything he had with my mom, that's for sure.

I-Man was in back watching this huge painting of a lion lying in the jungle with all kinds of other animals that it would normally slay and I was standing there by the door looking out across the terraced gardens with all the white red-eyed animals and down the valley to the sea and for a while I watched a couple of John Crows slowly loop their way up the long slope rising and circling without even moving their wings as they rose into the sky until I almost forgot why I was here, when I heard footsteps behind me clicking on the polished floor and I turned and there he was, my real father!

He didn't recognize me obviously, on account of me having changed physically so much since I was five and he looked slightly irritated like Evening Star'd interrupted his nap or something. He was incredibly tall, at least to me he was and skinny but with a good build just the same and he had a long brown-haired ponytail and a diamond stud in his left ear and he was wearing these loose tan shorts and sandals and a fancy white shortsleeved shirt that was silk or something. He was all tanned too like Evening Star only on him it looked like he'd gotten it naturally and not from sunbathing on purpose although I could tell in a second he was one of those guys who thinks about their looks a lot like ol' Bruce did except my father was much more normal-looking than Bruce. Plus he obviously had major bucks, being a doctor and all.

He goes, What can I do y' for? and then looking around the room he caught I-Man in back and he says, That I-Man? Yo, Rasta, wussup? Respect, mon. Everyt'ing irie? talking pseudo-Rasta like Evening Star which made me wince a little. But it was cool that my father knew how to do it.

Everyt'ing irie, I-Man said and went back to studying the picture of the lion like he was playing a video game.

Well, what about you? he says to me. Evening Star tells me you're here to see me. Do I know you? he says looking down at me now and giving me the big once-over. Evening Star was lounging behind a ways leaning against the banister and taking occasional draws on her fatty and nodding her head to the beat of the music in the background and shuffling her feet in a little dancestep with her eyes closed and suchlike. Really *into* it.

What's your name, kid? he asked me and he took out a pack of Craven A's and lit one.

My name's Bone, I said. But . . . but it used to be Chappie. Chapman.

Oh? he says and he lifts his eyebrows like he's made the big connection but doesn't believe it yet so mainly he's suspicious. What's your last name? Bone. Bone what?

Just Bone. But it used to be Dorset, I said. Same as you.

He held out the pack of cigarettes and I took one and he lit it for me and I saw that his hand was shaking which was a good sign, I thought.

Okay. Dorset, he says. Same as me. Well, does that mean we're related?

By now Evening Star'd picked up the drift of our conversation and came over with her eyes glittering and the dogs were excited too like they could read her mind. I decided then just to say it straight out and let whatever happens happen, Jah's will be done et cetera so I go, Yeah. We're definitely related, man. I'm your son.

His mouth dropped and he goes, My *son!* Chappie? He says, *You're* Chappie? like maybe he expected some six-foot All American dude instead of a short skinny scabby-kneed kid in a doo-rag and tee shirt and cutoffs.

But he grinned, he actually looked happy to see me and he said, Lemme see you! Lemme see what you look like, for Christ's sake! and he pulls off my doo-rag and studies my face for a second and keeps on grinning like he's actually ecstatic to see me now which relieves me a lot.

Evening Star says, This is so *cool!* This is so *wild!* and the dogs are jumping around and grinning too and I-Man has come over and has his old amused pursed-lip smile back like he'd arranged the whole thing and is pleased it's all working out so nice for everybody. There's a heavy Bob Marley song booming from the poolside speakers, I Shot the Sheriff, and some guy is hollering, Cynthia, Cynthia, watch this! and I can hear the diving board thump and a big splash.

My father put his cigarette into an ashtray and took mine and did the same and then he placed his hands on my shoulders. He held me away from him and looked into my face like he was looking into his own distant past and his eyes filled up.

Then he said, Ah, Jesus, Chappie, thank God you've finally found me, son, and he pulled me against his chest and hugged me hard and my own eyes filled up but I didn't cry because even though I knew that from now on everything was going to be different I didn't know in what way so in the middle of the moment that should've been the happiest moment of my life so far I was scared instead.

He stepped back and caught my crossed bones and he said smiling, What's that?

It's a tat. A tattoo.

Lemme see it, he said and he drew my arm toward him and turned it over like a mainliner looking for a vein to shoot. That's because of the name? Bone?

Vicey-versie.

Then he dropped my arm and looked at me from way up there and he laughed. Ah, you little devil. Yeah. Yeah, you're my son all right! he said and he hugged me again.

SEVENTEEN

HAPPY BIRTHDAY
TO THE BONE

After that there was a continuous flurry of activities you might say, except when my father had to go back to Kingston to work as a doctor which he did three or four days a week. Instead of calling the place Starport I named it the Mothership on account of how Evening Star ran it but only to myself and I-Man because nobody else up there seemed to have too good a sense of humor about the scene, not even my father. There were all these lost animals Evening Star took in, like dogs and cats and goats and birds. Plus the people who I called the campers. I-Man didn't know what campers were so I had to explain but it got lost in the translation I guess because he still didn't get it.

Mostly though the campers were from the States, the white ones at least and the females and the rest were

Jamaican dudes who were hanging mainly for what they could get out of the Americans who were like these artist types and older and compared to the Jamaicans rich. The really rich one it looked to me was Evening Star. I think she was like an heiress and the Mothership'd been one of her family's estates and she paid for everything, I noticed.

When my father wasn't there the campers pretty much ignored me, even Evening Star so I could lurk in the background so to speak and check things out on my own with I-Man. Except for the three or four little kids from the neighborhood who did yard chores and ran errands for tips the Jamaicans were natties, these good-looking young dudes with starter dreads and terrific builds most of them walking around barefoot in only loose shorts that sometimes showed their units and making out on the couches and suchlike with the white American women and I suppose hooking up with them later. The females were like middle-aged but generally pretty hip and good-looking and I guess single or else their husbands were still back in the States making some more money or something. There were usually two or three of them, different ones because whenever Evening Star'd drive one down to the airport to go home to the States she'd come back with a new one to replace her or a few days later a taxi'd drive up the hill with one. The natties more or less stayed the same. It was a little weird to see older women acting like that and I could actually understand the natties better since they were mainly into hustling anyhow, Jamaica being such a poor country and all but the whole thing made me want to puke sometimes.

It's hard to explain. I usually don't give a shit what other people do so long as it's what they want to do. But it was like the white American females were into young black guys and were probably scared of hitting on a regular black guy from the States who would've known where they were coming from and would've told them to fuck off so instead they hooked up with these black dudes who were basically permanently broke and didn't even know anybody they could steal off of for a living. I could tell the females felt superior to the natties, plus they could fly back to the States whenever they felt like it and live a regular life but the natties were stuck here hustling forever.

Rent-a-Rastas, I-Man called them but I think he was pissed more because of the way they pretended to be followers of Jah like him and went around Rasta-rapping all the time about Babylon and Zion and one love and suchlike to impress the females, than because of them selling themselves so cheap. They weren't exactly skeezers, those guys but when you thought about it if they were their price tag was too cheap. That's what bugged *me*, I think. Like they got to hang out around the pool and smoke a lot of free ganja and all and snort some coke and listen to reggae on boss speakers and I guess for a Jamaican the food was pretty good at the Mothership because Evening Star liked putting out these awesome meals on the porch every night with candles and everything and they got to have sex with white women, but that was about it. No actual money changed hands. People who have to sell themselves ought to be paid in cash is what I think.

Me the campers treated like just another neighborhood kid except when my father was around and suddenly I became the little prince. They handled I-Man though like he was a movie star or something due to him being a real heavy-dread Rasta-man from the olden days especially Evening Star and the natties who thought I-Man'd hung with Bob Marley and Toots and the Wailers and all which he probably did since Jamaica's such a small country and back then in the seventies there weren't that many real Rastas anyhow except for Bob and Toots and the rest of the Kingston reggae posse. They'd like ask him, I-Man, did you really *know* those guys? and he'd say, I-and-I an' Ras-Bob, we be like brudders, mon. Toots-him, Toots be cool too. I-and-I an' Toots an' Bob, we be schoolbwoys togedder, mon. Then he'd go all dreamy like he was remembering the olden golden days in the ghetto so you couldn't really tell, plus nobody'd push him very hard on the subject I guess because everybody even me wanted to believe we were hanging with this cool dude who'd been almost famous.

In general I-Man chilled and ignored the poolside activities on account of having to meditate a lot and not being into any of the females but when he came around and joined the campers at the chillum pipe which he did on a regular basis they'd all deal with him like he was Grandfather Dread full of Irie wisdom and in a sense he was. He was into it too, I could see. He'd talk the talk and walk the walk. They'd come up and check out his awesome Jah-stick and a couple times one of the natties reached out to touch the lion's head on top and got zapped just like the Delta Airlines lady in Burlington which really busted everybody's brains when it happened and made them go all wide-eyed and respectful although by now I knew from checking it out at the ant farm once when he was sleeping that he'd just planted these tiny sewing needles into the lion's head where the whiskers were and on the tip of each of the ears that you couldn't see unless you got real close and he'd like move the stick a fraction and stick you good with one of the needles and you'd think it was Rasta magic. To me it was a joke but I didn't say anything. I just made like I was used to magic from I-Man and touched the Jah-stick whenever I felt like it because you could avoid the pins easy if you knew they were there.

Basically though for I-Man the situation was cool because he got to sell a whole lot of weed to the campers and their friends, so much that he had to make a trip every few days back down to the ant farm for more. Plus I think he'd started using the resident natties to do some dealing in the neighborhood so for him it was like setting up a branch office. For me it was okay too at least for now. I liked Evening Star quite a lot mainly because she was my father's old lady but also she didn't ignore me as much as most of the others did and asked me questions like what was my sign and so on. Plus she let me help with the cooking since from living with I-Man I already knew quite a bit about how to make Ital food, the main kind of food they had up there except when somebody came in from the States and brought a lot of what she called goodies that they couldn't get in Jamaica like special canned hams and salamis and once even smoked oysters the same as I'd learned to enjoy during my days holed up with Russ at the Ridgeways' summerhouse. I-Man of course didn't eat any of that stuff but the natties'd all join in in spite of Rastafarians not being allowed to eat pig or any animal that comes from the ocean and doesn't know how to swim, which is smoked oysters to a T. Also other good things like crabs and lobsters. People sitting around eating ham and oysters and suchlike'd send ol' I-Man into a

funk for days and he'd diss everybody for it especially the
natties and then go hole up in the back of the livingroom
alone in the dark with his arms crossed over his chest and
like glower so I always ate the deaders in secret even
though I myself never made any great claims to being a
Rasta-in-training and didn't have any image to protect. I
just did it to be kind.

My father came and went a lot and the deal was I'd
help out around the Mothership for room and board
when he was gone doing chores like the kids from the
neighborhood and then when he was back at the
Mothership him and me'd work hard at being a real
father and son team going places together and talking
about the past and all. It wasn't like we went fishing or
played baseball or anything cheesy like that, he wasn't
that kind of dude and I wasn't either. It was more like he
took me into Mobay in the Range Rover to score some
coke off a guy who ran the Holiday Inn and another time
we went out to Negril to do a money deal with a Jamaican
real estate guy where you exchange American dollars for
Jamaican money at a different rate than at the bank and
he explained how this sort of thing worked which was
pretty interesting and all in case I ever got my hands on
some American cash.

He was cool but he wasn't what you'd call a normal
father. He didn't want me crashing with him in Kingston
he said because he was gone all the time and the apartment was only a one-bedroom but I figured it was a girlfriend. He was the kind of guy who'd have one and
Evening Star was the kind of old lady who wouldn't give a
shit as long as she didn't have to deal with her in person
and my father was too smart for that. I asked him about

doctoring and he said he worked in a hospital in Kingston but didn't seem to want to talk about it particularly so I didn't push it. I guess it was like he'd done in Au Sable at the clinic when he was an x-ray expert under false pretenses and had gotten my mom to cover for him. He'd done a lot of trampoosing since he left Au Sable and he sat up late sometimes with me and I-Man out on the porch when everybody else'd gone off to hook up, telling us about his travels to places like Florida and Haiti.

One night he even apologized for abandoning me back when I was five. It was your mother, he said. If it hadn't been for her I'd've never left you, Bone, he said. I liked it that he called me Bone when he knew he didn't have to. Those days I'd've let him call me anything he wanted. He could've called me Buck.

My mom'd wanted to throw him in jail for nonpayment of alimony, he explained and he knew if he was locked up he'd've only ended up ruining not just his own life but my life too because A, there was no way he could raise any money while he was in jail anyhow and B, he knew I'd have to grow up in a small town where everybody'd look down on me because my father was a jailbird, so before my mom and the sheriff could bust him he'd fled the country. He said he'd planned to make some money elsewhere so he could send it to me later like in secret but he was never able to figure out how to get it to me without my mom and the sheriff knowing. And there was no way once my mom got married again he was going to send her money so she could just hand it over to my stepfather who was a pure piece of shit. All these years, he told me, he'd been like waiting for me to come to him on my own. And now I'd done it.

*   *   *

The Mothership was huge like a hotel with all these bedrooms on the second floor and there was a small empty one at the end of the long upstairs hall that Evening Star gave me for myself the first night that had two beds in it. The very next day my father and I got my stuff from the ant farm including my old stuffed woodcock and the classical CDs which I still hadn't played and I moved in there more or less permanently and I-Man shared the room with me when he wasn't down at the ant farm himself loading up on fresh weed or traveling around the countryside setting up branch offices or dealing it himself. Most of the rest of the bedrooms up there were for the visitors from the States and whoever they happened to hook up with, plus there was the poolhouse that had its own bedroom and kitchen and then a couple of cabins they called cabanas out in the woods by the garden that people slept in.

Evening Star and my father who I'd started calling Pa by now so's not to call him Dad like I did my stepfather slept in the master bedroom which was downstairs in back. They had like their own bathroom and a private screened-in porch and everything back there but they didn't really sleep together like a married couple since Pa was a night owl, probably due to him liking coke so much and Evening Star was an early-to-bed early-to-rise kind of person which is generally true of people who're into weed but still want to be in charge of things.

Usually after a long day of slightly criminal activities with Pa and a night of father-son talk with him doing most of the talking and me most of the listening I'd go up the wide center stairs around two or three in the morning and crash. I-Man'd already be snoring but I'd still be wired especially if I'd had a taste of Pa's coke so for hours I'd lie there listening to Pa walking around downstairs in the kitchen or playing old seventies tunes like the Bee Gees on the stereo in the livingroom until finally I fell asleep myself. Then real early the sun would wake me up since my room was on the east side of the house and no curtains and I'd hear Evening Star down below running the vacuum cleaner and washing dishes and emptying ashtrays. I was starting to wonder when they ever got it on.

This one morning after the sun came up I couldn't fall back to sleep so I came downstairs and over coffee me and Evening Star got to talking in the kitchen about my sign which is Leo the lion and seemed to impress her quite a lot due to how the Rastas always talk about Haile Selassie being the Lion of Judah and all. Your astrological *sign*, she said, is your *entry* point to the *universe*. It's the place where y'all step off the *astral* plane, darlin', and land on the *planetary* plane, and that's why it determines your *char*acter and your *fate*!

Yeah but there's about eleven other signs, right? Twelve in all?

That's *right*! she said all excited.

Like fucking duh, I'm thinking. But I go, That means one-twelfth of all the billions of people on earth have the same sign as me, okay? Millions and millions of people all over the world and they're all like Leos, okay? With the same character and fate as me. Except so far like I haven't run into a single person whose character and fate're anything like mine. You know what I'm saying? Like maybe all the other Leos are living in China or someplace.

No, no, *no*, honey, she said. Listen. Everybody on this

planet is a unique creation. It's *very* complicated, honey. Listen. Y'all have a *rising* sign and a *falling* sign, and so forth, and the *other* signs have an impact on your *major* sun sign, which is your *birth* sign, depending on how *far* or close they are. It's very complicated, darlin'. They're like *planets* affecting each other's *orbits* around the *sun*. You know something, Bone, y'all should be more metaphysically *open*, she said. Then she asked me when my actual birthday was and I told her and she said that's this *week*, only three days from now which surprised me because I hadn't known what date it was for a long time, ever since I went back to the schoolbus after being at the Ridgeways' and I thought my birthday was still a long ways off. We've got to give you a *party*, darlin', she said. A *birth*day party!

That's cool, I said. And it was, even though I knew Evening Star was always looking for an excuse to toss a party and that's all it was, an excuse. Still, nobody'd given me a party in a long time.

My father had like his own driver who worked for the government or something and dropped him off and picked him up and stayed with relatives in Mobay when Pa was at the Mothership, and he was heading back over to Kingston the next day so Evening Star decided to put the party together that same night because like she said it'd be the first time me and him'd been together on my birthday since I was a teeny-weeny bwoy. That's how she talked, a little of this and a little of that so you never knew who you'd be hearing, it might be a white middle-aged southern rich lady one minute or a regular kid like me using words like buff chick and crankin' or a Rasta wannabe off on an Irie-rap or a kindergarten mommy at sandbox time which is what I got a lot of when it was just the two of us. I guess from being around so many different types of people all her life and smoking excellent herb all these many years she didn't have any more words left inside her that were strong enough to block out the words coming from outside and I wondered what her thoughts were like when she was alone. She was like an actress who was playing a bunch of different people in a bunch of different plays all at the same time.

Besides I-Man there were only two Jamaican dudes at the Mothership then, a heavyset guy in his thirties named Jason who said he was a champion dominoes player even though he wasn't too bright but he was giving me lessons so I liked him and this half-Chinese half-African light-skinned dude named Toker with a Fu Manchu mustache and a great build like Bruce Lee's who was into selling I-Man's herb locally and used the Mothership as a base to crash in and get laid sometimes and do his karate exercises. Plus there were two American females there that week, this tall bony college professor named Cynthia who spent all day lying by the pool and reading until she got toasted at the chillum around sunset and then she liked to drink rum and dance with Jason or Toker and wasn't bad at it either for a skinny white woman her age, and this other younger woman named Jan who was Evening Star's cousin from New Orleans and was a poet and I could tell didn't approve of the fun and games aspect of life at the Mothership but didn't want to diss anybody for it either so she went along and tried to make like she was having a lot of fun visiting her weird cousin in Jamaica.

Jan was more into the life of the natives so to speak than the others and she spent a lot of time trying to make

I-Man and the natties give straight answers to questions about unemployment and family life and suchlike which are subjects they're not used to talking about even though they know a lot about them from firsthand experience. I liked her though because she had a good low-voiced laugh and she'd break into it and shake her head when Jason or one of the other natties'd try to explain for instance how he wanted to go to the States to earn money to support his five kids and their three mothers and maybe she could help him get his visa et cetera. Or like I-Man'd get all somber and say, In Jamaica de 'oman be like a shadow, Jan, an' de mon be like an arrow, and Jan'd give out her laugh and say, Ain't *that* the truth, sugar!

All that day Evening Star and I-Man hung in the kitchen cooking for the party while the other campers lounged around the Mothership as usual. Me and Pa and Jason spent the afternoon driving all over Mobay looking for a guy but never finding him that Pa knew who'd sell Jason a gun which he said he needed to kill a guy over in Negril who'd burned down his brother's house. I didn't think any of it was true, you hear a lot of stories like that and neither did Pa, but I could tell Pa was going to pay for the gun since Jason didn't have any money of his own and then Jason'd end up owing it to him and it'd be like Pa having his own deputy with a gun who'd use it any way Pa wanted him to, which might come in handy someday. But we never found the guy.

When we got back to the house around six there were all these balloons strung around and a huge sign made out of three whole bedsheets and hung between some trees that said HAPPY BIRTHDAY TO THE BONE!!! Music was blasting across the hills from the speakers by the pool

where there were big flaming torches up on poles and
coolers full of ice and Red Stripe beer and tables with all
these platters of Ital food plus regular Jamaican beans
and rice and so on set out on them and bottles of rum
and other drinks and a whole goat roasting on a grill and
a big pot of soup made from the goat's head and guts
including his balls called mannish waters. It really looked
like an incredible party for a much-loved person was
about to begin.

Pretty soon practically the whole village started coming
up the hill to the greathouse, families with little kids and
old people and lots of natties from the neighborhood I'd
seen chilling day and night down by the road to Mobay
and I-Man's dreadlocked posse from the ant farm even,
Fattis and Prince Shabba and Buju who were real glad to
see me and high-fived me like crazy plus a couple of white
Jamaicans I'd never met before, heavy dudes with coffee-
colored females who wore spiky high heels and showed
lots of thigh, from Mobay I guess because they came in
Benzes, and Pa's driver was there with Pa's black Buick
and the customs guy I remembered from the airport, a
huge crowd until the patios and porches and all around
the pool and even the flower gardens were filled with people eating and drinking and dancing around to the
music. Every time I looked Evening Star was at the center
of the action like a dreadlocked white queen in a long
lace dress you could almost see through and no underwear hugging and kissing people when they came up and
telling them where the food was and the drinks and so
on. I-Man was like consulting with his posse over a
humongous chillum in the livingroom in front of his
favorite Haitian picture, the one with the lion lying peace-

fully with the animals it usually eats. Cynthia and Jan were dancing with various and sundry Jamaican dudes while Jason tried to look like he was one of the people in charge by running the sound system and playing mostly dancehall and in between songs rapping on the mike like Yellowman the famous DJ and Toker showed off swimming laps until the pool got too crowded with kids jumping in. My father kind of drifted from one group to another looking cool and above it all and once in a while he'd see me and wink like we knew something nobody else did although I didn't know what it was yet.

I was having a pretty good time just chilling by the pool smoking a J and packing back Red Stripes and watching people. I hate it when people sing Happy Birthday and clap but actually I was kind of waiting for the birthday cake to come out with the usual candles and all. I guess I'd figured it was going to be one of those Big Public Moments like where in front of a whole lot of people you mark the end of one life and the start of another even though I was only turning fifteen not twenty-one or forty and this wasn't like a retirement party. Still, I was imagining a scene with Pa taking the mike from Jason and making a little speech to everyone about how his only son Bone after a terrible childhood in the States had found his way to him at last for protection to be raised by him into manhood here in Jamaica and I-Man would lean over while Pa was talking and say to me, Whole new world, Bone, whole new ex-peer-ience, and maybe after Pa finished his speech with a tear in his eye he'd come over and hug me and say, Welcome home, son, and just then Jason and maybe Jan would carry this huge cake out with fifteen candles blazing and Evening Star'd hold up her glass and start singing Happy Birthday to Bone and everybody'd join in, even the little kids who didn't know me.

But it got later and later until eventually people started leaving except for the ones who'd crashed in the garden and bushes or passed out on the couches and pool chairs. Most of the booze and food was gone, even the mannish waters and the goat although there was still quite a lot of the Ital food left because not everybody likes that stuff, Jamaicans included. The dogs were wandering around looking for scraps and the cats were licking off the plates and up on the tables prowling among the leftovers and Jan and Jason were dancing real slow to a Dennis Brown song all wrapped up like snakes fucking which kind of made me sad even though I liked both of them better than the rest of the campers. I'd caught a glimpse of Cynthia the college professor tiptoeing off hours ago with Buju from I-Man's posse, and the others, Prince Shabba and Fattis'd left without him. Toker I think'd split with Pa's white friends in one of the Benzes for another party at the Holiday Inn. There was a cool breeze blowing that'd snuffed the last of the torches and knocked down two-thirds of the Happy Birthday to the Bone!!! sign so it just said Happy and the ten or so balloons that hadn't been popped by the little kids earlier had gotten soft and wrinkly and paper plates and plastic cups were floating in the pool.

The place looked pretty grungy but at least everybody'd had a good time, I was thinking but I still wondered about the birthday cake, like if maybe there'd actually been one but Evening Star'd just forgotten about it on account of the great success of her party. I wandered around the grounds for a while looking for somebody to

talk to but everybody was gone now or passed out. I figured Pa must've left with the white dudes and gone down
to the Holiday Inn party too. Finally I went into the
house, bypassed the livingroom and walked out to the
kitchen to check. But there were just piles of dirty pots
and pans from the cooking. No birthday cake.

No big deal, I said to myself and I opened the fridge
and pulled out practically the last beer and I'm like looking around for an opener when I hear these sick-sound-
ing groans from the room next to the kitchen which is
where the laundry is and a cot and shower and toilet for
the guy who takes care of the gardens. Maybe it's Jan puk-
ing or somebody else who needs help, I think so I push
open the door and go in. The room is dark but with the
door open there's enough light from the kitchen for me
to see Evening Star on the cot on her hands and knees
with her lace dress up around her waist and I-Man with
his pants down banging her from behind. He's half her
size and it's not a pretty sight.

Then Evening Star turns and over her shoulder she
catches me looking and she scowls and says Shit! but I-
Man just keeps on whaling it to her like he's about to
come so I let the door slowly close and back out of the
kitchen feeling hot and red in the face and incredibly
pissed off but confused because I don't know what I'm
pissed at. It's everything I guess. The no birthday cake
and I-Man banging Evening Star and my father gone without even saying goodbye. When I got out onto the porch I
saw I was still carrying the unopened bottle of beer and I
threw it as hard as I could into the darkness in the general direction of the pool.

I heard it smash against the tiles and one of the dogs,

the Lab I think yelped like maybe some glass had hit it which made me feel like a piece of shit. I ran over to the pool but the dogs were gone, even the cats. There was brown broken glass everywhere though. I didn't know what to do then. I guess I should've cleaned it up but I didn't.

For a while I walked around in the flower gardens below the house. The moon'd come out and in the moon-light the white animals with their red eyes and mouths started to spook me. Up above the gardens the wind in the palm trees sounded like the low mournful voices of the ghosts of the thousands of African slaves who'd been born there and worked in the cane fields down below for their whole lives being whipped and manacled if they tried to resist or escape and then they'd died generation after gen-eration like for hundreds of years and had been buried someplace out back in the bush where no one remem-bered now because the jungle'd covered everything up so you couldn't go and put flowers on their graves even. The wind was the saddest sound I'd ever heard and I had to get out of there before I started sobbing.

I was crossing the darkened livingroom headed for the stairs and my room when I heard my father's voice com-ing from his chair in the corner. That you, Bone?

I said yeah but didn't stop and he goes, What's happen-ing, son? I turned then and saw the light from his ciga-rette and went over and sat down in the chair next to him and I guess sighed because he said, What's wrong, son?

Nothin', I said. Well. . . *some*thing.

He laughed, a little too loud, like he does when he's been snorting awhile. Some sweet yellow gal break your heart, son?

I told him then. It was wrong and I knew it as soon as I

did it but I couldn't help myself. Plus I didn't think he'd react the way he did. Actually I didn't know *how* he'd react and I didn't think about it one way or the other. I told him just to tell him. I said it flat out, that a few minutes ago I'd walked up on I-Man fucking Evening Star.

At first he was calm and said Oh? and asked like did they see me and I said yeah but when he asked where did I see them fucking his calmness scared me so I lied.

Down below. In the flower gardens, I said.

He wanted to know exactly so I said I wasn't sure, maybe near the statues of all the lambs and foxes and so on. Next to the big birdbath, I told him which happened to be down near the gate and as far from the house as you could get without going onto the road. What're you gonna do? I asked.

Well, Bone, I'm going to have to kill him.

Jeez. How come?

Why? Because what's mine is mine. That's the rule *I* live by, Bone. And when some little nigger comes into my house and takes what's mine, he has to pay. He has to pay and pay, many times over. And the only thing that nigger owns is his worthless life, so that's what he'll have to pay with.

Jeez, I said. That's pretty harsh. He got up from his chair real slow and creaky and I said, I thought this was Evening Star's house.

She's mine, Bone. So whatever she owns I own too. He walked into his bedroom then and came back out a few seconds later and when he got close to the door the moonlight glinted off the gun in his hand and his face which was gray and cold as ice. Down by the birdbath you say?

Yeah. I was really freaking now and wishing like mad that I'd never said anything but it was too late. Listen, Pa, I think I'll stay up here if you don't mind, I said.

Up to you, Bone. I can understand that, he said and he stepped outside and in a flash I took off for the kitchen and the laundry room in back. When I got there I-Man was buckling his pants up and Evening Star was gone.

Bone! he says only mildly surprised to see me like he didn't know yet that I'd walked in on him and Evening Star. Wussup, mon? he said and strolled into the kitchen like he'd just taken a piss outside and planned to check out the fridge for a late-night snack.

Listen, you gotta get outa here, man. Doc's after your ass, I said. He didn't seem to register, just lifted his eyebrows and pursed his lips, then reached for the handle to the fridge.

He's got a gun, I said. That got his attention.

Serious t'ing? Where him at?

Down in front by the birdbath, I said. He's fucking deadly cold, man. And he's got his piece.

Why Doc wan' t' kill I-and-I, Bone?

For screwing Evening Star, for Christ's sake! Why d'ya think? Hurry the fuck up and book by the back way, I told him. There were some old paths crisscrossing through the bush there that the local people used instead of the road when they came over the hill on foot.

He nodded and walked slowly to the door to the back-yard and then stopped and turned to me. How Doc come to understand dat I-and-I jukin' Evenin' Star?

Yeah, well, I dunno about that. Maybe she told him. Maybe he like saw you himself. He was right here at the time, man, sitting out in the livingroom twenty feet away and even though he was coked to the gills his senses were alert, man. He might've even heard you.

Fe trut', Bone?

Yeah, the truth. Now get the fuck outa here, man. For Christ's sake, book it, willya?

You comin', Bone?

Where? Not back to the ant farm, man. That's the first place he'll look for you.

Not de ant farm. I-and-I goin' to Jah-kingdom. Up into de Cockpit, Bone, where I-and-I mus' sattar 'mongst mi Maroon brethren-dem and be I-lion in I-kingdom, mon. Time come, time go, time fly away, Bone, but I-and-I mus' return to Cockpit Country. Mus' return I-self to de mos' fruitful land of I-birth, de home of all de African I-scen-dants in Babylon. De Babylonians-dem cyan't come in dere 'mongst de Maroons. You comin'? he asked again. Or you stayin' on de dis a-yere plantation wi' Papa Doc?

You think I shouldn't?

Up to you, Bone. But I-and-I headin' fe de Cockpit now.

I didn't know what the Cockpit was exactly unless it was the little village in the boonies he'd talked about back in the schoolbus when he was homesick and all which if it was I had a pretty good mental picture of the place and at that moment it seemed to have a lot of advantages over the Mothership especially since I wasn't as interested as before in like turning into Baby Doc so I said, Yeah. Yeah, I'm comin'. Lemme get my stuff first and I'll meet you out back.

He said Irie and took up his Jah-stick and stepped out-side into the moonlit backyard while I ran upstairs to my room where I tossed my old stuffed bird and the classical

CDs which I still hadn't listened to and my few articles of clothing into my backpack. I was headed back down the hall toward the stairs when I looked over the railing and down and saw Pa with his gun in his hand walk through the door into the livingroom where he stood in a patch of moonlight and sniffed and looked around like he was a snake planning his next move. Just then the door to his and Evening Star's bedroom opened and she came out into the moonlit livingroom all naked and the two of them faced each other with me up above in the darkness looking down.

C'mon, Doc, she said in a low patient voice like she was calling in one of her dogs. C'mon in to bed now. Party's over.

Bone saw you and the nigger, he said.

She sighed like she was real tired and said, Yeah. I know.

I'll have to kill him, you understand. Or have him killed.

Not tonight, darlin'. C'mon in now.

Then he said like she looked pretty good standing there naked in the moonlight and she laughs and says he looks good too because of the gun in his hand which turns her on, and they start walking slowly toward each other with him already unbuckling his belt with his free hand so I take this opportunity to tiptoe back to my room at the far end of the hall. I went straight to the one window and opened it and crawled out onto the roof of the laundry room and with my backpack on I swung out and went hand over hand along the overhanging branch of this big breadfruit tree back there and then shinnied down the trunk to the ground where I-Man stood watching in the shadows.

Ready, Bone? he said.

Lead on, man. Babylon's behind us now, I said and he made his little chuckling laugh and turned and led me into the bush.

EIGHTEEN

BONE GOES NATIVE

It was late the next afternoon before we finally got up to Accompong in the Cockpit Country which turned out to be like I'd thought, I-Man's hometown that he'd been so homesick for back in the States. It took about four different rides to hitch in because Accompong is a long ways from Mobay and not many people go there so we had to spend a lot of time just chilling by the side of these winding country roads and rode sometimes in the back of pickups and had to walk the last four or five miles uphill from the main road in to the village. When we got there it was sort of the way I'd pictured, basically a single dirt street with grass growing in the middle and a dozen or so cabins and small houses and a few more you could see scattered around in the jungle and all these little veggie gardens and banana trees and kids running around in underpants and old guys snoozing in the shade of a breadfruit tree and goats and the occasional pig and females carrying baskets of yams on their heads or plastic pails of water from the well.

One reason they call it Cockpit Country must be on account of the way the land looks. For miles and miles around as far as you can see they have like these huge deep craters or pits where the ground dropped out way back in ancient times and they're all covered with trees and vines and thornbushes and so on and the people who live up in the Cockpit are more like ridge runners than they are mountain climbers and don't like to go down into the craters unless they have to for a lost goat or kid or to hide out from the cops or their other enemies. Due to the hundreds of caves down in the pits and the thickness of the bush hiding out is basically what people have been doing up there for like hundreds of years, I-Man explained to me. The people who live there are called Maroons, he said because of the reddish tint to their skin which the truth is I couldn't see, they all looked like regular black people to me only darker. But they're all descended from these incredibly tough Africans who were called Ashantis and after they were captured in Africa and shipped over to Jamaica they escaped into the bush the first chance they had and then kicked ass when the white slavecatchers came after them until finally the slavecatchers said fuck it and went back to their sugar plantations on the coast and just let the Maroons live out there on their own and said don't send us any more of those Ashanti warrior types and that's when the Queen of England signed a peace treaty with the head Maroon whose name was Cudjoe.

Nowadays though the place was full of ganja growers

and miscellaneous criminals who were raised here and went to the city and fucked up and came back plus some regular Jamaican farmers and suchlike but they still pretty much lived like their Maroon ancestors and didn't have electricity or running water or TV or cars or any of the other modern conveniences. Also a lot of Rastas had their groundations up there in the Cockpit and I-Man said the real reason it's named Cockpit is because it's always been the place where the Rastafarian ascendants of the old African Ashanti warriors sattar fe control de universe.

All the way up from Mobay throughout the long night after we'd made our escape from Papa Doc and the greathouse and while we chilled by the side of the road out of Mobay waiting for a ride I-Man was really into teaching me this stuff about the Maroons and Accompong and the old Ashanti warriors, like he'd decided I was ready now to learn these things and use them in my daily life even though I was still a white kid from America. But I was feeling weird and guilty from when I told Pa about how I-Man'd hooked up with Evening Star which was why we were on the run in the first place and I-Man wasn't making it any easier by treating me like his favorite student or something.

I hadn't figured out yet why I'd done it and I couldn't ask I-Man the way I usually did when I couldn't figure something out so I was slipping into blaming white people generally and saying to myself I must've done it because of my background in lying and betrayal that I'd learned as a child from my stepfather and other adults who all happened to be white. I-Man'd be running on about the old Ashantis and the slavecatchers and how they'd hunted the Ashantis down with these humongous man-eating dogs from Panama and I'd be thinking, Fucking Babylon, man, white people really suck, you can never trust them, et cetera, like that was letting me off the hook for almost getting I-Man killed by my own father.

There were maybe a few hundred people living in the village of Accompong and a few hundred more living in the surrounding area and everybody said they were Maroons and were related to everybody else or that's how it seemed anyhow and I guess it was true because you couldn't be one without being the other, so the Maroons were like a tribe, you could say. They owned all the land in the Cockpit together and shared it on account of the treaty their great-grandfathers'd signed with the Queen of England more or less like the Mohawks at home and other American Indians. Except the Maroons didn't call the Cockpit a reservation, it was more like an independent country called Accompong inhabited and ruled exclusively by the Maroons, at least the way they talked about it it was. They had a chief and everything and even a secretary of state who were these really old guys that I saw a couple of times from a distance but never got to talk to because I-Man right after we got there set me up out in the bush far from the village where he had his groundation and that's pretty much where I stayed.

He didn't exactly say it but I-Man was protecting me I think by having me sattar way out in the Cockpit a couple of miles from the village basically to watch over his ganja patch which was pretty sizable, hundreds of plants that I was also supposed to water from this spring way down in the bottom of the pit. But having white strangers or any kind of outsider camped in the village was definitely not encouraged or at least that's the feeling I got from I-Man because when we first got there and he introduced me to a few people like the woman he said was his kids' mother, not his wife I noticed or one of his cousins hanging in his yard he'd say Bone jus' be passin' through. Plus with his kids and all he didn't have any room for me in his cabin. They only had two little rooms where everybody slept, all the kids on one bed and I-Man and the kids' mother on another and the rest of the time everybody hung in the yard where they cooked under a thatched roof on poles and sat around on little stools and an old car seat.

Where I was was wicked cool though. Out there in the Cockpit up on a ridge with panoramic views and a cleared slope in front with these terraces where the ganja grew I had my own cabin made out of bamboo with a thatched roof and a hammock for sleeping in and a stone fireplace for cooking and the necessary pots and other utensils and lots of food around like breadfruit and yams and akee and coconuts and calalu plus stuff I-Man brought out from the village that his old lady made. It was the best squat I'd ever had. I was happy and besides I think I needed it, being alone way out there with plenty of time to like think and remember things except when in the evenings mostly I-Man'd come out with a couple of his Rasta cousins and they'd sit around and meditate over a chillum and do some African-style drumming on these excellent homemade drums and put out deep reflection until dawn some nights. Mainly I'd hang back and watch and listen because these were wicked heavy dudes who talked about killing guys down in Kingston and Mobay and except for I-Man they weren't too interested in me and probably just thought I was some American white kid who was into weed that I-Man was using as a watchdog.

Which was basically true. I was a regular herb boy then and I did work for I-Man who'd spent one whole day teaching me how to blow through a conch shell like a horn in case somebody tried to steal his crop. But there were other things in life that interested me even more than weed and watchdogging I-Man's crop and I-Man knew that so lots of times he'd come out to the groundation alone or with one of his pick'nies he called them, his kids of which he had four and after he'd checked his plants and talked to them awhile and done some weeding and nipping the buds and shown me some new tricks of the ganja grower's trade and so on he'd sattar in the yard by the cabin and Rasta-rap his way through another chapter in the history of the African captivity in Babylon.

By this time my hair was pretty long, down to my shoulders and in my eyes and I had this nervous habit when I was thinking of twirling it with my fingers and one day in the middle of telling me about how Marcus Garvey'd been poisoned by the capitalists for trying to take the Africans back to the promised land in their own ark I-Man noticed me doing it and got up and went into the bush and came back with a bunch of leaves that he crushed and squeezed some juice out of and said to rub it into my locks. The juice smelled like licorice but it worked because the next day when I woke up I had regular dreadlocks growing, not big time but these loose springy dark reddish-brown locks about a foot long that I couldn't really check out since I didn't have a mirror but I could feel them and could tell they were cool-looking. Also I'd only been wearing shorts out there on the groundation and no shirt and had gotten real tanned so this

one day I was standing alone dribbling water from a pail
onto the plants like I-Man'd showed me and I flipped my
head to chase off a mosquito and saw dreadlocks swirling
through the air in my shadow. Then I looked down at my
arms and hands which were like coffee-colored and when
I saw I didn't look like a regular white kid anymore I put
down the bucket and did a little Rasta dance right there
in the sunshine.

It's funny how when you change the way you look on
the outside even if it's only with a tattoo you feel different
on the inside. I was learning that it's true what I-Man'd
said, if you work at it long enough and are serious you *can*
become a brand-new beggar which is like if you're a car-
penter you go to the worksite and discover all new material to work with so you can change your plans and start
building yourself a bigger and a better house to live in.
I'd even started talking different, not saying cool and
excellent to everything anymore but instead I'd go Irie,
mon, and when I used to refer to myself only as I or me
now I said I-and-I which makes you feel slightly separate
from your body, it makes you feel that your true self is like
this spirit that can float through the air where it com-
munes with the universe and it can even travel backward
and forward in time.

All the drumming and long meditation and all the late-
night reflection sessions with the Maroons and their
Ashanti ascendants who were with us in spirit like I-Man
said and the detailed instruction in history and daily life I
was getting from I-Man plus the regular partaking of the
sacrament of kali at the chillum with the Rastas and the
everyday solitary exploration of I-self I'd been doing with
the assistance of excellent weed ever since the first day I

met I-Man at the schoolbus in Plattsburgh, all this'd been having a deep gradual effect on me without my actually knowing it, until one morning I woke up in my hammock and looked up at the thatched roof overhead and I knew I'd like finally cast off my old self and was lying naked in the universe as the day I was born fifteen years ago in Au Sable, New York, United States of America, Planet Earth.

Then on the night of the full moon when the ganja plants were taller than my head and were supposed to be harvested the next day I-Man and three of his Rasta brethren from Accompong came out to the groundation all serious and carrying machetes, and when they told me they were taking me to the secret Maroon cave fe see in de true lights of I-self, I was ready, man. I was fucking ready. In the old days I probably would've said cool or whatever and maybe tried to postpone the whole thing without them knowing I was scared but now I just said, Dat be irie, and followed I-Man in the moonlight straight into the bush with the brethren coming along behind and no one talking.

It wasn't like I wanted to be made into an honorary Negro or anything. The truth is I really believed in wisdom then, that there actually was such a thing, I mean and a few people had it, like I-Man mainly and under the right conditions they could pass it on even to a kid and I believed, with my background and being a white American and all I especially needed some wisdom if I was going to grow up and be better at living my life than most of the adults I'd known so far were.

We didn't seem to be walking on a regular path and sometimes I-Man had to hack the macca bushes away before we could pass through one cockpit and climb over the ridge and descend into another but I guess we were on some kind of known path because I-Man didn't hesitate any or change his mind about this way or that. We walked for hours it seemed like, up steep inclines in zigzags and then down again until I started feeling like I was on a whole other continent than the one I'd lived on all my life, like I was in Africa and I was a little nervous because I knew they had these wild pigs out here that people said were dangerous and I was glad the brethren and I-Man were carrying machetes.

I knew the brethren pretty good by then, Terron and Elroy and Rubber who were in their thirties or forties, older Rastas with wicked massy dreads. Terron and Elroy were I-Man's cousins and like junior partners in his groundation and Rubber whose name came from his face which he could twist into all these different expressions anytime he wanted but mostly looked sad was his nephew and had his own groundation in the cockpit next to I-Man's. They were heavy dudes, darker and fiercer than the ant farm posse, expert machete men with great builds who looked like they could pull your arms out if they wanted. I-Man who was a tiny old guy compared to them they treated with total respect and Terron once told me that someday I-Man when he ascended unto the fullness of his age and completed his trampoosing among the various peoples of the world would probably become the chief of the Maroons in Accompong or at least the secretary of state.

Finally we were way down in the bottom of one of the cockpits where the moonlight couldn't reach and you couldn't even see the stars and I was just following I-Man in pitch darkness by the sound of his footsteps now. Then suddenly I couldn't hear him anymore so I stopped and after a few seconds I said, Yo, I-Man, where you at?

Rubber who was right behind me said, Keep movin', Rasta.

But I-and-I cyan see nuttin.

No matter, mon, he said and gave me a little push on the shoulder with the tip of his machete and that got me going again. On and on I walked in total darkness like for a quarter of a mile maybe, thinking, Well, if I walk off a cliff I won't know it till it's too late so why worry, when I noticed that the air had gotten cool like a fan was blowing and I could feel through my sandals that I was walking on smooth flat rock now not dirt or grass anymore and I could hear water dripping. I knew I must be in a cave but it was like I had a blindfold on and I started imagining bats and snakes and shit darting at me out of the darkness and my skin got goose-bumped all over and for a second there I was scared I'd lose it completely and start trying to claw my way back out to the moonlight and for the rest of my life I'd have to live with the shameful knowledge that I'd panicked at the very moment I was supposed to be viewing the lights of I-self and ascending in that irie glow to the heights of I-and-I where I'd finally come to know Jah.

I heard a match then and saw the flame and I-Man's craggy brown face as he lit up a spliff and took a deep hit off of it and with the same match lit a candle and then took it and went around lighting more candles that were in these nooks and crannies in the walls of the cave. The darkness disappeared and tall shadows flashed and fell all around like I-Man was dropping solid dark gray wool blankets off of a clothesline and revealing behind them this humongous room with yellowish-white rock walls that were curved and smooth like they'd been carved out of solid rock by water over millions of years. It was like being inside a gigantic human skull and we'd come in through the mouth. Up above there were a couple more dark caves leading out that looked like eye sockets and in back where I guess the spinal column was I could see another dark hole and I could hear water running down there like that was the ancient riverbed and it was still carving its way deeper and deeper into the earth.

I-Man sat me down on a little ledge and sat beside me and pointed out a bunch of red pictures up on the top of the skull of these weird squiggly signs and a couple of animals I recognized like turtles and birds and snakes and stick figures of guys with spears who were fighting each other, some lying down with the spears sticking out and some with their heads cut off and the rest whaling on them. The pictures were way up on top, higher than you could reach without an extension ladder which they didn't have in those olden days so I wondered how they got up there to paint them.

Dem fly up, Bone, I-Man said. Dem ol' Africans could fly lak birds, mon.

I figured there'd be some kind of ceremony now and I was really hoping it wouldn't involve any cutting and blood but I'd come this far without turning back and was ready to go the whole route no matter what the drill was. So I was really relieved when Rubber reaches into the cloth bag where I'd been thinking they had the knives and bowls for collecting blood or whatever and instead he pulls out this cool little clay chillum made in the shape of a pregnant African woman sitting with her legs crossed and her arms folded under her huge tits and I-Man immediately fills it from a pouch and says, Dis be some special herb, Bone, and lights it. He passed the chillum down to Terron and Elroy and Rubber who all took huge hits and then to me and I gave it my usual medium-sized whack and passed it on to I-Man but before the tube'd even reached I-Man's mouth I felt myself whirling like in a barrel going over a waterfall and for a second it was completely dark again and I couldn't see anything except I knew I was still spinning in the barrel. Then my eyesight came back and I was in a totally different place than the cave and with different people.

I'm remembering it now while I'm telling it so I'm like in two places at once, here and now and then and there, but when it was happening I was only in the one place which was not a limestone cave in Cockpit Country in Jamaica with I-Man and his Rasta brethren, and it wasn't like any tripping on acid I'd ever done where you're also in two places at once and one of them is weird and the other normal. Even dreaming you're usually in two places at once. No, this was like real and I didn't have any memory of how I got there or any plans for getting out.

A drum was beating, real heavy and slow like thump, thump, thump, and it didn't let up or change, it just went on and on, a sort of sound track on a continuous loop that seemed to come from the place itself the way the sound of the wind does, like it was coming right out of the trees and fields and sky and not from outside. I wasn't scared or anything yet, I just went with it and discovered one thing at a time and dealt with it, like the fact that I was up on a wagon driving a team of oxen I guess they are, like cows only bigger slowly along a lane that cuts across a wide green cane field and my wagon is heaped up with cane stalks. There's the sea in the distance with waves breaking on a thin sandy beach and rocky ledges further on and a bright blue sky overhead and a burning sun and behind me the dark green mountains.

I'm all alone out there on my wagon and it's hot under the noonday sun and it takes me a long time to get across the cane field to the line of trees at the edge and when I pass into the shade of the trees it's cooler and a light breeze blows and I'm pretty happy for a few minutes then. There's a little stream flowing by and where the trail crosses it I stop the wagon and let the oxen drink from it and drink a little myself and wet my doo-rag and wipe my face with it.

Then I get back up on the wagon box and drive on and cross some more cane fields until finally I come into this little town where there's a regular stone church and some stores and so on and lots of people walking around, mostly black people barefoot and in work clothes and a few white people dressed more or less the same until I get to the town square where there's more white people than black now and the whites are wearing straw hats and these old-fashioned suits. Nobody pays any attention to me so I go by real slow and try to catch the scene although it makes me feel ashamed and I don't want to look. But I do.

The white people are buying and selling black people. A white guy up on a kind of stage in the middle is showing off a naked scared-looking black kid about my age, making him turn around and bend over and spread his cheeks and show his ass and balls to the crowd which has a fair number of females in it and different whites in the crowd are bidding on the kid while another white guy off to the side of the stage, the auctioneer I guess points to this or that bidder and keeps the price going up. Everybody acts like it's normal. Even the black people. Little pick'ny kids are running around and black women are carrying bundles on their heads and white men are smoking cigars and talking. Nobody's crying or looking embarrassed or pissed off, everybody's relaxed and easy and familiar with each other, white and black alike although obviously the whites are the bosses and tell the blacks to do this or that which they do but not too fast.

The auctioneer who's a tall skinny hawk-faced guy like Pa makes the naked kid on the stage squat down and jump like a frog and everybody laughs, even the few blacks who are among the crowd although there's a line of other blacks I now see standing on the ground behind the stage, men and women and some kids and babies all of them naked even the older ones and they're all chained together at the ankles and scabby and sorrowful and none of them laughs at the kid leaping around on the stage like a shiny black frog. I guess they're still Africans and to them this isn't normal yet.

The whole scene creeps me out so I give a little flick of the stick and keep my oxen moving on out of town along the track, keeping close to the sea for a while. After a few minutes I don't have any complicated thoughts or memories anymore or even any stupid or simple thoughts, I'm just catching the rays up on my box and digging the smell of the cane and the feel of the light sea breeze on my face and now and then brushing a fly away and letting the oxen make all the decisions. The track turns gradually uphill between more cane fields until I come to a big stone gate and turn in and drive the wagon up to a bunch of buildings like barns where there's a dozen or so black dudes and some women unloading cane from different wagons and carrying it inside this one barn and stacking it. There's also this huge grinder with a blindfolded ox hitched to a long pole going around in a permanent circle and a building with a tall brick chimney sending up a cloud of white sweet-smelling smoke and various other smaller buildings, offices and workshops and the such.

It's a sugar factory and as soon as I pull up in my wagon a bunch of older guys and women and teenaged kids, all blacks and really sweaty and filthy come over and start to unload it. Nobody talks. They just work. I don't know what to do now so I'm just sitting there waiting for instructions or maybe the oxen will know what to do when I notice off to my right a white man whaling on a black woman with a short whip. He's got her shirt pulled off and she's down on her hands and knees on the ground and every time he hits her her tits shudder and all the time I can hear the same drum thumping like before only now it's in time to the whip coming down. The white guy is all sweaty and has a mustache like my stepfather although it's not quite him and he's going about his business whipping the woman like he's splitting wood, nothing personal or emotional about it, just part of the job. I look around and the other black people are all going about their business too. Just part of the job.

Then suddenly somebody grabs my arm and yanks me down from the wagon to the ground. It's another white guy, shirtless and young, like in his twenties or so and tough-looking with muscles and a hairless chest with great definition like ol' Bruce but no tattoos or nipple rings or anything. For a second the blacks stop working and look at me but then they turn away and go back to work. The white guy's got kind of a blond buzz-cut and good teeth and he reaches down, clamps his hand onto my arm and yanks me up from the ground like I don't weigh anything which compared to him I don't and without saying anything he drags me around behind one of the barns like I'm a chicken and he's got to cut my head off for the cook. When we get back there out of sight of the others the white guy unbuttons his pants and flings a huge boner out which he makes me jerk off with my hand while he holds me next to him real tight and when he comes he gasps and kisses me hard on the back of my neck. Then he stuffs his unit back into his pants and buttons up and shoves me back in the direction of the wagons and the other people and follows along behind like nothing happened. I'm actually relieved that nothing worse happened but I'm feeling pretty shitty anyhow so I'm glad to see that my wagon's empty and when I climb back up onto the box the oxen turn and move back down the long curving driveway between the cane fields to the road by the sea the same way as we came before.

All day long it goes like that, real slow and mindless in the sun when I'm alone with the oxen driving the wagon across the cane fields and while the wagon's being loaded or unloaded by black people but then as soon as I'm around white people everything gets crazy and speeded up and violent. I see an old black guy get kicked in the balls by a white man who then throws a bucket of cold water on him and walks away. I see two white guys screaming at each other, the cords in their necks sticking out and spit flying while a young good-looking black female stands off to one side looking at the ground and waiting. I see a white man in a suit and broad-brimmed hat galloping toward me on horseback and I pull my oxen out of his way into a cane field and the wagon smashes some of the cane while he races past and afterwards another white guy comes running out of the field and beats the shit out of me with a bamboo cane and calls me a fucking idiot. I see a black man hanging from a tree at the edge of town and white kids throwing stones at his body and John Crow birds waiting in the top branches of the tree for the kids to get bored and go away.

And at night after everybody's come in from the fields and most of the blacks have gone to their cabins behind the greathouse which is a lot like Starport but not as fancy and not up in the hills, I have to carry food and drinks to the white people at their table who talk like I can't understand English and don't know that all they talk about is how lazy and stupid and dishonest the blacks are. There are four or five men, I can't remember them all individually because they kind of blend together and whenever I'm around them I'm scared and feel shitty or else I'm trying to get away from them but they're related, fathers and sons and brothers. Plus there are a couple of females, a wife and mother of the sons and a younger one who's either a sister or else is married to one of the sons, and there's some little white kids I try to ignore except when they tell me to bring them something or take something away.

Later the men sit out on the porch looking across the fields in front to the sea sparkling in the moonlight and I'm supposed to stand behind them and wave this palm leaf to keep the mosquitoes away while they drink and smoke and worry about money and slaves and tell weird stories about the sex lives of black people until finally they

say they're going to bed and they stumble off and leave
me by myself. With the white people gone I don't know
what to do next so I wander around the big empty house
for a while and then go outside and start toward the slave-
quarters in back when all of sudden standing in the path
in front of me there's I-Man and his Maroon brethren
Terron and Elroy and Rubber, all of them carrying
machetes and looking serious. There's blood on the
machetes and a big splash of blood across Rubber's shirt
that I figure came from the white overseer who lives in
the barn or the white clerk who has a room in the office
building by the blacksmith shop.

Before I can say anything I-Man puts his finger to his
lips to shush me. Then I see behind them in the shadows
a bunch more black people, mostly men but some women
too with little kids even, the black people I've been seeing
all day out in the fields and at the sugar factory and up in
the greathouse, the woman who was being whipped and
the old guy who got kicked and the young woman the two
overseers were fighting over, all the people who were
working alongside me like silent machines without any
thoughts or feelings.

They're carrying machetes too, plus scythes and sickles
and hatchets and they quickly brush past me following I-
Man and the other Maroons toward the greathouse. I
want to follow them but something stops me, like my feet
are suddenly made of lead and I can't walk so I have to
stand there in the bushy shadows at the edge of the big
wide lawn and watch the blacks enter the darkened house
at all the entrances, front and back and side. Except for
the steady drumming which I'm totally used to by now
like it's my own heartbeat and the sound of the wind off

the sea clattering the moonlit palms it's completely silent. I stand there for a long time wondering if maybe I was dreaming, when I hear a shriek that makes my blood go cold followed by screams and someone, a woman wailing for a second until she's abruptly shut off and then a white man is begging, No, no, please don't! and he's cut off too. Then silence again. Until I hear some glass breaking inside and then I notice someone, a child creeping on hands and knees across the porch in front. It's a blond-haired white boy barefoot in a nightgown, like five or six years old and he makes his way along the length of the porch and climbs down to the ground there and starts running straight toward where I'm standing. He comes up suddenly on me all wild-eyed and pumping his arms and legs like mad and just as he's about to pass me by I reach out and grab him and clap my hand over his shocked mouth and pull him back into the shadowy bushes and hold on to him tight.

A minute later I can see flames flaring up at the back of the house and up on the second floor somebody's smashing the windows and tossing stuff out, books fluttering down and dishes and piss pots and a tailor's dummy. The drapes on the first floor are on fire now and I can see black people with their machetes and so on coming out of the house and gathering together on the far side. Me and the white kid who's shivering in my arms back off a few more steps into the bushes as the blacks check each other out and then start running. There's about twenty or thirty of them waving bloody machetes and hatchets as they cross the great wide lawn in the moonlight headed toward a grove of live oak trees and a long sloping field where the cows are kept. The house is really on fire now, huge sprays of sparks're flying up and the sky is glowing orange and yellow.

Behind me the long driveway curves away to the road by the sea and I see in the distance the first of the white men on horseback coming with a second batch a short ways behind. The blacks have disappeared into the cow field and beyond the field is the woods and then the hills and beyond the hills is the Cockpit. There's no one left here now, no one alive but me and the little blond-haired white kid sobbing in my arms. And here come the white men riding up the driveway like mad with guns and swords glinting in the moonlight ready to slay the first black they see. They're hungry for killing a black and spattering his blood and no little white kid is going to be strong enough to save him.

Suddenly someone touches me on the shoulder and I turn and it's I-Man. He says, Comin', Bone?

What about him? I say and show him the little white kid.

Forget-tee, Bone.

Practically crying I say, Oh Rasta, I-and-I cyan't do dat!

Up to you, Bone, he says and he walks off toward the bush and disappears into the darkness.

I unwrap my arms from the white boy and release him and instantly he takes off running toward the men on horseback who have arrived in front of the house now and are shouting and firing their guns into the air look-ing crazy and wild until they see the kid. The head white man gets down off his horse real fast and sweeps the boy up in his arms, and right away the kid points straight at where I'm hiding in the bushes. The little bastard betrays me! The head white guy starts jogging toward me with his gun out ready to blow me away and several others come up behind him so I take off running, darting down behind the barns and the sugar factory where I scramble over a stone fence and plunge into the cane field there with bullets flying over my head and zipping through the cane snapping off stalks as I plow ahead like in a green endless head high sea of sugarcane expecting my next breath to be my last.

But it's not. Way out there in the middle of the cane field with my chest heaving and my legs almost too heavy to run another step I push away a clump of cane and see a hole in the ground. Quick as I can I check it out and observe that it goes a long ways in and is just big enough for a skinny kid like me to squeeze into but no regular white man can. I take one more look back at the greathouse which's all aflame now and the white guys're riding around it like they set it on fire themselves shooting their guns off in all directions even in mine still. Then I notice that a bunch of riders are torching the cane field on three sides and a bunch more are galloping their horses around to the fourth side by the road to wait there for me so I drop down on my hands and knees and crawl into the darkness of the hole in the ground.

I'm surprised and a little scared to find that the hole just keeps going, it's a tunnel and pretty soon it's pitch dark and I can't hear the gunfire and the roar of the fires and the white guys yelling anymore, all I can hear is the drumming, the same drumming as before only it's getting louder now as I crawl along the tunnel feeling my way with my hands out in front of my face. I squirm and crawl like this for hours it seems like and all the time the drums keep getting louder until finally I work my way around a sharp bend in the tunnel and up ahead I catch a glimpse of a flickering light and before I know it I've reached the end of the tunnel.

I pull myself forward and up out of it and when I stick my head up and look around I see that I've come out in the candlelit Maroon cave. I climb up out of the spinal cord hole at the rear of the skull and there's I-Man kicking back with a spliff and ol' Rubber's working out like a madman on one of those little square goatskin drums and the other Rastas, Terron and Elroy're rolling joints and everybody looks like even though they've been waiting patiently for me to get back they're relieved to see me and are ready to book. Rubber lays off the drumming and stands and stretches and the other guys do the same. Then I-Man blows out the candles one by one and leads the way back out through the mouth into the darkness.

NINETEEN

SECOND THOUGHTS

Things moved pretty fast after that and I didn't really have time like for weeks, until I left Jamaica actually, for digesting the experience of coming to know I-self so to speak and how coming to see with the lights of I-self'd changed the way I saw everything else like it was supposed to do. And did. But the next few days we just worked all day and even at night harvesting the ganja plants, me and I-Man and the other guys cutting the plants with machetes on both plots, I-Man's and Rubber's next door and then hauling them up to my cabin where the drying racks were that they'd built out of bamboo, and then as soon as the plots were cleared we chopped up the dirt again with hoes and fertilized it with this powdery old bat-shit that we had to bag and lug from a cave a long ways into the Cockpit. It was hard work, harder than any I'd done before and you had to concentrate so I didn't have much time for thinking or remembering, especially because it was so hot all the time. My head was like that kid's I'd been in slavery days, pretty much a blank except I wasn't scared or nervous about anything anymore especially white people.

After we had the dirt ready we planted the seeds for the new crop and hauled water and got the rows real soppy and for shading them while the plants were still babies we ran strings from poles and hung these humongous thin camouflage sheets that I-Man said'd been left behind in Grenada after the United States Army finished invading and went home. Dem hiding sheets spread all over de Caribbean now, mon. Dem de bes' t'ing 'bout dat invasion so as t' mek de ganja reach him fulfillment undisturbed 'neath de Jamaican sun an' den return to Babylon an' help create de peaceable kingdom dere. Jah mek de instruments of destruction come forward fe be instruments of *in*struction.

Then we spent days sorting the dried ganja plants and pressing and packing them into burlap bales, about a hundred of them that we stacked under a lean-to we built and inside my cabin so I had to move out practically and hang my hammock from a couple of trees out behind it. But only for a few days, I-Man explained. De Nighthawk soon come, he said referring I figured to some guy with a big truck because that was what he'd need for hauling this many bales out of here. I never asked much about the higher workings of the ganja trade, how it got financed and all, I just let I-Man tell me what he thought I needed to know which actually wasn't much since I was like a peon still and just did what I was told by the older heavier dudes in the posse. But I figured there were even heavier dudes in places like Kingston and Mobay or maybe the States who'd put up the money for the operation, for the camouflage sheets for instance and the plastic pails and hoes and all and for walking-around money since the only cash money I-Man or the other guys had came from dealing small load down in Mobay out of the ant farm. What they had going up here in the Cockpit was a major plantation though and that took cash no matter how much free labor we were putting in.

After a few days of chilling and mainly tending the new green shoots I got waked up in my hammock by Rubber one morning to tell me that I-Man was down in Mobay making the final arrangements with Nighthawk and he'd sent word that we were supposed to get ready for delivery the next night. What this meant was lugging all the bales of ganja on our backs, on our heads actually over hill and dale about three miles still further into the Cockpit where there was a flat space about the size of a basketball court cleared along the ridge of one of the pits and no road in or out so I finally realized that Nighthawk was a guy with a plane although it was hard to see how a regular plane could land and take off on such a small space.

We worked all that day and the next, me and Rubber and Terron and Elroy carrying the ganja from the groundation to the airfield where we stashed it under some more of Ronald Reagan's camouflage. I could only lug one bale at a time on my head but the other guys could handle two so I felt kind of useless. They didn't care though and we did a lot of joking and suchlike while we hauled the bales because spirits were up then. Everybody I guess was sniffing the end of another successful growing season and a big payday and I was starting to wonder if I

was going to get a share of the profits too and if I did
what I'd do with it. Rubber was going to buy a motorcycle,
a Honda he said all excited like it wasn't just Jap shit and
then he planned to go out to Negril and fuck American
college girls. Rubber was pretty weird-looking though,
almost comical and could only talk the native language so
I didn't think he'd score much with American females
even driving a Harley which I don't think they have in
Jamaica. Terron was into buying a huge outdoor sound
system and becoming a DJ with a friend who had a pickup
and could carry it around the island to all the dance par-
ties, and Elroy said he was going to pay for his mother to
have an operation on her hips so she could walk again
which I thought was cool. I-Man I didn't know about since
he never mentioned money except to put it down and
diss people who liked it although I'd noticed that ever
since I'd known him he always had a few bucks in his
pocket when he needed it which wasn't true of any other
Jamaican I'd met so far. Of course the only Jamaicans I
knew were really poor. But I think I-Man was one of those
guys who decided in the beginning to live the same when
he had lots of money as when he didn't have a penny and
it'd worked out that he lived somewhere in the middle all
the time and never had to think about it much one way or
the other. That's pretty much what I was planning to do
with my share if I got one.

Anyhow the next night around seven we'd finally finished hauling all the bales to the airfield and were sitting
around out there waiting for Nighthawk to make the
pickup. After a few hours of nothing happening I-Man
suddenly showed up, he like just stepped out of the bush
and touched us on our shoulders without us once hearing

him until there he was which was the way he usually came up on people, like he'd been beamed up invisible and then materialized right before your eyes. I was starting to take seriously all this stuff about I-Man being a magician that Rubber and the guys'd been telling me, an obi man they called him, even though I'd known him when he was an illegal alien escapee from an apple farm in upstate New York. Plus all the stories about those old Africans who could fly. There was even one I-Man'd told me about this famous Maroon female warrior named Nonny who could catch the slavecatchers' bullets in her pussy and turn around and bend over and shoot the bullets right back at them with her ass.

Sometime after midnight I guess it was I-Man stood up and said time to light the torches and led us out into the field where there were these sticks in the ground with dried palm leaves tied around the top. By the time he'd lit the first one I heard the plane that he must've heard earlier so we started running from one torch to the other lighting them real fast. When they were all going I saw they made like a rectangle of lights and pretty soon the plane buzzed past and cut a wide turn and came back the other way a few hundred feet from the ground just over the trees and then dropped down at the edge of the field and skidded across it and came to a stop at the end right next to where we'd stacked the ganja bales.

It went real fast then. The plane was like one of those old-fashioned two-engine jobs you see on the late movie and Nighthawk who was a fat white guy in a muscle shirt and Bermuda shorts and high-tops jumps out by the side door carrying an Uzi, the first I'd ever seen up close and says for us in American to hurry the fuck up, I'm running late, like he's got a dentist appointment. Me and the posse go right to work then loading the bales while I-Man and Nighthawk stand off to one side watching and smoking cigarettes and talking business I guess, but then as I'm passing by them with a bale on my head I hear Nighthawk say, Who's the white kid?

I pass my bale to Terron who's doing the stacking inside and go back and hear I-Man say, Baby Doc, and the guy says, No shit? Doc's got a white kid? and I keep going because we're like in a line and Rubber's practically stepping on my heels and grab another bale and come back. This time they're arguing a little, I-Man and Nighthawk who says, I don't give a fuck what you thought.

Next time I go by Nighthawk's saying, Don't sweat it, man, it'll be there tomorrow, next day at the latest. I-Man's pissed, I can tell, he's got that dark pulled-down face on with pursed lips and his arms crossed on his chest and a few seconds later he pulls away from Nighthawk and starts helping us finish the loading.

The second we're done Nighthawk without saying goodbye or thanks or anything takes his Uzi and climbs inside his plane, closes the door and cranks up his engines and while we're running off the field he turns the plane and aims it back the way he came in. It rumbles across the little field looking like a pregnant pigeon or something, real slow and heavy and I'm wondering if it can even take off with that load but at the end of the field it turns and comes back toward us again going faster and faster and then it's off the ground and zooms over our heads just clearing the palm trees behind us and in a few seconds it's gone and in a few more you couldn't even hear it.

*   *   *

What happened was the guy who was supposed to give Nighthawk the money for I-Man had come in from the States late and got hung up in customs in Mobay or something so Nighthawk had to fly out to the Cockpit without the money and without even his own pay, he said. But because the deal'd already been made for delivery of the ganja in Haiti the next day and couldn't be postponed or the whole thing'd come apart Nighthawk had agreed to go ahead as planned and get paid when he got back from Haiti and I-Man'd have to do the same.

I guess this kind of fuck-up happened a lot because once Nighthawk was gone I-Man didn't seem pissed anymore and the next morning he came out to my cabin and said for me to come with him to Mobay fe sattar at the ant farm which I figured meant I was going to get a share of the profits just like the rest of the posse. This was excellent because I hadn't had any honest money of my own for a long time. Since back when I was dealing weed to Bruce and the Adirondack Iron. Plus it was tourist season now and I-Man wanted me to follow up on my old idea of me dealing to the white party animals in the hotels who were too scared of black people to buy ganja from them. I'd thought he'd forgotten all about that but like he said, Everyt'ing in him season, Bone. Everyt'ing in him time.

We hooked a ride with a beer truck and got down to Mobay and out to the ant farm by late afternoon and chilled that night in one of the inner chambers with Prince Shabba who said the rest of the posse was playing in a reggae band downtown at Doctors Cave which is this famous beach and general hangout for rich white people and a good place for dealing small-load herb. It was a mellow night, just me and Shabba and I-Man listening to tapes on I-Man's box and smoking from the stash and talking Rasta and the next morning I left the ant farm early to check out the scene at the Holiday Inn and some of the other hotels where the package tourists like from Indiana and other places in the Midwest go.

Mainly I was on a research mission to see how hard it'd be to hang out by the pools and the bars and beachfronts which were off limits except to hotel guests and talk to people. And like I thought, it turned out real easy for me on account of being white to stroll pretty much wherever I wanted to and I talked to quite a few party animals of all different ages and interests and pretty soon had more orders for ganja than I could keep in my head and had to cop a pencil and paper from one of the waiters at the Casa Montego to make notes. It wasn't much, a quarter ounce here, a half there but it added up fast and I was psyched.

By around three in the afternoon I'm headed back to the ant farm to get the goods so I can make my deliveries before party time and I'm really stoked because this is the first time I've been able to do a job for I-Man and the posse that nobody else can do even though it's only on account of the color of my skin. The ant farm is located a few miles out beyond Rose Hall off the Falmouth Road and when I come up on the path that leads down through the bushes to it I see this same dark brown Benz parked by the side of the road that'd blown by me awhile ago right after I'd given up hitching and decided to walk the rest of the way in. Anyhow I'm thinking, Cool, this is the money guy from the States as promised so I bop on down but when I get there nobody's around. At least not out in the yard in front of the entrance where I'd expected them to be. Just I-Man's box playing a Black Uhuru tape real slow like the batteries are low again and his Jah-stick lying on the ground.

I pushed open the main door and walked into the first room, past the picture gallery of Martin Luther King and the other heroes and into the next, and so on through several more chambers but nobody's there and I can't hear anybody talking. Weird, I'm thinking but I was curious to see how a deal like this goes down in case I ever got the chance to do one myself someday so I kept on wandering through the many inter-connected chambers of the ant farm expecting every time I turned a corner to see I-Man being handed a leather briefcase full of crisp new American bills like on TV.

It's sort of like a video game maze back in there and you can wander around in circles for days but once you're used to it from living there like I was you pretty much know where you are all the time and can generally remember the way out in spite of there being no windows, even though all you can remember exactly is the last room you were in before this one and all you can predict is the next room off of it. Anyhow I'm standing in the middle of one of the center rooms where we sometimes gathered fe deal wi' de chillum and some mellow drumming when I hear a lot of movement on the other side of the bamboo wall and then the curtain is brushed away and in walks Nighthawk with his Uzi and right behind him is Jason who I remember from the Mothership and he's got a gun too, a short-nosed blue niner and right behind Jason is a white guy in a safari jacket I've never seen before.

They're looking real pissed all three and in a wicked

rush. Nighthawk grabs me by the shoulder and says, How the fuck d'we get outa here, kid! and the white guy who I guess is the American with the money says, Jesus, who's *this*? and that's the moment when I realized that something terrible'd happened.

Jason looks at me like he doesn't recognize who I am but Nighthawk says, Doc's kid the Rasta told me.

The white guy in the safari jacket goes, *Doc's* kid? Doc doesn't have any white kid, for Christ's sake. The fucking Rasta's fulla shit.

No, I seen him last night, Nighthawk says. He was workin' for the Rasta.

The American guy says, Well, get the little bastard to tell us how to get the fuck outa here and do him. And hurry the fuck up, he says and steps back like he doesn't want to get any of my blood on his jacket.

Nighthawk shoved me back against the wall and I banged off of it and fell down and when I looked up he was standing over me with the barrel of his Uzi staring me in the eye. C'mon, kid, where's the fucking exit?

I said to go out the door behind me and keep bearing left which was approximately correct and as close as I could say anyhow. I can lead you out better than tell you though, I said.

Just then Jason put his face down by me and said, Bone? Dat really you wid all dem dreadlocks, mon?

I go, Yeah. Wussup, Jason.

He smiles and turns to the American and tells him I'm Doc's kid all right and I used to live with Doc up on the hill but I ran off with the Rasta last summer.

Fuck! the American says.

Then Nighthawk says, We shouldn't do a white kid anyhow, man. No matter whose kid he is. Too much trouble, especially since he's American. The tourist board'll go nuts.

Yeah, fine. The fucking tourist board. Look, do what you want. I don't actually give a shit one way or the other, the whole fuckin' island's a fuckin' monkey house. I'm outa here tonight anyhow.

He moves for the exit and then to me he says, Kid, if you're smart you'll go back to Doc's house and you'll stay put there till you grow up. If you was one of Doc's black kids you'd be dead meat by now. I don't give a shit myself. Next time you might not be so lucky.

I go, Thanks for the advice, man, and he shook his head like he'd gotten real sick of me fast and disappeared into the next chamber. Nighthawk lowered his Uzi and followed him. When Jason got to the door he turned back and said, See you up on de hill, mon, and gave me a toothy smile that actually looked friendly and was gone.

After I couldn't hear the American and Nighthawk and Jason anymore and figured by now they'd found their way out I stood up and brushed myself off. I pretty much knew by then what I was going to find but I went looking for it anyhow. I headed for the rooms way at the back where I myself would've run if three guys like these'd showed up with guns and no plans to pay me for my services. In one of the rooms when I pushed the curtain away I saw poor old Prince Shabba lying facedown in a pool of blood with a bunch of holes in his back where the Uzi'd really ripped him up.

I stepped around his body and went into the next room and there against the far wall was I-Man sitting on the sandy floor all slumped over with his skinny little legs sticking out and his eyes and mouth open. His face was empty inside though. I-Man was gone, flown off to Africa. There was a jagged hole in the center of his forehead and a whole lot of blood running down the bamboo wall behind his head into the sand. Oh man, it was a horrible sight. Especially that single dark blue bullet hole which I could see had been put there by Jason's niner.

You can understand if I just keep talking here, okay?

I didn't know what to do then. I wasn't scared or anything although I probably should've been. All I wanted was to get out of there, to get as far from the ant farm as I could, so I could think about everything and try to make sense of my feelings and thoughts which at that moment were the most mixed up they had ever been in my life. Somehow the whole terrible thing felt like it was my fault and there was no way left for me now to make it right.

When I got back out to the yard I-Man's box was sitting on the ground finally silent and dead as ol' I-Man himself. I picked it up and put it on my shoulder and took up I-Man's Jah-stick and walked back up the path to the road where the Benz'd been parked and started hiking in the direction of Mobay. It didn't make me feel any better to think of I-Man as flown off to Africa. Actually when it came right down to it, like now, I didn't believe any of that shit.

TWENTY

BONE PHONES HOME

When you're in a country full of black people and you're a white kid and don't want to stick out the best thing is to go hang where the white folks gather. Which in my case was Doctors Cave in Mobay, this private beach club with a bunch of fancy shops and restaurants in the neighborhood and white people all over the place strolling hand in hand and buying things and getting suntanned and feeling safe from attack or deception by the natives. Plus since I didn't have any ganja to sell now it was an excellent place to spare-change a few bucks while I figured out what to do next.

That first night I crashed in the back seat of an unlocked Volvo I found in the lot behind the Beach View Hotel on Gloucester Avenue and the next morning after I'd successfully scored for change a few times despite my dreads with my story about being left behind by my teenaged Christian tour group I was sitting on a bench eating a meat patty for breakfast and reading a copy of the *Daily Gleaner* I'd found in a trashcan, and over on the second page I saw a little article stuck in the middle of all these other articles about shootings and machete choppings and suchlike about two unidentified men found shot dead in Mount Zion. That's the name of the town the ant farm was in so I knew it was about Prince Shabba and I-Man. Like no way I was going to go to the cops and identify their bodies, but I did think I ought to hitch out to Accompong maybe and tell I-Man's old lady and Rubber and the guys what had happened, so that's what I did.

I was all burdened down by guilt feelings then, partly on account of not being able to help I-Man at the moment when he most needed me although I don't know what I could've done to distract those dudes so he could get away. Still I might've thought of something. I'm a pretty good talker especially when it comes to bullshitting white people. That was the other thing that had me all twisted up. Whiteness. Even more than being Doc's son it was my white skin that'd saved me from being blown away like Prince Shabba and I-Man. I knew if I wasn't white, if I'd been a real Rasta-boy like I'd been pretending to be I'd be dead now.

When I got out to Accompong that afternoon though, right away I saw it was a mistake. They didn't need me to bring the news. I probably should've realized it but everybody already knew what'd happened at the ant farm—Jamaica's a really small country and news travels fast even without telephones especially when it concerns somebody as well known on the ganja circuit as I-Man. Anyhow I went to I-Man's old lady first but she wouldn't even talk to me. I'd never actually learned her name, I-Man'd only called her his 'oman and introducing people to each other by name wasn't his style exactly but I was ashamed I'd never even asked. She was a short stocky lady with a hard face and when I knocked on the door to her and I-Man's cabin she came to the door with a little pick'ny-kid on her hip and when she saw who it was she just waved me away like I was a fly and closed the door in my face.

Everybody else in the village, the guys hanging out at the general store and the bar and the kids who used to be real friendly all just turned away when they saw me coming or watched me from a distance with cold dark faces. It was grim. Finally I went out to I-Man's groundation where I found Rubber watering the baby plants by himself but even he didn't want to see me or talk about what had happened. I tried a couple of times to act friendly like before and introduced the subject by saying stuff like, You heard about I-Man I guess, but he just nodded and went on with his work like I wasn't there. It looked like he was taking control of I-Man's plants and didn't want me around to help him or even witness it.

People weren't like making physical threats against me or anything but for the first time it felt dangerous up there amongst the Maroons and I figured it'd be best if I got out of there before dark so I went up to my old cabin and got my backpack and my belongings. While I was there I saw my old machete leaning in a corner that I-Man'd given me and taught me how to use for all the different tasks. I'd used it as a plow and a shovel and a hoe and an ax and a gigantic jackknife and a sword all in one, and I thought, man, I've earned that at least, so I took the machete and the sharpening file too. I didn't say goodbye or anything to Rubber, just walked off toward the village and then down the long slope to the main road.

When I got out to the road I set my pack down and I-Man's box and leaned my Jah-stick against them to start hitching but for a while there weren't any vehicles coming so I checked out my machete and started sharpening it with the file. Pretty soon it was like razor sharp and I tried that old hair test where you pull out a hair and slice it in half and then all of a sudden I'm sawing off all my dreadlocks one by one. It only took a minute and they were gone, lying at my feet like a pile of dead snakes. I leaned down and scooped them up in my hands and carried them back into the bushes a ways and laid them gently on the ground there and patted them like saying goodbye to a sweet friend or a pet you have to abandon. Then I came back to the road where my stuff was and continued hitching and the third car that passed stopped and picked me up. It was a Baptist minister, a fat black guy sweating in a suit and tie who drove me all the way in to Mobay singing hymns in this deep loud voice and dropped me off right in front of Doctors Cave.

That night I couldn't find any unlocked cars behind the hotels along the Gloucester Avenue strip and finally real late I sneaked onto the St. James Hospital grounds which're like a park with a fence around it and camped under some bushes near the fence so I could climb back over and hit the street real quick if I had to. For a while I lay there with my head on my backpack for a pillow thinking about my troubles and how much I was missing I-Man already and what a little turd I was for trying not to be white when all the time I'd been enjoying many of the

benefits of the white race, like still being alive for instance.
I thought no wonder the Maroons were pissed at me, they
probably figured I'd helped set the whole thing up and
was working for Nighthawk and was only coming back to
Accompong to try and rip them off a second time.

It was hard to fall asleep, due to my turbulent thoughts
of course but also from the ambulances coming and
going plus the action on the street, mostly drunk or
stoned tourists heading back to their hotels from the
beach bars. But finally it quieted down and I was just starting my nod when I heard a cop whistle and heard somebody running real hard. I peered out through the fence
to the sidewalk which was right next to it and here came
two little Jamaican kids maybe ten or twelve years old running like mad and half a block behind them a red-striper
was in hot pursuit with his gun out blowing his whistle
and hollering for them to stop or he'll shoot. As the kids
race past where I'm hiding the one in front tosses something over the fence and it lands almost on my head, a
ladies' pocketbook and then they're gone and not till the
cop runs past a few seconds later and I can't hear them
anymore do I pull the pocketbook up to me and take a
look inside.

It was the usual ladies' items, makeup and Kleenexes
and suntan lotion and also a suede wallet with a snap but
when I open it it's empty, no money, no credit cards, until
I look inside this one compartment and find a Kentucky
driver's license with a picture of a good-looking silver-
haired woman on it and also a telephone calling card
from AT&T. Excellent discovery, I'm thinking. If only I
had the woman's phone number I could use the card and
reach out and touch someone, although up to that

moment there hadn't been anybody I'd wanted to reach out and touch except I-Man and not even AT&T could connect me to him now. Then I noticed this little black address book and inside the woman had foolishly filled in the ID section and there was her home phone number. Cool. Now I could call anybody in the world if I wanted to, at least until the woman from Kentucky reported her card was stolen.

I went into my backpack and pulled out my own wallet, a little canvas job that I always kept there because it didn't have anything in it except my phony ID and a few phone numbers people'd given me over the years and the clipping about the fire from the Plattsburgh newspaper, and there it was, Russ's Aunt Doris's number in Keene, New York that he'd given to me the day he split off from me at the Ridgeways' place on East Hill. I hadn't thought of it until that exact moment but once it was possible, once I like had that lady's AT&T card and her home phone number in my hand all I could think about was hearing my ol' compadre Russ's voice in my ear.

I shoved all my stuff further under the bushes so you couldn't see it unless you knew exactly where to look and walked across the hospital grounds straight into the lobby like I was there to visit my mom who was a patient and I did not realize it was after hours. But there was nobody in the waiting room except this nurse at the reception desk who was half asleep and she didn't even look up as I crossed the room to a pay phone by the elevator door.

I put all the numbers through and the phone rang and rang way up there in upstate New York and I thought, Shit, it must be really late there and they probably don't even know where Russ is now. I was about to hang up when I heard Russ himself say H'lo?

It's me, man. Wussup.

Who.

Me. Bone, for chrissake! My voice must've changed, I'm thinking.

Who? he said again so I finally had to tell him Chappie but when he heard that it really flipped him out and he goes, Wow, Chappie, no shit, where the fuck *are* you, man? and so forth.

I told him Jamaica and he said you mean the country? and I said yeah and that blew him away for a while. When he finally came back I tried to tell him a little of how I got there but as soon as I started I realized there was no way I could fill him in even if I had a year to do it. Too much had happened. Plus I'd changed in ways that even I didn't understand yet. Russ who was pretty smart was never what you'd call sensitive when it came to other people's lives so I mainly asked questions and when the conversation came back to me and what's happening in Jamaica and drugs and babes and all I just got vague and changed the subject.

I was surprised he was still at his aunt's but he said he'd gone to work in construction last summer for his uncle and stayed there because they'd let him live in a room in the basement. I'm like a fucking mole in a hole, man, he said. His mom'd basically washed her hands of him which was mutual, he said and everything that'd happened in Au Sable, the fire and all had blown over and been forgotten and he'd even gotten his old Camaro back.

Guess what my first job with my uncle was, he said.

Beats the shit out of me, man, I said already pretty

bored but starting to hatch an interesting new idea. Hey listen, I said, there's something I need to ask you, man.

My first job, right? I hadda clean up the Ridgeways' place that we trashed, you remember that? Oh man, was that place a fucking mess and it looked like you did some heavy damage on your own, man, after I split. Lots of busted windows, man. But don't worry, I never mentioned it was us. Or you.

Thanks. Listen, Russ—

Oh an' wait till you hear this, man. This'll fuckin' cheer you up. Your mom and stepdad? They split, man.

They got *divorced?* I said really psyched.

No, no, dipshit, they *split.* They moved away.

Oh. Where?

He didn't know. Someplace out near Buffalo where my stepdad got a job as a prison guard which sounded like the perfect job for him. I asked him when and he said right after my grandmother died.

Grandma *died?* I said.

Oh man, wow, like I'm sorry, I forgot you wouldn't've known that. How long you been in Jamaica, man? That happened in the fall, October I think. Heart attack or something, he said. He didn't know the details, he'd only heard it from his aunt who knew him and me were friends.

That pretty much settled it. My mom and my stepdad were gone which made my hometown of Au Sable all of a sudden look seriously tempting especially since Russ was doing okay over in Keene and we could still hang. Grandma was dead which made me sad and all but not too much because we hadn't exactly been buddies and besides it freed me from any possible future connections to my mom and stepdad. They wouldn't even know I'd come back. Any life I ended up leading in Au Sable now would be my own. I could even go back to school if I wanted. What had been only an interesting new idea now turned into a plan.

Listen, man, I said, I want to come back. I'm ready to come home now.

He was shocked. Here? Gimme a fucking *break*, he said and went on about what an asshole place Au Sable was and how everything and everyone there sucked the big one.

But I said no, it'd gotten too tense for me here and I needed to come back to the States and lead a normal life and get my shit together for the future. I was even thinking about college someday, I said although actually that thought'd never crossed my mind in my whole life until I said it and I might've been lying. It was a moment of weakness and I was pretty confused right then.

But I don't have any money for plane fare, I told him so I was wondering if he could maybe loan me three hundred bucks say and I'd pay him back as soon as I got a job which I'd do right away, probably at the mall.

Now he was really shocked. Stunned. You're shitting me, man! he said. The fucking Plattsburgh *mall*? And go to *school*? In Au *Sable*? When you could be kicking back in fucking Jamaica drinking excellent rum and cokes and smoking humongous spliffs of ganja and screwing Jamaican babes under the tropical moon! I heard Jamaican babes are the best, man, and they really dig white guys. That true?

Russ, it's not like you think, I said. Nothing is.

Yeah, sure, for you maybe but if like the two of us were down there together, man, everything'd be incredibly cool. You're too young to be there alone, man. There's like too much you don't know yet. I'm seventeen now and can kind of show you the way, you know what I'm saying? I'll tell you what, Chapstick. I'll raise some money, I'll sell my Camaro, that's how much I love you, man, only *I'll* come *there* instead of you coming here. This place rots, man. It truly rots. And besides, my aunt and uncle're trying to get me the fuck outa here anyhow. They want their basement back and they're always on my case to like join the fucking army. But I got this guy I know, he's willing to give me seven hundred bucks for the Camaro. Cash. It's a piece of shit anyhow. I'll sell it and be there in two days. Less, even. I'll fucking *be* in Montego Bay tomorrow. Like where'll I meet you, man? Just tell me where we can hook up and I'll *be* there. We can deal a little ganja, hang out on the beach, screw all the local babes and fucking *party*, man! And if you *still* want to be a wuss and like come back here and work at the mall flipping fucking burgers at McDonald's and go back to the little red schoolhouse, fine. Do it. I'll even pay your way home.

I didn't think he'd show up in Jamaica tomorrow, or ever. I didn't even think he'd sell his Camaro but I said okay anyhow and told him I'd be hanging out by the clock tower in the main square in downtown Mobay. It was a place I almost never went and now would avoid completely, just in case.

Mobay, huh. That what they call it?

Yeah. Montego Bay.

Cool. You just hang there, man, and if I'm not in Mobay by the clock tower tomorrow night I'll be there the next. And Chappie, he said.

Yeah?

Line us up a couple of buff Jamaican chicks, man. I got a permanent boner these days and it needs some of that black pussy to stroke it.

Yeah. Sure.

All *right*! he said.

I told him I had to go then so I said goodbye and hung up, wondering if Russ'd always been such a dickhead only I hadn't noticed on account of I was a dickhead myself. And I was pissed, pissed at Russ for everything he'd said and at myself for being such a wuss and wanting to go back to Au Sable in order to get my shit together like I couldn't do it just as good here or anywhere in the world. I'd been sad and lonely though when I'd called Russ due to everything that had happened and I couldn't blame him for not having the equipment to understand. He was who he was. But if I was sad and lonely when I called him I was even sadder and lonelier now.

I flopped down in this plastic chair next to the phone and was putting Russ's aunt's phone number back into my wallet when this other piece of paper slipped out and fell to the floor and just then a little breeze crossed the lobby and blew the paper across the room like in a dance. I was almost too bummed to do anything about it but I got curious suddenly about what was on the paper so I stood up and chased it across the tile floor of the lobby toward the open door and managed to snatch it up just as it got to the door. Then I took a look. It was my own handwriting and said *N. Riley* who I'd never heard of with what looked like a telephone number and area code I didn't know, 414.

I'm not usually superstitious but I guess I was kind of spacey then from not having smoked any herb for two whole days almost and my idiotic conversation with Russ. It's a message, I'm thinking, a secret coded message sent from I-Man imitating my handwriting with instructions about what to do next and as usual he wants me to do some headwork on my own in order to get it. I'm thinking maybe 414 is the area code for Jamaica and I-Man's secret name is N. Riley and like the N. stands for Nonny after the old Maroon female warrior who could catch the British bullets with her pussy and fire them back from her ass, and the letters in Riley are supposed to be rearranged. I studied them for a minute and came up with I-LYRE which made complete sense if it really was a message from I-Man since a lyre is like a harp that angels use. By now I was really psyched.

I went straight to the phone and punched the numbers in, using the AT&T card of my Kentucky friend like before. Man, I'm thinking, this is going to be wicked incredible. I was so stoked to hear I-Man's voice again that when a woman's voice came on and said, Yeah? I just blurted out, Lemme speak to I-Man.

Who?

Then I realized of course I-Man wouldn't be using his own voice anymore so I said, Jeez, I'm sorry, I hope I didn't sound rude. Is this like. . . Nonny?

Yeah. This's Nancy, she says and something about the voice is familiar. It's slurred and a little buzzed like it's coming through a cheap speaker even though it's a clear enough connection.

Ah. . . this isn't Nonny?

It sure ain't, honey. I thought you said Nancy. Sorry 'bout that. But you can talk to *me* if you want, she said and laughed like a crackhead, a little off. I remembered then.

The area code 414 was for Milwaukee, Wisconsin and I was talking to Nancy Riley. Sister Rose's mother.

Yeah, well. . . I guess I'm calling for Sister Rose actually.

Sister Rose? You mean my Rosie? Jesus Christ, whaddayou, some kind of church or something? I don't need this—

Wait, don't hang up! I'm like a friend of hers, of Rosie. I'm the one who sent her home to you, I'm the one who got her away from that guy Buster Brown. Remember? I. . . I'm just calling to see if she got there okay and all.

Oh yeah, she says. You're the kid with the money. Yeah, she got here fine. You know, that was Buster's money, I found out, and you stole it off him. If he ever finds you, kid, he'll fucking kill you, believe me.

That's cool, I said. So is Rose there? Can I speak to her?

No.

No I can't speak to her or no she's not there?

There was a long silence. I'm thinking if I ever get back to the States I'm going to find this woman and kill her and then I'm going after Buster. Finally she says, Both.

Both what?

You can't speak to her and she's not here. Rose. . . Rose passed on last September.

I didn't know what to say to that so for a long time we just listened to each other breathe. Then I said, C'mon. Sister Rose didn't die.

She was real sick when she got here. That was one sick little girl you put on the bus, mister.

The *fuck* she was! What'd she die of, bitch?

Pneumonia, if you want to know. And you don't have to talk to *me* that way. I've been through hell. I tried to save her but I'm sick myself, you know what I'm saying? Rosie was my little girl but they took her away from me like it was my fault she was sick. It was yours though. You never should've put her on that bus. That's what did it, she said.

I did some deep breathing so I wouldn't lose it on the phone and calmly asked her where was Rose buried. I knew someday I'd be able to go there and put flowers on her grave and I would, but I didn't tell her that.

The woman obviously didn't even know where her own daughter was buried and just said it was none of my business unless I was willing to help pay for the funeral costs. It's expensive, you know, and I'm broke, mister. I don't even have enough money to put a little gravestone up. You could help with that, if you're really her friend like you say. Five hundred bucks'd cover it, I think. You could just put it on your credit card and like wire it to me.

Lady, I said, for what you've done you should burn in hell forever.

Yeah, well, fuck you too, she snarled. I already am burning in hell. And I hope Buster finds you and cuts your balls off, she said and hung up.

For a few minutes I stood there in the hospital lobby with the receiver in my hand looking at it like it was a bug. Then I set it on the hook. I had I-Man's message in my other hand and still thought of it as I-Man's message even though it was about Sister Rose and not him or me so I put it into my mouth and chewed it up and swallowed it.

Later I was back under the bushes on the hospital grounds lying with my head on my backpack and trying to organize my thoughts and keep my feelings out of it at least long enough to decide what to do tomorrow so I could fall asleep tonight. My main man I-Man had flown back to lie beside his ascendants in Africa where I could never go. And all the doors of Accompong were closed to me forever and the ant farm was a busted-apart house of death that I never wanted to see again. Sister Rose was gone to wherever little kids go when they die, and I was too old to go there now and start life over with her—I almost wasn't a kid anymore and knew too much and was too strong and wily now to die without a struggle. And Russ, my homeboy, ol' Russ was basically off my screen. Permanent. My moment of weakness had passed over me like a dark cloud and gone and with Grandma dead and Mom and my stepdad moved to Buffalo, even though it would be more peaceful for me in Au Sable there was no more reason for me to go there than anywhere else in America. Au Sable was a town like any other where I'd be just another homeless kid scraping by trying to stay off drugs and not catch AIDS. Forget-tee, I said to myself.

Here in Jamaica though I was a foreigner and an illegal alien and white besides and I couldn't spare-change on the streets of Mobay many more days before the red-stripers busted me for vagrancy, and without a reliable source of ganja anymore I couldn't deal to the tourists for a living and raise enough money to rent a regular room. Things were truly grim. I'd never been so bummed.

I hated doing it but it was time to take the American guy's advice. Time to head for the Mothership.

TWENTY-ONE

BONE'S REVENGE

In the morning when I woke up to the sound and diesel smell of trucks and buses blatting past on Gloucester Avenue next to my head practically I didn't know this would be my next-to-last day in Jamaica, but I wouldn't've done anything different if I had. I would've gone up to the Mothership anyhow same as I did and I would've pretty much done up there what I did irregardless. I told myself I was going because like the American guy said at the ant farm, it was the only place on the island where I was safe now but actually I had some unfinished business with my father, with Doc, with Pa, and that's why I went. I didn't know what the unfinished business was exactly but I was pretty sure it had to do with me betraying I-Man to him the night that I-Man hooked up with Evening Star, the night of my birthday party. That was like a sin which is different from a crime and it still weighed heavily on my

mind so to speak and I guess I wanted to somehow undo
it if I could, especially now that I-Man was dead and I
needed my father, Doc, Pa, for that.

I spare-changed for a while and by mid-morning had a
few bucks in my pocket plus a meat patty breakfast under
my belt so I cut over to the marketplace where I caught a
bus like I-Man and I'd done the first time and rode up out
of Mobay on the long winding road to the village of
Montpelier and got off by the little grassy lane that led up
to the Mothership. It was a real pretty day with a fresh
breeze blowing and the sun out but not too hot and the
local people as I passed them were friendlier toward me
than I remembered from before, I guess on account of my
Jah-stick and backpack and the box which maybe made me
look like I'd come from a far place like Australia and was
returning home. Or probably they just remembered me
from my birthday party last summer and were glad to see
me back again. I liked the local people, the farmers and
suchlike and the women and kids who lived in the little
houses and cabins in the bush all around the greathouse
on the hill and who it's possible were the descendants of
people who'd been the slaves there, and it made me happy
that they seemed to remember and like me too, so when
they smiled and waved I smiled and waved back like mad
and shook my Jah-stick in the air like it was a spear and I
was on a sacred mission to deal with the dragon in his cave
who'd terrorized the villagers for centuries. That's a fan-
tasy, I know but that's how I think sometimes.

Finally I was over the top of the hill looking down at
Mobay and came to the sign STARPORT and turned in at
the stone gate and walked up the long driveway past the
terraced flower gardens and all the strange white animals

with the red eyes and mouths and marched up the wide front steps to the greathouse. It was real quiet and I couldn't see anybody not even the guy who worked in the gardens or the woman, his wife who did the laundry and all but I remembered it was the heat of the day and they never worked then anyhow, but there weren't any cars in the parking area I noticed and no one out at the pool either which was unusual. I'd never seen the place empty before and kind of liked it.

I hollered, Yo, Pa! and Yo, Evening Star! a couple times and finally decided the place was mine for the time being. I took a cold Red Stripe from the fridge and wandered into the livingroom where I'd dropped my stuff and scrounged around till I found some cigarettes, loosies in a silver box. I took a handful and started smoking and because I hadn't had any for a few days got instantly high although not like with skunk of course and it wore off right away. Then I noticed Pa's CD player by his chair and I thought I'm pretty nervous and this'd be a good chance to finally hear those classical CDs I took from the Ridgeways' summerhouse in Keene so I went into my pack and pulled them out.

I was thinking about that place in Keene now anyhow due to the similarities of me being alone there and alone here and with both houses being old and up on a hill with great views and I was noticing how different I was now from how I was then only a little less than a year ago. Naturally in lots of ways I was still the same person but the differences were real and pretty amazing and I hoped permanent because in spite of how things'd turned out I never wanted to go back to being the sad fucked-up kid I was a year ago.

The guys who'd made all the CDs had these mostly unpronounceable names which was definitely not like typical rock or reggae bands except for this one that attracted my attention not only because I could pronounce it, Charles Ives but because IVES was in big letters and seemed like an excellent Rasta name and plus some of the songs had names like The Unanswered Question and The See'r and All the Way Around and Back which sounded like they might be Rasta songs or at least spiritual, so I snapped that one in and kicked back in Pa's chair and listened to it. I guess I was like still wishing for a message from I-Man in Africa to tell me what to do next so I listened to this I'ves guy more careful than I would've otherwise and accidentally got really into his songs, most of which didn't have any words but that didn't matter because when they did have words they were sung like in opera and I could barely understand them. But it was the band music I was into, all these trumpets and violins coming at me from different directions at different speeds and loudness but linked together anyhow. No one instrument stood out so I figured Ras I'ves must be the songwriter and probably led the band too although he might've been the piano player. I don't think he did any of the singing.

I sat there for a couple of hours and played the CD over and over and the more I listened the stronger and steadier inside I felt until I was sure that I-Man was using his ol' compadre Ras I'ves to drum me into shape and clarity the same way the Cockpit Rastas late at night used their African drumming out on their groundations sitting around the chillum together to see into the depths and the heights of I. I figured Ras I'ves must be a white guy due to a lot of the songs having white names like Three Places in New England and General William Booth Enters into Heaven but it was obvious listening to him that he was a true heavy Rasta anyhow and I was starting to think that maybe *that* was the message I-Man was sending me, that even though I was a white kid I could still become a true heavy Rasta myself someday but only as long as I didn't ever forget I was a white kid, just like black people could never forget they were black people. He was telling me in a world like ours which is divided into white and black that was how you finally came to know I.

Along about five I heard a car coming up the driveway and it turned out to be the black Buick, Pa's government car. The driver stopped by the steps and let Pa out and then turned and went back the way he'd come. Pa I could instantly see was seriously toasted, swinging and swaying as he came slowly up the steps and grinding his teeth like from speedballs so I decided this might not be the best time to tell him his son had returned to the fold. I grabbed my stuff and ran up the stairs and down the hallway to what used to be my room at the end and didn't remember till I got there that I'd left the Ras I'ves CD playing. It was too late to go back so I just chilled and let him deal with it. I could hear Pa hollering downstairs for Evening Star and yelling, Where the hell *is* everybody, for Christ's sake! and mumbling to himself as he walked from room to room.

Then a little while later I heard another car drive up, Evening Star's Range Rover from the sound of it and here comes a whole bunch of white American female voices including Evening Star's plus one Jamaican guy laughing that when he said, Me gwan fe kill de goat now, I recognized as Jason. A couple of the females said like, Oh-h-h no-o-oo! but they were only kidding and laughed and pretty soon there was the sound of splashing and diving from the pool where I guessed everyone'd gone for a swim, except Jason I figured and Pa who I'd never seen swim even once the whole time.

Downstairs then I heard Evening Star in the livingroom saying, What the hell are you listening to? and Pa who was somewhere else, probably in the kitchen says, Beats the shit out of me. I dunno, I think it was on when I came in, he says sounding fairly mellow so I decide this's as good a time as any to make my appearance.

I don't know why but I put my pack on and brought my Jah-stick. I guess I wanted to like make a grand entrance descending the staircase which I did and they both watched me in silence as I came walking slowly down to the livingroom. Then when I got to the bottom step Evening Star came rushing over to me and wrapped me up in her arms smelling like bread and I could see on her shoulder and neck a light sweat and almost licked it but didn't. She said, Oh Bone, thanks and praise! Thanks and praise to *Jah*, Bone! We've been so *worried* about you, darlin'. *Look*! she says to Pa releasing me then and turning me around so he can see me better. He's *back*! she says. Your pick'ny's *back*! and Pa gets this squinty shit-eating grin on his face like he can almost see me through the haze.

Mi pick'ny, he said and he floated his hand out in the air toward me so I shook it but it was like shaking a cold banana and I let go of it real quick.

Doc's not feeling too good, Evening Star says to me

and I go, Yeah, I see. He looked really bad actually, even thinner than before and gray-faced with dark circles under his eyes and he didn't look like he'd had a bath in a long time either.

Hard week, dear? she said slightly sarcastic but Southern so you can't really tell.

Yeah, you could say that, he says and drops down in his chair and notices the Ras I'ves which is still playing and says, What the *fuck* is that? and twitches like it hurts him to hear it. Ol' Ras I'ves is deep into Central Park in the Dark then so that's what I say, Central Park in the Dark, and Pa cringes and turns away.

I *hate* that shit, he says. Turn it the fuck off!

Evening Star reached down to the player and switched it off and said to me, C'mon in the kitchen, dear. Your daddy's in a *foul* temper but *I* want to hear all about your adventures. I want to find out where you-all've *been* all these months. We were afraid you'd gone back to the *States*, she said. That is, until Jason told us he'd run into you out there at Mount Zion.

He said that?

Yes he surely did, only a few days ago. He said he saw you with I-Man, poor thing, and we were *so* worried about y'all after they found I-Man shot to death. It was drugs, wasn't it? I hope *you* weren't involved. Bone honey, tell me you weren't involved. You've *got* to tell me everything, darlin'. *Everything*. There's *so* many rumors floating around. What *happened?* she asked but immediately turned and headed for the kitchen. I dropped my backpack and Jah-stick and followed her with a few questions of my own but she'd already started rattling in her high excitement mode about tonight's menu, roast goat that

Jason's going to barbecue for us and some ex*qui*site basmati rice dear sweet Rita's brought us, whatever that was and whoever Rita was although I could guess as I heard squeals and squeaks from the direction of the pool.

Y'all want to take a swim, honey? You look plumb tuckered out. I've got to get supper going but you go ahead and meet Rita and Dickie, they're these *wonderful* lesbians from Boston, she said like I gave a shit they were lesbians. They're both artists and you'll *love* them.

Evening Star was wearing this loose red and white striped smock over a skin-colored bikini bathing suit and I could catch flashes of leg and belly now and then. Her tan was wicked good and probably all over because of the nude sunbathing she was into. She and the others'd spent the day at Doctors Cave, she said and later shopping for souvenirs for Rita and Dickie to take home. She was covered with dried ocean salt and itchy and was going to take a swim in the pool herself as soon as she had the supper under control. So you go ahead, darlin', she said. I'll join y'all in a few minutes.

I said no, I wanted to hear about I-Man and all that so while she cooked and I helped by chopping the veggies and grinding the coconut and suchlike she went on about how she'd heard that I-Man'd tried to rip off some bigtime American ganja dealer, she didn't know who and he and one of his posse'd gotten shot for it. I asked her what about Doc, did he know anything about it and she said no, although Doc did know some of the Kingston dealers and various and sundry unsavory types, she called them but this one was a mystery to him too. I asked if Doc was into dealing and she hesitated a second and said, Well, sometimes a little, I reckon, but don't say anything. Just a little ganja, you know. For the tourist trade. Basically, she said, Doc's become a consumer. As you can see.

Yeah, I said. Speedballs.

She sighed and looked at her hands. I'm afraid so, honey, she said. I'm afraid so. It ain't a very nice welcome home, is it, my love? she said and put her hands on my shoulders and looked sadly into my eyes. We were about the same height I noticed which meant I'd grown about four inches since I split with I-Man for Accompong last summer. Then suddenly she let go of me and pushed her dreadlocks back and went to work again. For a few minutes neither of us said anything and I just watched her from behind while she stirred the dreadnuts in a pan at the stove. There was some more squealing from the pool and I smelled woodsmoke from the barbecue pit out on the patio where Jason was getting ready to cook the goat. Doc had put one of his own CDs on, some old Ike and Tina Turner song and when I glanced back into the living-room I saw he was flopped in his usual place and was smoking a decent-sized J and looking blissed.

There's something I've been wanting to ask you, I said to Evening Star.

She turned and looked at me and smiled. What's that, darlin'?

Well, I was like wondering... I was thinking maybe you'd like to fuck me. You know, since I've never actually done it.

It sounds coldhearted and all probably, but it wasn't. At least not completely. I mean, Evening Star was definitely a hot babe irregardless of her age and from when she'd hugged me after I first came down the stairs to greet her and Doc I'd been pretty turned on and everything, plus somehow just being in that house always got my sex juices flowing. Right from the start with all the loose screwing that went on at Starport for me the place'd been a sex box. It was hard especially for a teenaged kid to ignore female poets from New Orleans slapping on suntan lotion by the pool and black natties with great builds and no shirts and their units showing in their shorts sneaking off to hook up with Evening Star's many white friends and relations, and I hate to admit it but it's true, I really was turned on by lesbians from Boston trotting around in bikinis and from the beginning I'd been way turned on by the sexual vibes that Evening Star herself gave off constantly, how she sort of suggested that her whole purpose in life was to give pleasure whether in the form of food or drugs or sex didn't matter, it was like the giving that mattered because that was the only thing that gave her pleasure back which is some weird kind of generosity that when you think about it and I did is more like constant desire than generosity and is very sexy to a guy. With all that going on for months and years and for all I knew for centuries practically, since slavery days, the place hung suspended out there in the darkness of normal life like Pleasure Island vibrating and twinkling and giving me a perpetual hard-on so to speak that up to now I'd tried to deal with on my own you might say.

But it's also true that it was coldhearted too, my asking Evening Star if I could fuck her or to be exact if she would fuck me. A, because I was wicked curious in a scientific sort of way about what it'd be like and had been wondering about the mechanical details of screwing for at least a couple of years, ever since I first found out about Russ and other guys my age or slightly older getting laid by girls they picked up at the mall and so on. And B, because of Doc and I-Man. More than my general on-going horniness and Evening Star's buff appearance and more than the Pleasure Island lifestyle of Starport and definitely more than the requirements of scientific curiosity, the force that drove me to hit on Evening Star in the kitchen that evening was my need to try and undo the sin I'd committed against I-Man.

When I told Doc the night of my birthday that I-Man'd screwed Evening Star I'd separated myself from I-Man and joined up with Doc. It only lasted a minute and I did it because Doc was my father but still I'd betrayed my best friend and teacher and he'd died for it maybe. Now though, by committing the same crime against Doc as I-Man'd done, which was to steal something that Doc thought was his but actually wasn't since it was a person, I'd be separating myself from Doc and joining up with I-Man again. Stealing is only a crime but betrayal of a friend is a sin. It's like a crime is an act that when you've committed one the act is over and you haven't changed inside. But when you commit a sin it's like you create a condition that you have to live in. People don't live in crime, they live in sin. I didn't know if it'd work, I was still new at this sin-versus-crime business but I had to try. I already had enough experience as a criminal to know that you can't undo a crime. Even a so-called minor crime. When it's done it's done. I'd known that since the day I got kicked out of my mom's and stepdad's house for stealing my grandmother's coin collection. But a sin which can go on forever irregardless of whether you're punished for it I was hoping could be *un*done. Even if I had to commit a crime to do it. Well, sort of a crime. Like I said, Doc didn't really own Evening Star, he only thought he did.

She stood there by the stove with this little smile on her lips for a long time not saying anything, like she was running a mental video on fast forward to see how screwing me might turn out. Finally she let go of the spoon she'd been stirring with and carefully lowered the stove flame. She turned back to me and smiled. Y'all want to do it now? she says.

Sure. Why not?

She glanced at the clock on the wall like this won't take long and said she had to get something from her bedroom first that I figured was some kind of birth control device which was cool as I was definitely not into fatherhood. Wait for me in the laundryroom, she said. I reckon nobody'll bother us there. Except *you* maybe. And I'll have y'all with me this time, won't I, darlin'?

Yes you will! I said and went through the door into the darkened laundryroom where there was a washer and dryer and various yard tools plus the little cot against the wall in back. I could tell I already had a wicked huge boner but I didn't take off my clothes or anything yet. I remembered from porn films and such that the female always takes off her clothes first so I just sat there on the cot like in a doctor's office until the kitchen door swung open and I could see from the daylight behind her that she'd taken off her bathing suit and was only wearing the striped gauzy shift now and nothing underneath. My breathing had definitely speeded up and I could hear my heart pounding and my hands were all sweaty. I was seriously scared, more of doing something bad than scared of Evening Star herself but no way I'd turn back now.

She came over and sat down beside me and started kissing me and putting her tongue in my mouth and all that and guided my hands around to her nipples but they didn't need much guidance so she let go of my hands and started unbuttoning and unzipping my cutoffs. I kicked off my old sandals then and wriggled out of my tee shirt and she let her shift fall off and lay back and pulled me straight to her and I went right up inside like despite everything of a sexual nature that'd happened to me in the distant past this was exactly what I was made for. I'll spare you most of the details but she pretty much controlled everything which was cool because otherwise on my own I probably would've hopped around there for a few seconds and that would've been it and I would've had to wait for five or ten minutes of downtime before I could do it again which would've been embarrassing. But she clamped onto my ass with her hands and drew me slowly in and out and taught me to make certain hinky little hitching moves and drifty swirls with my hips that seemed to really do a job on her and I was feeling kind of proud but then when she started moaning and pulling me in faster and faster I found myself getting incredibly excited and then just as I started to have some really good thoughts about this, like how sex with another person really does block everything out of your mind except that person herself who fills your mind and becomes like the whole universe, and it really helps your concentration and lets you finally forget all your troubles, and it's got so strong a pull on your attention that you actually can't think about yourself anymore, you can't even try, it even blocks out your thoughts, my thoughts got blocked out and I came.

She kept me moving for a little afterwards but then gave up I guess due to my thoughts having returned and let go of my ass and flopped back on the cot all wet with sweat and smelling like cake. She was smiling though, I could see in the dim light coming through the shuttered window and she looked wonderful to me, an amazing new creature on the face of the earth like from a different species than me and ten times more beautiful. She was a naked adult woman and I'd never seen one up close and leisurely before so I just kind of took my time and gazed at her.

I said I was sorry I came so fast but she said not to worry, I was really great and someday I'd be a worldclass lover. I had all the right moves, she said and she was proud and happy that she'd had the privilege of glimpsing my future which was a kind thing to do for a kid on his first try at regular sex, irregardless of his motives.

Well, she said, time for me to get back to makin' dinner for my guests. And then I'm gonna jump in the pool an' cool off. What about you, sugar? We won't eat till after dark, when Jason finally gets that goat barbecued. I wouldn't have done it but I promised Rita and Dickie some irie Jamaican roast goat an' they're holding me to it, bad girls.

I had my clothes back on and was standing next to the cot still kind of gazing at her beauty but my mind was clicking through the gears and moving rapidly on to the rest of my life. You know, I said to her, when I was out there like in Accompong I heard a few things. About Doc.

Oh? she said all suspicious.

Yeah, but nothing bad, you understand. One thing though I wanted to ask you before I talk to him about it myself.

What's that, honey?

I heard he had another kid. Maybe more than one. Over in Kingston, you know? And I heard the mother was like Jamaican. I mean, some people knew he had a kid but not a white kid. That true?

There's a lot about Doc that nobody knows, sugar. He's a mystery man.

Yeah, but c'mon, you'd know if he had another kid than me. I don't think it's *wrong* or anything, you understand. It's not like a *sin,* or a crime even. I just want to know and I can't exactly ask him. Not right now anyhow.

No, not now for sure. But. . . well, yes, he wouldn't mind me telling you, I'm sure, he's just a little embarrassed to do it himself. But yes, he does have another son. Actually two, I think. But who knows with Doc? There could be other families in other lands. He's that kind of man, you know. Anyhow y'all shouldn't be jealous or anything. Doc loves you the most, I know that *per*sonally. He's told me that a hundred times.

What about the mother, is she Jamaican?

Yes. Yes, she is. A good woman too, as I've been led to believe, and Doc stays with her and Paul and his little brother when he's in Kingston, and he stays with you and me when he's over here! she said brightly.

His son's name is Paul? I said. The same as Doc's?

The older one is. I'm afraid I can't recall the name of the other one or even if there's but one. Paul's the only name I've heard Doc say. Listen, sugar, I've got to get back to my stove now.

How old's the son named Paul?

I don't know, about ten, I guess. I've never met the boy. Not a teenager though. Now c'mon, we can chat about all this later. Right now I've got work to do, sweets. What're you gonna do? Whyn't y'all cool off in the pool?

No, I'm gonna book, I said.

Whatever do you mean, Bone?

I'm leaving now.

Oh Bone. Didn't you like it with me? She made a pout. Don't you want to do it again?

Sure, but I'm leaving. Don't take it wrong, it's not about you.

Oh now, Bone, you *mustn't* be upset about Doc's other family. I *never* should've told you.

Naw, that doesn't do anything to me one way or the other. In fact I feel a lot sorrier for them than for me. Especially the one named after him. I was only curious, that's all. No, it's on account of Doc himself that I'm leaving. If he wasn't here, yeah, I might stay. But he is here.

Listen, Doc won't *ever* know about us, sugar. *Trust* me, she said. Who's gonna tell him anyhow? You? she said and laughed.

Yeah, well, I would if I could.

Now don't you get any bright ideas, sugar, she said and cinched her shift tightly at the waist. She was really in great shape for her age. She said, Y'all just wait till later this evening, sweetie. I'll come tippy-toein' down the hall to your little room an' I'll show you some tricks that'll make your *hair* stand on end. Wait till everyone else's gone off to bed. The evening star, don't you know, is *Venus.* The goddess of *love,* sugar. An' don't you forget it.

She gave me a kiss on the lips and ran her forefinger down my tee shirt from my collar bone to my belly button. Then she turned and smiled over her shoulder and pushed open the door and went back into the kitchen

leaving me alone in the darkness with my thoughts which
were setting up in my mind like slabs of concrete. They
weren't many but they were tough and hard and as I've
found out since pretty near permanent.

Dealing with my father was eased a lot due to him having passed out on the couch. The CD was silent now and
when I came out through the kitchen once I knew Evening
Star'd gone swimming I stopped at the doorway and for
quite a few minutes stood watching Doc lying there on his
back and he didn't blink or move even afterwards when I
came into the livingroom and picked up my backpack and
Jah-stick. The sounds of naked women playing in the water
drifted in from the pool and the bump of the diving board
and so forth, and then somebody put a heavy reggae album
on the big outdoor sound system and started blasting the
jungle with it. Peter Tosh it was, Steppin' Razor. Party time.
Doc stirred but then lapsed back.

For a few minutes more I stood over my father's unconscious body and looked down and wondered how I
could've thought once that he looked like JFK. He didn't
look any more like JFK than ol' Buster Brown had or my
stepfather Ken. I'd sure run into a lot of evil men in my
short life so far, at least that's how it seemed to me and I
hoped it wasn't going to be like this the rest of the way even
though I was much better prepared now to deal with them
than before. I was thinking probably John F. Kennedy himself if I'd've known him personally wouldn't've looked anything like the man I'd imagined him as. Not necessarily
worse or evil, just different. But Doc, my father, he looked
evil. Even passed out like this. I almost felt sorry for him,
like he was possessed.

Anyhow I had my plan and started to put it in action then. No time for feeling sorry. Over on the end table next to the phone was a notepad and pencil and I ripped off a sheet and in large letters wrote out, THE BONE RULES, NEVER FORGET-TEE! At first I was going to just pin it to Doc's silk shirt but I couldn't find a pin anywhere. Then I had a better idea. I reached down into my pack and came out with the stuffed woodcock that I'd hauled around with me ever since the Ridgeways'. Inside the hollowed-out place where I'd once stashed Buster's porn money I put the note with just enough of it showing so it wouldn't get overlooked and then I stood the woodcock carefully on Doc's chest facing him with its long beak almost touching Doc's nose. The bird looked stupid standing there but sad and stern too, like the woodcock was me and I was giving my father the evil eye that when he came to it'd be the first thing he'd see, and if it didn't make Doc change his ways of living right then and there maybe it'd give him a heart attack instead. Either way, it didn't make no never-mind to me. Not anymore.

I was in a mood to study for a while the one Haitian painting that I-Man'd loved so much but it was getting late in the day and the sun was fading fast so I had to get a move on. I was headed for the marina at Mobay and wanted to get to it before they closed and locked the gate. A couple of times last fall I'd gone there with I-Man to deliver herb and knew the routine and after around nine you can't get out onto the docks where the boats are. I took the machete out of my pack then and hitched my backpack straps over my shoulders, picked up the machete in my left hand and my Jah-stick in the other and went straight out to the patio to deal with Jason.

He was standing on the other side of the waist-high barbecue pit which was about six feet long and made from cinderblocks with this long grill and a spit where he was slowly turning the charred body of the goat over the fire. I have to admit it smelled delicious. The pool was on the further side of the patio and beyond a high wall so up here by the barbecue you couldn't see it or be seen from there either except by someone standing on the diving board. The females must've been paddling around calmly now though or chilling with a J because I couldn't hear them anymore even between songs on the sound system. Jason didn't notice me until I was almost up to him with the barbecue still between us and when he saw it was me he grinned like we were pals and said, Hey, Baby Doc! Respect, mon. Welcome home.

No, mi not called Baby Doc no more, I said. I actually didn't know what I was going to do or say to Jason, my plan wasn't all that detailed. All I knew was that I was going to deal with him, whatever that meant. He saw the machete in my hand though and got suddenly serious and reached down beside him and grabbed up a machete of his own which was all bloody from butchering the goat and at that instant I felt like *I* was possessed, not by an evil spirit like Doc but possessed by the good spirit of I-Man. It was like my voice and words weren't mine anymore but his, and my movements weren't guided by me but by him.

In a low dark voice I heard myself say, Me nyan come fe slay a mon when Jah can do de job more properly. Lissen mi, Jason. Mi come fe place a curse 'pon you, mon. Lissen mi, dis be de curse of Nonny, dat him who live by de sword shall die by de sword. Then I took a step forward and he raised his machete like to chop at me if I attacked him but I didn't, all I did was gently place my machete on the grill below the body of the goat and step quickly away from it.

The coals were red hot and the smoke made like a shifting gray curtain between me and Jason. He seemed confused and upset, maybe even scared a little. Y' know, you fren' him, I-Man dat ol' Rasta-man, it be de Nighthawk who shoot him, de white man. Me couldn' stop him, Bone. Him go crazy when him see de Rasta, jus' pow-pow-pow like dat! Wid de Uzi, mon.

I knew he was lying and if it hadn't been for being possessed by I-Man I probably would've told him so but instead I said, Dat sword dere in de fire gwan kill you, Jason, gwan sattar in de fire till it red hot and den it rise up an' fly 'cross de air an' chop off you head from you neck, mon. De sword of virtue it be an' it gwan slay de liar an' de hypocrite wit' a single stroke!

I think he figured at that point I was looney-tunes and basically harmless because he laughed and grabbed the machete off the grill and now he had two machetes, one in each hand and he jumped up on top of the barbecue, not on the grill but on the cinderblocks around it which still must've been hot on his bare feet but he didn't seem to mind. He was standing up there towering over me shirtless and in shorts with a machete in each hand and a wild crazy stoned look on his face. It was like a white man's worst nightmare and if it hadn't've been for I-Man still holding me under his control I'd've been outa there that second, no way I'm hanging around to discuss things, but instead the Jah-stick like takes on a life of its own and pulls itself forward in my hands and even though I'm yanking back on it trying to keep it from jabbing at Jason

I can't and the lion's head at the top of the stick heads right for Jason's face and jacks him in the eyes. He howls in pain and the machetes go clanking and he slips and falls onto the grill knocking the goat off the spit and burning the shit out of himself and now he's really screaming in pain and I don't know how to help him except by running around the barbecue to the other side and steering him as fast as I can down the steps toward the pool where the females are out in the middle with their hands over their mouths and looking on in horror as I push Jason into the pool.

And book. As fast as I can and without once looking back I race up the steps again and grab the Jah-stick and run full speed down the long driveway past all the sad little red-eyed rabbits and foxes and so on and through the gate to the lane and down the long hill past the cabins and houses of the local people who watch me and a few wave but I don't wave back. I just keep on running.

TWENTY-TWO

SHIPPING OUT

And that's about it, pretty much the whole story up to now. Except to tell how I got off of the island of Jamaica which is no big deal since it was basically pure luck.

The reason I'd decided to light out for the marina once I'd made my exit at Starport was I knew quite a few yachts and private charter boats came and went from there to all over the Caribbean and some of the captains of those boats weren't too fussy who came and went with them so long as you were willing to work hard for bad food and no pay or almost none. How I knew this was I-Man'd done a little lunchtime dealing over the years with the various guys who worked in the boatyard and on the docks and he'd gotten to know the crews and even a few captains who made regular stops there for water and gas and other supplies, including Jamaican mountain-grown ganja for themselves and their customers too sometimes, the rich people who either owned the boats and just liked to ride around in them or the not-so-rich people on vacation who rented them.

Last summer before we fled into the hills of Accompong there'd been three or four times that me and I-Man'd made ganja deliveries at the marina and hung out there chatting up the customers like I-Man always did when he made a delivery. It was part of the service I guess, plus it was how he got information about the cops and so on and how he made new contacts for future sales. I used to think I-Man was too sociable in general and not such a hot dealer of weed, nothing like ol' Hector the Spanish guy at Chi-Boom's in Plattsburgh say, but later I came to view him as one of the best, actually the best I'd ever known.

Anyhow up at the Mothership that night while I was sitting alone on the cot in the laundry room making up my escape plans I'd suddenly remembered this one guy named Captain Ave from Key West, Florida originally who ran this charter boat called *Belinda Blue* out of Mobay and was a regular customer of I-Man's. *Belinda Blue* was a short fat commercial fishing boat from Maine or someplace that he'd like converted for taking people on two-week-long charter cruises to the various islands, families mostly and honeymooning couples and suchlike who'd thought when they signed on that a boat named *Belinda Blue* that they had to fly down to meet in Montego Bay, Jamaica would turn out to be one of those sleek three-masted schooners like you see in magazines. I think maybe Captain Ave misled them too, with pictures of other guys' boats and had gotten in trouble doing the same thing in the States and that was the real reason why he worked out of Montego Bay instead of Miami or Key West.

The point is Captain Ave who was a decent enough guy himself usually had seriously pissed-off customers who thought they'd been cheated and like anyone they took it out on the crew who on these kind of boats have to be like the servants. Which meant he had a hard time keeping his crew and was always looking for new guys. That was the word around the marina at least, and Captain Ave himself once when me and I-Man dropped off a couple ounces told me he always needed an extra hand and if I ever felt like doing a little island-hopping I should look him up. He asked me did I have any experience and I said sure, I'd spent a lot of time on the frigid waters of Lake Champlain which I admitted wasn't exactly the Atlantic Ocean but they had a lot of big boats and ferries and so on there and I could crew, sure.

Okay, anytime, kid, he said. I think he sensed I was pretty good at bullshitting white people which was something he definitely needed on the *Belinda Blue*. But back then I was still newly arrived in Jamaica and was employed full time at the ant farm as I-Man's apprentice and was totally turned off by the idea of serving food and cocktails at sunset and doing laundry for rich white Americans too pissed off to lighten up because they'd expected to be cruising the warm romantic waters of the Caribbean on a white-sailed windjammer instead of a fat wallowing old tub which was pretty comfortable actually and cool the way Captain Ave'd fixed it up with bunks and a galley and all, even two staterooms, he called them.

Now though everything was different. I was nobody's apprentice now. When I finally got down off the hill and stepped off the bus from Montpelier in front of the marina it was dark and I was hoping the gate hadn't been locked yet, and it hadn't. And when I ran through the open gate into the marina and made my way down the crisscrossing docks where all the boats were tied up I was hoping I'd see the *Belinda Blue* where it used to be, I was hoping hoping hoping, and it was. All I had to hope for then was that Captain Ave'd need another guy to crew for him and that the *Belinda Blue* was set to go out real soon, before Jason or any of his coworkers or even Doc found out where I'd gone. On an island like Jamaica you can hide all right from the rest of the world but you can't hide from the people who live there.

Captain Ave was loading cases of beer and soft drinks aboard by himself and when I walked up and asked did he need any help he said, Yeah, stash this shit below and c'mon aboard, kid, and we'll talk. Which I did and a little while later we were sitting in the stern doing business. It turned out that a husband and wife and their two little kids were flying in from New York City tomorrow to take the *Belinda Blue* to this island called Dominica where they'd rented a house for a few weeks, sort of a month-long surf-and-turf family vacation that this phony New York rental agent Captain Ave knew had cooked up for them. Nobody at the marina wanted to crew for Captain Ave as usual and for the usual reasons, I knew although he didn't say that, but also because it was a one-way cruise with no guaranteed return trip.

The husband was supposed to be this famous singer from the sixties who'd kicked drugs and booze and got married and had kids et cetera and become like a regular citizen but I wasn't even born until 1979 so I'd never heard of him. Captain Ave thought that was weird but he was a sixties guy. The beers I'd been lugging below were for Captain Ave and his crew, he said because the cruise was supposed to be drug and alcohol free. He was pretty disgusted by the whole thing. Plus he'd just found out the whole family were vegetarians which he said he didn't know from Unitarians. Can you handle that? he asked me and I said sure, I'll cook Ital. He said fine so long as he didn't have to eat that shit. Then we agreed I'd get two hundred bucks when we got to Dominica and we shook hands.

We each drank a beer over it and afterwards he showed me where the crew bunked. It was way up in the bow of the boat and tiny like a pointed coffin with no window and two foot-wide benches with sponge rubber mattresses for sleeping on. I was glad then that I was the only member of the crew and decided that unless it rained I'd be sleeping up on the topdeck anyhow and proceeded to haul one of the chunks of sponge rubber up there and lay down on it and probably due to the excitement of the last few days plus relief for having found a way out of Jamaica I didn't have any thoughts left and almost instantly fell asleep.

There's only one other thing that happened to me in Jamaica worth telling about. Not because it's so interesting but it's kind of sad. In the morning Captain Ave who had to go meet the singer and his family at the airport gave me a bunch of money and dropped me off at the Mobay market to buy enough veggies to get us to Dominica. Get about a week's worth, he said, and bring me the change plus receipts. No problema, I said although I wasn't too happy about making any public appearances so to speak especially at the marketplace where I'd stand out and certain people I knew did their food shopping. Still, Captain Ave didn't know about my various adventures and I couldn't tell him so I did what he asked and went around to the different stands buying breadfruits and akee and calalu and coconuts and various fruits, the usual components of an Ital menu which was basically all I knew how to cook anyhow. Him and me he said could eat the fish we caught and there'd be several islands we'd stop at along the way where we could get regular American food which was fine by me since I hadn't had any in a long time.

I was pretty close to finished and was buying this huge bag of oranges from a lady when I looked up and spotted a white person in the crowd on the other side of the market and even though I hadn't seen him since the Ridgeways' I recognized him at once. It was Russ. He looked the same at first except I could tell he was really confused and scared especially by all the black people whose native language he probably couldn't understand a word of. For a minute there I had to fight off a desire to rush over and help him but I quickly overcame it and ducked down behind the fat lady selling the oranges and peeked out under her table at him. Russ's eyes were darting around and he was licking his lips a lot and kept pushing his hair off his forehead. He was trying to seem cool. He had on a sleeveless shirt and cutoffs and black hightop Doc Martens and no socks and he'd cut his hair with a buzz on the sides and a rattail in back. I noticed then that he had a bunch more tattoos, all over his arms and legs even, all kinds of snakes and different-colored dragons and various slogans. They were pretty much everywhere. He looked really pathetic and I wished we could still be friends but it was definitely too late.

His eyes were like cruising the marketplace crowd, for
me no doubt since I hadn't been at the clock tower where
I'd promised but then I saw he'd locked onto something
and I followed his gaze across the crowd to a group of
three whites, females they were, Evening Star and her
campers Rita and Dickie. Evening Star being the experienced Jamaican shopper and all was pointing to this and
that and explaining everything to the other two who were
like nodding and being politely amazed. Russ though was
already zeroing in on them like a teenaged heat-seeking
missile. I really had to fight with myself to keep from
standing up and waving my arms and hollering, Russ!
Don't, Russ! Come with me to Dominica, Russ!

But it was too late even for that. Evening Star'd picked
him out of the crowd and was already smiling in his direction and he was smiling back and I knew was rehearsing
in his mind the line he'd use. He'd say like, You guys
come here often? and she'd say, Every Saturday, darlin',
and he'd say, Wow, you must live here, I'm new in town,
just arrived from the States and looking for my homey
named Chappie who was s'posed to meet me blah blah
blah, and the rest would be as predictable as the first part.

I watched for a few minutes more while Russ and
Evening Star yakked it up. Then she introduced him to
her friends from Boston and turned aside and said something private to Russ which was probably that her friends
were lesbians and which knowing Russ would turn him on
and knowing Evening Star that was the point of telling
him. Anyhow a second later he was carrying their groceries for them and talking like they were all old friends
and I figured it wouldn't take more than another few minutes for Evening Star to realize that Chappie, Russ's

homey from upstate New York was the very boy she'd
known as Bone. And in an hour Russ'd have a blunt-sized
spliff in his mouth and be doing the backstroke in the
pool at Starport.

They strolled toward the parking lot and I finally stood
up and watched them get into Evening Star's Range
Rover and drive off. Poor ol' Russ, I thought. I wished I
could've saved him. But I knew that even if I'd tried he
wouldn't've let me. That could've been me, I thought,
that poor bewildered kid in the Doc Martens and the rattail haircut with the painful-looking red and blue and
black newly drilled tattoos all over his pink skin climbing
into the fancy car and riding up the hill to the
greathouse, a stoner boy amazed at his incredible luck
and looking forward already to getting coked with some
weird dude named Doc on the patio before the sun goes
down and laid by this buff older chick named Evening
Star in the laundry room before it comes up again.

It *would've* been me, if it hadn't been for Sister Rose
and I-Man and everything I'd learned about myself and
life from coming to love them out there at the schoolbus
in Plattsburgh and being with I-Man afterwards at the ant
farm and up on the groundation in Accompong. I'd even
loved big bad Bruce because he'd died trying to save me
from the fire in Au Sable and that'd taught me a lot too.
They were the only three people I'd chosen on my own to
love, and they were gone. But still, that morning in Mobay
when I saw Russ for the last time, I saw clearly for the first
time that loving Sister Rose and I-Man and even Bruce
had left me with riches that I could draw on for the rest of
my life, and I was totally grateful to them.

*   *   *

We cast off from the marina at around four that afternoon and headed in bright sunshine and a light breeze for open water. From the galley I could look out onto the foredeck while I was working and watch the kids Josh and Rachel who were supposed to be twins but they didn't look anything alike and I wondered if they were adopted because neither of them resembled the parents either. Josh was moon-faced and blond and freckled and Rachel was dark and curly-haired and wore glasses and was taller than her brother. They were maybe eight or nine, spoiled rich kids I suppose but basically decent and surprisingly considerate to each other, considering they didn't get much out of their parents one way or the other.

I remember the singer and his wife lying in their perfect bodies on the foredeck on these plastic chaise longues getting tanned and zoned and not saying anything which was their style even to each other. They were like in the middle of a ten-year fight and they didn't know if you were going to come in on his side or hers so they weren't talking till you declared yourself. No smiles, no jokes, no questions, except like where's the bathroom and so on. They weren't unpolite, just into themselves a lot and each of them into blaming the other whenever something went wrong. Like already their whole vacation'd gone wrong on account of the *Belinda Blue* not being a clipper ship but instead of just making the best of it they seemed to prefer giving each other dirty looks and ignoring the rest of us, including their own kids.

I don't mean to go wandering off on the subject of the singer and his family but there was something about the kids, Rachel and Josh that really got to me as we pulled out of Mobay late that afternoon and headed southeast along the coast of Jamaica. Probably instead I should've been paying attention to my departure from this place where so much good and bad had happened to me in less than one short year. I was sure I'd never get back again unless someday I came searching for I-Man's grave up in the churchyard cemetery in Accompong to put flowers on it. My natural father lived in Jamaica but that didn't exactly provide a draw, not anymore and I'd had my first total-immersion sex experience with a woman there but that's something you can only do once. And I'd come to know I in Jamaica, I'd seen the lights of I at the heights and at the depths, but you can't do that more than once either. Either the lights of I kick in or they don't, and if they don't you keep going back to the heights and depths until they do. But when they do kick in like they had with me that night in the cave you're supposed after that to look out from I and forward, not in to I and back. You're supposed to use those bright new lights strictly for seeing into the darkness.

Which is what I was doing I guess by not looking back over my shoulder at the quickly shrinking green hills of Jamaica and peering instead through the small square window of the galley at the children up on the foredeck. The parents were stretched out on their chaises in the middle, their pale skin glistening with lotion and their eyes shut behind sunglasses. Josh was sitting on the starboard side and Rachel was on the port. With his knees drawn up to his chin and his arms wrapped around his shins the boy stared solemnly out to sea, and just as serious as him the girl was pointing her toes out in front of her like a ballet dancer and gazing at the opposite sea.

They were totally alone, those kids, like each had been accidentally sent to earth from a distant planet to live among adult humans and be dependent on them for everything because compared to the adult humans they were extremely fragile creatures and didn't know the language or how anything here worked and hadn't arrived with any money. And because they were like forbidden by the humans to use their old language they'd forgotten it so they couldn't be much company or help to each other either. They couldn't even talk about the old days and so pretty soon they forgot there even were any old days and all there was now was life on earth with adult humans who called them children and acted toward them like they owned them and like they were objects not living creatures with souls.

I could see from their expressions and gestures that those two little kids, Josh and Rachel were probably going to grow up to be just like their parents. They were already practicing. But who could blame them? No one in his right mind would want to stay a kid forever. Certainly not me.

We put in late that night at Navy Island which is just off Port Antonio at the eastern end of Jamaica and real late after everybody'd gone to bed I dragged my mattress up on the topdeck. It was actually just the roof of the main cabin but that's what Captain Ave called it, the topdeck. The night was totally clear and the stars were awesome, like zillions of tiny lights bobbing on a wide black ocean. I was still thinking about the kids Josh and Rachel and wondering which star up there they'd orginally come from and if they knew it, or say I found out somehow and pointed it out to them would they want to go back there and be among their own kind again?

Probably not. The experience of being born on earth and living among humans even for only a few years changes you forever. I guess all you can do is make the best of what's clearly a bad situation. Still, it would be nice to know that on this one particular star or maybe on that one over to the right of it there were people who loved you for yourself.

I was thinking that and other such thoughts when suddenly I noticed that it was true, the biggest stars or at least the brightest ones were related like in a family and you could connect the dots so to speak and make a picture if you wanted, same as the old shepherds did who watched their flocks by night. I'd tried lots of times to see them before but it'd never worked so I'd figured constellations were just one of those things like atoms and molecules that people tell you exist but you can't see them so you say yeah, whatever.

But it *was* true. There was a bunch of bright stars here and another there and several other bunches that stood out from the zillions of stars in the background. The trouble was, even though finally I could see with my own eyes that there really were such things as constellations up there I couldn't remember any of the names or pictures anymore. I knew there was supposed to be like some guy with a bow and arrow and a chariot and horses and various Greek gods and goddesses but I couldn't tell which was which.

So I tried connecting the dots on my own. There was this one cluster of stars fairly low in the northern part of the sky and when I connected them they made like a perfect barbell. That's the constellation Bruce, I thought. Only not to have it sound stupid I decided to call it Adirondack Iron, the sign of the bad boy with the brave heart.

Another batch of stars that floated all by themselves in a really dark part of the sky turned out to be a long-stemmed rose, and I looked at that for a long time and almost cried it was so delicate and exposed out there on its own. It had little thorns on it and beautiful red petals. It was the constellation Sister Rose, the sign of the rejected child.

A third cluster of stars hovered right above me and I lay there on my back looking straight up until it came forward in the shape of a lion's head with a crown, the constellation Lion-I, the sign of the open mind, and among those stars, even though I couldn't see him I knew I-Man sat looking down on me with his lips in that little pursed smile and his eyebrows raised in slight surprise at the way things'd turned out.

All the rest of the night I passed my gaze from one constellation to the other and watched them float slowly across the sky until finally along toward dawn it began to get a little pink out on the ocean in the east and the stars started sliding into the darkness behind the mountains. First Adirondack Iron passed into the dark, and then Sister Rose, and finally Lion-I. They were gone and I missed them but even so I was very happy. For the rest of my life no matter where on the planet earth I went and no matter how scared or confused I got, I could wait until dark and look up into the night sky and see my three friends again and my heart would swell with love of them and make me strong and clearheaded. And if I didn't know what to do next I could ask I-Man to instruct me, and across the huge cold silence of the universe I'd hear him say, Up to you, Bone, and that's all I'd need.